PRAISE FOR THE WORK OF RICHARD C. WHITE

"Entertaining, old-school sword and sorcery, in the tradition of Fafhrd and the Gray Mouser."
—**Jim C. Hines**, author of the Magic ex Libris, Jig the Goblin, and The Princesses series, on *For a Few Gold Pieces More*

"What a fantastic ride! If you like sarcasm and snark reminiscent of Harry Dresden, good doses of magic, treachery, and myth, this is the book for you."
—**Goodreads**, on *For a Few Gold Pieces More*

"White's *Terra Incognito* is a solid introduction to the subject of world building. It succeeds in helping the apiring writer in creating a skeletal framework on which to hang the moving parts required of a believable fictional setting."
—**The Gaming Gang**, on *Terra Incognito: A Guide to Building the Worlds of Your Imagination*

"A very good spin on the tried and true 'good-guys-for-hire' formula. All in all, an enjoyable read that I would recommend to anyone."
—**Word of the Nerd**, on *Troubleshooters, Incorporated: Night Stalkings*

"An accurately dialogued epic set in a place and time of fantasy. If you like pirates or elves or fantasy adventure or pure swashbuckling, then pick it up."
—**Comic Genesis**, on *The Chronicles of the Sea Dragon Special*

Starwarp Concepts Titles
By Richard C. White

Fantasy
Harbinger of Darkness
For a Few Gold Pieces More
Chasing Danger: The Case Files of Theron Chase

Science Fiction
On Wings of Steel

Writers' Reference
*Terra Incognito: A Guide to Building
the Worlds of Your Imagination*

Graphic Novels and Comic Books
The Chronicles of the Sea Dragon Special
Troubleshooters, Incorporated: Night Stalkings

ALSO BY RICHARD C. WHITE

Novels
Gauntlet: Dark Legacy: Paths of Evil

Novellas
Battletech: No Rest for the Wicked
The Dark Leopard: Mouse Trap
Strikeforce Falcon: Flashpoint
Star Trek: S.C.E.: Echoes of Coventry

Anthology Contributions
Charles Boeckman Presents: Johnny Nickle
Doctor Who: Short Trips; The Quality of Leadership
Monsters!: The Origins Game Fair 2014 Writers Program Anthology
Space: The Origins Game Fair 2015 Writers Program Anthology
Robots: The Origins Game Fair 2016 Writers Program Anthology
Star Trek: The Next Generation: The Sky's the Limit
Star Trek: Corps of Engineers: What's Past
One for All: Tales of the Musketeers
The Ultimate Hulk • Tales of Freeport
Liberty Girl: Fight for Freedom

ON WINGS OF STEEL

The Darkside Chronicles · Book One

RICHARD C. WHITE

StarWarp Concepts

www.starwarpconcepts.com
New York, NY

StarWarp Concepts
P.O. Box 4667
Sunnyside, NY 11104

Visit our website: **www.StarwarpConcepts.com**

Visit Richard C. White on the Web at:
www.richardcwhite.com

Library of Congress Control Number: 2025934978

ISBN: 979-8-9864432-0-1 (trade paperback)
ISBN: 979-8-9864432-1-8 (e-book)

First Print Edition: 2025

Front cover art by Beto Lima, www.artstation.com/betolima

Back cover photograph by Leva Nevsky, Courtesy of Pixabay

Edited by Steven Roman

Book design by Mike W. Belcher

Printed in the USA

Here's to the dreamers who swallow their fear, spread their wings, and reach for the sky.

ACKNOWLEDGMENTS

As with any project, there are a number of people who have been invaluable to helping this book come together:

Heather McCorkle, who suffered through some of the early drafts of this manuscript and gave some much needed advice and encouragement to keep this moving forward.

Mike W. Belcher, who stepped in to handle the cover and book design for us.

Beto Lima, who created the magnificent cover for this book.

Steve Roman, my long-suffering editor, who has been working with me for over thirty years now and still speaks to me, which says a lot for his patience. *grin*

And, of course, my wife, Joni, and the daughter-unit, who put up with seeing the back of my head for long stretches while I work on my various projects.

Honestly, without all of you, this book never would have happened. Thanks!

Chapter One

The sound of pounding feet up the stairs echoed in the small stairway. A wave of bodies spilled out onto the roof of the imposing building, forming up in ranks as each woman adjusted their flight uniform and ensured her gear was in place. The low rumble of thunder in the distance warned of a storm heading their way, but it paled in comparison to the storm that came out of a nearby glass-enclosed room and strode to the front of the formation.

"When I say the formation will be at fifteen hundred hours, I mean I expect to step out at fifteen hundred to find everyone standing tall and waiting for me. Not some last-minute grab-assing and shifting around in formation."

Erica Halgrim gulped and not for the first time was grateful she was both short and on the back row of the formation. Not that it always helped—Flight Commander Kralowitcz had almost a sixth sense when it came to something not being right. As the flight commander continued expressing her displeasure, Erica stole a glance to the lit office and noted a large number of visitors for today's training session.

"Cadet Halgrim, do I have your attention?"

"Ma'am, yes ma'am!"

Erica met the wizened woman's steel-blue eyes and, after a few moments, the flight commander turned back to the formation at large. "Today is your final test. Pass this and you'll no longer be trainees, but members of the Angels of Steel. Fail and you can reapply in a year...if you survive. Now, take a moment and check your teammates' gear. We are standing on the sixtieth floor of Angels Tower. Now is *not* the time to find out your flight gear is nonoperational."

Erica moved almost mechanically, checking the metallic wings and the small engines attached to the back of the young women to the front, right, and left of her position in the formation. She could almost see the checklist in front of her eyes as she started at the top and worked her way down, checking connections, and straps, and inspecting for anything that seemed out of place. Satisfied with her teammates' equipment, she stood still while they did the same for her.

1

Once the formation had come back to attention, the flight commander resumed speaking to the assembled women. Erica heard the thunder growing closer and risked a glance upward. The Dark Cloud, the mass of miasma that separated Southwatch into Dayside and Darkside, spread across the sky as far as she could see, hiding the approaching storm from view. As she watched, the mass churned as if waiting for the oncoming rain clouds, daring them to try and break up the never-ending storm that doomed those who lived below it to eternal twilight.

Kralowitcz must have noted Erica's wandering attention, but her voice didn't carry its usual sting. "We fully expect the storm to break during your test. You have protective gear with you. Do *not* attempt to don it midflight. Find a perch, gear up, and then continue the test. Do *not* attempt to finish the test without your gear, no matter whether you're behind schedule or not. You've seen what happens to people who get caught in the rain. Now imagine that happening when you're a couple hundred feet in the air."

Even at the position of attention, Erica could see the involuntary shudders running through the formation. The flight commander waited a few seconds to let her words sink in before speaking again. "When I give the command, you will line up by name. Each of you will be given a set of six locations. You will fly to each of these locations and procure an item that will be waiting for you. You have three hours to acquire these items and return. No two people have the same route, so tagging behind someone else will not help you. You find your points or you fail. You arrive back here in three hours or you fail. If you get hopelessly lost or injured, hit the panic button on your wrist armor and we'll try to find you—but you'll still fail. Any questions?"

The only sound on the rooftop was the wind rising as the storm front approached.

"All right, line up as we call out your names. The test starts the second you step off the roof."

Erica twisted her body to the side as she maneuvered through a narrow alleyway. It was a tight fit, but she'd always excelled at the acrobatics part of flight school. The servos in her wings strained to keep her balanced, but it was a short alley and she was able to level off before she'd lost too much altitude. The thalisium motor helped her wings overcome the pull of gravity as she arched her back and climbed almost straight up toward her fifth destination.

According to the chronometer on her wrist, she still had almost fifty minutes left but there was no time to dawdle over this pickup. Her last destination was in Bakerstown, on the far side of Southwatch from Angels Tower. It was going to take every bit of her knowledge to map out the shortest route there and back.

I know one way, but I'd rather not use it unless I have no other choice.

The rain continued to pelt down as the winds tried to shove her back toward the gray streets below. She tried to angle beneath a walkway to get a bit of relief from the stinging drops that splatted against her goggles and mask. She hated flying with the rebreather on, but nothing came through the Cloud untainted and that went doubly for the rain. At this rate, she was going to need a new flight jacket and helmet at the least as she could imagine the acidic water hissing against the treated leather. She did a pirouette in midair, trying to fling the water drops away from her, but the rain mocked her attempt by increasing in strength.

Finally, she spotted her target and swooped down to a small balcony where the package rested. She noted the two gargoyles stationed on either side of the balcony and eased her wings in to not disturb them. She knew it was just an urban legend, but the flight instructors had told them to avoid touching *any* gargoyles, so it took her a moment to center herself on the balcony and make a soft landing. A quick glance at the package reassured her it had her name on it, and seconds later it was safely tucked into her pouch and she was winging her way south and east toward Bakerstown.

As she emerged from the tangles of Downtown and crossed over in the more residential section of town, she glanced at the card listing her destinations. She pulled up in shock as she saw the final destination was blurred. Apparently the acid rain had eaten its way into her wrist holder and the ink had run. She stared at the card through her rain-streaked goggles and wasn't quite sure if her package waited at 33 Thompson Place, or 38, or 83, or 88 for that matter.

Well, there's nothing to be done for it now. Going to have to move and check them all out until we find it. Looks like it's a good thing I know of that short cut. After all, the flight commander didn't forbid us flying through the Underground.

3

She tucked her arms and legs in tight and focused on coaxing as much speed out of her wings as she thought she safely could. Just because the housing complexes in Bakerstown didn't reach into the Cloud did not mean they didn't have dangers all their own. Take clotheslines, for example. In good weather, it was easy to spot them hung between the low buildings when housewives hung their clothes to dry. However, in the rain, they were virtually invisible, turning them into deathtraps for flyers who could snag wings or propellers in them with nothing to break their fall but the cold concrete streets below.

Erica said a small prayer to the Goddess and focused on trying to spot obstacles as she wove in and among the buildings trying to find her last package. As she had feared, it was at neither 33 nor 38 Thompson Place, which meant she had to move even farther east, away from the finish line, as she searched.

A small movement caught her eye as she approached 83 Thompson Place. It looked like an arm waving her closer, but after she wiped the rain off her goggles, she realized it was only a gargoyle perched on the corner of a building. The huge stone statue couldn't have moved, so she chalked it up to the lack of visibility. Still, her instincts told her she might want to check in that direction. Glancing down, she saw something sitting on the edge of a balcony.

Hang on, there it is. If I can just reach it...

Erica angled her wings and dove toward the package. With luck, she'd be able to snag it as she went past and shave some time off her trip. She tucked her wings tight to gain speed and stretched out her arms.

"STOP!"

A voice rang out in her head, startling her. She flared her wings and the thalisium motor strained as she backpedaled in midair. She'd just brought her flight under control when a Sky Patrol gyrocopter came whizzing around the building, passing directly in front of her, the rotors missing her by only a few feet. The pilot shook his fist at her and continued on, his flashing lights disappearing in the distance.

Erica shuddered and fought to get her emotions under control. This wasn't the first time she'd had a premonition while flying around Southwatch, but it was the first time she'd actually *heard* something instead of just feeling something was off. She glanced around to see who had given her the warning, but the only thing she could see was

4

the stone statue, glistening underneath the water running down its body.

Shaking her head to force herself to focus, she moved forward on jerky wings, barely maintaining her altitude until she reached her final package. She glanced at her chronometer and saw she had just a bit over thirty minutes to get to Angels Tower. There was a chance if she flew out over the Docks and Bricktown, she could make up time since neither of them had buildings that rose above Midtown. However, it was a roundabout way and if she ran into any delays, she'd never make it to the finish in time.

No, there's no choice. Head straight back into Downtown and then head for the entrance at the Grand Canal. I'll have to keep my head on a swivel to avoid running into anything, but it's the closest thing to a straight line there is in Southwatch.

Erica glanced at her chronometer one last time, convinced herself that there was no time for a Bricktown detour, and clawed for sky. She pushed herself as close to the Dark Cloud as she dared and then began a steep glide pattern back toward the Great Steamworks that dominated the center of Downtown. She wove in and among the buildings, using the feathers on the tips of her wings to slow her plunge toward the huge building rising toward her.

After a few minutes, the multiple smokestacks of the Steamworks rose into sight and she knew she was on target. Diving beneath a covered walkway, she spotted the entrance she was looking for, a road that disappeared beneath the Grand Canal. Taking a deep breath, she swooped down toward street level, startling several pedestrians who weren't used to seeing one of the Angels this close to the ground. Electric cars and trucks swerved when they spotted her, their horn blares echoing after her as she plunged into the darkness of the tunnel.

She maneuvered to the center of the tunnel, trying to avoid the few trucks moving goods in both directions as she flew deeper underground. The tunnel began leveling out and then suddenly opened up into a sprawling cavern beneath the Steamworks, filled with the smoke of numerous giant engines. A large waterfall filled the north end as the waters from the Grand Canal were funneled beneath the Works, turning the turbines that provided electricity to the majority of the city.

Erica pivoted slightly and, checking her gyrocompass, she headed toward a tunnel system leading to the northwest. Dodging in and out between smokestacks, aerials, cranes, and the occasional jet of flame that rose from one of the buildings she passed over, she sped across the part of Downtown that most people never saw. A couple of autonomous mechanicals flew up near her, showing a remarkable amount of curiosity for what were usually simple-minded machines. Normally, she might have been tempted to converse with them, but time was of the essence.

Her flight path took her out of Downtown's Underground into the caverns beneath Webster Groves. Here large factories dominated the caverns beneath the city and huge mechanicals moved cargo and raw materials beneath her. She continued to hear the countdown in her head as she struggled to make up time. She had to follow a tunnel deeper into the Underground as she passed below the East River, and then she began weaving her way toward the exit tunnel.

She sped along, staying as close to the ceiling as she safely could to avoid traffic. These tunnels had never been designed for someone to fly through them and from the sound of horns and the occasional curse from a startled driver, she was certain the Angels would be getting some nasty letters.

I'll worry about that when it happens. Right now, I have to reach the finish line.

She burst out of the tunnel at the border to White Cliffs. The storm had apparently blown itself out while she was underground and visibility had begun to return to normal. Pushing herself, she climbed as high as she dared and then angled her flight toward Angels Tower. Going more on instinct now instead of actually plotting a course, she wove in and out of the buildings, diving below and then arcing above crosswalks and balconies, trying to cut off every second of flight time she could.

Finally the tower rose above the buildings around it. She put on a spurt of speed, depleting her thalisium levels to a dangerous low, but it only had to last a few more minutes. She saw another Angel landing on the roof and the flashing light on her own wrist as the flight controllers began to signal for her to go into an orbit around the building. She glanced at her chronometer; only a few minutes were left before her deadline.

She waggled her wings, signaling the tower she was not going to orbit, and dove for the roof. At the last second, she saw another Angel, wings outspread and catching air, attempting to land in the center of the roof. She turned and aimed for the far corner of the tower. She flared her wings and arced upward, cutting her flying speed below stall as she crossed the lip of the roof. The sudden loss of momentum dropped her toward the brick landing pad and she bent forward and spread her wings as far as possible, letting them act as a drag on her downward plunge. She hit the roof harder than she wanted, but she was able to stand up and tuck her wings into place before a rush of bodies surrounded her.

Flight Commander Kralowitcz stepped forward, her nose only a few inches from Erica's. "Halgrim, what the hell were you doing with that stunt?"

Erica glanced at her chronometer. "Flight Cadet Halgrim reporting in. Six packages retrieved. Landed at Angels Tower two hours, fifty-eight minutes flight time."

The flight commander's rage was not appeased by that bit of information. "Turn in your wings and gear at Operations and then report to the main conference room in thirty minutes." Kralowitcz didn't even bother dismissing her, just turned and walked back toward the control room to await the next Angel who was attempting to land.

The longer Erica waited outside the doors to the main conference room, the more she noticed the little things, especially how quiet the hallway had become. It felt like the entire building was holding its breath, waiting to see what was going to happen to her. The few people who passed by seemed to hug the far wall and avoided talking to her outside of saying hello. A few of her fellow candidates were congregating in a room at the end of the hall, peeking in on her from time to time through a small glass window in the door.

I wish I knew what they were discussing in there. If they're going to fail me out for that landing, then just go ahead and do it. I've thought it over a dozen times standing out here and I'd do it again if the situation called for it. If they didn't expect us to make forced landings from time to time, then why do they teach us how to do it at Base Camp?

Erica glanced down at her chronometer and sighed. *Twenty minutes? That's it? It feels like I've been standing out here for hours. Still, how long does it take to come to a decision?*

Erica leaned against the wall and puffed a breath of air upward, forcing her bangs out of her eyes. Then she heard the sound of footsteps approaching the door and drew herself up to the position of attention before the doors swung open next to her. A member of the training cadre stepped into the hall and faced her.

"Cadet Halgrim, please report to the committee."

Erica took a deep breath to calm herself and stepped out sharply. She entered the room and saw the table at the far end. Six training instructors and Flight Commander Kralowitcz were gathered with, to her surprise, Lady Kitsune Orisaka, the founder of the Angels of Steel herself, who sat in the center position. There was one isolated chair on her side, centered directly across from the lady, and Erica marched up to the chair and stood ramrod straight as she stared just above the assembled personnel.

"Cadet Halgrim, reporting as ordered."

After what seemed an eternity, she was directed to take a seat. She sat there, keeping her head straight, but glancing with her eyes at the faces staring back at her. She wasn't sure what the issue was or what kind of decision they had reached, but after a few seconds, Erica decided she never wanted to play poker against any of them.

Finally, Kralowitcz spoke up. "Cadet Halgrim, how many hours of flight training do you have?"

Erica thought for a second and dredged up the number from her flight log book. "Ma'am, I have two hundred fifteen hours, counting the three hours for the test I took today over the past three months. I believe that is the standard for all Angel cadets."

"Two hundred and fifteen hours. Do you consider yourself to be an expert after all that time in the air?"

"Negative, Flight Commander. I believe I am very good at flying, but I would never consider myself an expert."

"So, if you are not an expert with your wings, what in the name of the Seven Sisters made you think flying through the Underground was acceptable in any way, shape, or form?"

So, apparently word gets through the city faster than I thought.

"It was desperation more than anything, ma'am. That and the fact I've spent years exploring the Underground when I was in elementary and high school. I do not claim to be an expert flyer, but I do know parts of the Underground better than most street dwellers."

There was a bit of a buzz as the members of the committee whispered among themselves. After a moment, the flight commander started to speak again, but she halted when Lady Orisaka laid a hand on her forearm.

8

"Cadet, even though you know the Underground as you say you do, have you ever flown through it before?"

"No, Lady Orisaka, I have not. However, I was running behind on my test and I knew if I avoided the main smokestacks at Fletcher Dynamics, the area between the upper levels and the ceiling are relatively free from obstructions. There are the giant cranes that track along the ceiling and the emergency gyrocopters that fly through there, but they're well lit. The only other route I could think of aboveground would have taken me through Bricktown, and I'd have failed the test for sure."

The lady favored her with a smile before her face became serious again. "But, do you realize how many guy wires you missed during your flight?"

Erica felt her face go pale and she slowly shook her head. "Guy wires? I don't believe I saw any down there. None registered on my goggles."

"The route you took had thirty-eight guy wires stretching from the tops of poles and chimneys to the ground or adjoining buildings. You avoided most of them by a safe distance, but missed at least three by less than a foot. Do you remember what happens when a wing and a guy wire intersect?"

"There's usually a jolt and either the wing collapses or is ripped off at the shoulder, immediately followed by a crash."

"Exactly, which is why we have you intentionally run into one at about three feet off the ground. However, during your flight, you were aimed directly at several of these wires only to veer off at the last second. Yet you claim not to have seen them. Can you explain that?"

Erica thought hard about her plunge through the Underground. "No, I can't. I knew I had a feeling I should make a turn several times during the flight, but it was just that. The instructors always taught us if you feel something's wrong, you're probably right, so adjust accordingly. I guess I must have seen them without registering them."

Erica's eyes grew wide as she realized the implications of what the lady had said. "Wait. I can believe you received reports about my flight—enough people weren't happy about my entering and exiting the Underground. But there's only one way you could possibly know whether I narrowly missed any wires down there. Someone was following me."

The flight commander allowed herself a ghost of a smile. "I'd have been more impressed if you'd have spotted your tail, but yes, you were followed. We assign our best flyers to tag along with the fledglings. I have to congratulate you, Halgrim—you gave your partner a run for her money. She said you were the hardest person she's ever followed in the eight years she's been flying for us. Said you scared her to death going through the Underground like you did."

Her face hardened back into its usual expression before she continued. "However, your reasoning for taking that risky path is unacceptable. Yes, you would have failed the test, but it's more acceptable to fail and retake the test than to wind up as a street pancake, Cadet."

Kralowitz leaned forward in her chair and spread her hands in front of her on the table. "I've heard the scuttlebutt among you cadets. 'We're just a delivery service, not the military. Why do they push us so hard?' It's simple. It's the rare Angel who survives making mistakes. When you step off the edge of a building and open your wings, there's nothing but your equipment, your training, and your judgment between you and a rather abrupt stop on the pavement below. I'm not sending a single one of you out there until *I'm* convinced and *Lady Orisaka* is convinced you are coming home. In the future, when you are delivering packages, remember it's better to be a minute or two late and arrive in one piece than to rush into a dangerous situation."

Erica's eyes grew wide. "When I deliver a package?"

Lady Orisaka held a hand up to her mouth to hide a smile. "Of course, Angel Halgrim. Did you not pass the final test? Did you not finish in the top ten of your class in classroom work and practical exercises? The Angels of Steel have been accused of many things, but not recognizing talent is not one of those things."

Flight Commander Kralowitcz added, "But don't think your little stunt will go unnoticed. The way you flew to pass this test, you just volunteered for the drill team. See Flight Leader Zwyer to get your assignment."

Chapter Two

"Join the drill team," they said. "It'll be fun," they said.
They lied.

Erica pushed herself to keep up with her teammates as they slowly circled above the Great Steamworks in the Downtown district. She had just completed her eighteenth month with the Angels of Steel and between her regular delivery runs and practicing with the team, she'd barely had enough time for herself, much less spending any time with her boyfriend, Michael Shay. And Flight Commander Kail had been merciless these past few weeks getting them ready to perform for the Founders' Day celebration.

The great thing about the celebration was the new wings they were going to be using today. They were more streamlined than their usual wings, built more for acrobatics and precision flying than their more durable, but slower wings. Erica checked the thalisium level once again and saw she had more than enough lift to last through the day. The small electric engine centered on her back purred as it drove her wings into the air.

A small light flashed twice on her wrist and she glanced up to see Flight Leader Sophie Zwyer break out of the formation known as the Angel's Halo and begin making her way up toward the forbidding black mass above them.

Time to leave the Darkside behind, Halgrim. We're headed for Daylight.

She took the opportunity to adjust her rebreather one last time before she angled upward, keeping her distance from her teammates. The only advantage to rising up to the Aerie here was there was nothing above the Steamworks, so no chance on hitting a walkway or passage while passing through the Cloud. A few seconds later, she saw her partner disappear into the Cloud ahead of her and she switched on the small lights at her wingtips.

Darkness surrounded Erica as she maneuvered higher through the Dark Cloud. The only sounds she could hear were the flapping of her wings and her breath through the rebreather. To her left, she could barely make out the dim lights attached to Kim Fitz-Simmons's wings. Erica pushed herself harder to ensure she stayed level with her teammate as they climbed through the Cloud.

I hate being in the Cloud. It's like flying through soup. Hopefully they'll give the signal soon.

A sudden flash on her wrist caught her attention. She took a deep breath through the rebreather and focused on picking up speed as her teammates banked to the right and spiraled up toward the daylight barely visible above them.

Almost before she realized where they were, they burst out of the inky darkness and began circling the city of Southwatch, their wings spread out to catch the updraft of warm air bouncing off the top of the Cloud. Erica suppressed a shudder as she noticed the buildings looked like macabre fingers clawing their way out of the Cloud, greedily reaching high into the sky.

They wove in and out of the towers of Downtown, gaining altitude with each wing stroke. Erica slipped her rebreather off and glanced at the canopy of airships anchored above her, their glistening bodies of bessum reflecting the sunlight down toward the Cloud. Wisps of smoke rose from their steam-powered engines, curling above the gas-filled balloons fighting against the anchors that tethered these gas giants to the tops of the Downtown towers. Erica could almost watch the individual blades of the propellers as they churned lazily, providing just enough power to help maintain the airships' station.

She snapped herself out of her reverie as she remembered Flight Commander Kail's briefing. *"This is an important ceremony today. Don't follow too close. Don't lag behind. Hold your position in formation and move as if you all were one person. The eyes of Southwatch will be on you. Make the Angels of Steel proud."*

After a few circuits of the city, she and the others came on line with the upper reaches of Downtown known as the Heights. Erica noted how much cleaner these buildings looked compared to the grime and gray that made up the three levels below the Cloud. It was hard not to be envious of those wealthy enough to afford clean air, but she forced herself to concentrate on the pair of boots just ahead of her. No time to get sloppy now.

There was another flash and, as one, the Angels broke formation and climbed through the maze of airships, anchor cables, walkways, and lighting rods that made up Aerie, the playground of the nobles of

Southwatch. Each of the Angels followed her preplanned course to maximize attention on their flight—curling in and out to ensure specific airships were treated to a sight of one of the Angels flying past before the cadre regrouped in the skies above Aerie.

This was the part Erica loved. She seldom had the freedom to move without restriction and bask in the golden sun high above Southwatch. While she loved the challenge of banking and twisting her body through the maze of buildings below the Cloud or weaving through Aerie's convoluted paths, neither matched the pure exhilaration of simply flying in any direction the open sky presented. Still, the ceremony was not over and she quickly found her spot in the spiral of winged women forming up above her.

Again, Flight Commander Kail's voice rang in her head as if the older woman was standing right behind her. *"Look, Halgrim, you're the newest person on the team. Everyone's gonna be watching us. Don't screw up. Got it?"*

The flight began circling the *Avantian Temple*, the largest single airship in Southwatch. The golden dome of the craft sparked in the early afternoon sun and it dwarfed Baron Amberville's ship stationed at the center of Downtown Aerie. Erica glanced to the west and saw the smaller cluster of airships that made up the White Cliffs Aerie, but she'd be visiting that part of town later. Around her, she saw the windows of the Aerie crowded with onlookers gazing at the circling women. More and more walkways and balconies began to fill and she knew it was almost time to begin.

A triple flash from the light on her wrist-com told her Sophie had gotten the signal from the baron. The women expanded their wings to maximum and flipped a control on their wrists. The small servos running down their arms to the wings whirred and metal coverings pulled back, revealing the multicolored bessums in the linings. Like light through a pane of stained glass, their wings cast a kaleidoscope of colored steaks across Aerie. The golden bessum skins of the airships reflected the beams back. Other beams fell on the Dark Cloud, causing multihued patches to appear, changing its swirling black miasma into a cacophony of color.

Erica heard the oohs and aahs from the crowd below and saw children running around trying to "capture" the dots of light like kittens chasing a sunbeam. The Angels spiraled closer and closer together until they could grab each other's feet. Once the circle was joined, they spiraled slowly down toward the courtyard of *Avantian*

13

Temple. About forty feet above the *Temple*'s spiral roof, the Angels broke formation, swooping down on alternate sides to land in the courtyard,

One of the hierophants motioned to them. "Quickly. This way. We've got a room ready for you to change in. The baron, the lord mayor, and the hierarchs will be here soon to greet you." He directed them to a small room off the main hall. Once inside, they took off their wings and went into the dressing room beyond. Erica grabbed the package marked with her symbol and stripped out of the dirty jacket and pants she'd worn for the flight through the Cloud. She could hear the voices of her teammates as they rushed to wash before changing.

"Halgrim. You did pretty well out there for your first time."

Erica turned to see Sophie, leaning against the locker next to her. Sophie towered over her, her curly blond hair pressed against her head from wearing her helmet. "Thanks, Sophie. I couldn't have done it without your help."

"Don't mention it. Oh, there are things you can do better next time, but we'll worry about that at the debrief. Hurry up and get changed."

Erica grinned before answering. "You need to relax, Sophie. You don't always have to be on duty."

Sophie started to respond, but Rachel Walker, one of her teammates, stuck her head around a corner. "Sophie? She's always on duty. She probably sleeps at the position of attention."

"At least I understand discipline, Walker. You were late twice on beginning your maneuvers. What happened?"

"My wings were sluggish. I need to talk to Crystal and have her check my thalisium levels. It was tough to gain altitude today."

Sophie started stripping out of her gear. "I asked everyone if they had their wings checked before we took off. You *know* the Cloud is tough on the servos. I don't want anyone spiraling out in there. We'd never find you."

"They were fine yesterday. I'm not sure what happened. That's why I want Crystal to check them out."

Erica had heard this conversation a dozen times since she'd joined the Angels of Steel. Sophie had graduated first in their class at training, with Rachel a close second. For all their skills, they couldn't be further apart in temperament. The one thing they both excelled at was getting on each other's nerves. Erica grabbed her towel and left the two of them carrying on their long-standing feud while she took a quick shower.

A few short minutes later, she came out of the shower and nearly bumped into someone trying to enter at the same time. She pushed her wet hair out of her face to see Christina Bronson step back, blushing furiously. "Oh, I'm so sorry."

"My fault, I was in a hurry. Are you excited to meet the baron?"

"I still can't believe it," Christina said, slipping past her. "I told my folks as soon as I heard. I think they were more excited than I was." She continued talking, but Erica couldn't hear her over the rushing water. She hung around outside the door until Christina reappeared and the two of them hurried over to the lockers to get into their dress uniforms.

Compared to their flight gear, the dress uniforms were impressive. They were form-fitting silk dresses with a floral pattern, matched with a silk over-jacket with long flowing sleeves. They were designed to be worn with or without wings attached, but for this ceremony the baron had requested they appear with their wings.

Erica noted with a touch of envy how the outfit made Christina appear even more shapely than usual, while she felt she looked more like a boy than usual. Unlike most of the Angels, Christina had kept her brunette hair long, which made her stand out even more compared to the others who'd cut their hair short to fit under their helmets better.

"Come on, Erica, we're going to be late."

"Right behind you."

Erica finished putting on her boots and joined her friend near the door. On Sophie's signal the twelve women of the Angels of Steel drill team left the dressing room and moved toward a small set of risers behind a group of seated dignitaries. They took their positions as the smell of flash powder filled the room. The three main seats up front were still empty and Erica could see Sophie checking everyone out to ensure Lady Orisaka would have nothing to complain about when she saw the pictures in the *Southwatch Gazette* in the morning.

A sudden burst of music from the assembled orchestra caught everyone's attention as Baron Thomas Amberville, Lord Mayor Peter Mulvihil, and Hierarch Pamphile entered together. The baron was a middle-aged man, graying slightly at the temples, but it was obvious

15

he was still at the peak of health. Only the faintest hint of an expanding stomach betrayed his age. The lord mayor showed both his age and his lifestyle in the elaborate and woefully out-of-date outfit he wore.

The hierarch moved at a slow, steady pace to allow the baron and lord mayor time to stop and visit with some of the other visiting nobles in the crowd. Still, Erica could see she moved with the grace of a much younger woman, only a few lines and her carefully coifed gray hair betraying her age. Apparently being one of the leaders of the *Avantian Temple* agreed with her.

The party arrived at the podium and stood in front of the three empty seats. The hierarch gave the ritual blessing of Avanti to the assembled nobles before the head party took their seats. The rest of the assembled gathering sat down, leaving only the Angels standing on the risers. They all hoped the ceremony wouldn't drag on, but those who'd done this before knew that was a vain wish.

Once everyone was settled, Hierarch Pamphile rose and moved to the podium. "Children of Avanti, we welcome you to the Founders' Day Celebration. Two hundred and eleven years ago, the city of Southwatch did not exist. There was only a pile of rubble, left over from yet another useless war. Our forefathers saw the beauty of this site and realized a new city could arise from the skeleton left behind — a city that would be a beacon of hope for the rest of the world. A city dedicated to peace, yet able to defend itself against those who mistook our desire for peace as a sign of weakness. And so, now, here we stand, two hundred and eleven years later. Look around you—look at the gleaming city in the sky we call home."

The hierarch continued on in this vein and Erica tried her hardest to look like she was paying attention, but inside she was seething. *Sure, look at the bright and clean city you get to live in. You should come off your high perch and come down to Darkside. You've been in the clean air so long, you've forgotten what it's like not to be able to see the sun. You've forgotten about the acid rain and the lack of vegetation. It's all gray and black and concrete and soot down where people like me have to live.*

To calm down, Erica let her eyes wander and noted how many of the city's nobles were gathered in the *Temple.* Apparently Founders' Day was something everyone wanted to be seen at. She wasn't sure she'd seen this many people at the *Temple* before, even during Festival Week. She hooked the edges of her wings onto the riser and leaned forward, letting the wings and her harness hold her up while she tried not to fall asleep. After a while, the hierarch completed her speech and the baron took her place.

A soft whisper caught her attention. "Erica, check out the far doorway."

Erica slowly stretched her head to the side as if she was working out a stiff neck. A young man, about her age, stood there in full military dress uniform. She recognized the Imperial Air Corps insignia on his collar, even from this distance. He was handsome and she knew Christina would waste no time going over to introduce herself once the presentation was over. Even though Erica would never admit it, she was envious of Christina's ability to just meet people. Christina currently was between boyfriends, but Erica knew that wouldn't last long.

However, it was the middle-aged man standing right behind the Air Corps officer who caught Erica's eye. He was obviously a pilot but he was dressed in a battle uniform instead of a dress uniform and he wore no visible insignia. He leaned forward and whispered something to the younger man, who suddenly stiffened and blushed. The older man turned and winked at Erica, who fought to keep her features still. She blushed all the way up to her red hair and pointedly went out of her way to avoid his gaze for the rest of the ceremony. Somehow she knew that amused him more.

The pain in her lower back and legs was becoming intolerable when the baron finally wrapped up his own speech and motioned to the orchestra. A trumpet call rang out and everyone rose from their seats. On cue, the Angels spread their wings as the window behind them opened to let in the afternoon sun. Again the cascade of colored lights flickered through the room. Erica concentrated on standing still as the soft music played and the crowd seemed enthralled with the lightshow inside the *Temple*'s main chamber. After a few minutes, the music came to a close and the mayor wrapped up the ceremony, inviting everyone to join him for food and drinks in the next room.

Christina rushed off to catch up with the young officer, but Erica just moved to a place where she could sit down without her wings bumping on the ground behind her. *Oh my Goddess, my legs. Between standing and these heels, I think I'm going to fall over. Next time, I'm going to make sure these shoes are broken in before another dress uniform assignment.*

"Nice ceremony."

Erica managed to keep from screaming as the voice came from right behind her. She spun around to see the man in the combat gear standing there. "You startled me."

He flashed an unapologetic grin at her. "Yeah, I hear that a lot."

Erica felt her heart rate coming back to normal. "I'm Erica Halgrim," she said, bowing her head slightly but keeping him in her field of vision.

He bowed in return. "I'm Captain Tony Blaylock. I'm with Majowski's Marauders. We're supporting the Southwatch Air Rangers."

"I don't think I've ever met an Air Ranger before."

Tony laughed. "And, I hate to tell you, you still haven't. I'm a mercenary. We've been hired to beef up the Rangers for the ceremony. Apparently the powers that be thought having all these nobles and visiting dignitaries from the capital might be a tempting target for sky pirates. So they hired us. If nothing happens, we get a couple weeks' work, some good food, and then we move on to the next contract."

"Sounds like you travel a lot."

The older man laughed again. "Don't get out much, do you?"

Erica felt herself bristling. "There's no need to be rude."

"Sorry, your question just startled me a bit. Yes, we travel a lot. I think I've pulled duty in fourteen different countries on five continents. However, Colonel Majowski's originally from Brabant, in the north of Dalriada, so he prefers to take Imperial contracts whenever they're available."

"I'm sorry. I've only been with the Angels of Steel just shy of two years. I'm hoping I'll get a chance to travel, but I suspect most of my work will be delivering goods around town."

"Trust me, Miss Halgrim, there's something to be said for having a steady job and a regular place to sleep. I'm hoping once I finish saving enough for an airship of my own that I'll find a place like this to settle down."

Erica's eyes widened. A small airship was an incredible amount of money. The only airship owners she'd heard of were nobles, wealthy industrialists, the Church, and sky pirates. Still, it would be rude to point that out, so Erica changed the subject. "What did you think of the ceremony?"

"Well, the pre-ceremony was incredible. I loved watching you all out there. I wish I could do what you do, but I'm too big for those wings. That's why I pilot a gyrocopter."

Erica stretched her legs one last time and gingerly climbed to her feet. Tony was easy to talk to, but the Angels were supposed to mingle with all the guests, not sit in the chamber and visit with one gentleman, no matter how personable. "I probably should join the others. Hopefully they left a little something to eat."

"Miss, I saw the waitstaff going into the other room. If that crowd ate *that* much food already, this *Temple* would be sitting on the ground from all the weight."

A scream stopped them in mid-laugh. There was a sudden movement and a dark figure plunged past one of the windows and landed in the courtyard with a sickening thud. Erica and Tony rushed through an open door and looked around.

Over in the far corner lay the broken body of a young woman. Tony rushed toward the body, but a shadow passing over the courtyard caught Erica's attention. She glanced up to see a gyrocopter bank away, angling down toward the Cloud. Two other gyrocopters roared past the *Temple*'s central spire and dove, trying to intercept the first craft. She unfurled her wings and started to step onto the rail when she felt a hand on her shoulder.

"What are you doing, Halgrim?"

"Sophie. That woman . . . I think she fell from that copter. I've got to stop them."

"No."

Erica watched as the gyrocopters faded into the upper layers of the Cloud and disappeared from sight. "But, Sophie . . ."

"What were you going to do? We're not the police or the army. We are a messenger service. Do not allow emotions to get you in trouble."

Three gyrocopters bearing the markings of the Air Rangers roared by, heading in the same direction as the other gyrocopters. Sophie turned Erica around to face her. "Did you see her actually fall from the gyrocopter?"

Erica felt the warmth as tears began running down her face. "No, Tony and I heard the scream. Then there was a horrible thud and the scream stopped. The next thing I saw was a gyrocopter disappearing into the Cloud, with two other copters chasing it."

Sophie looked at her intently. "Tony? Who is Tony?"

Erica glanced around but the middle-aged man was nowhere to be seen. "He was right there . . ."

"We'll worry about that later. Now think, Halgrim, what could have caused the girl to fall from the sky?"

"A very good question, Flight Leader."

Erica felt a presence behind her and turned to see the mayor with two inquisitors standing behind him. He was wringing his hands and there was no questioning the worried expression on his face. "Terrible, this is a terrible thing to happen. Especially on Founders' Day in front of all these people." He turned to look directly at Erica. "I'm sorry, miss, I'm going to have to ask you to accompany Sergeant Black here. I'm sure he's got some very interesting questions to ask you."

Chapter Three

"What were you doing in the main room of the *Temple* after the ceremony? Why didn't you join everyone else at the reception?"

The voice of the dark-haired man sounded like the crack of a whip. It was all Erica could do to not scoot back in her chair to escape it. His eyes bored into hers, looking for the slightest hint of falsehood. She took a deep breath and tried once again to answer his questions.

"I remained behind because my legs hurt after standing through the entire ceremony. I just wanted to rest for a few moments. Then someone approached me and we began talking. We talked for a few minutes before I heard the scream and found the girl's body lying there."

"Yes, so you say. Now, do you know who the girl is?"

Erica turned her head before speaking to the inquisitor, an involuntary shudder running through her. "I never got close enough to see her face. I could tell she was dead. I've seen enough accidents when I was in training to recognize a neck shouldn't bend that way. She landed face-first on the balcony, so all I saw was her back. Tony may have recognized her. He was checking her vital signs the last time I saw him."

"Ah, yes. This elusive Tony. And where is he?"

"I don't know. He seems to have disappeared about the time my flight leader showed up."

The inquisitor rose and walked to one of the windows, staring down into the swirling maelstrom below. "Miss Halgrim, I wonder if you can appreciate the severity of this situation."

Erica looked up in surprise. "A girl is dead. I don't know how much more serious it can get."

"That was not just any girl, Miss Halgrim. I don't know if I should tell you this, but that girl is—excuse me—*was* Iriana Bogdanovich, the daughter of the Coritanian ambassador. He was at the reception when the incident occurred. He has not only filed a formal complaint with the baron, he is insisting we deal with this immediately or he'll be forced to raise this to the Imperial council."

Erica nodded. "I hope it gets solved quickly too. Even if it turns out to be an accident, the man on the gyrocopter should have landed to see if she was all right."

The inquisitor's head snapped around at Erica's statement. "A man? I thought you said you didn't see how she fell? Describe this man."

"I *didn't* see what happened. I told you, I saw the gyrocopter flying away. I was going to pursue it before I was stopped. It looked like a man. I mean, I never got a good look at the pilot, it just seemed like it might have been . . . Oh, everything is so confused. Sophie's right, it could have been an accident. Maybe whoever was flying the gyro was afraid and panicked."

"There could be another explanation. Perhaps it was murder?"

Erica's eyes widened. "Murder? But why?" She stopped and bit her lip and then looked up at the inquisitor. "That would explain why the pilot was in such a hurry to leave."

"If there was a pilot."

Erica did a double take at that comment. "What are you saying, Inquisitor?"

The dark-haired man spun around and slammed a hand down on the desk in front of her. "Perhaps you know more than you're saying. Who knows? Maybe *you* stayed behind so you could fly off unobserved. What's to say *you* didn't meet this young woman—a woman who was supposed to be attending the same reception you were absent from? What's to say you didn't argue with her and then grab her, fly up into the sky and hurl her headfirst to the courtyard below? You had time to do that and then land to 'come to her aid.' It makes as much sense as a mystery gyrocopter."

"That's preposterous!"

The inquisitor smiled at her before sitting down. It was not a reassuring smile. "Perhaps, but it is *an* explanation. Not necessarily a good one, but it is plausible and it would work. You see, Miss Halgrim, if we cannot solve this incident, there will be consequences, both political and, Goddess forbid, militarily. Coritani is a powerful ally, but they would be a worse enemy. After all, they have opposed Dalriada in the past and they're a much more militaristic society than we are. If we have to provide a *solution*, it will not really matter if it's the truth. It merely needs to be close enough to the truth to be believed."

Erica felt the walls closing in on her. "You couldn't. That would be . . . I mean, that's not right . . . I didn't do anything wrong."

"Perhaps you didn't. Then if you recall anything or discover anything in the future, contact me at once." The dark-haired man turned around and stared out the window. "You may go."

Erica rose and left, her mind going in a thousand different directions. Sophie and Christina were waiting just outside for her, along with Sergeant Black. He escorted the three of them to the stairs leading away from the administrative rooms beneath the *Avantian Temple*. The soft throbbing of the motors that kept the airship afloat only served to make Erica's head hurt worse than it already did.

They stood in front of a desk as the sergeant filled out some paperwork and then he looked up at them. "You three are allowed to go. However, do not leave Southwatch without coordinating with us first. You are free to resume your duties with the Angels without restriction as long as you remain within the city limits. If for any reason your duties would require you to leave the city, you must notify us forty-eight hours in advance. Do I make myself clear?"

The three responded in the affirmative and he gestured with a big, meaty thumb over his shoulder toward the door. The three women walked out of the office and caught their breath at the base of the stairs leading to the central chamber.

Christina stared at Erica and then rested a hand on her shoulder. "Are you all right?"

Erica nodded. "I think so. The inquisitor was pretty rough on me."

"How—" Christina began.

Sophie cut Christina off. "Of course he was. That's his job. He's trying to get to the truth. Anyway, we're several hours late returning to headquarters. I contacted Lady Orisaka and she wants to talk to us first thing tomorrow. We need to get going."

The three young women returned to the changing rooms. Erica noted her gear had been rearranged in the locker. Someone had searched her belongings, no doubt looking for evidence of her possible "crime." Christina's sharp intake of breath told Erica she'd encountered the same thing. A quick glance at Sophie told her nothing— her flight leader was as expressionless as usual.

I wish I could accept everything the way Sophie does. Nothing flusters her. She's all business all the time. No wonder Lady Orisaka takes such a personal interest in her career.

23

The women, now clad in their flight gear, climbed onto the balcony and went through their preflight checks. The sight of the two acolytes trying to scrub the bloodstains off the courtyard brought the image of the young woman's broken body back. That ensured preflight, normally the most boring part of flying, became a nerve-wrenching series of events as Erica tested and retested her equipment to ensure her wings responded to the servos and the thalisium levels were sufficiently high enough to provide lift to counter the effect of gravity.

Sophie's voice cut through the fog in Erica's brain. "All right, Halgrim, you've tested them enough. Let's go."

The three women brought their goggles down and stepped off of the balcony. Spreading their wings, the three glided in ever-widening circles until they were evenly spaced apart. On Sophie's signal, they plunged toward the swirling darkness below.

The Cloud rose to meet them, almost welcoming them into its inky embrace. Erica always hated that momentary loss of vision before the goggles reacted to the Cloud's chemical makeup. Slowly her vision cleared enough for her to be able to control her flight. Eddies and clumps of thicker pollution swirled as the winds that bound the cloud shifted the darkness in a clockwise rotation, ever circling the city. She banked to take advantage of the wind and slowed her descent. Sophie and Christina were blurry, indistinct shapes ahead and she tacked against the wind and followed them deeper into the Cloud.

While the Cloud appeared to be a solid mass when viewed from above or below, there were pockets of clear air here and there, well, clearer than other parts. The Cloud twisted and turned through the towers that rose from Midtown and thrust their way into the sunlight to create the Heights. This was the Dead Zone, the place where no one could survive without artificial rebreathers and protective clothing— at least not for long. However, that didn't mean there weren't *things* in the Dead Zone.

She noted a group of winders nearby. The almost mindless robots made up the majority of Southwatch's mechanicals. These were making their way up the building, inspecting for any sign of structural damage. Their control wires streamed behind them toward the ground below, probably leading to an inspection team guiding them.

Over in the distance, she caught a glimpse of a gyrocopter negotiating its way down toward Darkside, gingerly maneuvering around an abandoned walkway that connected two of the towers. Erica could imagine how picturesque the view might have been back before the Cloud formed. Now, it was simply a navigational hazard. She glanced up and noted Sophie had circled back and was motioning for her to pick up speed. She realized the signal light was going on her wrist and instantly tapped it to signal back to Sophie "message received."

I'm going to hear about that when we get down. Sophie is always warning us to pay attention when we're in the Cloud. I was paying attention, but not to her, which is going to bother her more.

A sudden movement on the walkway caught her attention. Two figures in protective suits rose up; each one held some type of tube tucked under their arms. Sophie and Erica banked rapidly to the side and tucked their wings in tight, diving into the darkness as two nets whistled narrowly overhead, disappearing into the darkness behind them. Before the two could drop their net guns and make another attack, Christina swooped down from behind them; the small electro-guns mounted on the edge of her wings glowed with a full charge. Pulling up, she released the charge, sending two bolts of miniature lightning toward the men. One of them froze as the electrostatic charge ripped through him and he slumped forward, the back of his suit smoking. Her other bolt missed, sending a shower of sparks up from the walkway as the second figure ducked away.

Erica pivoted and began to charge her own weapons when Sophie maneuvered between the other two women and signaled for them to follow her. *Sophie's right. There could be more scavengers hanging around. Speed is our best friend now.* She tucked her wings in again and the three dropped into the darkness.

After falling several dozen feet, Sophie spread her wings and Erica and Christina followed suit. The bottom of the Dark Cloud was visible, and seconds later they broke through the Cloud into Darkside. The rest of Southwatch spread out below her, the stark grays, blacks, and off-white of the city in stark contrast to the colors and brilliance of Dayside. They circled for a moment to get their bearings and then kicked off toward Angels' Headquarters in White Cliffs.

They bled altitude as they moved toward the edge of Downtown, catching glimpses of life in Southwatch as they descended. The Midtown portion of the towers teemed with business people, as men and women made their way between the towers on covered and open walkways. Some carried briefcases, others boxes, and a few just moved in small groups talking. A few stopped and waved at the Angels as they passed by, but most seemed too engrossed in their own issues to notice.

Down lower, the smells of cooking and the sound of children became more prominent as they moved closer to the Streets. Here, the roads and alleyways were crowded with people moving around and the occasional car or truck rumbled on the cobblestone streets, honking their horns to get the kids playing to move so they could get through. She heard a child call out and soon a small parade of children were chasing the Angels through the streets as the women flew overhead. Sophie pulled up and hovered for a moment to wave at the children before the Angels moved on.

Well, I'll be. She does have a heart after all.

Leaving Downtown behind, the Angels crossed the Khyber River and entered Riverside. This was a more residential area than Downtown and none of the buildings reached high enough to pierce the Cloud. They flew over the low buildings until they crossed the Whitefish and entered the White Cliffs district. Sophie motioned upward and they soon were climbing toward the tallest building on the outskirts of White Cliffs. They circled the building, gaining height with every circuit until they crested the building and saw the landing area with its guards on duty. The three Angels circled until the challenge came over their wrist-coms. Each Angel had to respond with that day's acknowledgment before being allowed to land.

Erica was the last down and she hurried to catch up with the other two, who were entering the only structure on the roof outside of the guard shacks in each corner. Sophie motioned for her to hurry. "Come on, Halgrim, We've been waiting for you all day."

"Sorry, Sophie, I had to wait for the landing signal."

"Yes, yes, come on. Grab the rail."

Erica took a good grip on the metal bar next to her as Sophie pushed the nearby lever down. There was a rumbling sound as the steam engines below gathered speed and the pneumatic shaft that held the elevator in place descended rapidly. Erica always felt more nervous in this shaft than she did flying, even if she knew the elevator was safe. Nearing their stop, Sophie lifted up on the lever in a steady motion until the shaft ceased contracting on itself. She moved the lever until it was parallel with the floor. The floor monitor showed they were on the seventeenth floor and Sophie opened up the door grate and pushed another lever to open the main door.

"Go get your gear checked in. Take your wings down to Crystal for inspection. Meet me in Conference Room C in thirty minutes. I have to go report in to Lady Orisaka." Erica heard Sophie mutter as she walked out of the elevator, "Although, I'm certain she already knows we're here."

"Wow, Sophie is really spun up about this," Christina said as she helped Erica remove her wing harness. Once Erica had done the same for her, Christina unzipped her flight jacket while they walked down the hall. Erica noted again how quiet the halls were in the headquarters. It reminded her of her first time waiting to get called before Lady Orisaka.

"She may act like she's been doing this forever, but don't forget, we went through basic together. This was *her* first ceremony as an Angel too. Since she was the flight leader, she's responsible for whatever happened."

"What really *did* happen up there, Erica?"

Erica saw too many people wandering around, many staring at them with unabashed curiosity. "Let's talk about this in the conference room, Christina. I don't think this is the time or place. Besides, we have to get to Crystal's lab before she shuts down for the day."

"Who're you trying to kid, Erica? Crystal lives with her equipment. I doubt she's slept in her room for months. Especially since your *friend* designed that companion for her. She may never come out again."

Erica blushed and put a hand over her friend's mouth. "Chris, let's leave my boyfriend out of this conversation," she whispered furiously.

Christina nodded and began pointing at her mouth. After a few more seconds, Erica let go and Christina took in huge, dramatic breaths and fanned her face. "I thought I was going to die. I wish you wouldn't do that."

Erica gave her a dirty look and then started walking down the hall. "Come on, I'm getting changed and heading for Crystal's lab. You can dawdle here and be late to Sophie's meeting if you want."

"Oh no, you're going to have to get in line behind me," Christina called as she sprinted down the hall with Erica in close pursuit.

Chapter Four

Erica felt a shiver run down her spine and it had nothing to do with the air circulators that seemed to be working overtime in the conference room. Lady Orisaka sat at the end of a long table, flanked by her flight commanders, trainers, and a number of people Erica had never seen before.

Sophie led the three of them into the room and they stood at attention until Lady Orisaka motioned for them to sit down. She looked over some notes and one of the men sitting near her, dressed in a waistcoat and wearing pince-nez glasses, whispered something to her and bobbed his head toward the end of the table. He appeared to be concerned about something but Lady Orisaka continued to look at her papers.

She began without looking up at the trio. "Bronson, did you witness the events at the *Temple*?"

Christina gulped before answering. "No, Lady Orisaka. I was one of the first to arrive, but I didn't see the actual incident."

The older lady raised her hands in front of her, her long fingernails visible even at this distance as she clicked them together unpleasantly, almost like the sound of a large crustacean's claws snapping shut. "Did you overhear or observe anything not in your report?"

Christina glanced at Sophie, whose face remained impassive as usual. She then looked at Erica before looking down at the floor. Eventually, she raised her eyes to meet Lady Orisaka's and meekly replied, "No, ma'am."

"Very well, Bronson. You're dismissed. Continue with your regularly scheduled activities for the day. If we need you, we'll send for you."

Christina gave Erica an apologetic look and Erica wondered what exactly Christina had put in her report. Christina rose, bowed to Lady Orisaka, and moved quickly toward the door. It shut quietly behind her and the room seemed a little colder with her friend's absence. Erica knew Christina wanted to stay for moral support, but her dismissal didn't surprise Erica.

Lady Orisaka's voice brought her back to the here and now. "Now, Flight Leader Zwyer, you were in charge for the ceremony. How is it we find ourselves in the middle of a diplomatic scandal? Do you know the baron's chief attorney and his chief of staff have already visited me three times since your meeting with the inquisitors? It wouldn't surprise me if the Imperial Legate arrived any moment now, wanting to know how we're going to explain this to the Coritanian ambassador."

The older woman rose and began pacing at her end of the table. "All you had to do was fly up, do a small performance at the *Temple*, mingle with some guests, and then fly back to headquarters. How do you explain this fiasco?" With each new word, her voice rose in volume and she moved down the table toward the two young woman. As she reached the end of the table, she stopped and rested her hands on one of the chairs, leaning forward to ensure both of them were looking at her.

Sophie stared straight ahead, still as placid as if she'd walked off the training grounds. "There is no explanation that would suffice. From my point of view, there was no failure on our part. Most of the guests responded to the sound of the girl's scream and subsequent fall. It is just our misfortune Halgrim was the first one on the scene."

Lady Orisaka stared at Sophie the same way a butterfly collector might stare at their latest trophy before pinning it into place. Then a small, wry grin formed at the corners of her mouth and she straightened up. "Correct answer, Zwyer. It *does* appear to have been an unfortunate set of coincidences, at least on the surface. This is why I pay high sums of money to some of the people seated around this table. It is their job to run interference on situations like this. However, answer one question—do you think Halgrim is involved?"

Erica started to say something but a sharp pain in her ankle stopped her. She waited as Sophie glanced down the table to ensure everyone was watching her and not Erica before responding. "I do not believe Halgrim had anything to do with the death of the ambassador's daughter."

Lady Orisaka walked back toward her end of the table before spinning around. "Zwyer, you did not answer my question."

The room got deathly quiet and Sophie nodded. "I do not know the full circumstances of Halgrim's presence. It could have been bad fortune. She could have been delayed to ensure she would be one of the first to arrive on the scene. There is the matter of the unidentified man who detained her in the assembly room. According to my research this morning, this man has not been located yet. Few remember seeing anyone resembling his description. His name did not appear on the guest list. If Halgrim is not hallucinating, it would be advisable to find this man and soon. She may need someone to alibi her presence if she is called in front of the inquisitors again."

"You seem rather familiar with this investigation, Zwyer."

Sophie nodded. "As you stated, I was in charge. I have friends who keep me up-to-date on things like this, ma'am. It pays to have friends in high—and low—places." To Erica's surprise, there was the faintest hint of a smile on Sophie's lips, as if she and Lady Orisaka were sharing a private joke.

Erica felt the weight of the eyes in the room focusing on her as Lady Orisaka eased back into her chair. "So, Halgrim, you say you were visiting with Captain Anthony Blaylock of Majowski's Marauders? He was there when the incident occurred but he disappeared shortly after the incident?"

"That is correct. He went to provide aid to the woman. I was going to join him when I saw a gyrocopter flying toward the Cloud, pursued by two others. I attempted to follow when Flight Leader Zwyer intercepted me. I didn't know if the girl had fallen from the gyrocopter, been pushed from it, or if they simply witnessed the incident. However, I was reminded we are neither the Southwatch Police nor are we Air Rangers. The next thing I knew, I was being escorted to the inquisitor's office since this happened on church property."

Lady Orisaka inverted her elbows on the table and brought her fingers together in an inverted V in front of her face. She stared at Erica and the only movement was the slow clicking of her nails in an arrhythmic fashion. Erica tried not to look away, but it was difficult meeting the woman's intense gaze. After what seemed an eternity, Lady Orisaka broke the stalemate.

"That all sounds so plausible—except for one small matter."

Erica felt a sinking sensation in her stomach when her leader said "except." She took a deep breath to try and steady her nerves before responding. "I don't understand. I've told you everything I told the inquisition."

"Would it surprise you to learn the man you claim to have met could *not* have been Captain Anthony Blaylock?"

"I didn't *claim* to have met him. I *did* meet him."

"No, you didn't."

That last statement brought Erica up short. There was such an assurance in the lady's delivery, Erica felt the first twinge of doubt. "With all due respect, Lady Orisaka, you were not there. You cannot say I didn't meet Tony."

Lady Orisaka picked up a sheaf of papers from a folder and held them casually in front of her. She glanced over the top of the papers, spearing Erica with her eyes. "I cannot say you did not meet *someone*, but what I *can* say is you did *not* meet Captain Tony Blaylock. Captain Blaylock died three years ago. He was a glider pilot working for Majowski's Marauders. The last time anyone saw Captain Blaylock, he was engaged in combat against Mad Dog McCue's pirates over the Gray Mountains. His glider was engulfed in flames and corkscrewing into the side of a mountain. So, either you saw someone who claimed to be Tony Blaylock for reason or reasons unknown, you saw Blaylock's ghost, or you're making up your story whole cloth. So which is it, child?"

Erica felt her hackles rising. She didn't appreciate being called a liar and at this point didn't care who she annoyed. "The person I spoke to in the *Temple* identified themselves as Captain Tony Blaylock. I'd never heard of Tony Blaylock, or Majowski's Marauders, before yesterday, so it defies imagination I would not only make up a name, but make up a name associated with a former pilot of that specific unit." Erica paused for a moment and then an idea came to her. "If that's his dossier, are there any pictures of him in there?"

Lady Orisaka's eyes narrowed, but somehow, Erica thought she was pleased by the question. The Angels' founder extracted something from the folder and handed it to a well-dressed man sitting next to her. He walked it down the table and sat it in front of Erica.

She picked up the photograph and felt her jaw drop. Her voice came out in a startled gasp. "That's him. That's the man I was speaking to yesterday."

"That, Miss Halgrim, is impossible."

"Impossible or not, it is true."

A buzz began around the room, but it was cut off by the sound of a hand slapping the table. "Very well, Halgrim, we'll investigate this phantom pilot of yours further. Now I also understand from Flight

Leader Zwyer's report, you were attacked in the Cloud while you were returning?"

"Correct. A pair of scavengers intercepted us during our descent. They set up an ambush on a walkway approximately thirty feet from the bottom of the Cloud. Flight Leader Zwyer and I conducted evasive maneuvers, and Angel Bronson took one of the scavengers out with an electro-shock attack. The other scavenger avoided the attack and escaped in the confusion."

"That verifies your flight leader's report. Now, did anything suspicious occur before the attack?"

Erica thought back on the incident. "There was a gyrocopter off at the far edge of my vision, descending toward the Great Steamworks district. It appeared to be a typical gyrocopter and it made no suspicious moves, but it did appear just before the attack." Erica paused and then continued, "I did notice it near the walkway where we were attacked when I first saw it from above."

"That too agrees with your flight leader's report. Very good. Until further notice, you are restricted to sub-Cloud flying. Please report to flight operations and ensure they restrict the thalisium in your wings to ensure you cannot break that ceiling. You are dismissed."

"What?"

Sophie grabbed Erica by the shoulders and tried to drag her out before things could deteriorate further. The older woman stood up and glared down the table at the two. "Did I stutter, Halgrim? You are restricted to sub-Cloud flying. If I had my way, you'd be grounded until this was all over. Since you're still in your probationary period, we need to see how well you handle stress and *follow orders*. Do I make myself clear?"

"Crystal, ma'am," Erica said through clenched teeth.

Even though the older woman stood ramrod straight, Erica still felt she could hear a sly tone in her voice as she continued, "Do try to stay out of trouble, Halgrim."

Erica bowed and turned to leave with Sophie trailing along behind her. She started walking toward Ops without waiting to see if Sophie was following or not. *Lady Orisaka knows more than she's saying. I feel like she's trying to tell me something, but I'll be damned if I can figure out what game she's playing.*

"Wait up, Halgrim," Sophie called, trying desperately to catch up without actually running. "We need to talk."

Erica continued her march toward Ops without looking back at Sophie. When she spoke, she surprised herself with the anger in her voice. "What is there to talk about? You heard her. She's convinced I'm crazy, a liar, or both. Sophie, why the hell did I go through four months of training, and now probation, if this happens the first time there's trouble?"

Sophie reached out and grabbed her shoulder, making her wince from the pressure. "You went through the training for the same reason I did: You want to fly so badly you took everything they threw at you and survived. You made it and now, the first time you run into adversity, you want to whine and quit? Is that it, Halgrim?"

Erica shook loose, surprising Sophie. "No, I'm not quitting, but I'm tired of everyone accusing me of lying."

"Then prove them wrong."

"What the hell are you talking about? I'm restricted to sub-Cloud, remember? I can't exactly go back to the scene of the crime and search for clues—like I'd even know what to look for in the first place."

Sophie pointed toward the elevator to take them to Ops, a thoughtful look on her usually stoic face. "Lady Orisaka gave you quite a bit of information about this mystery person. I've got some connections with the Mercenary Guild. My cousin works there since his accident took him off active duty. It might be possible to get a copy of that dossier. Plus he can check to see if some guy is passing himself off as Tony Blaylock."

Erica felt her mood lighten. "Great idea. The more I can learn about this guy, the more likely I can drag him out into the open to vouch for me."

"No. you've got other things to worry about."

Erica paused at the elevator. "Like what? You're not assigning me for more training, are you?"

"No, Halgrim. I'll work on finding your mysterious flyboy. *You* need to figure out who attacked us in the Cloud and why. Those weren't scavengers. They dressed like them and acted like them, but the weapons they used were significantly more sophisticated. If I were you, I'd use your contacts and your boyfriend's contacts to figure out who's gunning for you and why."

Erica turned a little green at that thought. "Gunning for me?"

"If I were to commit a murder and you and 'Tony'"—Sophie paused to make quote marks when she said his name before continuing—"were the only potential witnesses, well, I'd ensure there *weren't* any witnesses. You saw the gyrocopters. We have to assume they may have seen you too. Face it, our dress uniforms are hard to miss, even at a distance. They don't know you didn't see them clearly. The fact you saw them makes you a threat. Plus, people saw the inquisitors take you away for questioning. It probably wasn't hard to get your name given the way the nobles gossip. So, kidnapping you, or killing you, is the quickest way to be sure you can't talk to anyone else."

Erica let all of that sink in and then said in a lower voice, "So, Lady Orisaka wasn't grounding me because she's mad—"

"—she's grounding you for your own safety. Personally, I wouldn't give you your wings back either, but I know you need them to get to certain places."

Erica blushed furiously. "Does everyone in this flight know what I do on my days off?"

"Are you ashamed of him?"

"No! Of course not. It's just, well, he's a private person and he'd prefer if not everyone knew where his laboratories were. He has enough trouble protecting his work from his rivals. If everyone here knows where he's working, then I'm going to have to quit meeting him there."

"And that would be a problem, why?"

Erica was never so glad to see an elevator arrive. She ducked inside, but Sophie followed. The elevator began its breakneck descent toward the basement of Angels' Headquarters before Erica spoke again. "Look, Sophie, with all of my duties here, I barely get to see him as is. He can't always just drop an experiment to meet me at my place—like there's any privacy here in this building—or at a restaurant. So, I go to his lab. It's easier on the both of us."

Sophie brought the lever into place and drew the elevator to a smooth stop before motioning Erica out. The sound of machinery humming and the increased heat told Erica they'd arrived at Operations. There was a loud clank and then the sound of running feet before a muffled explosion went off around the corner they were walking toward.

34

A small smile reached Sophie's face. "Ah, looks like Crystal's gotten here ahead of us."

They turned the corner to see a girl in green coveralls wiping soot off her face, her feet covered in fire-retardant foam. Three large wrenches hung off a belt around her hips, making a clanking sound as she approached them. "I don't understand, Sophie. That mixture should have worked."

The flight leader patted her on the head and spoke soothingly. "I'm sure you'll get it figured out, Crystal. Have you had a chance to work on those wing modifications I asked for?"

Crystal's eyes lit up, her failed experiment forgotten. "Oh yes, Sophie. I'm not quite finished, though. They need more testing but it was a brilliant idea. In fact, I was able to get more lift from that design than we anticipated. I can't wait for us to get a chance to try them out soon."

The young technician grabbed Sophie by the arm and dragged her to a pile of equipment showing recent fire damage. She maneuvered like a ballerina through the piles of gear, tubes, and wires strewn all around the room until she reached her destination.

Erica was always a little nervous around Crystal. She had been born to one of the royal families, the Digby-Smythes, and sent to the finest schools in the Empire. No one doubted her genius in mechanical aeronautics. However, sometimes she got so wrapped up about designing wings she forgot about the person who had to wear them. There were times Erica believed Crystal had put test Angels into danger, just to see how her designs would react in extreme conditions. Crystal wasn't malicious, but she was so damned focused on her work she never considered what might happen if something went wrong because nothing *should* go wrong.

Not like someone else I know, she admitted to herself ruefully.

She caught up with the pair. Sophie was inspecting a new type of servo Crystal was installing on a large set of wings and Crystal was bouncing all around trying to explain her modifications, tripping on her words in her enthusiasm. Erica found it rather endearing that Sophie called Crystal by her first name—the only Angel apparently afforded that bit of friendship. The two were a contrast in personalities and style, but they worked well together.

"We'll talk more about this in a bit, Crystal. There's a reason we're here. Did Lady Orisaka call down ahead of us?"

Crystal's face fell as she turned away from her new project. "Yes, and I don't like it. Wings should be free to carry you anywhere you want to go. It seems wrong to put limiters on them."

Sophie nodded sympathetically and patted Crystal on the shoulder. "I agree, but there is a good reason for all of this. Can you make the adjustments on Halgrim's wings and harness?"

"If she can't go higher, can she go faster?"

Erica started getting nervous the way Crystal was grinning at her, but Sophie interceded. "Crystal, can she still control her flight if she's going faster? It doesn't do any good if she can't turn before she runs into something."

"Oh sure . . . I mean, she'll have to practice so she's used to the change, but I've got a new wing design I've been wanting to try. It'd be easier to adjust them with a height restrictor than to modify her current wings."

Crystal walked over to Erica and pulled a tape measure off her belt. She took measurements while Erica tried to stay still. "Height, check. Shoulders, check. Bust, check. Waist, check. Leg length, check. Weight, approximately one hundred twenty pounds. Yes, I think these new wings will fit you perfectly. Oh sure, we'll have to make a few adjustments, but yes, yes, I think you'll do fine. I can't wait to see you try them out."

Sophie had found a seat on a nearby drum and watched the probing and prodding with an amused look on her face. "So, Crystal, what's so special about these wings?"

"Weight ratio. I managed to get some Black Diamond steel from Atragon. I've used that for the main struts while using bessum for the feathers. Unfortunately, my initial design didn't work. Bessum just isn't flexible enough to do those dragon wings I wanted to make."

Sophie shook her head before responding. "Crystal, there's a reason we're called the *Angels* of Steel, not the *Dragons* of Steel."

Crystal nodded slowly. Erica could almost see a miniature Crystal standing in front of a blackboard making notations and erasing others as she thought. "Although I could possibly—"

Sophie spoke up hurriedly. "We can discuss this later, Crystal. Now, the new wings?"

Chapter Five

"All right, Halgrim, time to see if you can beat your old record. Ten laps around the course. You know the drill. Get ready."

Erica drew her goggles down and adjusted her harness one last time.

"Get set."

Wings spread for maximum lift on the first sweep, knees bent, arms down by her waist.

"Go!"

Erica sprang from the platform and felt the momentary thrill of free-fall before her wings caught and the servos kicked in. With a powerful movement, the wings bit into the air and provided the lift she needed to get stabilized. Then she was able to concentrate on her balance, turning and leaning to minimize anything that would slow her down as she moved through the winding course in the valley. She found herself weaving between narrower and narrower slalom poles. She had to rapidly adjust her altitude to either climb over or duck under gates as she powered through the course.

She felt her breathing match the flapping of her wings. There was euphoria in her flight. Mechanical wings be damned, these were *her* wings and she and the wings moved as one.

Concentrate, Erica, concentrate. Keep your arms tucked in, keep your legs straight. Let the wind flow past you like you're not there. Let the wings do the work and focus on staying as close to the barriers as you can without touching them.

A few seconds later, she was through the speed portion of the course and into the obstacle course. Now, instead of poles and gates, she had to avoid objects sliding through her flight path on wires, or rising out of pop-up blockades, and even other instructors who attempted to interfere with her flight. She turned, banked, flew sideways, and even upside down to avoid being struck by everything coming at her from multiple directions at the same time. And when she flashed past the last obstacle, there was nothing but a long straight flight a few feet above the ground down a valley toward the finish line at the lake.

The countdown timer in her head told her she was doing well, but it was not time to relax. She concentrated on focusing her servos to the maximum, getting every erg of power out of the wings to propel her faster. The finish line was in sight. She was going to make it. She was—

buzzzzzz

"Erica, aren't you up yet?"

Christina's voice sounded a thousand yards away, but Erica couldn't hold onto the dream and her eyes slowly opened. She eased into a sitting position in bed and slumped forward, letting her arms dangle toward the ground. "It can't be seven o'clock yet."

Christina walked into the room, her toothbrush still in her mouth. She pulled it out and pointed it at her sleepy roommate. "Seven fifteen. You hit the snooze button twice. Now, come on. You've got to report to Crystal at nine. If you want to eat before then, I'd get moving."

"A little sympathy for the dead? I feel like I didn't sleep a wink last night."

"You've been having some wild dreams. You spent the entire night tossing and turning. I nearly had to move into the other room. Crystal working you that hard, huh?"

Erica flopped back onto her bed, her arms akimbo above her head. "I feel like I'm starting all over at basic training, Chris. These new wings Crystal developed? Oh, my Goddess, they're so light and comfortable but they're touchy." She turned to face the bathroom door where her friend had been standing a few seconds ago. The sound of running water told her Christina was washing her hair. She waited until the water shut off before continuing. "If you get out of trim for a second, you're spiraling out of control or swerving into an obstacle before you can correct. A few times, I wasn't sure the harness would stop me. If I hadn't insisted we work in a padded area, I wouldn't be here to talk to you."

Christina's voice echoed out of the bathroom. "Are they as fast and responsive as Crystal keeps saying they are?"

"And more. That's the problem—they're so responsive I keep overcorrecting, but if I slow down too quickly, it's easy to stall. I swear she used a hummingbird as the design model."

Christina came back into the room, her hair tied up in a towel. She rummaged through her dresser and pulled out a fresh duty uniform.

"Well, then, think like a hummingbird. If you want to hover, you're going to have to flap faster."

"But I don't want to burn up the servos."

Christina turned toward her, slipping a set of diamond studs into her ears. "Can you? Have you asked Crystal what their top end is?" Christina arched an eyebrow at her, looking for all the world like their old classroom instructor, Flight Trainer Gibson. "Halgrim, are you sure you know what you're doing, or are you just relying on your gut again? There's a reason we issue manuals and have instructors, you know. That's to keep you from killing yourself out there."

The two girls collapsed in laughter and then Erica pushed herself out of bed toward the bathroom. "Point taken. Maybe I'm making assumptions because I already know how to fly. What I don't know is how to fly with Crystal's wings. I guess I need to take it slower and ask questions."

"Look, Crystal is a good person, she just gets hyper-focused. Don't keep shying away from her. She wants to succeed as much as you do. You *do* know there's a big gathering of the city's scientists at the end of summer. She may be up for an award if she can get this to work."

Erica paused for a second. "You think Crystal pays attention to awards?"

Christina finished lacing up her boots and turned to Erica. "From people like us? Probably not. From her peers? Absolutely." Christina checked her watch and leaned into the bathroom. "I'm heading out for chow. I'll see you down there, okay?"

"Yeah, yeah, I'll be there in a moment." Erica walked back into their dorm room as Christina slipped out into the hall and shut the door quietly behind her. Erica ran her brush through her hair and grabbed her least rumpled duty uniform.

Now, where did I take my boots off? Hell, I don't even remember coming back to the room last night, much less going to bed. That last session with Crystal really wiped me out. At least I have the weekend off and Michael's free. It'll be nice to get away from this place. Since the incident at the Temple, I feel like someone's constantly with me or watching me or something. I just can't be myself.

Erica leaned back in the chair and watched Michael cut off the welding torch he was using and push the welding mask up to the top of his head. She reached up and pushed her own goggles onto her forehead. She glanced around the room, taking note of the disorder—boxes and crates shoved here and there among half-completed experiments and tools lying everywhere. The clutter was accumulating faster than Michael's work mechanicals could pick them up and sort them into the right spots. Plans and blueprints hung from the walls in an existentialist representation of chaos, one tacked up over the next one without any worry about plumb or level as Michael got a new idea.

If he could ever focus on one project, he'd probably make a fortune on his designs, but he's always rushing from one to the next as his muse changes gears in his brain.

Michael blew on the spot weld he had just made and watched as the metal slowly turned from cherry red to a dull bronze color. He set it down on a small tray of sand to ensure he didn't set his desk on fire—again—and turned to Erica. "So, how was training this week?"

"Beastly, Michael, simply beastly. Can we talk about something else? It seems the only things people want to talk about at work are my training and the incident at the *Temple*. It's like I have no other purpose than to be their source of entertainment these past few days."

"I'm sorry to hear that, darling. But, you have to admit, it's not every day someone gets involved in intrigue, murder, and political machinations."

Michael took off his mask and set it gently down on the table in front of him. A small winder resembling a spider with an additional set of arms scurried up onto the table and grabbed the mask and hauled it off. Erica watched in amusement as the small robot tried to balance the heavy mask as it climbed down the desk leg and made its way over to the wall where similar pieces of equipment were stored on pegs.

"Thanks, Sparky," Michael told the winder. It paused momentarily to whirr at him like a cat before continuing on its way.

"Personally, they could take all the politicians in a rowboat and sink it in the Khyber River for all I care. I mean, Lady Orisaka has had me in her office three times since the ceremony. I've seen her more since the incident than my entire career up to now. Honestly, Michael, I think she knows more than she's saying. Her questions keep changing slightly, but I'm pretty sure my answers are still the same."

"Pretty sure? That's not a very scientific way of measuring success."

She leaned over and poked him on the nose. "That's because I'm not a scientific genius like you. We mere mortals sometimes have to rely on estimates. I recognize the scientific method in her line of interrogation, though. If you ask your questions slightly differently, it's possible the answer may change because the stimulus is different. It's no different from the way you say you test your hypotheses before committing actual equipment. It's just not as much fun being the subject at the short end of the microscope."

Michael gave her a leering grin. "I love it when you speak science at me."

She swatted his shoulder that time and got up out of her chair to walk around the lab. "Seriously, Michael, I'm tired of everyone staring at me like I've grown a new head or something. I just want to take this weekend and relax. Do something different for a change."

Michael put the rest of his tools down and the various winders began trekking toward his desk to start gathering them up. "I am sorry to hear things have been so rough. What do you say we go to that new theater in White Cliffs? Not only do they have a new show straight from the capital, but there's a new restaurant that opened just across the way that is incredible."

"Who are you and what have you done with Michael? All right, let me check to make sure you're not some high-tech mechanical," Erica teased as Michael turned a bright shade of red. "No, that sounds incredible. You've seen most of my dresses. Do I have time to pick out a new one or will I be all right?"

Michael rose from the desk and held his hands up, framing her like a photographer might. "I think you'd look incredible no matter what you were wearing, but your dark blue dress would be perfect for the theater. How long do you think it will take you to get ready?"

"Probably not more than an hour, unless there's more traffic than I think."

"Fine, I'll have a cab waiting for you out in front of Angels' Headquarters on the Streets in an hour. I'd have suggested using one of the carriages, but my weather equipment thinks it'll rain this evening and I really don't look good in sludge and tails. Besides, if I go for a ride with you, it's bad enough having to look up at the bottom of the Cloud instead of seeing stars overhead. I don't think acid rain is that romantic."

"Still, it'll be nice to do normal stuff for a change."

"It's never just a normal time with you, Erica. Any time I get to spend with you is special. Besides, I know you like getting dressed up and I love *seeing* you dressed up, so it's a win/win for me too."

Now it was Erica's turn to blush. "I'm going to have to take it easy with this scientific talk. I don't want to overload your circuits."

"You're right, though. I've been up to my neck in commissions and haven't been out of the lab in a while. It's not fair you only get to see me with all this clutter. Let's enjoy each other's company for once. I'm assuming champagne will be acceptable with dinner."

"Just a glass, Michael, you know it goes right to my head. All right, I'll see you in an hour. Will you be wearing the tie with the brown or red stains?"

Michael waved a thumb over his shoulder toward one of the doors in the back of the lab. "I'll have you know Theo picked out an entire new wardrobe for me. It even matches this time, or so he claims."

There was a rustling at the far end of the room and a very human-looking mechanical rose up from behind a crate with a couple of boxes in its arms. The cybernaut's bronze skin shone in the gas light and his golden eyes glowed as he responded. "It's not my fault, Michael. You failed to program me to recognize shades of color. I think I did very well this shopping trip. I may have even gotten your size right."

Michael and Erica laughed at the mechanical's indignation and then Michael waved a hand in Theo's direction. "I'm certain you did fine." He turned back to his human companion and smiled at her. "I'll call right now for the reservations. The theater owner owes me a few favors, so I think I can get a good box seat for the performance tonight. I'll make sure they have fresh flowers at the box and the champagne on ice waiting for us."

Erica gave him a hug. "You do that, Michael. I can't wait to see you."

She slipped out of his embrace and headed toward the entryway to his laboratory, but he called her back before she reached the door. "Oh, here's a little something I'd like you to wear tonight," he said, handing her a narrow box. She flipped it open and there was a beautiful silver necklace consisting of a series of interlocked chains, supporting a large clear crystal.

"Oh, Michael, it's beautiful, but it's too expensive. You shouldn't have."

"I wish it *were* that expensive. That's an artificial stone I created. It's ninety-nine percent as clear and as hard as a diamond. Still, I think it will accentuate your eyes wonderfully in the candlelight at the restaurant."

Erica blushed again and gave him a kiss before turning to leave again. Theo came over and assisted her into her wings, ensuring everything was hooked up properly before he opened the outer door. She stepped out onto the landing and looked down the forty-six floors to the street. Michael's lab wasn't the easiest place to reach, considering there were no connections to the floors above, below, or beside. The only way in or out was to have one of his mechanicals walk you up the side of the building or to be able to fly to the small landing she now stood on.

Then again, it helped when you dated a girl with a set of wings.

Taking a dramatic step out into space, Erica free-fell down the building with her wings tucked in tight. She held that position for a few seconds before opening her wings and swooping up into the air. She heard the *oohs* and *aahs* from the children watching from the walkways and balconies nearby and she paused to wave and speak to a few of them before turning to the west, leaving Webster Groves and heading toward her home in White Cliffs.

No matter how many times I take flight, each time is almost better than the last. If there was a way to package this feeling, I'd make a fortune.

Erica saw a couple of Angels flying in the distance carrying packages. They waved but Erica couldn't make out who they were in the fading light. Still, seeing them reminded her of Sophie's warning. Someone could be lurking, waiting for her to let her guard down. She tried to focus more on her surroundings as she flew.

One thing she noted was the number of mechanicals around the city. A veritable horde of winders were doing menial jobs too dangerous for regular people, especially anything that required scaling the tall towers that made up Southwatch. Some washed windows, some cleaned chimneys or air purifiers, and some scrubbed the ledges from the filth and debris that gathered there over a period of time. Some, she noted, stood motionless at corners atop certain buildings, their glowing red eyes staring out over the city. She resolved to ask Crystal or Michael if they were familiar with them.

The streets below were filled with cars, trucks, carriages, wagons, and people. No matter what time of day it was in Southwatch, you could count on finding someone out wandering about. The wagons had always interested her as a child. She knew the farmers from outside Southwatch brought their produce into the city with real horses, but they exchanged them for the mechanical horses she saw below. Horses did not do well beneath the Dark Cloud. In fact, *few* living things did well under the Dark Cloud, but the humans who still lived here refused to give up Southwatch without a fight.

Landing atop the Angels' building, she took the elevator down to Operations and put her wings away in her locker. She hurried back up to the dorm level and rushed to get changed. She found a note from Christina saying she was going to be out late this evening. Apparently she'd gotten the name of that handsome Air Corps officer and they were going out to dinner.

Good for her. She hasn't been out with anyone for a while. Not since she and Rafe broke up. It'll do her good to get over him.

She grabbed her dark blue dress and thanked the Goddess she'd just gotten it back from the cleaners. She fixed her hair and put on her best jewelry, not that it was that impressive compared to the pendant Michael had given her. Still, she wanted to fit in with White Cliffs society. It was a long way from Camden Town Midtown to living at Angels Tower in the White Cliffs. Even though it didn't rise all the way to the Aerie, it still commanded a beautiful view of the Thorn Forest off to the southwest as well as gazing down from the Cliffside over the rest of Southwatch. Unfortunately, as a probationary member of the Angels, she didn't qualify for an exterior room, yet.

She frowned slightly, thinking about this evening. White Cliffs still saw itself as separate from Southwatch. Many of the inhabitants still resented being absorbed by the city-state and looked down on people born in the city proper. Then again, people back home used to call anyone acting snobbish a "cliffer." Personally, she didn't care; all she wanted was for tonight to be perfect with Michael.

Checking her watch, she saw she had a little time before she was supposed to meet Michael, so she took the elevator down to the ground floor. She signed out with the duty officer for the weekend before stepping outside. Glancing up, she could tell Michael's weather prediction machine was right on the money again. Angry lights and rumbling noises began to reach the streets. It was only a matter of time before the rain started to fall.

And it begins again. Sunsiders will get clean rain to restore the sparkle to their ships and water the flowers that grow in the Heights. We Darksiders? We'll get the toxic sludge that forms when the rain falls through the Cloud. Michael says there must be a scientific reason for why the Cloud persists overhead, but it just feels like there's a curse on the city.

Erica twirled the specially treated umbrella she had brought with her and then turned as she heard a familiar clopping on the street. A produce wagon came rolling up in front of the building and a number of children appeared out of nowhere to visit with the mechanical horse. Other young men came out of restaurants and stores to pick up crates of tomatoes, corn, and other fresh vegetables.

She put up her umbrella and stepped out onto the sidewalk to see the horse. The children had already disappeared, chasing after another phantasm only the young could see. Erica petted its head absentmindedly and walked around to see what else the wagon might be carrying.

The first warning something wasn't right was a feeling that someone was behind her. She started to spin around but someone grabbed her roughly and put a cloth over her mouth and nose. She recognized the smell of chloroform and as she started to go limp, she felt people lifting her and sliding her on something cold and hard. And then darkness closed in and she didn't know anything more.

Chapter Six

"Welcome back to the land of the living, Miss Halgrim."

Erica's eyes opened and then shut tightly as the bright light made her eyes water. She realized she was sitting in a chair but she couldn't move her head, arms, or legs. Turning her head slightly, she felt something soft against her throat, holding her head against the back of the chair. Her mouth and throat were parched and she croaked out a short sentence.

"Water, please."

"Of course, Miss Halgrim," the deep male voice replied. She heard rustling and she chanced opening her eyes a bit. She saw a shadowy movement nearby and then her head was pulled backward roughly and water poured onto her face. She coughed a few times but managed to swallow some of the liquid as the rest ran down her face and neck.

"Now, now, not so rough," the voice chided. His disapproval was palpable through the stage whisper he was using. "Miss Halgrim is our guest. We should treat her with respect."

The shadowy figure let her chin drop back down against the restraint and then moved silently away. Several bright lights shone in her face. She tried to squint through the lights to make out who was speaking to her, but he was merely a black lump stationed between two of the lights. It hurt too much to stare in his direction for very long.

She waited for someone to explain why she was here, but there was nothing but the measured breathing from the man just beyond the circle of lights. She eased her eyes open, a little at a time, to try and get used to the brightness. She had to compromise at open just enough to peer through her eyelashes into the darkness. A door opened and closed behind her and she guessed whoever had given her the water had left since the figure in front of her hadn't moved yet. Minutes passed and she gingerly turned her head from side to side, but no matter which angle she turned her head, all she found was the bright glare of the lights. There were no signs of windows and since she couldn't hear any noise, she guessed she was in an interior room, which meant there was no sense in calling for help.

Finally, she couldn't stay still any longer. "Why am I here?"

"An intelligent question. I'm impressed." The voice almost purred as he responded to her. "You didn't start threatening me or screaming or anything useless. Therefore, I *shall* answer you. You are here because you witnessed something you should not have. You are here so we can determine what you saw and what you did not see."

"I already told the inquisitors everything. Why all the—" She took a deep breath and shifted uncomfortably before she continued. "You're not with the inquisitors. You're with the people on the gyrocopter."

There was no mistaking the delight in his voice. "Oh, this is going to be so much fun. I can't tell you how much I appreciate working with an intelligent young woman. You have a keen grasp of the situation, Miss Halgrim, so this will make things easier. So, tell me, what did you see?"

Erica took a deep breath and began reciting her story to the shadowy figure. She'd told it so often, it was almost by rote at this point. It took a while but eventually she reached the end and then stopped. "Is that what you wanted to hear?"

"Very good. Almost word for word what you told the inquisitors."

His comments shocked her and she blurted out her next words. "How do you . . . ? Never mind. You probably found that out the same way you discovered my name and where I lived."

The deep voice sounded pleased, but she wasn't reassured by its confident sound. "By the goddesses, you *are* brilliant. By the way, do you mind if I call you Erica? It would be much simpler."

"I don't see how I could stop you, but yes you may since you asked nicely."

"A remarkable woman. I must say, Erica, I *am* glad you were the one we had to interrogate. I *do* appreciate meeting someone as levelheaded as you."

Erica flexed her arms and legs, but there was no give in her restraints. If she was going to escape, it wasn't going to be by strength alone. She had to play for time and hope either Angels' Security or Michael could track her down. If she relied on the Southwatch police, they'd find her body years from now and probably fine her for littering.

She tried to focus her eyes on the shadowy figure and spoke with a confidence she didn't really feel. "It does me no good to lie. So, since I told you everything I know, are you going to kill me now or do you have other plans?"

The deep-voiced man laughed heartily. "Kill you? Oh, my dear, it's certainly not on my agenda. Honestly, that would be a waste of your talents. Still, that's not up to me. We all answer to someone if you go up the chain far enough." He paused and laughed again, a little more sarcastically than before. "Still, your life depends on how interesting your answers remain. After all, this interrogation has just begun. You have given me the basic synopsis of what you told the interrogator, but there may be details you're withholding. You may not even realize you know more than you think you do. We will continue this discussion until I am satisfied. Now, from the beginning . . ."

The hours blended into one another as the interrogation continued. Her captors were polite to the point of being grating. If she needed to pause for a drink, they provided it. If she desired a small snack, they provided it. What they did not provide was a respite. They asked her questions, then asked questions about the answers she gave, then about the question they had just asked. It felt like an endless recitation, asking the same question a hundred different ways, but Erica's answers remained consistent.

The man had her give him an approximate timeline and then had her give them the timeline in reverse order. She had no idea what time it was and she didn't even care any longer. She just wanted the questions to stop so she could sleep.

"Now, Erica, tell me more about this gentleman you were visiting with before all of this started."

"I don't know what more I can tell you. He's in his late thirties or early forties. He's about six feet tall and in good physical shape. He's got dark hair, graying at the temples. He's what you would call ruggedly handsome—I think it's the eyes; they're unusually expressive. I remember he had a mischievous look on his face, like he's the only one in on some joke. He said his name was Captain Tony Blaylock. He claimed to be with Majowski's Marauders, a mercenary group. However, I've been told that can't be him, because Captain Blaylock's dead."

"And you believed them?"

That question stopped Erica cold. "Given the source of my information, I have no reason to believe they'd lie to me. Identifying the man as Captain Blaylock, a dead man, cast more suspicion on me than anything else I'd said to that point."

The man made a tutting noise before responding. "Indeed? That's too bad. You see, his identity has not been determined by anyone. He is quite the phantom. Personally, I'd keep an open mind. After all, until someone proves otherwise, who's to say he's not Captain Blaylock?"

"Wouldn't that be tough since Captain Blaylock died in an air accident? He crashed into the side of a mountain."

The man sounded insufferably pleased with himself. "And you saw the body? Did anyone see a body?"

Something in his tone of voice brought all the frustration Erica had been under to the fore. "Don't be daft. Of course I didn't see the body. I didn't even know he existed until we met at the *Temple*. It's not like I dug through his old military records or looked for a charred skeleton on a mountainside."

She paused and then it felt like scales fell from her eyes. "However, I have the distinct feeling if I *do* manage to live through this, you're suggesting I should consider that exact course of action."

The sound of applause from the darkness surprised and annoyed her. "Oh, Erica, you are a delightful pupil. It's too bad you already work for Lady Orisaka. If you were a free agent, I'd hire you on the spot. Still, as you noted, there's no guarantee you will walk out of here. After all, many people besides you and me have an interest in this incident. People in high and low places but all of them quite powerful. But, enough depressing talk, let's return to something you said earlier . . ."

She was going through a particular part of her story for the eighth or ninth time when the door opened behind her. A figure moved through the shadows and stopped next to her interrogator. They whispered for a while and then her interrogator rose to his feet. She saw he was tall and thin but, beyond that, there were still no distinguishing features—just a black shape against a slightly darker background.

"You'll have to pardon me for a moment, Erica. There's a small matter I need to deal with. I'll be back shortly."

"I'll just wait here."

He laughed before responding. "Yes, I suppose you shall."

49

He bowed at the waist, bending forward but not enough to allow the light to hit his face, before disappearing with the other shadow. She heard two sets of footsteps disappear and then the sound of the door easing into place. She counted to twenty and then tried rocking her chair to tip it over, but as she feared, it was bolted to the floor.

There's nothing to do now but wait. What was it Lead Trainer Zimbalist used to say before a sparring match? "When you know you're fighting a superior opponent—relax. Defend yourself and look for an opening. If you look helpless, your opponent may not take you seriously and relax their guard. That's the one opening you need to win."

Well, I'm pretty darn helpless now. Let's see if they relax and give me a chance to escape.

She waited with her eyes closed against the lights, trying to relax. After a few minutes, she heard the door open and close quickly. A soft whirring sound approached and she glanced down by her feet to see two spiderlike winders gazing up at her, a series of glowing red eyes going all around their squat oval bodies. They looked so out of place she knew she was starting to hallucinate.

Might as well just go with it and enjoy the dream. "Hello, there. Are you in trouble too?"

One winder moved toward the foot of her chair and vanished from sight as the other began climbing up the chair. She watched with growing anxiety as the winder moved from the leg of the chair to her lap and then moved closer to her right arm. It seemed to study her bonds for a moment and then a large pair of scissors and a scalpel rose out of its back on mechanical arms. It moved closer to the leather strap holding her arm in place. She also felt pressure against her left leg. She had to assume the other winder was working on the strap on her leg.

"You do know what you're doing, don't you?" she asked with some trepidation.

The small winder paused and turned slowly toward her. Even though there was no obvious face, she had the impression it was gazing at her as one might look at an exceptionally slow student. It moved closer to her arm and slipped the edge of the scissors beneath the strap and made a small snip in the leather. It used the scalpel to weaken the strap while it worked on the strap with the scissors. Finally, she was able to snap the remaining leather on her own.

She felt the pressure on her left leg give way at the same time. The winder on her lap turned around and started to work on her other arm strap. She fumbled with the latch on the strap holding her neck into place. All of a sudden, her right arm seized with cramps and a tingling sensation. She had to remind herself that she hadn't moved her arm for hours. She flexed as best she could until the feeling started coming back.

Once she could move her fingers again, she bit her lip to ignore the pain. On the third try, she managed to undo the strap and her head fell forward in relief. She heard two more snips and suddenly the pressure was gone. She tried to stand up, but her legs buckled beneath her and she barely managed to grab onto the arm of the chair.

The two winders waited at the door, watching her. Moving like a day-old colt, she wobbled behind them until she could grab the door-knob and rest on it. It turned easily beneath her touch and she opened the door enough to see there was a dark hallway beyond. Two glowing red lamps illuminated doorways at either end. She saw the door to the right led to a stairway, but the doorway to the left was dark. The winders began scuttling in that direction.

I don't know if they're testing me or if this is a rescue, but at this point, I don't care. As long as I'm not in that chair, I'm good with whatever happens next.

She worked her way down the hall, using the wall to support her. The feeling was coming back to her legs, but she still felt tingling sensations every time her feet touched the ground. Reaching the darkened doorway, she discovered it was a stairwell leading down. The winders were taking turns going down the stairs, gingerly extending their long spiderlike legs as they navigated the drops. She walked cautiously behind them, even though her instinct was to grab them and run down the stairs. She had to keep convincing herself they knew the way out and she didn't, so she had to be patient.

They descended four flights of stairs, inching past open doors at each landing until they came to a concrete floor. She followed them down a small hallway toward a door in the left wall. The winders waited for her to open the door and then they scuttled out, motioning for her to follow.

As she stepped into the darkness, there was a small commotion on her left and then suddenly Theo appeared with a large cape and a cap for her as well as a small rebreather. The pure oxygen revitalized her and she realized she was in Bricktown, the true slums of Southwatch.

From the smell of the salt air, she knew they were close to the docks. She started to ask Theo what was going on, but he simply motioned for her to remain silent and follow him. He picked up the two winders before opening a small compartment in his chest. They scurried inside and once he was sure they were secure, he took Erica by the arm and guided her toward an alleyway.

A small truck with a canvas cover on its back waited there. Theo helped her into the back and she saw Michael sitting there with a strange pair of goggles on his face and two small antennas rising from something covering his ears. He was speaking into a small crystal set through a microphone and showed no sign he had noticed she was there.

"Michael?"

"*Gah!*" He started and nearly fell off his chair. "Theo, didn't you warn her?"

"I'm afraid not, Michael. We just arrived." The cybernaut looked abashed, but Erica suspected he wasn't that concerned. Michael had programmed him too well; the two picked on each other as if they were brothers instead of creator and creation. Theo continued, once Michael regained his seat, "Are you ready to recall your flyers?"

"Yes, we need to get going." Michael spoke into the microphone once more. He pushed two buttons on a machine at the front of the vehicle before removing the ridiculously large goggles off his head. "They'll be landing in a few moments, Theo. Grab them and stow them back here. I'll get the truck started."

"Very good, Michael. Shall Miss Erica stay back here or ride up front?"

"Probably best if she stays here. I'm hoping my distraction kept her captors busy but they may have discovered her absence by now."

She wobbled and Michael finally noticed what kind of shape she was in. He rushed over to help her over to a bench in the truck and then sat down beside her. He hugged her close and then looked her over. "You're all right, aren't you? They didn't hurt you?"

She was too tired to fuss at Michael for being Michael. "No, I'm fine. I'm just very tired. That interrogation went on forever. What time is it?"

Michael pulled a large pocket watch out of his vest pocket and clicked it open. "Four in the morning. You've been missing for nearly eight hours. Sorry it took so long for me to find you."

Erica jumped when she heard a large thump outside, but relaxed when Michael patted her hand and moved toward the end of the truck. Erica watched with amusement as Theo lifted two large winders resembling birds of prey into the truck and handed them to Michael. They had large antennas coming out of the backs of their heads and their oversized eyes resembled Michael's goggles.

"There we are. Let's get going before we're spotted. Sorry, Erica, but I haven't taught Theo how to drive or I'd ride back there with you. Do you want me to take you to the police?"

"No, take me to Angels Tower. I think Lady Orisaka needs to know what happened first. Besides, as soon as my kidnappers realize I'm gone, they'll break down their gear and leave. They're professionals. They won't leave clues obvious enough for the police to spot."

Michael frowned, but after a few moments of contemplating, he nodded. "Fair enough. You can always talk to the police tomorrow after you've had some rest. No sense in going from one interrogation to another. We'll take a rain check on that dinner. Maybe tomorrow—" He stopped and laughed. "I mean, later tonight?"

"Maybe, Michael. It depends on what happens next. Lady Orisaka may lock me in my room after this."

She yawned as the events of the evening began to catch up with her. Theo sat next to her to support her as the electric motor of the truck spun to life and the truck made its way out of the alley with only the faintest whisper. Erica looked out the back through an opening in the truck's canvas flap and tried to memorize the path from where she'd been held captive to Angels Tower. Even though she knew there was no point in coming back, she knew Angels' Security would be there shortly to see if they could find anything useful.

A shiver ran up her back. *I don't know who those people were, but they've got serious connections if they can access inquisitor files. I don't know what's going on, but I'm convinced the Church, Lady Orisaka, or those guys know. I'm going to have to find out for myself if I don't want to spend the rest of my life as a sitting duck.*

She nodded off somewhere on the way home. The next thing she knew, Theo was tapping her on the shoulder as Michael was letting down the tailgate on the truck. Michael helped her get down and walked her to the front door.

"Are you going to be all right?" he asked, giving her a hug.

"I think so. I'll get word to you as soon as I can."

"Do that. I can't wait to see you again . . . in less exciting circumstances, that is. Take care of yourself." He gave her a quick kiss and hopped into the truck. Theo had secured the tailgate and climbed into the passenger compartment next to Michael. The bronze cybernaut waved a hand to her out the window as the truck disappeared into the morning gloom.

Erica went into the main lobby to get the guard to call Lady Orisaka when she stopped dead in her tracks. *How* did *Michael find me?*

Chapter Seven

"Halgrim!"

Erica rolled over in her bed. According to the clock Michael had designed for her, it was 11:00 on a Sunday morning. She started to roll back over when she realized that was Sophie's voice, this was not a dream, and Sophie was standing at the end of her bed.

Oh, crap.

"Halgrim, you have to report to the main conference room in fifteen minutes. You've got just enough time to clean and get there if you start moving *now!*"

Erica started to protest but remembered this was Sophie she was dealing with. If she didn't start moving in the next three seconds, her bed would likely be on top of her after Sophie dumped her out. *That girl has a great future ahead of her as a drill sergeant.*

"Halgrim . . ." Sophie's voice had just moved from warning to threatening. Erica spun in her bed and put her feet on the floor as Sophie grabbed the bottom of her bed.

"I'm up! I'm up! Just leave me alone, I'll be there on time."

"I am your official escort. Do not make me bring you in there over my shoulder, Halgrim."

Erica grabbed a towel and stepped into the bathroom. Over the running water, she could hear Sophie's voice muffled through the closed door. "You scared the sludge out of everyone, Halgrim. The duty officer saw you get attacked, but they had slipped something through the handles of the door. By the time he could get out to the street and we had people in the air, you had vanished. Are you all right?"

Erica paused for a second. She wasn't used to Sophie showing any emotion when dealing with her subordinates. "The doctor said I'm fine. Just a little stressed. Thanks for asking."

"Just checking on your status, Halgrim. A good leader takes an interest in the physical and mental condition of the personnel under their command."

Of course they do, Sophie. Of course they do.

A quick change of clothes and Erica and Sophie were standing outside the main conference room with one minute to spare. Erica flicked the wet hair out of her face as Sophie knocked. There was a muffled sound of admittance from inside and the two young women stepped through the doorway.

Erica was surprised to find the large conference table gone. Several chairs were arranged in a semicircle and a group of women were discussing something intently. There was a pause as the two entered the room. Along with Lady Orisaka, there were four women Erica had never met before along with Dr. Lopatka, who'd examined her last night. Everyone was wearing business wear except for the doctor, who was in her usual uniform, so Erica had no illusions this was a social call.

Lady Orisaka stepped forward as the other women settled into the chairs facing the two young women. "Thank you for retrieving Miss Halgrim so quickly, Flight Leader Zwyer. Please stay—this is going to involve you also." She pushed a button on her chair and a side door opened. She motioned toward Erica and Sophie and attendants brought additional chairs for them, arranging them at the focal point of the semicircle. Erica and Sophie exchanged glances and took their seats.

Once everyone was settled, Lady Orisaka faced Erica. "Now, I know you told our security people everything last night, so I'm not going to make you repeat your story. From what I hear, you should be tired of answering questions."

"Yes, ma'am. It was a pretty long night."

Lady Orisaka turned to the other women. "You have the files there, so please make full use of them as you need to." She turned back to Erica with a sympathetic smile. "So, to make this easier, we're going to talk and you may ask questions as they come to you. We apologize for not letting you sleep longer, but it was hard enough to get everyone here, much less this quickly. Still, Dr. Lopatka tells me you're in good shape. You were lucky to escape. I hope to meet this young beau of yours someday to thank him personally."

"I'm sure Michael would love the opportunity to meet you, ma'am."

She waved her hand toward the other women. "I don't believe you've met the other people her, so let me introduce them. Miss Miles here is with Angels' Security. Miss Casciato is a detective with the

Southwatch Police Force; her focus is primarily the Brickyard, which is why she's taking a personal interest in this case. Miss Cameron is a legal representative for the *Temple*, and . . ." She paused as if not quite sure how to proceed, but the youngest of the four spoke up.

"I'm with the Black Watch. You can call me Jessica."

Erica felt her blood chill. The other three women made sense to her, but the Black Watch was the baron's personal secret police. They answered to no one but him and there was some question as to whether they even did that. Erica swallowed hard and smiled at Jessica. "I'm honored to meet you all."

Lady Orisaka nodded and then continued. "There have been a number of discussions about you since the incident at the Founders' Day celebration. However, no one anticipated you might be the target of . . . well, let's just say none of us suspected you might be kidnapped."

Erica noted the pause in Lady Orisaka's conversation, but she decided to wait and see if it was explained later or if that was one of the questions she'd be allowed to ask. She noted the detective seemed anxious to speak, so Erica turned her attention to Detective Casciato. "Did you get a chance to check out where I was held last night?"

The dark-haired lady looked uncomfortable speaking in front of the others, but she pulled out a notebook and consulted her notes before responding. "We did. Our officers secured the building and made entrance approximately twenty minutes after you arrived at Angels' Headquarters. There was *no* sign of occupation. Any equipment they had used was gone. In fact, there was no sign of occupation period—waste cans were empty, ice box was warm. There was a coating of dust on the fourth floor that appeared undisturbed. However, there was a spike on the building's electric meters last night. Someone was there, but they removed any trace of their visit. Almost too thoroughly, if you ask me."

Erica felt disappointed, but Detective Casciato didn't sound like she disbelieved her, so that was a good thing. "I tried to get a glimpse of them, but they were careful to keep the lights in my eyes at all times. All I can do is give you some approximate heights and weights and the fact they all seemed to be male."

Jessica spoke up, before Detective Casciato could say any more. "Are you sure, Erica? Is it possible you may have seen something but just can't make sense out of it?"

Erica turned and saw Jessica watching for her reaction. "No, I'm sure I told Angels' Security everything in my initial report. I thought about it before I went to sleep but I can't think of anything I can add."

Jessica nodded. "I know Lady Orisaka said we weren't going to ask you any questions, but I just wanted to verify you hadn't remembered anything else."

Erica gave the woman a wan smile. "No, but I've only had a few hours' sleep. If I think of anything, I'll be certain to let Detective Casciato know and I'm sure she can get word to the rest of you." Erica felt like a sheep being measured by a wolf. She forced herself to turn away from Jessica's piercing eyes and she could almost feel Jessica's smile at her actions.

Miss Cameron spoke up, breaking the tension in the room. "I have reviewed your interview with the inquisitors. We are disturbed about your report that your interrogators had a copy of a sealed report. Trust me, we are already investigating this breech of *Temple* security."

"I'm glad to hear that, ma'am."

Miss Cameron continued, "You may not be aware, but we have interviewed nearly all the attendees at the Founders' Day celebration with one major exception: Mr. Blaylock has avoided all of our attempts to contact him. There is general agreement a man of his description attended the celebration and he was seen on the observation deck with you by several others. That part checks out. We thought you'd like to know this since we understand there was some doubt to your veracity on this point in the initial interviews."

Erica laughed, but there was little mirth in it. "I understand the confusion considering I spoke to a man who's supposed to be dead."

Miss Cameron nodded, barely looking at her notes. "While the circumstances around Mr. Blaylock's accident seem quite convincing, it is possible he may have survived, or another man is passing himself off as Captain Blaylock."

Sophie spoke up, a puzzled sound in her voice. "I know many people use aliases when they join a mercenary unit, but I've glanced at his record. Blaylock was a decorated pilot in the Imperial Air Corps before joining a mercenary unit. Wouldn't this person take a big chance coming to the celebration? What if he had run into someone who knew the real Tony Blaylock?"

Jessica spoke up again. "He may have been testing his disguise. If he's passing himself as Captain Blaylock, he needs to establish a presence. After all, it was more likely he'd run into people who knew him by reputation but not necessarily by sight. According to our records, Captain Blaylock was stationed in Southwatch for only two years and *that* was six years ago."

Miss Miles broke in, "I'm sure the Black Watch and the *Temple* have a vested interest in learning how this Blaylock person penetrated your security and attended a gathering of some of the most important nobles in the Empire without being detected. However, unless you're saying he had something to do with Miss Halgrim's kidnapping, I think we're going astray from our purpose here."

Erica watched the unspoken conversation going on between Miss Cameron and Jessica and the two women nodded slowly. Miss Cameron blushed slightly. "Excuse me, Miss Halgrim. Miss Miles is correct. However, it seems clear the unfortunate death of the Coritanian ambassador's daughter and this kidnapping are connected. Outside of your statement about being interrogated about the incident, there is no evidence linking the two, though. If we had an idea who conducted Miss Halgrim's interrogation or who abducted her from the very doors of Angels' Headquarters, or if one group was hired to deliver her to the other . . . it's just so tenuous. We need something to build a case on."

Jessica glanced at Erica through half-closed eyes. "What *exactly* were you doing when you were abducted?"

Erica cocked her head to the side for a second before answering. "I was waiting for my boyfriend to pick me up for a dinner date."

"No, my dear, what were you *doing* while you waited? How did they sneak up behind you?"

Erica thought back to the incident and tried to recall everything that happened. "I walked out of the building. There was a cart delivering groceries and a mechanical horse out front and children playing near it. I've always been fascinated with horses, mechanical or otherwise, so I approached the horse after the children took off. I walked toward the back of the cart to see what they had and that's when I realized someone was behind me. Before I could move, something was put over my nose. I think it was chloroform—at least it smelled familiar. My mother worked as a nurse and I helped her when it was busy."

"We found no signs of a sedative in her system, but between the time of her disappearance and her return to Angels' Tower, all but the strongest known sedatives would have processed through her system. I suspect they gave her the lowest dosage they could since they wanted to question her that evening." Dr. Lopatka flipped through her notes. "We did find a few abnormalities in her blood but we were unable to identify them. I sent the sample down to our lab for further analysis."

"Abnormalities?" Jessica asked, drawing out the last syllable.

"There was evidence of a foreign element in Erica's bloodstream. However, as we said, it was very faint. Given her general state of health, it does not appear to be anything she should be worried about."

Jessica smiled at the doctor. "Most interesting. I'd love to get a sample to take back for our scientists to review."

"I'm afraid that's not possible. That would be a violation of doctor-patient confidentiality."

Jessica's eyes narrowed. "You know I can get a court order to make you surrender that sample."

Lady Orisaka broke in, "And you know we have some of the finest lawyers in Southwatch on our payroll. Pick and choose your battles, Jessica."

There was an awkward pause and then Jessica bowed her head to Lady Orisaka. "Of course. Lady Orisaka, Dr. Lopatka, please forgive my overzealousness. Let me phrase this differently. Should you wish to take advantage of the best scientists in the barony, we stand by to provide any assistance in determining what that substance might be."

Dr. Lopatka nodded slowly before replying. "Thank you. I'll keep your generous offer in mind." She smiled at Jessica, but there was no way to miss the ice in her eyes.

Erica realized Jessica was not used to being denied and she didn't care for the sensation one bit. It was becoming obvious Erica was a prop in a play with much larger stakes. It felt like the Black Watch and the *Temple* were working in conjunction and Angels' Security and the Southwatch Police were the opposing team.

Detective Casciato spoke up, breaking the silence. "You say you were looking at a mechanical horse right before your attack?"

"Yes, ma'am. It resembled a draft horse. Most of the mechanical horses in Southwatch look like thoroughbreds or racing stallions— there's even a lady in White Cliffs who rides a mechanical unicorn."

She chuckled a bit at that memory and then continued. "Seeing an ordinary draft horse was quite a surprise."

The police woman smiled probably the first honest smile Erica had seen since entering the room. "Indeed? That is something to add to the report. Since you seem to be a bit of a horse connoisseur, I'll have our men start looking for it. Do you think you might recognize this horse if you were to see it again?"

"It's possible. It might be tough to pick it out from a photograph, but if I were to see it in person again—yes, I think I could."

"Thank you. Between your description of the wagon and now this, we might be able to find it. If we can find it, maybe we can find someone who saw what happened and go from there."

"That would take a load off my mind. I've been thinking about this ever since the ceremony—trying to figure out what's going on. I mean, I feel horrible for that young woman. Still, there seems to be an awful lot of people interested in learning what specifically I know about this. No one seems to believe it was a case of wrong place, wrong time."

Detective Casciato made a few more notes in her notebook. "You have to appreciate the unusual circumstances here, Miss Halgrim. You are the closest thing we have to an eyewitness, unless we can find those gyrocopters. You've got an outstanding memory. Most people wouldn't recall half of what you have, but I've noticed people's memories sometimes get jumbled when they witness something shocking. Sometimes they focus on little details and miss big things out of self-defense. It's natural. That's why we visited with you last night, today, and probably will again next week after you've had time to process things more. Let's see what you remember after you've had a chance to relax." She paused and then made sure Erica was looking at her before she continued. "However, take it easy for a few days and avoid any unnecessary trips."

Erica smiled. For the first time since she'd walked into the room, she started to relax. "Thank you, Detective Casciato. I appreciate your concern."

Jessica motioned toward Sophie. "As long as we're reviewing Erica's movements, what was she doing earlier in the day? Before she left to go to visit her boyfriend?"

Sophie looked a little uncomfortable but Lady Orisaka nodded. "Halgrim has been reassigned to our Research and Development team pending a resolution to this situation. She is testing some devices we are developing. She is an outstanding flyer, so this seemed to make the best use of her talents rather than reassign her to administrative duties."

"New flying devices, hmmm? Erica—may I call you Erica?—did the people who kidnapped you ask about these devices? Did they ask you about your boyfriend or anything he might be developing? Is he working on something that might have been of interest to them?"

Erica was taken aback at Jessica's request to call her by her first name. The phrasing was eerily similar to the person who interrogated her last night. She tried to keep her face impassive before she answered. "No, they only asked about the accident at the *Temple*."

"Accident? Did they call it an accident?"

"No, but I'm assuming it was an accident. Unless you're telling me it wasn't?"

"Touché, Erica. No, I'm calling it an unsolved incident at this particular moment. Whether it was an accident, intentional, or something somewhere in the middle has yet to be determined. The Coritanian ambassador is growing impatient with the current state of the investigation. Then again, if that were my daughter, I'd be turning Southwatch upside down to find the truth."

Lady Orisaka looked over at Erica. "Miss Halgrim, how can we reach your boyfriend?"

The question confused Erica. "I gave you his address last night. I told him that Angels' Security would probably stop by, so he wouldn't be surprised. He sounded like he would be expecting you."

Miss Miles spoke up. "We did stop by there. After that visit, I can appreciate how much he likes his privacy. He did not respond to several attempts to reach him and it took us over two hours to breach that location. No one was there. The room showed signs of having been recently abandoned. There was nothing there but some old burnt-out parts, half-eaten food, and broken boxes. All of his equipment and experiments were gone."

"I wish I could say I was surprised," Erica replied. "Michael has issues with people knowing where he works. Apparently his rivals spend an inordinate amount of time to discover his latest projects or to cut him out of his contracts. I know he has alternate laboratories where he does his more dangerous experiments, but he's never taken me to any of those. When he goes there, it's just him and Theo."

"Theo?"

"Theo's an advanced cybernaut Michael built to serve as a lab assistant and occasionally his valet."

Jessica spoke up again. "Doesn't it concern you he showed up, rescued you, and then disappeared?"

"Well, yes, however, Michael's a very private person. Sometimes I'm surprised he comes out of his lab as often as he does. I suspect he'll contact me soon and let me know where he is."

Lady Orisaka turned to her security person. "Were you going somewhere with your questions, Felicia?"

"Yes, my lady." She turned back to Erica. "Did he ever say how he found you?"

Erica thought for a bit. "No, he never did. Actually, I talked more to Theo than Michael. Once he was certain I was all right, he drove the truck back to here. Theo sat in the back but I'm afraid all I did was sleep. I'm guessing he used his flying winders. He was wearing strange goggles and speaking to them through a crystal wireless."

"But you were inside a building?"

"To be honest, I was so tired and just happy to be out of there. I figured we'd talk about it tonight."

Miss Miles nodded and wrote some more notes on the pad of paper she had with her. "That's all I have right now. If you hear from Michael, I'd love to speak to him, after Lady Orisaka, if he's up to it?"

Jessica spoke up. "I think we'd all like to talk to him."

Erica nodded to their expectant stares. "Agreed. Once he contacts me, I'll let him know you'd like to see him."

Lady Orisaka looked around at the other women and then back at Erica. "All right, Halgrim, Zwyer, you're dismissed. Zwyer, ensure Halgrim is relieved from duty today and gets plenty of rest. After the night she had, I think she's earned it."

Sophie and Erica rose and bowed to the assembled women before walking quickly out of the room. Sophie motioned to the right and led Erica down to the break room. She went to the ice box and withdrew two bottles of beer. She sat one down in front of Erica and cracked the other one open. "Go ahead, I think you've earned it."

Erica couldn't remember seeing Sophie drink on duty before but she welcomed the cold liquid and a chance to relax. She rested the

63

cool bottle against her forehead and sighed. "For being there so I could ask questions, I don't recall being able to ask many."

"I think you handled it well. This is not going to go away anytime soon. Too many political issues are involved in this death."

Erica snapped her chair around to look at Sophie. "To hell with politics. I'm tired of being hauled here and there and even kidnapped to answer the same questions over and over. I'm sick of it and I'm about ready to tell them to do something anatomically impossible with a set of wings and to do it sideways."

Sophie looked at her without batting an eye. "I'm certain the sentiment is heartfelt, but it's not useful. There is no way to separate politics from practical in this matter. This happened at the baron's event at the Temple to an ambassador's daughter. That's about as political as it gets."

Erica froze at that comment then pointed back at the conference room. "Sophie, did you hear how Jessica asked if she could call me by my first name? That was almost word for word how my interrogator did it last night."

Sophie nodded. "That doesn't surprise me. Sounds like a standard interrogation technique. But keep it in mind, just in case."

"Just in case...what?"

"Just in case." Sophie took a sip of her beer and set it down on the table. "We don't know if whoever kidnapped you was working for the baron, the ambassador, some crime syndicate, or agents from another country. Although, I think we can eliminate a crime syndicate. There's no way the local gangs are as efficient as the men you met last night."

Erica laughed. "And you would know how the syndicates work here in Southwatch?"

Sophie just pointed her beer bottle at Erica. "Everyone did something before they joined the Angels, Erica. We're given a clean slate when we join, but it doesn't mean something wasn't written there before." She took another drink and then stood up. "Come on, we can finish them on the way. We're still meeting Crystal this afternoon after you've had time to get some sleep. I know you're off duty, but Crystal has some new ideas she wants to try out and you're obviously not hurt from your kidnapping. It'll do you good to get your mind off of stuff."

"Provided Crystal doesn't kill me in the process."

"Think of it this way: If she kills you, you won't have to answer any more questions."

"Good point." Erica took one more swig and jumped out of her chair. "I can sleep later. What are we waiting for?"

Chapter Eight

Crystal slipped a strap of leather through an anchoring bolt in the floor and cinched it as tight as she could before looking up at her subject. Erica watched with trepidation as she stood in the middle of what appeared to be a spiderweb of leather straps and thin metal wires that was attached to the floor, walls, and ceiling.

I can't believe it's been a week working with Crystal. Actually, I can't believe I've survived a week of this. I'm going to kill Christina when this is all over. Ask Crystal what the maximum capacity of these wings is. What's the worst that can happen?

"All right, Erica. This time I've got the harness set for maximum stress. I want you to *really* push those wings. I'm certain the harness will hold you in this time."

"I'm glad to hear that, Crystal," Erica said, flexing her shoulder to work out the kinks. "I felt that last trip even through this padded suit."

Crystal looked at her with a sheepish grin and adjusted her thick glasses, brushing her long black hair back out of her face. "I'm certain I have all the slack out of the harness this time. I didn't expect you to bounce off the ceiling and into that pipe over there. Luckily, the pipe seems to be undamaged."

"The pipe?" Erica shouted indignantly.

Crystal looked at her as if she were explaining how a screwdriver worked. "Yes, the pipe. That supplies coolant to another experiment I'm working on. If you had bent *it*, this whole floor might have exploded."

Erica swallowed hard. "Shouldn't we be testing in another room if that pipe is that important?"

"Oh, I'm certain you won't hit it again. At least, I'm *mostly* sure you won't. Anyway, let's get to work."

This wasn't the first time Erica had second thoughts about working with Crystal. However, she knew Sophie was receiving daily reports, so she just nodded grimly and prepared for the next phase of training with Crystal's new wing design.

Once she had inspected the rigging one last time, Crystal grabbed her clipboard. She made sure Erica was paying attention as she went over the next test. "This time, I want you to try to hover using the wings. Do not try to catch an air current in here. I've blocked all the vents so you'll have to concentrate to keep yourself aloft. You'll have to flap faster than you ever have in your life."

Erica nodded. She bent her knees slightly and waited for Crystal to move back. The scientist absentmindedly adjusted her glasses as she walked through the room one last time, gathering any small objects or tools she had left out to ensure they didn't become projectiles. Once she was satisfied, she stepped into a small booth in the far corner of the room. She moved some switches on a control panel and then looked through the clear glass walls before keying her microphone. "Anytime you're ready, Erica."

Erica began flapping her wings slowly at first, trying to build up momentum. Her feet lifted off the floor, but she forced herself downward while increasing the rhythm of her wings. Finally, the upward thrust overcame her weight and she rose into the air. She continued to focus on remaining where she was as her wings fought to lift her into the air. She felt warmth on her chest and knew the thalisium was reacting to the electric stimulation created by her wings, helping support her weight against the pull of gravity.

"That's it, Erica. Keep it up! Faster, now."

Sweat broke out on her forehead. Even though the servos kept her wings operating, she had to focus on maintaining body position, keeping her balance steady, controlling her position in midair, and regulating the sweep of the wings. The tips of her wings became blurs, going faster and faster trying to hold her in the same spot without drifting forward or back.

"Now, Erica, maneuver your body parallel to the ground and maintain your hover."

She's got to be kidding. It's all I can do now to stay in place.

Erica bit her lower lip and inched her arms and legs out. For a few seconds, she thought she was going to be able to hold it, but then her body turned fractionally off line and her wings caught air. She shot forward and only the harness prevented her from slamming into the padded wall. Her wings tangled in the wiring as she rebounded toward the center of the room and all she could do was try to keep still as the harness bounced her around.

Crystal rushed out of her booth as Erica hung upside down suspended from the harness. Before Erica could say anything, Crystal began hooking tubes and cables to the wings, taking measurements, and checking the web harness.

"Uh, Crystal, can I get down?"

"Just a few more moments. I need to take these measurements before the webbing can settle back into place. It's important to determine how much thrust you generated before you shot forward. Even if you weren't able to hold the hover, there's still valuable information to be harvested from this experiment."

Erica knew Crystal wasn't trying to be obnoxious. They weren't called *storms* for nothing after all. Once a "brainstorm" started, it seemed like the whole world disappeared except for the current project. So, Erica waited, the blood rushing to her head while Crystal took notes, poked and prodded the gear, and finally looked up.

"Erica, your face is all red!"

"That happens when you stand on your head for too long, Crystal. May I please get down now?"

Crystal rushed to the emergency release button before Erica could stop her. A second later, the entangled Angel found herself sprawled on the floor beneath a mountain of harnesses, wires, and tubes. The shock sent Crystal's test gear crashing down on top of her. She let out a small moan and lay very still to keep from making things worse.

"Eeek! I'm so sorry, Erica. Are you all right?"

Erica made sure everything still worked before raising her head to give Crystal a halfhearted grin. "I think so. I'll know more after I get all this stuff off me."

Crystal pushed a button on her belt and a small door opened in one of the walls. Erica saw a flurry of motion out of the corner of her eyes and then she felt the weight lifting off her. A familiar whirring noise sounded next to her and she turned her head to see a group of winders, with four legs and four arms, lifting the gear. Others were sorting the debris into neat stacks and gathering up the loose cables and putting them back onto their reels.

"I see you have your own cleanup crew."

"Sophie insisted. Said she couldn't keep sending people to help pick up. So, I designed some assistants. They've gotten pretty good at this."

Erica managed to keep herself from saying "They've probably had plenty of practice," and concentrated on getting free of the pile. After the winders made their third trip carrying gear away, she

68

managed to climb to her hands and knees and reached up to detach the harness gear from her flight suit. As her hand hit the first snap, Crystal came running up.

"Wait! Wait! I need to check those. I need to see how much stress you put on them."

Erica's temper snapped at yet another delay. "I stressed them. I know that. I felt like someone shot me from a cannon with a rubber band attached to my feet. I'm probably two inches taller than I was when I started. It was not a pleasant experience, let me tell you."

"I'm sorry about that, Erica. However, I need to see if I have to replace them. You may have come close to popping them open, which would have been bad. If you think you hit the ceiling hard the other day, today would have been catastrophic. Your wing speed hit almost forty miles an hour while you were hovering. That's almost twice as fast as the average flyer goes. Do you realize what that means? The wings held up beautifully and you did so well keeping focused. It was simply magical."

Erica saw that dreamy look in Crystal's eyes and poked her on the shoulder. "Yes, I'm sure it was wonderful. Now, measure, so I can get out of this, please?"

A few minutes later, Erica extricated herself from the harness and limped toward the door. Crystal opened it and guided her to a small locker room. While Erica stripped out of her gear, Crystal went to an intercom system and sent word for a physical trainer for Erica.

A hot shower and a good massage later, Erica plopped down in an overstuffed chair in Crystal's office. She noticed Crystal had the wings hung from a rack on her far wall and hooked up to some odd-looking machine. She was inspecting the servo connections to one of the steel feathers. Erica decided to take advantage of Crystal's absorption in her work to get some rest. She had almost fallen asleep when there was a knock at the door. Crystal showed no signs of answering, so Erica forced herself upright and went to see who was there.

A young woman in an administration uniform stood there. There was a small pushcart standing next to her. "Excuse me, is Miss Erica Halgrim here?"

"I'm Erica. What can I do for you?"

The young woman reached into the cart and handed a small package to Erica with a smile. "This came for you earlier. Please sign here."

Erica absentmindedly signed the slip of paper and returned to the chair with the box. Crystal showed no sign she'd even noticed Erica's absence. Erica saw the plain brown paper on the box bore her name but there was no return address. She slipped the string off of it and undid the wrapping, carefully folding it up. Opening the box, she found a small metal bracelet with wires and glass beads on it. There was an unsigned note tucked inside the box next to the bracelet.

Erica,

When you get the opportunity, I need to see you. Go outside and ensure you're wearing this bracelet. There is a small switch that will turn on a signal so I can find you. Do this only if you are certain you're alone. Tell no one I have contacted you. It is important I speak to you before I speak to anyone else.

Erica slipped the note back into the box and closed it. She tucked the narrow box between her leg and the arm of the chair. A few more minutes passed in silence before Crystal turned around with a big smile on her face.

"I think that's done it."

"Done what, Crys?"

The scientist walked over to her desk and sat down. "We're ready to move on to Phase Two of the testing. We'll head out to the training camp. Remember how you used to go through the obstacle course out there? It's a perfect place to try these new wings' mobility. Plus, I have a couple of other designs we could put through their paces too. I'll let Lady Orisaka know and we'll leave Monday."

"Monday? That's just a few days from now."

Crystal's smile grew like a kid getting a double helping of ice cream and her voice picked up speed. "No sense in waiting. After all, since you're still restricted to sub-Cloud flying, why not go out to the training ranges where there's no Cloud? No Cloud, no restrictions, right? I want to see what you can do with these wings—height trials, speed trials, maneuver trials, dive trials. It'll be a glorious advance for science."

Erica recognized the look in Crystal's eyes. When a brainstorm hit, she was going to be like that for a while. "Tell you what, Crystal,

70

why don't I leave you here to get things ready? I'll need to go through my gear and decide what to bring. Just let me know what time you want to leave."

Crystal nodded absently and then grabbed a pen and a stack of paper from her desk. "Let's see, I'll need to be sure and get some of these . . . and I can't forget this . . . and . . ."

Erica slipped her box under her flight jacket and eased out of the room, but she realized she could have carried a bull elephant out of the room and Crystal never would have noticed. By the time she reached her quarters, Sophie was standing outside her door. Erica shifted her suit to be sure the box was hidden before she joined her flight leader.

"Halgrim, I just received word we're heading for the training camp. Lady Orisaka thinks it's a good idea to take the entire flight. Bronson and you will be the testers for the speed wings, but Crystal has several other designs she needs tested. Angels Walker, Chen, Iewarren, and Sorenson will be joining us. We can use this time to work on flight drills too. We haven't flown together since the . . . well, since that day."

"Do you have an idea how long we'll be gone and who else is coming?"

"I don't have a full itinerary yet, but I suspect at least a few weeks. There will be a number of technicians coming along to assist Crystal. I will be supervising when I am not doing training myself." Sophie paused and then spoke in a softer voice. "Oh, and Miss Miles and a team from Angels' Security will be going along."

"That makes sense. We don't want any of these wings falling into the wrong hands. People would make a killing selling these on the black market."

"The wings are of secondary importance. The security team will be along to keep an eye on *you*."

Eeep!

Erica thought for a moment. "I remember there were a ton of guards when we went through initial flight training. Do we really need Angels' Security too?"

Sophie gave her a pitying look. "Think, Halgrim. This is a top secret training mission. We will be isolated from anyone else at the camp. There won't be any guards beyond the skeleton crew manning the front gate and the perimeter guards—and they're only there to keep the local kids from sneaking onto the range, not to keep out a determined force. Besides, if someone's bold enough to kidnap you literally at our front doors, I suspect they'd love a chance to intercept you on a trial run. No, you will be supervised the entire time you're there."

Erica felt her shoulders slump in defeat. "Is this ever going to be over?"

"Yes. When we figure out who is behind this. Now, quit feeling sorry for yourself. Trust me, you don't want to know what Jessica had in mind to 'protect' you."

Erica suppressed a shudder. "Let me guess—live bait?"

"Precisely."

Erica walked to her door and paused to look back at Sophie. "I need to start packing. At least now I know how long we'll be gone. Crystal wrapped herself into her planning as soon as she made a decision. Didn't tell me anything."

Sophie let a small grin reach her face. "That sounds like Crystal. Get packed and get some rest, Halgrim. We may not be leaving for a few days, but I'll be here at seven sharp to go over the training schedule with you and Bronson."

Erica snapped to attention and saluted. "Ma'am, yes, ma'am."

"Can it, Halgrim. However, congratulations on your tests so far. Crystal has had nothing but compliments on how hard you've been working. You may not think she's paying attention, but she really does care. She just is more comfortable dealing with machines than people."

"Thanks. That makes the bruises feel a little better."

"Well, think of it this way: When we're on the training range, there won't be many walls and no pipes."

"There is that. See you in the morning."

Erica slipped into her room and listened as Sophie's footsteps faded in the distance. She tossed both uniforms and civilian clothes onto her bed to make it look like she was in the middle of packing and then changed into a nondescript outfit. She tucked her hair up under an unflattering hat and looked at herself in the mirror.

I swore to Christina I was never going to wear this ugly thing, but now I'm glad she got it for me. It'll come in handy. No one would expect me to be wearing this!

She hurried and caught an elevator before anyone saw her. As it headed down, she leaned against the wall and tried to relax. She didn't need to draw attention to herself now. After a short search, she found the service exit she had found one day by accident and let herself out into the dark alley between the Angels' building and a small restaurant.

If we're leaving in a couple of days, I don't have much time. I need to see Michael before we go, though. Surely he knows the police want to speak to him. Why is he hiding? That's not like him. Something's going on and people are trying to keep me in the dark. Maybe he can figure something out while I'm at the camp?

Besides, if I'm going to be gone for a couple of weeks, he still owes me dinner.

Chapter Nine

Erica made her way to the mouth of the alley and waited until she was certain no one had noted her exit, then put the bracelet on and pushed the small switch she found between two of the glass beads. Shortly, a small Barrymore Javelin truck pulled up along the curb. Theo leaned across the narrow seats and opened the door from the inside.

"Quickly, Miss Erica, we mustn't dawdle."

Erica avoided the puddles on the sidewalk from a recent rain and slid into the truck's seat. She shut the door while Theo adjusted the controls and the steam in the engine purred to life. He guided the car down the street and turned to the east.

A thought occurred to Erica as they entered traffic. "I thought you didn't know how to drive?"

"I didn't until today. Michael programmed me to follow this specific route. Should our way become blocked, you'll have to take over driving, Miss Erica. I apologize in advance should that happen."

Alarmed, she nervously watched traffic but everything seemed to be flowing smoothly. "So, where is Michael now?"

"He has relocated to one of his laboratories in the Underground, Miss Erica. Beyond that, I am not at liberty to say."

Erica turned so she could watch Theo closely. For a mechanical, there were times his reactions were more human than she would have guessed. "So, we're not going to his new place?"

Theo honked at a couple of kids who had started to walk into the street and swerved to avoid them. Erica winced as he missed them by inches. The mechanical continued to watch the road ahead and his baritone voice showed no sign of the narrow escape. "No, Miss Erica. He arranged a special place to meet you this evening. You both will be safe there."

Erica frowned. This was not shaping up to be the evening she had envisioned when she started packing for the trip. Then all of a sudden, something Theo said struck her. "Wait a minute. You said we'd *both* be safe there. Is Michael worried about something specific? Has something happened or is that a general statement?"

Theo deftly maneuvered between two other cars trundling down the street, then avoided a streetcar crossing the intersection ahead of them. Erica caught herself holding her breath as Theo steered the car through the congestion, but his mechanical reflexes seemed up for the challenge. After he had found a relatively open spot in the road, he spoke again. "I honestly can't say, Miss Erica. It is merely something I overheard him say while he was arranging this meeting. I see you received the package without incident."

"Yes. Michael needs to understand a number of people would like to speak to him."

Erica thought she could hear a tone of resignation in the mechanical man's voice. "Yes, Miss Erica. He understands *that* very well. However, that is why he closed down his old lab as soon as we rescued you. Michael always has a reason for doing what he does. I am only a mechanical. I do not claim to understand how a human brain works. You are most difficult to program."

Erica smiled at him. "Is it easier to have someone telling you what to do?"

"I don't know if it's easier. I notice humans seem to resist that." Theo shifted lanes before continuing. "He obviously doesn't mind explaining things to you, Miss Erica. After all, he sent for you as soon as possible."

"Thanks, Theo. I'll feel better when I hear what Michael has to say." She allowed herself to be mollified by the cybernaut's seeming concern for her feelings. That was the problem with Theo—she could never tell how much of what he said or did was based on his programming, and how much seemed to be spontaneous. He was incredibly advanced for a mechanical either way.

"You're welcome, Miss Erica. We'll be arriving shortly."

Erica followed Theo into a run-down building on the north edge of University Heights. Theo directed her to an elevator on the far wall. Before she could ask what floor, Theo removed a floor panel and pushed a button hidden beneath it. He then lowered the lever and the elevator sank through the floor into a subbasement. They descended for quite a while before Theo brought the elevator to a halt. When the doors opened, there was only the faint glow of a gas lamp and a long, dark hallway ahead of her.

"Michael is waiting, Miss Erica. I have to return the elevator to the ground floor. I will join you later."

Erica felt a nervous shiver go through her as she stared at the dim hallway. "Michael's down there?"

"Oh, yes, Miss Erica. About thirty feet down, there'll be a door on the right."

Erica took a deep breath and started down the hall. Three steps later, she tried not to flinch as the elevator doors slid shut behind her, cutting off the only escape route she knew of from this building. She could feel the weight of the earth above her almost as if it were physically pressing down on her. She had never considered herself claustrophobic before, but she certainly could understand why it affected some people. She hurried down the hall, her heels making a staccato sound against the concrete floor.

She found the outline of the door in the faint light. There was no knob, but she pushed against it and it slid backward and to the right. Soft light came flooding out, making her feel better. She stepped into the Spartan room and saw Michael sitting at a table, working on something. She heard the door softly slide shut behind her, but she kept her focus on Michael to push her claustrophobic feelings down inside of her.

Michael put down his tools and looked up at her. "I'm glad you came. I was afraid it would be a while before you could get away and see me."

"I had to come tonight. We're leaving in a few days for Camp Falcon. I'm going to be there for a minimum of two weeks."

"That's unfortunate, but I guess it can't be helped."

She looked at him with a quizzical look on her face. "No, Crystal was insistent we leave as soon as possible. She's almost as focused on her work as you are on yours."

Michael coughed and shoved the machine he'd been working on across the table, out of reach, and turned back to face her. "Well, you will have my undivided attention tonight. I hoped things would calm down by now."

Erica walked past him and took another seat at the table. "Michael, where have you been? Everyone's been looking for you. I was afraid something had happened or you had run into the dark men."

"The dark men?"

76

"The men who interrogated me. All I ever saw of them was dark shapes. Don't try and change the subject, Michael. I was worried about you."

Michael took her hand. "I am sorry, but I had to close down my lab because I knew you'd pass on its location to the authorities. I hadn't told you not to, after all. I work on a number of classified projects for a number of different clients. Sometimes I work through a middleman, so often I don't know who my clients are and vice versa."

"But, Michael, Lady Orisaka and others want to talk to you. They have questions about how you rescued me. They think you may have information they could use in their investigations."

Michael paused before responding. "I understand their desires but you understand I'm not fond of authority figures. I prefer to be left alone to do what I do best. Your friend, Sophie—she's much better adapted to deal with those kinds of people than I am."

Erica moved her chair closer to Michael and put her arms on his shoulders to make sure he was looking her in the eyes. "Michael, this is serious. If we can't find out what's going on, the baron may try to pin the death of Ambassador Bogdanovich's daughter on me. To make matters worse, I think the Black Watch wants to use me as live bait to lure the people behind this into the open. If there's anything you can do to help, it's important that you tell someone and soon."

Michael stared at her and then leaned back, catching her hands in his. "Tell you what. I'll write up everything I know, explain how I found you without revealing any trade secrets, and give them my theories on what's going on, as sketchy as they are. Once I have everything compiled, I'll have Theo deliver a copy to Lady Orisaka. She can distribute it appropriately once she's had the chance to read through it."

He paused and ran a hand through his hair. "That should work. They'll have the information they need and I'll still be free to continue my work. I have so much to do and I can't afford to spend hours answering questions for people who don't know the right questions to ask in the first place."

He must have noticed the expression on Erica's face because he quickly continued. "I know this is hard on you, darling. However, you're going to be out at Camp Falcon for a while. That should give the police time to complete their investigation and apprehend the people involved. By the time you get back, this should be all wrapped up."

"I'm not so sure, Michael. This doesn't seem like something that's going to just go away. I have a bad feeling about the interest the Black Watch is showing. This has gone beyond a simple criminal matter. I'm really getting scared about this."

Michael stood up and gave her a bear hug, almost taking her breath away. "I know this can't be easy, Erica." He awkwardly patted her back and then held her out at arm's reach, a silly grin on his face. "I know. I still owe you a dinner. Maybe we can't go to that fancy restaurant in White Cliffs, but I have something that's better and it's closer. What do you say?"

Erica knew Michael was trying to change the subject, but she knew as long as she stayed with him, there was a chance she could find out what *really* was going on. She waited for Michael to put his equipment away, aided by his ever-present spider winders. A few minutes later, he stepped into another room and shortly returned wearing a fresh shirt, vest, and jacket, before offering her a hand up from her chair.

She thought he would lead her to the door, but instead, he led her to an interior room and through the door on the far side. To her surprise, this opened up onto what appeared to be a platform. Waiting there sat a small electric train engine and a single passenger car on a set of rails leading into a dark tunnel.

"Michael, where *are* we going?"

"Camden Town. This is a small private line used by friends of mine to get around the city without drawing attention. It won't take very long at all."

Michael helped her into the car and settled into his seat beside her. He flipped a few switches on the armrest and the lights in the tunnel began to switch on, illuminating the path ahead. The engine purred to life and, toggling another switch, the private train began pulling away from the platform, picking up speed as they went. Erica sat back and tried to relax.

She tried to continue her conversation with Michael as the train rumbled down the tracks, but he was busy watching the lighted screen in front of him, showing the network of tracks. He gleefully pointed out the other lights on the screen, showing other private cars moving beneath Southwatch, the winder work crews inspecting the tracks, and so on. He was so engrossed in explaining how they had built it and all the different techniques they had to use to keep the seawater from seeping in from the bay that Erica couldn't get a word in edgewise.

By the time Michael wrapped up his dissertation, the train was slowing down and eased into an isolated platform. He flipped some switches and the lights in the tunnel flickered out and the whine of the electrical engine came to a halt. It was an eerie feeling being in the quiet station with only one lonely light illuminating the passage ahead. Michael hopped up and escorted her onto the main platform and toward the passage.

At the end of the chilly stone hallway was a sliding metal door. Erica wrapped her arms around herself to stay warm while Michael rang for the elevator. He draped his jacket across her shoulders and she tucked it tight around her, enjoying how it smelled like him. After a few moments, she heard the soft whirr of the elevator descending.

The elevator door opened and an unusual mechanical motioned them forward. Erica knew some winders were built in where they worked, specifically ones in the factories in the Underground. However, she'd never seen one attached to the wall of an elevator before. He seemed to simply consist of a head, part of a torso, and one arm to work the elevator switch.

"What floor, sir?" the winder said. His voice sounded like metal grating together. Obviously, whoever built this device had spent as little time and money on it as possible. However, its appearance and condition seemed not to faze Michael in the least.

"Forty-seventh, my good man."

"Very good, sir. Please be sure you're inside the car before we start."

Erica moved toward the back of the car and tried to guess where they were going. There weren't many towers in Camden Town that reached that height. It was more of a residential area with some businesses. Downtown and White Cliffs were known for fancier businesses and restaurants. However, he had never led her astray before whenever he had recommended a restaurant, so she was willing to cut Michael some slack this time.

They rode the elevator in silence. The winder moved only slightly to maintain a steady speed and seemed completely unconcerned by their presence. After being around Michael's and Crystal's mechanicals, it seemed strange to find one that showed no signs of curiosity. She started to feel warmer and handed Michael back his jacket. He shrugged back into it as the elevator slowed and then came to a stop. The winder used its arm to slide the door back, revealing a well-lit walkway and a crowd of people milling about, going from storefront to storefront.

"This is the Celactian market. A number of the expatriates from Celacti live in this block of buildings. It's become my home away from home. There's a restaurant here that serves dishes with foods imported from there. I'll bet you've never tasted anything like them before. I guarantee, you'll remember this visit for a long time."

"Michael, I've got several weeks of intensive training ahead of me. Do *not* feed me something that's going to make me sick."

Erica gave him a stern look, but he just grinned. "You're going to have to trust me, darling. I can't even pronounce half of the items on the menu, but I've never had anything I didn't like."

He grabbed her by the elbow and guided her through the milling crowd until they reached a small door hidden between two large stands of strange-looking vegetables. If Michael hadn't been leading her, she would have walked past it without another thought. He paused to open the door and then ushered her in. He waved to one of the waiters and they were guided to a secluded table in the far corner.

Michael held her chair until she sat down and then flipped open her napkin, laying it in her lap before taking his own seat. "I like this table. It's closer to the kitchen."

Erica tilted her head backward and sniffed the air. "I don't know what they're serving but I admit, it smells heavenly."

"Told you."

She leaned across the table and touched Michael's sleeve. He started at the sudden touch. "Michael, we have to talk. Is this private enough?"

Michael looked around and then pulled a small wind-up device out of his coat. He gave it several twists and set it on the table. "A little toy of mine. It doesn't affect conversation nearby, but it adds just enough noise to keep our words private at a distance."

Erica relaxed a bit but made sure she had his attention. "Look, as I said earlier, there are a lot of people who want to talk to you. Even if you don't want to talk to them, you need to give me—or someone— enough information to satisfy them. If you don't, they're going to keep after you. How long do you think you can keep hiding?"

"Long enough if I play my cards right. Besides, I told you, I will send a complete report to Lady Orisaka in the next day or so. I promise. After all, once you leave, I'll go to one of my labs and hole up there for a while. I've got supplies and water stored away for emergencies like this. Still, you keep hinting there's something specific they're trying to learn. If you could tell me what they're looking for in particular, I could always give you the answers. You deal with people like that much better than I do."

"Michael, I know you don't want to be tied down to one company or one university. Still, it's not good to have no one to fall back on."

Michael laughed, a little too self-consciously. "I'm not quite as alone as you think. There are other storms like me and we support each other—maybe a little too much sometimes—but there's always someone out there to pick up the experiments if something happens to one of us."

"So you've hinted at before, Michael. Still, the first question is, how did you know how to find me?"

"That? That was child's play. Remember the necklace I gave you when you visited me—right before you were kidnapped?"

"Yes?"

"Remember the artificial stone? It has a unique chemical makeup but its signature is virtually undetectable if you don't know what to look for. Well, since I created it, I knew to send a cadre of chemical analysis winders around the city searching for that signature. Took a while—Southwatch isn't exactly a small town." Michael paused and then continued in a rush, "Now, get that look off your face, it's perfectly safe. I wouldn't give you something that might hurt you."

"What else have you given me that I should know about?"

"Nothing, I promise. However, you have to admit it was a good thing I did give it to you."

Erica hated to concede the point, but he was right. "Go on."

"Well, once we caught a hint of the chemical, I dispatched those flying winders you saw. I've come up with a way to control them via radio waves. You saw the helmet I was wearing. That lets me see through their eyes. It's still very experimental. I have to admit, I didn't know if it would work or not. It still needs a lot of fine tuning to get them to work all the time. But . . . as you can see, they worked well enough."

"And so, once you located the building I was in . . ."

81

Michael leaned back in his chair with a satisfied grin on his face. "Well, I sent in the cavalry and voilà, a few minutes later, you were out of there."

Erica started to ask the next question on her mind, but the waiter showed up bearing a sizzling platter. She didn't recognize most of the food there, but the smell was incredible and from the way Michael was digging in, if she wanted any, she'd better grab some right then. She had just filled her plate when there was a sudden motion and someone stopped by their table.

"Hello, Erica. I was wondering where you got off to today."

Erica swallowed hard and turned to face the newcomer. "Hello, Jessica. I didn't expect to run into you here."

Jessica pulled up a chair and sat down at their table. Erica noted she had the chair positioned so neither Michael nor she could get up easily without going past her. Jessica's shark smile was firmly affixed as she gave Michael an approving look. "So, is this the man of the hour? We've been hoping you would introduce him to us one of these days."

Michael's voice sounded emotionless as he looked up from his plate at the newcomer at the table. "Erica, I don't believe I've had the pleasure of meeting your friend here."

Erica took her cue from Michael and tried to stay as calm as possible. "Michael, this is Jessica. Come to think of it, I don't think you've ever told me your last name."

"Call me Jessica Black. I assume this is Michael Shay?"

Michael bowed his head forward in a small salute. "I am Michael, yes. I don't believe for a moment that Jessica Black is your name, but it will do for now. What can we do for you, Miss Black?"

"Oh, please, call me Jessica. There's no reason to be so formal. Go ahead and eat. I'll talk and then you can answer at your leisure."

Michael started to say something, but Erica noticed he thought better of it and began attacking his meal. Erica decided to follow his lead and took a healthy bite out of her dinner. The food tasted as good as it had smelled, but her appetite had flown with Jessica's appearance. Still, there was no reason to let the food go to waste.

"Actually, Erica, we were concerned when we learned about your upcoming trip. We're not enthusiastic about you going to that camp. We think you're being needlessly exposed to danger, but your boss was quite insistent about keeping to a normal schedule. I guess she has a point, but it's unfortunate she's so insistent we're not allowed to help provide protection. Says the area is outside Southwatch's and, more specifically, the Black Watch's jurisdiction."

Erica swallowed her food and took a drink before replying. "I'm afraid I can't do much about that. After all, I work for Lady Orisaka, so if I want to keep my job, then I go when she says go."

"I guess that's true. Still, we're worried about you."

"I'm sure she'll arrange for proper security. Besides, I'm also sure you'll have everything wrapped up soon. You've certainly got access to more resources than *I* do."

Jessica's smile slipped for just a second, but she reached out and patted Erica's arm. "Yes, *we* do. Don't ever forget that." She turned back toward Michael. "And we've so been looking forward to meeting you. Your reputation is quite impressive."

He leaned back in his chair and let a hint of a smile turn up the corners of his mouth. "I'm really no one. I just tinker with things. I'm more of a mechanic than anything else."

"Oh, you sell yourself way too short, Michael," she said, after a short laugh. "Your papers on chemical reactions to human sweat are incredible. Your old mentor would be quite proud to see how you're adapting his chemistry classes and applying them to mechanical technology."

Michael's response was light, but Erica could tell Jessica's knowledge bothered him. "See, that's the problem. I had to adapt his papers. I don't create much on my own. I just tinker with other people's ideas."

Jessica's smile was a little more forced, but her voice remained pleasant. "We should sit down and talk sometime, Michael. Some of my friends are curious about more practical applications of our work. It could be quite profitable for the two of you to work closer with me."

Michael took a sip of his drink and smiled at her. "I'm booked rather solid at the moment, but I can try to work them into my schedule. I'll contact your people and let them know when I'm available."

"You do that."

"Jessica, I do hate to be a bore, but as you see, Miss Halgrim and I are trying to enjoy our evening before she has to depart. Perhaps we could take up this conversation at a later date?"

Jessica glanced over her shoulder and Erica couldn't help but notice a number of large men standing near the front door of the restaurant and a few suspicious shadows near the door of the kitchen. Michael's eyes never left Jessica's face, though.

I can't believe how calm he's being. He's up to something to challenge her this blatantly. I know the Black Watch is many things but patient isn't one of them. What has he got up his sleeve?

"Michael, I think you don't quite understand your position," Jessica said, the smile disappearing from her face.

Michael leaned forward and placed his elbows on the table. He picked up the salt shaker and toyed with it for a bit and then turned to Jessica. "No, I completely understand."

With that, he sat the shaker down in the center of the table and Erica saw him push it down on the table. Jessica realized something was going on. Just as she started to move, the floor fell away beneath the chairs Michael and Erica were sitting in and then snapped back into place. She screamed as they fell into darkness and then Erica hit and bounced out of the chair onto something soft. Michael grabbed her by the shoulder and pulled her to her feet. Jessica's voice could be heard through the flooring and from the rumbling of feet above, she knew the rest of the Black Watch was rushing to find a way down to this level.

Erica stumbled along behind Michael on a floor that shifted with every step until they reached a wall. Michael fumbled with something on the wall before a door slid open and a soft light lit up the room they were in. They were on the largest stuffed bag she'd ever seen. She had a few bruises from where the chair had bounced off her when they landed. Michael wasn't in much better shape, but he also had a rather large bruise coming up on his forehead.

"You're hurt!"

Michael reached up and touched his forehead, wincing as his fingers found the spot. "Seems I clipped the table on the way down. I knew putting that trapdoor there would come in handy. Now, come on, we have to secure this place before they break through the ceiling."

"You knew they were going to show up?"

"No, but I had this room designed for an escape ever since I decided I liked that restaurant enough to go back there more than once. Damn it. Now I'll have to send someone to pick up their food for me. Another place I can't go back to."

He led her into the small room and then slid the door back into place. He took what appeared to be an oversized fountain pen out of his pocket and pointed it at the edge of the door. He moved a lever on the pen, sending a small stream of clear liquid into the crack between the door and the wall. The liquid bubbled as it landed on the wall and then solidified. He sprayed the liquid around the door and then motioned for her to follow him through a door at the back of the small room.

Stepping through that door, she found herself back in an elevator. Michael pushed the lever down and the floor began sinking rapidly beneath their feet. She was afraid they were descending too fast but once it reached a certain speed, she felt brakes kicking in and the elevator came to a smooth stop. Her stomach caught back up with her moments later and she stumbled out of the elevator after him.

They were in an area in the Underground she wasn't familiar with, but Michael seemed quite comfortable there. He took her hand and led her past several factories until they reached a store. Michael exchanged a few words with the proprietor and he escorted them into a dressing room. The door closed with a click and the floor began sinking. Another floor slid into place over their heads and the small compartment soon deposited them in the underground railway they'd used earlier that evening.

"I'm sorry, Michael. I didn't mean to spoil your evening."

"No worries. However, I *am* concerned we were found so easily. They may have implanted something in your clothing. I'd ask Lady Orisaka for an entire new wardrobe to take with you to the camp, just in case. I'm going to dump my clothing far away from any of my labs. Luckily, I wasn't going back to where you met me tonight for a long time."

"And that food tasted so good."

"I'll see if they'll ship some to you at the camp." Michael's voice grew more serious as he continued. "And now you see why I have to keep moving my labs. It's not just the fact I'm doing confidential work. The damn, bloody government is scared to death about unlicensed storms. It's all right if we are officially tagged with a university position or work for the military or the government directly—and an official minder just in case. However, try to make a living on your own terms? Not on your life."

"I had no idea, Michael."

He spun around at her, an angry look on his face, but as quickly as his temper had blown up, it blew over. "I've tried to protect you from this. However, the Black Watch has had its eyes on me for quite some time. As you may have noticed, they're not much for taking 'no' for an answer. Honestly, if I wanted a patron, your boss has a great reputation, but I like my freedom to work on whatever project I want. I hope you understand."

"Not completely, but I trust you, so I believe you."

He squeezed her hand. "Thank you. That trust means more to me than anything someone like Jessica could ever offer me."

They rode in silence and soon the train pulled up at a stop and Michael escorted her to an elevator. They rode up and to Erica's surprise, they were only a few blocks from Angels' Tower. He kissed her quickly and stepped back into the elevator. "I think you can make it from here."

"Wait, if you had an elevator here, why did you have Theo drive me all over town?"

"A guy's gotta have some surprises."

She could still hear his laughter as the doors shut and the elevator sank back into the darkness.

Chapter Ten

The next day came and went without any major incidents. Erica had been looking over her shoulder the entire day, waiting for someone to bring up the incident with Jessica, but the most excitement she encountered was sitting in on planning sessions for the upcoming training. Crystal and Flight Commander Kail argued about which tests should come first, where they should be held, and so on until Erica found herself sleeping with her eyes open.

She started when she felt a poke on her shoulder and she guiltily glanced over at Sophie, who made a wiping motion on her chin. Erica quickly ran a hand across her mouth and flushed red as she realized she'd been drooling. She sat up, but to her great fortune, the meeting broke up and she joined the rest of her flight beating a rapid retreat out of the room.

They hit the break room and Kim leaned forward against a chair and arched her back to stretch out her muscles. "Oh my Goddess, I thought they were never going to come to a decision. There was *no* reason for us to be there."

"Fitz-Simmons, we were there because we were told to be there. I admit Crystal and the Flight Commander dominated the conversation. Still, one of the agenda items was who'd be training with the variant wings while Halgrim and Bronson are working with the main training mission."

"But, Sophie . . . they didn't need us there. If they had simply come out and said 'you're doing this, you're doing that,' that would have been fine. Honestly, I think Crystal already knows. She just hasn't told us yet."

Sophie sighed. "You're right, but do you want to tell either Lady Orisaka or the flight commander you're skipping their meeting?"

"Not on your life."

A uniformed Angel appeared at the doorway. "Is Miss Erica Halgrim here?"

"Yes, that's me."

"Delivery for you. Can you please sign here?"

Erica took the thin envelope from the administrative assistant as the others, except for Sophie, crowded around. She shooed them away and walked over to one of the tables in the room. Again, she had to chase them off, asking them for a little privacy.

I swear it's like we were back in high school. "Oh, let me see that note." You'd never believe we're college graduates. At least Sophie is keeping her curiosity to herself. She paused as another thought came to her. *It's not like Michael to send two packages so close together. I wonder what's going on?*

She stood up suddenly and started out of the break room. She announced she was going to open it in the privacy of her room, which drew a chorus of boos from the other women. She waved coyly and retreated before they could chase her down. She entered her room and shut the door before walking over to her desk.

She opened the end of the envelope with a small letter opener. She pulled the single sheet of paper out and carefully unfolded it. She knew immediately it wasn't Michael's handwriting. Then she read the first few words and stopped dead, the letter falling from her nerveless fingers. Taking a deep breath, she picked up the letter to start again.

Miss Halgrim,

I know the truth about what happened at the Temple.

I am sorry to contact you in this manner, but I fear there is no other way. Too many people are trying to stop me from telling what I know. I fear for both my life and yours. I heard about your troubles and feel it is only right you know the truth. Hopefully, between what you and I know we can compile a complete story that can be told to the authorities.

I cannot come to your location, too many people are watching. To be honest, I am not sure there are any safe places within Southwatch these days. Can you come to Emerald Park, just across the river from White Cliffs, Sunday at noon? There is a small lake on the west side of the park with a fountain nearby. Go to the lake and feed the fish. I will join you there and tell you everything I know.

Please come alone. Do not bring the police and, for the Goddess's sake, do NOT bring the Watch. If I see any signs of people watching you will never learn what happened.

If you agree to these terms, I think both you and I will sleep better at night.

The black gyrocopter pilot

Erica read the letter twice to ensure she understood what was going on. She carefully folded it back up and slipped it into the envelope. She stared out the window of her room and looked at the city stretching out around her, trying to get her thoughts under control.

This is either a really lousy joke or a trap. Or is it? How is it possible the pilot I've been looking for—we've been looking for—just pops up out of nowhere to contact me? And why me? If he knows something, why doesn't he go to the police? There's no way I'm going to something like this out in the middle of a park, much less alone.

She stared out the window, turning the envelope over and over in her hands. *But, if I don't, am I passing up the one opportunity to learn why everyone is after me? Or will learning the truth put me in even more danger?*

Eric heard the door opening and put on a smile as her roommate came in, her uniform soot stained and her hair matted down against her head. "Another trip through the Cloud today?"

Christina spread a cloth out on the floor and began setting her dirty uniform in the middle of it. "Third one today. While you and the others were tied up in meetings, someone had to make the deliveries. I didn't realize how many packages we delivered between Darkside and Sunside before there was no one else available to do it. It's getting to the point I'm not going to need to review maps of the Cloud anymore. Luckily, I'm done for the day."

Erica moved to her bed and sat on the end. "Chris, you ever been to Emerald Park before?"

Christina cocked her head to the side, surprised by the sudden change of topic, but she smiled fondly before responding. "Yeah, we used to go there when I was younger. There were neat picnic places and it's outside the Dark Cloud, so we could actually enjoy the sunlight. Mom and Dad used it as a reward if my sister and I behaved during the week. There are statues, fountains, hiking trails, and several ponds and lakes. There's also an open-air swimming pool if you can believe it. Plus, there is plenty of room to run around without worrying about being run over by a cart." Christina looked over at her with a big smile. "Are you thinking about going? When? Can I come?"

"I've never been there, but I've heard about it. All I've done since I've been on restriction is wake up, train with Crystal, come back here, shower, and go to bed. I'm starting to go stir crazy sitting around here. It feels like I've been stuck in this complex forever. It might be a nice change of pace if we could go there tomorrow."

Christina laughed. "Oh, I *don't* know. You've been outside more than you want to admit. After what happened last night, I'm not sure Lady Orisaka will let you out of here without someone to keep you out of trouble."

"Nothing *happened* the last night. Well, nothing major. I just had a nice dinner interrupted by some rude guests."

"Nothing happened, she says," Christina said in a mocking tone. "I guess you didn't hear about this morning?"

"This moring? No one has said anything to me."

"Oh, something happened—you weren't around to hear about it. Jessica Black raised a huge stink with Lady Orisaka this morning. Something about willfully disobeying a law enforcement official conducting their duties, fleeing the scene of an incident, trespassing, and defrauding a restaurant."

"There were no orders, just a bunch of threats coming from her. Of course we fled the scene. We didn't want her around. And, for pity's sake, we did *not* defraud the restaurant. Michael sent them money this morning to cover the bill. And he has a charge account with them anyway."

"Oh well, at least *that* has been taken care of. Now, I wasn't invited to the meeting, but I have it on pretty good authority Lady Orisaka blew off Jessica's threats, thanked her for her report, said she'd look into it, and had Jessica escorted off the premises. However, this Jessica person seems to have taken a personal interest in you and not in a friendly way, if you catch my meaning."

Erica flopped back on her bed. "What did I ever do to her?"

"You probably didn't bow and scrape enough to her the last time you saw her." Christina got up and sashayed around the room, tipping her head back and staring down her nose at Erica. "Obviously, she lowered herself to walk among mere mortals and you weren't sufficiently impressed."

Erica watched her roommate and then got the giggles. The two wound up collapsing from laughter and nearly missed the knock on their door. Erica finally got herself under control and went to see who was there: It was her flight leader, with a puzzled look on her face, trying to determine the source of all the laughter.

"Come in, Sophie. We were just—"

"Yes, I know. I heard you two from down the hall. Anyway, I wanted to review your progress with Crystal, if you have a moment."

Erica sobered up and stepped to the side to let Sophie come in. Christina finished preparing her uniform to go to the cleaners and gathered up her shower gear. She excused herself from the sleeping area and a few minutes later, the sound of running water echoed from the bathroom.

"Halgrim, I'm concerned with your progress the past couple of days. I don't think your mind is completely on your testing."

"No, it's not, Sophie. I'm burned out. I can only slam into the ceiling, walls, or floor so many times before I start thinking of ways to minimize the bruising rather than stressing the wings. Come to think of it, I don't think I've ever come close to stressing those wings."

Sophie nodded in sympathy. "I realize Crystal can be a bit unsympathetic when she gets into testing mode. But, she really wants these wings to do everything she dreams they might do. This is probably the biggest project she's ever directed for the Angels and she wants Lady Orisaka, *and* her peers, to be proud of her. She's not pushing you any harder than she's pushing herself. I think she's been running on two or three hours of sleep a night since this testing began."

"I'm sorry. I'll really try to do better, Sophie. I just need to get out of here and enjoy myself a bit. At least when I was delivering packages, I had new scenery to look at as I flew. I think I've already counted every hole in the wall panels in Crystal's lab."

Sophie stretched and stared up at the ceiling for a bit. "I agree completely."

"You agree with *what* completely?"

"You need a change of pace."

"That's why she should go to the park this weekend." They both turned to see Christina wrapped in a towel, standing in the doorway of the bathroom. "She was talking about Emerald Park earlier. Why not make a day out of it? We could go there, have a picnic, hit up the flavored-ice man, listen to the band on the main stage, and then catch the fireworks in the evening. Have you ever seen fireworks when you weren't under the Cloud? It's a-maz-ing!"

Erica thought about the letter sitting on her desk. She knew it said to come alone, but if she could get Sophie and Christina to go with her, then the security people might approve her leaving the building. She didn't like the odds of being able to sneak out of the building again.

"What do you say, Sophie?" Erica asked. "You could come along to 'keep an eye on me,' which should make everyone happy. What kind of trouble could I get into in a park?"

"Don't ask, Halgrim. I know you too well."

"Ouch. That hurts."

The people mover came to a halt in Emerald Park and Sophie, Christina, and Erica stepped off, with their gear in hand. Christina ran ahead with the picnic basket as Sophie and Erica made their way through the gates and strolled along, taking in the surroundings. Erica felt sorry for Sophie—she looked so uncomfortable with her hair down and wearing civilian clothing. Christina and she must have told Sophie a dozen times that she looked fine.

Erica was surprised to see Sophie looking unsure of herself. Erica moved closer. "Sophie, are you all right? If you're really this uncomfortable, we can go back."

Sophie straightened her back and picked up her pace. "No, I am perfectly fine, Halgrim. It's just been so long since I've worn regular clothing out in public. The high school my mother picked out for me required us to wear a uniform. By the time I was done with extra-curricular activities at school and homework, there was no point in changing before bed. When I got to college, I joined the Imperial Air Corps Reserve Officer Training Corps, so I just traded one uniform for another." She let a small smile reach her lips as she reminisced. "I guess I was pretty gung-ho back then, because I wore my uniform to class, even days I didn't have training. To be honest, if the Angels' recruiter hadn't approached me my senior year, I might have been a senior lieutenant by now."

"Wow. Somehow, knowing you, that doesn't surprise me. You act like you were born to wear a uniform."

Sophie slowed down and stared off into the distance. "No, not born to it. Mother insisted I go to the strictest high school she could get me in. She worked two jobs to afford the tuition, but she wanted me to have opportunities she never had. She told me it was more important to concentrate on school than to worry about what to wear."

She smiled to herself, almost as if Erica wasn't there. "Of course, I fought her tooth and nail when I was a teenager. My old friends were wearing the latest fashions and I was stuck wearing a uniform. Still, because she kept pushing me, I graduated top of my class and got into college on a full scholarship. If she were still alive, I'd like to think she'd be happy with what I've achieved."

Erica put a hand on Sophie's shoulder. "I know she is. Everyone in the flight looks up to you. Your mom did a great job."

Sophie blushed faintly and then glanced ahead, not looking at Erica. "Thanks, Halgrim. Now, let's see where Bronson went."

And that's the Sophie I've come to know.

They moved deeper into the park and, through some subtle nudging, the three women wound up over by the western pond. Erica checked her watch and noticed it was a few minutes until noon. She let Sophie and Christina go ahead and set up the picnic area while she excused herself and walked over to the lake. A young man was walking along, selling food to feed the fish, and she angled his direction.

"One bag, please."

"Of course, Miss Halgrim."

She started and then looked carefully at the man. Even through the makeup he was wearing to make himself look older, she could see he was about her age. However, he looked like he hadn't slept in days. Handing her a bag, he leaned against the railing going around the lake. She stood a few feet away and began tossing the bread crumbs into the pond, watching the fish strike the floating pieces.

He spoke just loud enough for her to hear. "I thought I asked you to come alone."

"I'm here. If they hadn't come, Security would have. These events have everyone on edge."

"Understandable. That's actually rather resourceful of you."

He paused as another couple walked up and he sold them a couple of bags. He returned to the railing and waited for them to move out of earshot before turning back toward Erica. She frowned. This wasn't going the way she envisioned. He seemed awfully calm for someone who had such a burden to get off his chest.

"I believe you said you had something to tell me."

"All in good time. I'm making sure we are alone."

"I didn't tell anyone anything."

He nodded. "I'm certain you didn't but some people have a bad habit of turning up when you least want them to." He moved away as if looking for another customer and then returned to his spot by the railing. "As I said, I am the pilot of the black gyrocopter."

"So you said. Can you prove it?"

"No. But, that's for another time. I don't know what you've heard, but what happened that day was an accident. Well, sort of an accident. She accidently fell from my gyrocopter, but they forced me to make an evasive maneuver before she was strapped in. If I had known she wasn't, I would have done things differently. It's hard to explain."

Erica walked over to get another bag of food. "You're not making sense."

He handed her the bag and waited until she returned to her spot. "It's not easy to talk about. It wasn't supposed to have happened. I'm still trying to figure out what happened myself."

"What wasn't supposed to happen?"

"Wait. Let me start from the top and I'll—"

There was a sharp gasp and Erica turned to see the young man turn pale.

"I thought I told you not to tell anyone about this."

"I didn't."

"We'll try this again someday . . . I hope." With that, the young man walked casually away, not looking back. She heard a shout off in the distance and turned to see two men and a woman running across the grass toward her. It took her a second to realize the woman was Jessica Black.

How the hell did she find out about this?

She turned to warn the young man, but he had abandoned his gear and disappeared into some bushes near the far end of the lake. She heard running feet coming up behind her and she saw the men motioning to each other. They split up, each heading around the lake, while Jessica came straight toward her.

There was a sudden roar and then a gyrocopter lifted into the sky from the bushes. Before the men could pull out their weapons, the gyrocopter tilted its propellers forward, gaining both height and speed. It disappeared over a clump of trees and flew off in the direction of the river.

Erica heard more running feet and Sophie and Christina joined her at the railing, staring up into the sky. She knew they both had questions, but now was not the time to ask. She pointed up and spoke to Christina. "I didn't know they allowed gyrocopters in the park. I thought you said this was restricted to foot traffic."

Christina looked puzzled. "I didn't know either. I can't imagine why that was here."

"You know perfectly well why that was here, Erica," Jessica said, breathing heavily from her run.

"Miss Black? What a surprise. What brings you to Emerald Park?"

"I'm certain you were just innocently talking to that man?"

Erica looked at Sophie and Christina with a helpless look. "I'm going to say I was here at the park with my friends, getting ready to enjoy a picnic and relaxing. I was feeding the fish while they set up the blanket. I only spoke to that man to purchase the fish food."

"Then why did that man flee when he saw us? Why did he have a gyrocopter hidden over there?"

Erica smiled her most innocent smile. "I have no idea. Then again, I'm surprised you don't know. After all, you are the Black Watch. I thought you all knew everything."

Jessica turned red, but before she could say anything, Sophie swooped in and hooked her arm through Erica's. "Come on, Halgrim. We need to get to those sandwiches before the ants carry them off. Miss Black, we hope you manage to catch that man. Best of luck. Let's go, Halgrim, Bronson."

The three women retreated to their picnic area, leaving Jessica standing there openmouthed. Erica started to turn around to say something else, but Sophie applied enough pressure on her arm to make Erica's eyes water. Erica took a deep breath and let herself be led to the blanket Sophie had spread on the ground.

They ate their meal while listening to the band tuning up at the nearby pavilion. Erica made sure to keep her eyes either on the band or her food. After a while, Sophie looked over at her. "I don't know if they've gone completely, but the Black Watch has left the immediate area. Now, Halgrim, would you like to explain what's going on?"

"If I could, I would, Sophie. I was just as surprised as you were. I certainly did not invite Jessica to the picnic."

"I am certain of that." Sophie craned her neck and looked around. "However, you cannot tell me you arranged this little visit to the park out of the blue any longer."

"No, that's true. I received a message to meet the gyrocopter pilot I saw at the *Temple*. I'm not sure if he was or not, but after seeing that gyrocopter, I don't disbelieve him. He claimed he wanted to tell me what happened. I thought having the two of you here would minimize the chance of getting into trouble. I didn't count on Jessica showing up and spoiling things."

Sophie didn't say anything for a moment and when she spoke, the disappointment in her voice was almost more than Erica could handle. "So, you decided to go off on your own and put yourself at risk—and us."

"No, it wasn't like that. This might have been my only chance to learn the truth from the one person who knows it. If I had told you, you would have insisted on going to Lady Orisaka. She would have sent Security, which would have ruined everything. He almost took off without speaking because he saw Chris and you. Anyway, he started to tell me what happened when Jessica and her goon squad showed up." She paused for a moment and then continued while she was still brave enough to face up to Sophie. "I wouldn't have asked you to come if I thought there was a risk. I just couldn't pass up the chance to learn why this is happening. I'm tired of being scared every time I walk outside."

Christina started to say something but a look from Sophie stopped her. There was an awkward silence, only interrupted by the band practicing. Finally, Sophie came to a decision and nodded to no one in particular.

"Very well, Halgrim. You did what you believed you had to do. You are right, I would have reported this to Security and I *am* going to report this to Security when we return. But, we came here to enjoy ourselves and to watch some fireworks. I suggest we do just that. After all, we do have an early morning tomorrow to get out to the training range. Perhaps with you out of town, things will calm down and Miss Black will forget the incident."

Sophie looked at her again. "However, I seem to recall someone asking how much trouble they could get into in a public park. I find my opinion validated."

Erica blushed but said nothing. What could she say?

The band started up a lively tune and the women sat back with their own thoughts as the music washed over them. Erica concentrated on enjoying the sunlight and white fluffy clouds in the distance and vowed not to think of gyrocopters or annoying women the rest of the day.

To her credit, she almost managed to do so.

Chapter Eleven

"Hey, Halgrim, does this bring back some memories?"

Erica grinned at Sophie. "Memories? Like I could forget Flight Leader Ramirez's melodious voice at oh-four-thirty?" She tried to drop her voice as low as she could go. "'Hurry up, ladies. Chow is at oh-five-thirty. If you ain't there, you ain't eatin'. An' watch your step. Never know if ol' Jake the Snake is hiding out there in the darkness. Step lively and maybe he'll bite the slow'uns.'"

The two shared a laugh and then Sophie pointed off in the distance, to a group of young women hurrying from one group of buildings to another, calling cadence as they ran. Sophie looked at her. "I wonder if Flight Leader Ramirez is in charge of that group?"

There was a soft cough behind them and they turned around to see Flight Commander Kail standing behind them. "I'm sure you ladies enjoy reminiscing in these familiar surroundings, but we *do* have work to do. If you're available, that is?"

Sophie snapped to the position of attention and saluted. "Yes, Flight Commander. We're ready to begin the first training session."

The flight commander walked around the two women, eyeing them up and down. "Zwyer, your reputation precedes you. However, Halgrim, yours does too. There'll be no sneaking out of camp to meet your boyfriend here. In fact, there'll be no sneaking out at all. You might get away with that crap back in Southwatch, but here, you're under my command. Are we clear?"

"Ma'am, yes ma'am!"

"Well, at least your enthusiasm is a good start. Now, building sixty-two, if you please?"

Sophie and Erica saluted and fled from the flight commander toward the designated building. "Glad to see some things never change, eh, Sophie?"

"Less talking, more running."

The two finished in a dead heat as they reached the door to the low wooden building. Erica leaned against the building, trying to catch her breath, while listening to the strange noises coming from inside. She noted Sophie looked like she was ready to go another couple of laps around the complex. Sophie glanced at her and *ts*ked disapprovingly.

"Halgrim, we need to work on your physical conditioning. This will be a strenuous testing session. While you're meeting with Crystal and the rest of her team, I'll start working on your physical training plan."

"I feel guilty making you do the extra work."

"Think nothing of it." Sophie pushed against her stomach with a finger. "I could stand to tighten a bit more too. No sense in getting too heavy to fly."

Erica noted Sophie's finger couldn't have gone in more than an eighth of an inch, but once Sophie got an idea in her head, there was no point in arguing about it. She was almost as bad as Crystal at times. Erica pulled herself erect and knocked on the door. After a few minutes, the noises inside quieted down and someone approached the door.

A member of Angels' Security peered through a small window to verify who was outside before opening the door. Erica and Sophie stopped dead in their tracks when they saw the wings covering the walls of the large room—wings in all shapes and sizes, in differing states of construction. There were six or seven winders moving around the room, carefully placing hydraulic lines on tables and tools where the scientists could easily reach them.

Erica continued to scan the room until she saw what Crystal was working on in the center. As soon as she saw it, Erica felt her whole body freeze. Its face was blank except for two eyes, but otherwise it was Erica done in wires, gears, and chrome. The cybernaut slowly turned its head and looked at Erica before returning its attention to Crystal.

"Sophie, am I seeing what I think I'm seeing?"

There was a pause and then she heard Sophie's strained reply. "If you're seeing a mechanical built to your body measurements, then yes, we're seeing the same thing."

"Creepy."

"Very."

Crystal walked over to the pair, trailed by a couple of people in lab coats carrying clipboards. "Oh, good, you're here, Erica. I need to get some more measurements from you."

Erica ignored the technicians who began running tape measures around her body as she stared at her mechanical doppelganger. After a couple of tries, she found her voice, but it came out in a breathy croak. "Crys, what is that thing?"

"Oh, I thought I'd already introduced you to your twin. I started working on her as soon as you were assigned to this project. Erica, I'd like you to meet Eve."

Crystal motioned to the mechanical and it sat up on the table, lowered itself to the ground, and walked over to Erica. When it stopped, it dropped one hand on its hip and bent one knee slightly in perfect imitation of the way Erica was standing. It was as if Erica was watching herself walk in a full-length mirror—if she were wearing a full set of power armor.

Sophie positioned herself halfway between the two. "This is incredible, Crystal, but why?"

"Well, Erica can fly only so many hours a day. Plus, to be honest, some of these designs are a little less developed than the set she had back in Southwatch. It would be dangerous for Erica to be the first to try them out. She's going to be busy enough testing all the wings I'm reasonably sure should work."

"Thanks, I think," Erica mumbled with her eyes still fixed on her doppleganger.

Crystal ignored Erica's sarcastic reply. "I built Eve so I could finish getting the wings fitted and balanced. Eve is a mediocre flyer—she lacks Erica's natural instincts and pure ability—but she can make a lap or two around the complex here. She tests the new designs and then returns so I can check the readings. Plus, should a wing design fail catastrophically at five hundred feet, she's more likely to survive than Erica."

Erica gulped, trying not to think about what Crystal had just said. She let her gaze wash over the vast array of wings surrounding her. "So, what's up with all of this? I thought we were coming here to test the wings I'd been using back in Southwatch?"

"Oh, we will," Crystal said, reassuringly. "However, those were prototypes. I had to limit them to work in my lab. Out here, we have room to test different combinations of materials, elements, angles . . ." She wandered off, still talking to herself, the two assistants dutifully following along behind copying down her statements.

Erica continued to stare at Eve until she felt a touch on her shoulder. She jerked her head around to see Sophie standing there, pointing at a door at the far end of the room. "There's the changing room. You need to go get in your test gear."

"Oh, right. Back in a second."

Erica let the wings slowly unfold behind her, trying to be sure not to catch the test equipment in the remiges. The flight feathers were powerful, but delicate. She did not want one dislodging while she was in midair. She spread the wings, watching how the primaries, secondaries, and tertiaries slowly separated to catch as much of the wind as possible. Crystal circled, checking the connections attached to a small machine on Erica's hip.

"I tried to keep the measuring device as light as I could, but there's no way around the wiring. If you feel the wings getting bound at all, abort the flight and land as quickly as possible."

"Don't worry about that."

Crystal laughed at the expression on Erica's face. "It's unlikely to happen. I wouldn't send you up there if I hadn't already tested this with Eve. She had no issues and I don't think you will either . . . unless you try acrobatics, which are certainly not on today's schedule."

"No acrobatics. Check," Erica repeated and then grinned back at Crystal. The young scientist's enthusiasm was infectious. Erica couldn't wait for the preflight checks to be finished so she could get back into the sky. Her grounding in Southwatch had been tough to live through. She hadn't flown without being hooked up to one of Crystal's harnesses since the day after her kidnapping and she missed the feel of the air on her face.

Finally, Crystal gave her the heads-up and Erica moved a switch on the small box on her chest. She felt the soft warmth as the thalisium began to react with the electrical charge and her wings began to sweep back and forth. Once they were moving, she took two running steps forward and leapt into the air.

For a split second, Erica was afraid she'd mistaken her wings' lift, but right before she face-planted in front of the Goddess and everyone, her wings bit into the air and lifted her up and forward. She worked on keeping her legs and arms stable as she climbed into the sky, trying to minimize drag. Finally comfortable with the wings, she circled the field and the assembled people while Sophie prepared for takeoff. Unlike her, Sophie was wearing her regular wings and was coming along as a security measure. Flight Commander Kail had insisted someone flew with her because of the earlier kidnapping attempts. The fact they were testing Crystal's new designs didn't help matters either.

Scuttlebutt says the Imperial Air Corps is funding part of Crystal's work. These wings aren't suited for combat, but they'd be great for the observation corps or courier duties. I can't imagine a set of these wings will be cheap, though. Probably less expensive than sending a warship across the Empire to deliver a message, though.

Erica circled the camp until Sophie joined her. The initial course was simple. Fly along the edge of camp until they had completed one circuit, then come in at a lower altitude and do two runs through the slalom course Crystal had laid out—once at moderate speed and then as fast as she safely could—before flying a course between the buildings as close to the ground as she could to check the wing's stability. Crystal thought that would give her enough data for the first day of testing.

Sophie swept by and took her position about fifty feet higher than Erica. A flash on Erica's wrist-com told her Crystal was getting a signal from the box on her hip. Erica adjusted her goggles and signaled to Sophie to begin the run. She spread her wings to their fullest extent before beating a trail toward the camp's boundaries.

The first part was uneventful. These were the wings Erica had been practicing with back in Southwatch, so she knew what to expect from them. It was all she could do not to do a loop or something to break up the monotony of the simple circuit around the complex. Still, she heard Flight Commander Kail's warning in the back of her mind and forced herself to play it straight . . . at least today.

She caught herself picking up speed as they reached the far end of the complex and noted Sophie falling behind. She pulled up to let Sophie catch up when she realized they weren't alone. Sophie hadn't fallen behind; she was trying to position herself between Erica and an oncoming gyrocopter. Erica turned and with a burst of speed caught up with her flight leader as Sophie dived to one side, narrowly avoiding the gyro. Erica noted the pilot was wearing dark goggles and a mask covered his face.

"What's going on, Sophie?"

"No clue," Sophie shouted back over the rush of wind. "Get low and get back to the compound. I'll delay him as long as possible."

Erica forced her wings to flutter as quickly as possible, hovering in place as Sophie made lazy circles around her. In the distance, Erica could see the gyrocopter circling around for another pass. "Sophie, you don't have any wing weapons. What are you going to do?"

Sophie reached into the small pack on her waist and pulled out a small electro-gun and a stick with a metal case on the end of it. "Just because they didn't issue me weapons doesn't mean I'm helpless. Now, get out of here. This is my job. Yours is to protect yourself and those wings."

The look Sophie gave her said she wasn't in the mood for an argument. Erica nodded once and dove toward the ground. The sound of the gyrocopter grew in volume as she pulled in her wings and let gravity aid her dive toward a grove of trees below.

She heard an odd noise and flicked open one wing, sending herself rolling to one side. A metal net, sparking as the electricity in its capacitors was released, whipped through the space she had been a moment before. She spread her wings and rolled onto her back to glance up and saw the gyro maneuvering to line back up on her. Sophie valiantly pursuing, but the gyrocopter was quicker than she was.

Erica knew she should focus on getting away but, in that instant, she saw an opportunity to end this quickly. She slowed her descent and then hovered about one hundred feet above the grove. Sophie frantically waved at her, but Erica ignored her flight leader and kept her attention on the gyrocopter.

It was hard playing chicken with an onrushing vehicle, but Erica focused on keeping the pilot's attention on her instead of worrying about Sophie rapidly closing the distance. She saw the pilot looking through his sights at her, centering his craft. When she couldn't take it anymore, Erica wrapped her wings around her and dropped.

The gyrocopter's motor screamed as it went overhead and Erica quickly opened her wings. She fought to gain control of her wings in the gyrocopter's downwash as the vortices of air tried to suck her down into the trees. At the last second, she managed to gain control just enough to swoop upward, her boots ripping through the upper branches of the taller trees.

The gyro pilot fought the controls to swing around before Erica had the opportunity to land and disappear into the woods. Erica saw Sophie maneuvering into position above her. She had caught on to what Erica was doing. It was an old technique they'd learned back in training but Erica had never tried it against a real flying machine, much less one driven by someone trying to knock her out of the sky.

Erica swooped back up and hovered again. Crystal's wings were responding even better than back in the lab and Erica was growing more confident about what she could do with them. Again, the gyrocopter dove at her, but this time, she saw the pilot coming in under control, waiting for her to dive away again.

Erica forced herself to wait until the pilot committed himself before suddenly spreading her wings and clawing air, rising above the flashing rotor blades. Erica passed Sophie diving toward the gyrocopter. As she passed Erica, Sophie pulled a small ring from the bottom of the stick she was carrying and lobbed it in the gyrocopter's path.

The pilot slowed his craft to pivot after Erica. At the last second, he spotted the falling object and jerked the gyrocopter's controls to the side, but it was too late. Sophie's bomb exploded a few feet away from the gyrocopter, sending bits of metal scattering in all directions. Erica watched as one of the rotor blades detached from its housing from the shock wave, sending the wounded gyrocopter spinning erratically toward the ground.

Sophie and Erica circled as the flying machine crashed. Off in the distance, Erica saw two Lances and an Elephant speeding toward their positions. As they drew closer, Erica could see the large flatbed trucks were loaded with security personnel and the Elephant, with its large water tank and hoses, carried the compound's firefighters.

Sophie swooped close enough for Erica to make out her words. "Halgrim, I appreciate what you did, but you disobeyed direct orders."

"Look, Sophie, you couldn't keep up with the gyro and I knew after the first pass he wasn't good enough to keep up with Crystal's new wings. I figured if I could get him to focus on me, you'd get your chance—and you did."

"We'll talk about this later. Let's land down there. I think the flight commander is in the first truck."

I wonder how long I can stay afloat? I don't really want to have to go through this debriefing. I don't know what's going on, but I know it's not my fault.

Still, she found herself descending alongside Sophie. They landed near the crashed gyrocopter. The pilot had been thrown several feet from the wreckage. They started walking toward him when the trucks came rolling to a stop and the security people poured out to secure the area.

"Halgrim, Zwyer, come here now."

"Yes, Flight Commander."

They meekly walked over to the dark-haired woman standing there with her arms crossed over her chest. An angry breath escaped her lips, sending one lock of her hair flying skyward before it settled back into place. She glanced from them to the crashed vehicle and back. "Report."

Sophie stepped forward and saluted. "Ma'am, we were halfway through the initial lap of the training session when I spotted an unauthorized gyrocopter approaching, using the terrain to mask its approach. I signaled for Halgrim to flee while I attempted to engage it. However, it was faster than I was and it nearly netted Halgrim, who had to take evasive actions."

"Halgrim, were you not warned not to make any extreme maneuvers while you were on this test?"

"In the absence of higher authority, I made a command decision to avoid capture in an electro-net, especially given my current height and speed. If I was wrong, I willingly accept my punishment."

"We'll take that into consideration. Continue, Zwyer."

"Halgrim recognized her new wings gave her an advantage over the gyrocopter. The pilot seemed unprepared for her speed and ability to hover. She managed to distract it, giving me the opportunity to toss a stick grenade near the gyrocopter. It lost a rotor blade in the explosion and crashed where you now see it."

"So, Halgrim, along with not following orders to withdraw from this situation, you then allowed yourself to be drawn into air-to-air combat unarmed with an untested set of wings and carrying additional testing gear?"

"With all due respect, Flight Commander, I did not allow myself to be drawn into anything. I was *attacked* without provocation. I did not initiate the situation and the opponent was not going to let me meekly withdraw from the field. Since he was attempting to capture me, I saw no reason not to go on being the bait."

Flight Commander Kail stared at her for a moment and then a ghost of a smile flickered onto her face, before returning to its normal severe look. "Halgrim, Zwyer, continue this training session and then report directly to me. If you two ladies think you've got what it takes to confront combat aircraft on your own, then, by the Goddess, I'm going to train you how to do it right. I see there's a four-hour block between morning and evening sessions with Chief Scientist Digby-Smith. No sense in letting it go to waste. Take five, get yourselves refocused, and then let's get back to training, shall we?"

Erica and Sophie saluted and were turning away when there was a sudden shout to hit the dirt. They both dove forward onto their stomachs as an explosion ripped through the air above them. There were screams of pain and the sound of people running as dirt rained down.

Erica turned her head and saw flames rising from where the pilot's body was. One of the singed security people rushed over to Flight Commander Kail. "Ma'am, he was wearing a booby trap set to go off if someone moved his mask. We have to assume the gyro may be trapped also. Please move everyone back until we can get the bomb team in here."

Who wears a booby trap to ensure they can't be identified? What's going on and why am I at the center of this?

Chapter Twelve

Erica felt the board bend beneath her feet as she landed on the end of it, just before it propelled her forward into the air. She bent her body until her fingertips touched her toes and then straightened out to hit the water square on. She felt the rush of water past her arms and head, running along her body before she felt her hands brush against the concrete floor of the pool. She turned her body and thrust upward with her hands and feet until she broke the surface.

Wiping the water out of her eyes, she watched Sophie already completing the second spin before she plunged nearby. She treaded water until Sophie appeared and then they moved toward the far end of the pool with long, slow strokes. Touching the far side, she did a dolphin turn and then keeping her arms by her side, frog-kicked her way to the diving board end of the pool, only letting her face break the surface to take a breath.

"Not bad, Halgrim. You show some promise as a diver, but your swimming needs a lot of work. Don't worry, we've got all summer to work on this."

The voice of the flight commander broke Erica's concentration and she hesitated for a second, losing her momentum and sinking deeper into the water. She had to fight to get back on top of the water without using her arms and resumed her trek to the far side. Feeling her cheeks burning as she climbed out of the pool, she got back in line at the board to prepare for another dive/swim trip. Sophie emerged from the water and joined her. Erica felt a twinge of jealousy at the way Sophie looked in her bathing suit and resolved to stick to the diet she'd been assigned by the flight commander.

"I wish I knew why we got extended out here. This was only supposed to be a two-week training session. Why are we going to be out here until the end of summer?" Erica whispered as they made their way to the ten-meter board.

"I guess Crystal has more wings ready than they thought she'd have. But I can't complain. I don't think I've ever seen the stars this often in my life."

A voice growled at them from below. "If you two princesses are done gossiping, maybe you could get this drill started?"

Erica gulped loudly and hurried to the end of the board to take her turn.

"All right, you two, take five. You're starting to make me feel tired. Grab your towels and come here."

Soon, Erica and Sophie were sitting in front of a portable blackboard near the pool and were being quizzed about the training conducted earlier in the day. It had been two weeks since the attack by the unidentified gyrocopter and tensions were still high at the camp. Erica could have sworn she'd seen two members of the Angels of Vengeance at the camp, but Lady Orisaka's enforcers almost never left Southwatch.

Maybe I'm overreacting, but if that really was Ranulf DuPree, then things are a lot more serious than I thought.

"Am I keeping you awake, Halgrim?"

Erica blushed furiously and turned her attention to the flight commander. "Sorry, I was trying to apply what we've been going over to the incident. Was that Ranulf DuPree I saw a couple of days ago?"

That question earned her a scowl from the flight commander and two hours of extra training after the evening shift was over.

Coming out of the base library with her paper completed, she found Sophie sitting on the steps reading something. Erica coughed softly and Sophie slipped the book into her shoulder bag. She joined Erica at the bottom of the steps.

"Were you waiting long?"

"Not too. I was talking with Crystal about the upcoming trial while you were doing your extra assignment. This new set of wings will be a radical departure from anything you've used before. They're designed for long-distance gliding. We'll actually be heading to an alternate camp in the Gray Mountains. You and I will both be testing these. Crystal swears there's no way I'd keep up with you on a standard set. We'll also have to carry oxygen bottles since we're likely to hit some significant altitude."

Erica's eyes lit up. "You mean, free soaring? Not having to worry about obstacles, mooring lines, or the Dark Cloud?"

"I believe that's what I said, yes."

Erica was about to say something when she heard footsteps approaching. She turned to see Eve standing there. It was disconcerting to hear a voice coming from a face that had no mouth, but the message was clear enough. "Please come with me. Crystal would like to see you."

The two followed the cybernaut through the dark camp toward the main laboratory. Apparently Eve was fitted with some type of sensors because she managed to dodge every chuck hole and hump that Erica and Sophie tripped on en route. Finally, the trio reached the lab and Eve motioned for them to go inside.

The two women stepped into the darkened lab. Erica saw a soft light coming from beneath the doorway where Crystal's office was, but there was no sign of the scientist anywhere. Sophie went to switch on the light when there was a voice in the darkness—a voice Erica never expected to hear at Camp Falcon, or anywhere else to be honest.

"Please do not turn on the light, Flight Leader. I think it best if we have this discussion in privacy. If someone saw the light, they might investigate and that could lead to dire consequences."

Erica took a couple of steps forward before being brought up short by a table that caught her across the thighs. She sucked in air in pain but still managed to speak. "Tony, what are you doing here? And who the heck are you anyway? Tony Blaylock is dead."

A low chuckle greeted her questions. "I'm glad to see you too, Erica. I'm here to pass on some information. I'm afraid I'm not dead, no matter what the records say. Yes, my craft crashed into the wall of that canyon, but that was not my body they found. See, there are always hikers and climbers who fall to their deaths in those mountains every year. They found *a* body and assumed it was me. It suited my purposes and I never bothered straightening out the record."

Sophie's voice sounded from somewhere in the darkness. "So, why tell us now, Blaylock? Doesn't this threaten your anonymity?"

"Flight Leader, my anonymity was blown the day that poor girl fell to her death at the *Temple*. Because of that fuss, my contact never showed and I've been on the run from a whole mess of people since then. But, I hear you've been having your own set of adventures."

"For a dead man, you have a wealth of resources, Blaylock."

"I do my best, but Erica, I have some information that may be useful."

Erica tried to keep her voice level. She knew Sophie was up to something and wanted to keep Tony's attention on her. "I'd appreciate any information I can get, Tony. Things seem to keep happening but nobody wants to tell me why."

"Probably because everyone keeps trying to pin this on us instead of figuring out what really happened. We're the easy solution. Why should the authorities try to find the truth? That would be work. However, when you get back to town, I'd visit the ambassador. He knows more than he's letting on. Plus, people are asking a lot of questions about you in some of the low spots in town. Places I'm more likely to be at home than you or your buddy there. I don't think you're out of the woods quite yet."

"So, you want me to just waltz up to the ambassador's airship and invite myself in?"

"Do you want to learn the truth? Figure out a way. You're a resourceful young woman."

"You say people are asking questions. Got any names to go along with that bit of information? Given what's going on, I suspect there's a lot of people asking about me . . . and you."

"Don't know all the names myself, but you've got contacts I don't have. Check out the *Bloody Lynx*. I suspect the boys asking about you have something to do with that ship. However, I'd ask softly. They don't mind asking people questions, but they don't like being under the magnifying glass themselves."

Erica knew Sophie had moved into position. "And speaking of getting a closer look, why don't we discuss you?"

With that, there was a loud crash and Erica switched on the lights. She spotted Sophie tangled in wires and tubes and rushed over to help her to her feet. They realized the wires were hooked to a speaker and led back to Crystal's office. They inched the door open to find a microphone and an open window. They looked into the darkness but Tony, if he was indeed Tony Blaylock, was long gone.

"Halgrim, you've got a lot of explaining to do." Sophie attempted to pick up the mess she had made tackling the chair where the speaker was laying.

"Me? What makes you think I know any more about this than you do? What I want to know is, how did he convince Eve to come fetch us? And where is Crystal?"

The door sprang open and two security personnel rushed in, weapons drawn. Erica and Sophie slowly raised their hands into the air and kept very still. Flight Commander Kail and Crystal walked in behind them. There was an amused smile on the flight commander's face but Crystal seemed confused.

"Why are you two here in the lab after hours?" the flight commander asked.

"Eve brought us a message Crystal wanted to see us. However, someone else was waiting here. He got away before we could catch him."

Flight Commander Kail's eyes narrowed. "Who was it?"

"Just some dead guy named Tony Blaylock."

The flight commander motioned to the security people and they rushed out. Crystal walked around the room doing a quick inventory while they watched. Finally, she stopped and turned to the other three women. "Nothing is missing or even out of place except for a spool of wire and a couple of speakers. My schematics are right where I left them."

"No, Tony just wanted to talk. I doubt he had a clue what kind of gold mine he was sitting in."

"You seem awfully familiar with this intruder, Halgrim."

"He was the person with me when that young girl died at the *Temple*. He's been on the run ever since. He came out here to pass on a warning to me. Apparently the attacks the other day were just the start of our troubles. He suggested looking into something called the *Bloody Lynx*, whatever the heck that is." She decided to keep the advice to talk to Ambassador Bogdanovich to herself unless Sophie brought it up. She knew what the flight commander's reaction would be to *that*.

Crystal continued wandering about the lab muttering and then her head came up, staring at Erica. "Wait a second. Did you say Eve told you to come here?"

"Yes, she found Sophie and me at the library."

"But I didn't send Eve to get you."

Erica nodded. "I don't think you did either. So, either he tricked Eve into going to get us or else he figured out a way to make Eve think he was you."

Crystal turned and headed for the door. "We're going to get to the bottom of this. Come with me."

They glanced at the flight commander and she shrugged and pointed at the door. When Crystal got her back up, there wasn't much

111

point in getting in her way. The glow from their electric torches made them realize how dark the rest of the camp was. Only the occasional light over a doorway broke the darkness. Everyone stayed together, not wanting to get separated in the darkness. Somehow, knowing Tony had gotten in and out of the complex didn't make Erica feel comfortable. If he could infiltrate the grounds then so could a lot of people—too many of whom had shown a lack of respect for her well-being. The quartet searched around all the buildings in their complex and found no signs of the missing cybernaut. On a hunch, Crystal headed toward a warehouse over by the slalom course.

They neared the front doors to the warehouse when Crystal tripped on something. Erica rushed forward to help and stopped dead. There was a familiar body lying on the ground, except now there was something very different about it.

The last time they'd seen Eve, a long metal spike wasn't sticking out of her chest.

Erica arrived at the lab the next morning to get the final fitting for her gliding wings. She found Crystal working feverishly on repairing Eve, wires and tools scattered all over the table. From the rumpled condition of her clothing and the bloodshot eyes visible through her thick glasses, it was obvious Crystal had been working on her cybernaut protégée since they'd found her staked out like a butterfly the night before. Erica waited for a few minutes and then coughed to get her friend's attention.

Crystal gave Erica a halfhearted wave. "Oh, hi. I'll be with you in a few moments. Just a few more connections and Eve will be functional again. I want to get her functioning so she can test the wings before you. Even though they should work, I'd feel better if someone other than you used them first."

"I guess the damage wasn't too bad from last night?"

"Actually, the damage was pretty extensive. However, I had a number of spare sections shipped here ahead of time. Remember, I developed Eve to test-fly your wings. I expected her to take severe damage from time to time and she'd need to be repaired fast."

Crystal poured herself a cup of coffee and took a few sips before picking up a spanner and a screwdriver. She continued to talk to Erica as she opened up a panel and maneuvered something into Eve's chest. "When I examined her damage, I saw someone attempted to slit her throat from behind first. Once they realized it was a mechanical, that's when they used one of the slalom poles to spear her body. It went right through her power plant and shorted a number of her major components. That's why it's taken me all night to get her repaired."

Erica put her arm around Crystal. "All night? Crys, you have to get some sleep. We're going to need you to be sharp when we get into the mountains. If something goes wrong, you're the only one who knows how to fix these things."

"Trust me, I plan on sleeping all the way there. Once we arrive, the excitement will keep me going. Besides, today is just basic testing. We'll send Eve up for a few circuits and then Sophie and you will take one trip so I can take measurements and adjust the wings. Tomorrow we'll go for some height and duration testing. Day after tomorrow, we'll do the main test."

Erica listened intently as Crystal laid out the training plans in detail, going into one of her technical waves of words that left Erica washed up onto the shore. Then something Crystal said echoed in her mind. She backed away slowly with a hand to her mouth. With a squeak, she said, "Crystal, tell me again about the damage to Eve."

Crystal stopped mid-word, unused to people interrupting her. She took her glasses off and absentmindedly rubbed them against her lab coat. "There was a slalom pole shoved through her chest area. Destroyed her power plant and shorted out a bunch of her servos."

"No, the part before that."

"There was damage to her neck. It looked like someone tried to cut her throat first. Which is silly. I mean, she's a mechanical. I don't even have oil lines running close to the surface, so cutting her throat wouldn't damage her in the least bit."

Erica rubbed her neck involuntarily. "But it would me."

"Don't be silly, who would—" Crystal's laugh cut off and she stared at Erica, who had gone pale. "You think someone attacked Eve thinking she was you?"

"I think we need to talk to the flight commander."

Chapter Thirteen

The truck jerking to the side jostled Erica wake. She'd been going in and out of sleep ever since the convoy left the main camp. She bounced into the air and then felt a shot of pain as her rear end met the solid steel floor of the truck bed. She winced and not for the first time wished this trip to the Gray Mountains' camp was over.

After the events at Crystal's lab, Flight Commander Kail locked down the entire camp. That morning additional security arrived from Southwatch. According to the flight commander, Lady Orisaka ordered all testing discontinued until security was in place. They were ordered to proceed to the mountain camp and security would be joining the convoy by airship later in the day. Crystal protested against the delays, citing the possibility of storms later in the week. Erica learned from Sophie that Lady Orisaka made it clear to Crystal that if she appreciated her employment with the Angels of Steel, she would be well advised to follow orders.

Sophie lifted up the canvas flap covering the back of the truck's cargo bed and looked into the distance. Erica felt a shiver run down her back as the opening revealed the ground dropping away a few feet away from the road into a ravine. The mountainside rose just beyond the edge of the road on the other side, leaving only a path wide enough for one truck to pass between the mountain and the cliff. Erica hoped the advance team had secured the north end of the road. There was no room to maneuver if another vehicle approached from the other direction.

Erica climbed onto the wooden bench that lowered from the side of the truck's bed. *Okay, maybe I'm being paranoid, but if I were going to try something, this would be the perfect place. There's nowhere to hide and nowhere to maneuver. We're stuck on the side of the mountain until we get to the next checkpoint.*

Suddenly, the truck ground to a halt and Erica bolted upright, watching the machinery and boxes in the truck shift with the change in momentum. For a second, Erica was afraid she'd wished her imagination into reality. However, one of the guards jumped onto the back bumper and lifted the canvas.

"Just taking a little break to refill the steam boilers. Takes more water to keep pressure at these altitudes. If you want to stretch for a bit, we'll be here for about fifteen minutes."

The two women glanced at each other and nodded to the guard. He pulled the pegs that held the tailgate into position and lowered it while Sophie flipped the flap up. With a fluid movement, she dropped onto the bumper and then down to the ground, landing easily on the balls of her feet. Erica gingerly lowered herself, still feeling the lack of sleep from the revelations of last night.

"Halgrim, if you want to wait by the truck, I'll get some fresh water and fruit. Back in a few moments."

Erica waved distractedly and Sophie disappeared into the swirl of drivers and guards taking advantage of the momentary rest stop. She moved to the front of the truck and gazed at the goat trail someone jokingly had called a road. It curved to the left but she could see where it reappeared along a ridge closer to the top. She knew once they crossed that ridge, the camp was just on the other side. She could probably fly there in less than ten minutes, but given the way the road snaked, they probably were looking at another three hours of driving.

A noise caught her attention and she saw steam rising into the air from a truck two ahead of theirs. From the way the drivers scattered, someone's engine had a boil-over. Two mechanics rushed past her with their tool kits and she followed to see what was going on. Steam-powered machines still fascinated her—her father had been a steam engine mechanic and she had loved working with him in his shop, even if she'd never shown any aptitude at fixing them.

A medic led one of the drivers. Erica saw him applying a cotton compress to the driver's forehead. From the talk, a piece of hose had broken and whipped around inside the engine, catching the driver square on the forehead. Erica watched the mechanics work on the engine and soon it was purring along again. She turned around to return to her vehicle and bumped right into Eve.

"Pardon me, Erica. I did not mean to startle you."

Erica recoiled from the mechanical in horror. The line running across the cybernaut's neck from the attack the night before was still visible. Erica pushed past Eve before the cybernaut could react and ran blindly toward her vehicle. She heard Eve's measured steps following her but Erica could not stop her headlong flight away from the reminder of what could have been.

115

"Erica, please stop. I have a message for you."

She clambered back into the truck and dropped the flap, curling into a ball with her head in her hands. She spoke to Eve between sobs. "Just stay out there. Don't come closer."

"Very well. May I relay the message through the canvas?"

Erica shuddered but managed to stammer out a yes. Eve moved just outside the opening and spoke softly. "Tony had another message for you. One he could not tell you while Sophie was with you."

That brought Erica's head up. Even though she was afraid to see Eve again, she needed to understand where Tony fit into all of this. "All right, Eve. Are we alone?"

"No one is passing the truck at the moment, Erica."

Erica swallowed hard and dug her nails into her palms to help calm herself down. "Go ahead."

There was a strange noise and then Tony's voice emanated from Eve's voice synthesizer. *"Erica, I'm working with a friend of yours. He's helping me contact you through Eve. Someone in your camp is working with the* Bloody Lynx *pirates. Unlike the Watch or the Southwatch Police, they want to ensure you* don't *speak about what you might remember. We'll try to help you through Eve, but trust no one. When we know who the infiltrator is, we'll let you know. Michael sends his love. Blaylock out."*

Erica sat there, wide-eyed at what she had just heard. Finally, she stirred herself and moved to the edge of the truck bed. She insured the canvas was between her and the female cybernaut, but her voice was steady. "Eve?"

"Yes, Erica?"

"Erase that message. We'll talk later."

"As you wish. When it does not conflict with my orders from Crystal, I have been ordered to assist you any way I can."

Erica's eyes widened at that, but somehow knowing Michael was involved made her feel safer. "Thank you, Eve. Please leave me alone for a bit."

Erica heard the mechanical's footsteps withdraw. She reached out with trembling fingers to lift the canvas flap. Eve was nowhere in sight so Erica tentatively climbed onto the bumper and then dropped to the ground. She found Sophie standing next to the truck, gazing at her curiously.

Erica panicked, wondering how much Sophie might have heard, and fought to keep her voice steady. "I ran into Eve. I'm sorry. I know it's silly, but I'm not ready to deal with her yet."

"She's returned to the truck Crystal is riding in. I noticed she was standing outside the truck before she left."

Erica paused before answering. "She told me Crystal wants to meet as soon as we get to camp. She wants to fit Eve and me before we lose the light. I guess Crystal wanted to be sure I didn't forget."

"Considering how often Crystal gets busy and forgets appointments and mealtimes, it might be good to have Eve work as her personal alarm clock. Oh, here's the water."

Erica saw something else was on Sophie's mind. *I wonder if she overheard what Eve really said to me? If she did, there's nothing I can do about it. She'll either confront me later or report it to the flight commander. I wish Christina were here. I like Sophie and we've gotten a lot closer on this trip, but she's still my superior. Chris is someone I can just talk to about stuff.*

Erica heard shouting and spotted people hurrying to their vehicles. She climbed into the truck and took the water canteens and the small box of fruit before giving Sophie a hand to climb into the truck. A sudden vibration told her the driver started the engine. It was only a matter of time before they were moving again.

"I wish they'd let us fly ahead. It's frustrating, knowing we could get there so much faster than this. Back in Southwatch, I know sometimes not flying makes sense—especially when the Cloud is dripping acid during a nasty storm. But, out here in these blue skies? It's like they're torturing us making us sit in these snails."

Sophie glanced into the sky before responding. "I sympathize with you, Halgrim. Normally, staying together makes sense from a tactical point of view, but I feel exposed here. I'd rather take my chances in the air. Isn't that what the flight commander has been training us to do?"

"To be honest, I thought she was training us to be diving and push-up champions. I see how learning to shift your body weight like those dives could come in handy during combat. But, we're messengers. Our biggest threat is a daydreaming gyro pilot or someone tossing something out a window without looking first."

"Sometimes I wonder."

"Huh?"

Sophie's soft comment caught Erica by surprise. She looked over at her flight leader and saw Sophie staring out into the distance, holding her canteen in loose fingers. "We are supposed to be a messenger service. But, we go through military-styled training to learn how to fly. We're organized with a military chain of command, and we mount weaponry on our wings as well as having to qualify with small arms. I know the Angels do a lot of confidential work and we carry valuable items both in Southwatch and around the Empire, but it feels like we're being trained for something else."

Even with the noise coming from the truck and the bouncing of the gear in the back, Erica could see Sophie felt awkward talking about this. Erica moved closer to Sophie and kept her voice low. "If so, for what purpose? I don't see Lady Orisaka mounting an assault on the Sunside anytime soon. There certainly aren't enough Angels to declare Southwatch independent of the Empire."

Sophie turned to her and then laughed. "Don't be so melodramatic. We're not the forefront of a revolution. It's just odd we are doing this training, though. I sometimes wonder if this testing is for us or for the Imperial Air Corps."

"I've heard the Air Corps backs some of Crystal's work. If I had to guess, I suspect they're trying to develop a courier corps for themselves."

Sophie got a thoughtful look on her face and paused before answering Erica. "While that makes sense, I still don't see why the Angels are organized like the military. While it's an efficient structure, it still feels wrong. It's like we're guinea pigs in someone's pet project."

"So, what are you going to do about it, Flight Leader Zwyer?"

"I'm not sure yet. I'm not sure anything needs to be done, Wingman Halgrim. Still, keep your eyes and ears open. If your friend Mr. Blaylock can find his way into the compound, others may have done the same. I doubt he was responsible for the attack on Eve. After all, he sent Eve to get you."

Erica reflected on the message Eve had given her and then shook her head. "I just can't see Tony attacking Eve either. Besides, he didn't have enough time before the alert went out. If it were me, I would have been hightailing it toward the nearest escape point."

"So, if it wasn't him, then someone else is concerned about you. Unlike your earlier interrogators, this one wants to ensure you don't suddenly remember something."

Erica's emotions came welling up again. She saw the concern on Sophie's face and tried to keep from falling completely apart. She slid back on the bench and looked at the bed of the truck until she was sure she was under control.

"Halgrim."

The tone of Sophie's voice caught her attention before she noted the vehicles slowing. Erica saw Sophie reaching over the lip of the tailgate and pulling the pin. "Give me a hand, Halgrim. We're taking off."

"What's going on?"

"Give me a hand with this tailgate. I don't know what's happening but we're not waiting. We're going to the truck with our wings and take off. This is not a scheduled stop. We need to move before anyone notices. Hit the ground and roll to the side."

Erica rushed over and reached for the pin. It was tough to maneuver the piece of metal as the truck was rolling, but with a little effort, they managed it. They lowered themselves onto the bumper and then jumped lightly to the side. The reduced speed of the convoy worked to their benefit and both of them landed well beyond the following truck. They rushed to the vehicle third from the rear of the convoy where their wings were. Sophie caught the bumper and helped pull Erica up. They flipped over the tailgate without opening it, surprising Crystal, who was sitting there.

Crystal adjusted her glasses and stared at them. "What's going on? Why are we slowing down?"

Sophie opened a box and handed Erica's harness to her before responding. "We don't know and we're not sticking around to find out. We need our wings."

"The long box there. But, why?"

"There may be a roadblock ahead or maybe bandits. After what happened last night, we're not sticking around to find out. We'll fly ahead to the camp and wait for you. If it's nothing, send Eve to find us. If we don't see her or you, we'll return to the main camp and get reinforcements. My mission is to keep Halgrim safe and that's what I'm going to do."

The truck shuddered and came to a stop as Sophie finished strapping her wings on. Erica finished a few seconds afterward and Crystal craned her neck around the tarp at the end of the truck. "I can't see anything," she whispered, "so if you're going, I'd go now."

Sophie accepted the goggles Erica handed her and motioned for Erica to follow. They climbed out of the truck and moved toward the ravine side of the road. Faint noises were echoing from the front of the convoy. Erica wanted to know what was going on, but she realized there was no time to waste. Sophie brought her arm forward and they rushed toward the cliff's edge before diving off. They kept their wings tight to their sides to build up momentum and then snapped them open.

The wings pulled hard against their harnesses, but Erica kept herself under control as the two women swooped outward from the cliff face into the open air. She heard faint shouting behind them but didn't turn to look. She maneuvered into a tight position just above and behind Sophie and followed the flight leader as they headed into the Gray Mountains.

Once out of sight of the convoy, Sophie signaled and they made their way north toward the advance camp. Sophie kept as close to the natural terrain as she could to minimize any chance they'd be spotted before they arrived. Erica concentrated on holding her position. She checked over her shoulder on occasion to ensure no one was following in a gyrocopter or a glider, but she saw nothing.

Approaching the camp, Sophie signaled for her to move up beside her. "I'll circle the field, Halgrim. If it looks safe, I'll signal your wrist-com and you come in hot. Be ready to head for cover once you're on the ground. I've never been to this camp. I don't know what kind of shelter is available or what kinds of hiding places exist. Use your best judgment."

Erica felt the air getting cooler as they gained elevation and signaled that she understood. *I hope there are buildings here. If the convoy is delayed until after sundown, it's going to be a very cold night ahead.*

Erica and Sophie climbed until they cleared the ridges and then Sophie dropped behind them while Erica climbed just high enough to keep her flight leader in sight. Sophie circled the small collection of buildings and then overflew a small copse of trees near the top of the ridge. She waggled her wings, signaling for Erica to maintain her distance. The flight leader landed near the buildings and moved quickly toward the first but apparently the door was locked. Checking the other two buildings resulted in no better luck for Sophie as far as Erica could tell.

Sophie motioned to the copse of woods nearby and took off at a run. A few seconds later, three flashes on her wrist-com told Erica it was clear. She dove toward the ground, spreading her wings to brake at the last second, touching down on the bowl side of the ridge. She brought her wings in and hurried into the trees, finding a spot where she could observe the camp and still be out of sight.

She found a natural depression and began lining it with pine needles. A few minutes later, Sophie appeared and joined her, and together, the two turned the small depression into a makeshift fort. They dragged a couple of logs into position to give them cover, before weaving a small roof out of pine branches and other plant material. It was starting to get dark by the time they had finished and still there was no sign of the convoy. They slipped off their wings, but kept their harnesses on.

"Have you seen any sign of Eve? I hoped Crystal could get her into the air if there was no problem."

Erica shook her head. "Not a sign of her, unless she landed while we were moving that log. I wonder what's going on with the convoy? If it was just some rocks on the road, they should have been here by now."

"I don't know. We'll stay here tonight, like we told Crystal. In the morning, we'll go for help."

Erica's stomach growled and she looked at Sophie with a sheepish grin. "You didn't grab a canteen or some of that fruit before we left, did you?"

"No and neither did you. We'll have to wait until morning. Won't hurt either of us. Go ahead and get some sleep, Halgrim. I'll take the first watch."

Erica lay down after making sure her wings were within arm's reach. The pine needles helped, but there was no mistaking they were laying on cold, hard ground. She watched Sophie sitting there, gazing at the camp below them, before her eyes closed and sleep overcame her. Still, one thought kept pulsing through her mind.

What is going on?

Chapter Fourteen

"Halgrim? Halgrim?"

Erica rolled toward the sound of Sophie's voice and cracked her eyes open. The woods were still dark and it took her a bit to spot Sophie lying on her stomach, peering between the logs surrounding their hiding place.

"Yeah, Sophie, what's up?"

"Shhh. Something just pulled up to the camp."

Erica sat up, smacking her head on the weave of limbs forming their roof. She managed not to yelp as she bit her tongue, but she was instantly awake. The throbbing helped her focus and she crawled over to join Sophie. Even in the darkness, she could see Sophie gazing at her with a mixture of annoyance and pity.

Erica lifted her head until see could just enough to see two sets of lights moving near the buildings. The vehicles made almost no noise as they entered the clearing. She stared into the darkness, but besides the two vehicles, the rest of the convoy was missing. There had been seven trucks in all, so either this was an advance guard or something was seriously wrong.

"Should we see what's going on, Sophie?"

"I think we should stay here for now. I was hoping Eve would arrive and let us know. If they're with the convoy, they should be calling for us soon . . . I hope."

Erica was surprised. She'd seldom seen Sophie without all the answers. It was comforting, and yet a bit frightening, to see Sophie had doubts and fears the same as her. She glanced into the bowl and saw lights coming on in one of the buildings. Figures moved in the distance, but they were black silhouettes against the light coming through the open door. She craned her neck to see better, but a sudden pressure on her head shoved her back into place.

"Not so high, Halgrim. Remember your training—don't expose yourself needlessly."

"Sorry, I was trying to see if I recognized anyone in the light."

Sophie picked up one of the spare pine branches and held it near her forehead, letting the pine needles hang down in front of her. Then she lifted her head to gaze at the milling figures. If someone glanced up the hill, it was unlikely they would spot Sophie's blond hair. Erica found a small branch to provide some camouflage for herself and looked again. She flinched when someone came out of the building with a flashlight, shining it around the camp and into the woods.

Erica watched Sophie ease to the back of their hiding place and crawl out, dragging her wings behind her. Erica grabbed her wings and joined her. They moved deeper into the woods and helped each other gear up. Sophie noticed Erica's confusion and spoke up. "It makes good tactical sense to have a way to escape quickly if we run into trouble."

"Oh."

"We're going to circle around and check it out. I don't want to approach directly from our hiding place. Follow about twenty feet behind me and stay in the shadows as much as possible. If anything happens, don't try to help. You'd probably just wind up interfering as jumpy as you are. Take to the sky as quick as you can. I'll try to join you."

Sophie's comments stung, but Erica knew she was right. She nodded and watched Sophie move into the darkness. When her flight leader threatened to disappear completely, she followed, trying to imitate Sophie's gliding steps. It was amazing how smoothly and quietly Sophie moved in this darkness. Erica felt like she stepped on every twig and rock in the woods trying to keep up.

After a while, they reached the far side of the camp and Erica realized they'd been spiraling closer as they approached. She could almost make out the forms at the camp through the trees. The vehicles were not the trucks she had been expecting. Instead, they were small vehicles obviously designed for off-road travel. From the soft whirr coming from the camp, she realized they weren't steam powered at all. That meant they had electric engines, but *that* was impossible. No vehicle she'd ever heard of had the range to make it up the mountains on a single charge. And there certainly weren't charging stations in the Gray Mountains.

Sophie raised one hand and Erica froze in place. A second later, Sophie brought her arm down to her side, and both women lowered themselves to the ground as quickly as they could without making noise. Two men swept around the corner of the building, carrying flashlights. Erica couldn't make out their faces, but there was no questioning they were both armed. One had an electro-static gun of some kind and the other had a rifle. Not for the first time did Erica wish they'd grabbed wings with weapon mounts.

The lights swept past a few inches in front of Erica's nose but the guards' steps never paused. She lay there until they turned the corner and slowly turned her head until she made eye contact with Sophie. Sophie glanced around and then signaled for Erica to follow. They pulled back into the woods until they were sure they were out of sight of the camp.

"Who are they, Sophie? None of our guards had weapons like that. And how the heck did they get electric vehicles up here?"

"There's only one explanation—pirates. I suspect there's an airship hovering around somewhere. We've got to get out of here before dawn. We're not equipped to fight off armed gliders or gyrocopters and I suspect they have both."

Erica felt goose pimples rising on her arms but tried to maintain her cool. "Pirates? Any idea who it might be?"

"I'd suspect the *Bloody Lynx*. After all, didn't Blaylock mention they were interested in you?"

"Oh . . . yeah. Do you think *they* intercepted the convoy?"

"It's possible. The good thing is the *Lynx*'s crew is known for ransoming captives instead of killing them. They also don't like confrontations. They're a hit-and-run gang. If we can get back to camp and send reinforcements, they're likely to take off without the captives. Let's get out of here."

Erica followed Sophie through the darkness until they reached the top of the ridge. A thin sliver of moon hung between the circling clouds, barely illuminating the ground around them. Erica started to move forward, wings spreading for launch, but Sophie grabbed her arm.

"Wait."

Erica saw her friend pointing into the sky and her eyes followed Sophie's arm until she noted what had caught her friend's attention. A dark shape silently appeared out of one of the clouds, moving in a counterclockwise manner around the mountaintop. A soft glow shone from the ship-like gondola hanging below the oversized balloon. The tops of the smokestacks glowed from the heat from the huge steam engines powering the airship. The balloon strained against the restraining cables as if resentful of being forced to go where others wanted it to go. Erica listened carefully and heard the beat of multiple propellers pushing the ship through the air.

"The *Lynx*?"

Sophie nodded, stepping back into the tree line. "I suspect so. I heard it was originally a cargo ship. I suspect they've modified it significantly since 'acquiring' it. Note the three stacks. I'd guess it was designed more for lift than speed. That's probably how they got those electric vehicles up here."

Erica watched until the ship passed back into a cloud and then checked the thalisium levels on her harness. She had three-fourths of a charge, which should be enough to get back to their camp, but it was going to be close. Sophie went through her own preflight checklist before turning to speak softly to Erica.

"It's going to be a tricky flight, Halgrim. With that ship up there, we're not going to be able to fly at a safe altitude. We have to stay low and hope we don't get spotted. However, you have to stay right on my tail. We're likely to be dodging trees and mountains until we get some distance from here. Are you up for it?"

"I don't see any other way, Sophie. It's either that or hope we can stay hidden until they leave." She was finishing her checklist when a thought struck her. "Sophie, did it seem they were awfully familiar with the camp? It's like they've been there before."

Sophie paused before answering, a curious look on her face. "Now that you mention it, it seemed like a rather cursory search. I have a feeling since the Angels don't use that camp all the time, the *Lynx* may have taken advantage of the isolated setting and appropriated it for their own use. It may simply have been bad timing that our convoy was en route when they were returning."

Erica wasn't sure how much was true and how much was Sophie trying to bolster her confidence, but she appreciated the effort. Glancing up at the sky, she saw there was no sign of the ship. She pointed to the ridge and this time Sophie nodded. They hurried to the top and then climbed down a short way until they were hidden in the deep shadows on the reverse side of the slope.

"Ready?" Sophie asked, adjusting her goggles.

Erica's response was to launch herself down the slope, spreading her wings wide to gently glide into the night sky as the ground fell away below her. Sophie joined her a few moments later and Erica fell into position behind her. They circled a nearby mountain to take one last look at the camp when a bright spotlight suddenly lit up underneath the airship, scanning the ground below.

"I think they just found our hiding place. Time to go," Sophie said with the same tone of voice as if she was telling Erica the mail just arrived. The two women swooped away into the darkness as the searchlight began swinging through the night sky obviously looking for them. There was a faint noise and then six smaller searchlights arched through the sky, illuminating the clouds behind them. Erica guessed the pirates had launched gyrocopters to search for them.

The gyrocopters meant there were no options left but speed and good flying techniques to escape safely. Erica didn't consider herself religious but she fired off a quick prayer to the Goddess, thanking her for the darkness and asking her to please not let her crash. They dropped as low as they could, hoping they'd spot any obstacles before they flew headlong into them. After the third or fourth time taking evasive action to miss a treetop appearing out of nowhere, Erica understood why most birds were diurnal. Unless the clouds lifted soon, it was just a matter of time before something happened.

Looking up, she saw just the opposite happening—the clouds were closing in around them, cutting off what little light was left. Sophie rolled onto her back for a moment and then pointed into the sky. Erica nodded and followed her into the clouds. She knew they were trading one set of problems for another by climbing. Still, the fact they were less likely to pancake into a mountain offset the reduction in visibility. She thanked the Goddess they didn't feel like rain clouds, so hopefully they wouldn't encounter winds or lightning. She focused on keeping Sophie in her sights. With the swirling mist and the darkness, if they got separated now, it might be morning before they could find each other again.

The sweep of their wings were the only noises Erica heard as they made their way southward—or at least, that's the direction she hoped they were going. There was no way outside of climbing out of these clouds to get their bearings by the stars and there was no way to know how high these clouds went. She had a small compass mounted next to her wrist-com, but she was too busy watching Sophie to try and read its small dial in the darkness.

At least flying through this cloud was more pleasant than the Dark Cloud back home. Still, back in Southwatch, she'd have had the proper equipment for when visibility dropped to zero. *Of course, when things get too bad, I find a perch and wait. Eventually, there'll be an opening to proceed. The faint wind holding the Cloud in place keeps it from forming up too solidly. I've never been so lost in the Cloud I couldn't find my way eventually. This soup could be a problem if I lose Sophie. At least this cloud doesn't make me want to run immediately for the shower.*

Sophie suddenly banked to the left and dove. Erica followed as a large dark shape broke through the clouds ahead of them. The soft whirring of propellers told her it had to be the *Bloody Lynx* passing overhead and she pushed herself steeper into her dive to be sure to avoid the propeller blades moving the giant ship.

She barely kept sight of Sophie's feet as they plunged out of the sky. After a few seconds of near free-fall, Sophie spread her wings and slowly began spiraling downward. Erica let the distance between them grow as she followed. If Sophie made a drastic course correction, she needed as much room as possible to react. She heard the air ship cruising above them, but they seemed to have managed to avoid detection this time.

She broke through the clouds and saw the trees a few hundred feet below them. There was just enough light filtering through the breaks in the clouds to see they were in a mountain valley. Sophie motioned to her left and Erica saw what might have been a small opening in the trees. Erica followed and popped her wings full open as they arrived at the clearing, catching as much air as she could to slow rapidly. The two women glided to the ground and made their way deeper into the trees.

"That was too close. Are you all right, Halgrim?"

"Yes, Sophie. I don't think we were spotted. At least, they didn't turn on their spotlights."

"That's a good sign. We'll stay here for a bit. I don't know if they're doing a grid search to try and find us or if they have a way to track us through the clouds. If that's the case, it's just a matter of time before we're spotted."

"What do you think they could be tracking?"

"It could be anything. They could have planted something on us if one of them who infiltrated the camp the other night. They could be tracking our thalisium—it's a rare enough element. I can't imagine them developing such a sophisticated tracking device, though. We don't carry that much thalisium on us."

Erica pondered for a second. "Maybe they stole one. But who would build it in the first place?"

"If they had access to a storm, they might. But, how would they do that? There aren't that many storms in the entire world. Most are under the control of some government or the other. I can't imagine one voluntarily working for a small pirate group like the Lynxes."

Erica thought about how hard Michael worked to remain out of sight and wondered if there weren't more storms than most people thought. It was said they saw the world in ways regular people never would. Still, she agreed with Sophie. It was hard to imagine a storm working for pirates willingly.

She jumped at a sudden touch on her shoulder and had to pull herself together over Sophie's laughter. "Sorry, Halgrim, I thought we ought to get moving. Didn't mean to startle you like that."

"No problem. What's the plan?"

Sophie pointed into the woods. "I think we should hike for a while before we take to the air again. I don't want to stay here in case they did spot us diving. However, we can't stay here too long without food or water. I haven't seen anything to make me think there's a stream nearby."

"How far away do you think the main camp is from here?"

"Honestly, I don't know. I think we're going in the right direction. However, we could be flying the absolute wrong way. The smart thing would be to wait until dawn, but I'm not sure we can do that. My thalisium charge is getting low, so we need to fly while we can."

"So, you want to hike to the top of this mountain and see what we can see up there?"

"I know it's not a great plan, but it's the only one I can think of."

"Maybe we can find a shelter, at least until dawn. I think we can make it to the camp in a couple of hours once we're sure where we're going."

"We'll see, Halgrim. We'll know more when we get to the top."

Erica had more questions, but before she could ask, she found herself concentrating on simply walking and breathing. Sophie's pace forced her to almost jog along to keep up. She knew she was getting tired because it became an effort to keep her wingtips from dragging on the ground. She stumbled more than once climbing in the dark, but somehow she managed to keep up with Sophie. They reached the summit just below the tree line, so they were able to view the area from relative safety.

The clouds were starting to break up, so Sophie worked on determining their position while Erica scanned the sky for any sign of the *Lynx*. It was tough given the pine branches overhead, but as far as Erica could tell, the airship had moved on, which suited her just fine. A few minutes later, Sophie looked up from her compass and pointed to her left.

"We drifted a bit off course, but all things considered, we're closer than I thought we would be. Come on, let's take advantage of the clear skies and make up some time."

Erica and Sophie were soon in the air again and hugging the terrain as best as they could in case the *Lynx* was lurking around. After fifteen minutes or so, they began to relax and focused more on speed than stealth. Erica checked her harness and saw her thalisium levels were down to about fifteen percent. They were going to have to reach the base soon or she'd be landing and walking. The wings provided most of the lift, but not all and without thalisium she would start losing altitude whether she wanted to or not.

The pair swept around a low peak and spotted the camp's lights in the distance. Pushing as hard as they could, they soon swept over the camp and landed near the main buildings. Sophie immediately stripped out of her wings and handed them to Erica. She tucked them under her arm and headed toward the lab while Sophie went to report in.

Erica found the lab open and went inside to put the wings away. Hanging up her own set, she collapsed into a chair exhausted. She knew she should get up and at least find some water before falling asleep, but the chair was *so* comfortable. She leaned back to rest for just a second and then sleep washed over her.

Chapter Fifteen

Erica opened her eyes, trying to figure out where the bright light was coming from. A few fuzzy seconds later, she realized she was in bed, with nothing on but her undergarments. She shot up, pulling the sheets up around her before it sank in she was back in the barracks. Her uniform had been folded and laid on the metal frame at the foot of her bed and her personal items were carefully placed on the night table.

How in the hell did I get here? I remember hanging up my wings in Crystal's lab and then sitting down to wait for Sophie. Everything after that is a blank. Did something happen last night?

She inched her way off the bed and tentatively placed one foot on the ground. When nothing happened, she climbed out and crept to the door of her room to listen. She didn't hear anything unusual, so she opened the door enough to peek into the hall. From what she could tell, no one was in the barracks except her.

She locked the door behind her and went to the window. Moving the curtains a few inches, she saw people but they were too far away to identify anyone. They were wearing Angels' gear, so that at least was comforting. Erica realized she'd been holding her breath and let it out in a long sigh. She started to relax when there was a knock at the door. She moved out of direct line of the door before answering. "Who's there?"

"Zwyer. Are you all right, Halgrim?"

Erica hurried to the door and unlocked it, opening it wide enough for Sophie to enter. Her flight leader gave her a disapproving look and then sat in one of the room's chairs. "Interesting choice of uniform, Halgrim. I see you just woke up?"

"Uh, I've been up for a little bit. I was about to hop in the shower when you knocked. I must have really been out last night." Erica blushed furiously and then headed toward her locker to get her shower items. "I don't remember walking here from the lab."

Sophie shook her head. "That's because you didn't. One of the guards carried you here and I got you ready for bed. It would have been counterproductive for you to spend all night lying on that chair.

There's too much to do today. You need to be ready in in about an hour."

Erica stopped in the bathroom entrance and turned to face Sophie. "Ready for what?"

"You and I are going back to the camp with a flight of the Vengeance. They arrived during the night along with additional members of Angels' Security. While you were sleeping, they've already brought all the trucks back."

Erica started the shower, but kept the door open so she could talk to Sophie. "Sounds like a busy night all the way around. Is everyone all right? What happened after we left?"

"Our escape angered the raiders more than you'd think. They kept the convoy at that location until a gyrocopter landed during the night. A vehicle appeared and they loaded Flight Leader Kail, Crystal, and Eve on to it and drove off. All the rest of the convoy members were left behind. Apparently the pirates spotted security en route and made the best of a bad hand."

"That's horrible. You don't think the *Lynx* is still around, do you?"

"Not a chance. However, even if they're not at the advance camp, it's possible they left something to give us a clue where they've taken those three."

"Did they take Crystal's gear with them?"

"That's the odd part. They didn't take anything. Didn't even seem interested in the gear. It's beyond strange they'd pass that up. Even if they couldn't sell it on the black market, they could have ransomed it back to the Angels . . . or tried to, anyway."

While Erica rinsed off her hair, a sudden thought came to her. "Did you say we were flying with the Angels of Vengeance? With what wings? The ones we used last night need serious maintenance."

She heard Sophie move closer to the bathroom door before answering. "We're going to use those new gliding wings of Crystal's. The head assistant says they should work. Besides, gliding will be simpler than the flight we made yesterday."

Erica grabbed her items and walked out with a large towel wrapped around her. She slipped past Sophie and started putting on a fresh uniform. "They think they *should* work? That's not very comforting."

"The last time Crystal checked them they were at ninety-five percent efficiency. That's significantly better than our wings from last night."

Erica slipped her feet inside her calf-high boots, gave herself one last look over, and turned to face Sophie. "Is this uniform a bit more acceptable?"

Sophie called her to attention and then methodically walked around her, gazing at her from head to toe. "Your collar's crooked, you've got a button coming loose on your blouse, those boots haven't seen a polish brush in weeks, and your uniform cap is canted the wrong direction. Otherwise, you'll do."

Erica sighed inwardly while keeping a straight face. She should have known better to ask Sophie for a friendly opinion. The question was something she asked Christina every morning before reporting for the morning training sessions. *Speaking of which . . .*

"Sophie, have you seen Christina or Kim today?"

Sophie walked back to her chair while Erica plopped down onto the bed. "Yes. Rachel and they were being debriefed. They will not be accompanying us on this mission. The Angels of Vengeance specifically requested you and I come along since we encountered the *Bloody Lynx*."

"That's the part that worries me. Those Vengeance flyers are always armed to the teeth. Are they issuing us weapons also?"

The expression on Sophie's face reminded Erica of the same look Jessica Black had given her when they first met. "They weren't going to at first, but I think I made an impression on their armorer. We'll have two electro-rods mounted on our wings and personal weapons assigned. If I remember correctly, you're up-to-date on your qualifications."

"I'm fully qualified on all weapons the Angels normally carry. However, I'm not qualified on heavy weaponry or lethal weaponry. Per Angel regulations, we're supposed to discourage pursuit, not engage hijackers one-on-one."

"I understand that. The question is, can you do it if necessary?"

Erica paused and then looked Sophie square on. "I don't know. Maybe…if I had to…but I've never been put in that situation before."

"I hope you never have to be, Erica. Taking a human life should never be easy. But, if you're coming, assume it could happen. It could be to protect someone else or yourself. If something happens, you won't have the luxury of being a bystander. Don't get someone else hurt because you can't take care of yourself."

"I'll do my best."

"I never had any doubts, Erica. You handled yourself like a pro last night. My report to Lady Orisaka noted your exemplary performance. You're a lot tougher than you let on. I'll be back in about fifteen minutes. We'll draw some supplies and meet the others at the main parade field after that."

Erica watched Sophie leave and then spent a few minutes instinctively making the uniform corrections that Sophie had pointed out. Halfway through polishing her boots, she stopped suddenly. *Sophie called me Erica. She never calls me anything but Halgrim. Something's got her scared. I don't think I've ever seen her flustered before. Whatever we're getting into, I think she knows it's going to be a bad situation.*

She nervously finished and secured her barracks room key, identification papers, and a pocket knife and put them in the small pocket on her upper left sleeve. Her father had given her the pocket knife when she was a little girl. She'd carried it as a good luck charm ever since she'd joined the Angels. She knew it was a silly superstition, but it was the only thing she had from her father and it helped her remember him. She gave the pocket one last familiar pat to ensure everything rested comfortably there and headed for the front door to wait for Sophie.

Surely the plan will be get in, rescue Crystal and the others, and get out? It doesn't make any sense to start a fight after we've got them safe. But, from what I've heard about the Angels of Vengeance, they'll want to leave a clear message not to mess with the Angels in the future.

But how do you prepare to kill another person?

Erica walked through the warehouse door Sophie held open. The room buzzed with technicians maneuvering equipment while others loaded boxes onto an armored vehicle with tracked treads. Sophie pointed to the far corner and Erica saw the eight men they'd be accompanying into the mountains. Six were going through preflight checks while the other two mounted some unusual objects on the handlebars of their steam-powered bikes. One of the men said something to the group and the talk ceased. The first man joined the young women as the others stared at the newcomers.

The approaching man could have walked off a recruiting poster the way he carried himself. Erica was certain he'd spent some time in the Imperial Marine Corps before joining the Angels. As soon as he began speaking, her suspicions were confirmed.

"Good morning. I'm Flight Leader Vetrano. I'm the tactical commander for this mission. Flight Leader Zwyer will be in overall command unless we encounter the pirates. If that happens, you two will withdraw from the fight." He paused and a hint of a smile ghosted across his lips. "Nothing against you two, but you're not trained for this kind of mission and we've never trained with you. We don't need added distractions if we get into combat."

Erica saw Sophie draw herself up straighter and she swore she heard Flight Commander Kail's voice in Sophie's. "Understood, Vetrano. While Halgrim and I are capable of defending ourselves, you've never worked with us. You focus on your job and we'll focus on ours."

The Vengeance flight leader's smile was big and honest at Sophie's response. "I'm glad to hear that, Zwyer. Too many people get their nose out of joint when we tell them to let us handle things. I suspect you two can fly rings around me, but we can't take a chance on someone going right when the rest of us go left. However, I've seen your profile. If you ever think about leaving the Angels proper, I'd love to talk to you about joining our team."

Sophie smiled. "That is a generous offer. I'll consider it after all this is over."

He turned to rejoin his team. "Toby over there will help you into your wings and explain the small mods we've done to them. By the way, call me Phil. We're not much on last names in this group."

"Thanks, Phil. I'm Sophie and this is Erica."

"Pleased to meet you, Erica. Get harnessed up. We're pulling out in about fifteen minutes."

Two of the Angels helped them into the oversized wings. Toby turned out to be a rather average-looking young man with thick glasses. She had noticed him working on one of the motorcycles earlier. He introduced himself and then motioned for them to join him a bit away from the others who were checking their weapons one last time.

Toby talked them through arming and discharging the wing-mounted "shock sticks," as he called them. Then he measured their hands and arms quickly and verified if they were right- or left-handed. He disappeared behind some crates and then came back with an oversized suitcase. He set it on a bench in front of them and opened it, gazing over the top of the case at them, still measuring them with his eyes.

"Sophie, right? Here you go." He held some items up over the edge of the case for the blond flight leader. "One revolver, caliber .45, and it comes with six sets of reloads, one shock knife, and a compressed air dart pistol. The shock knife has a button on the handle. If you press it, it starts an internal capacitor that'll let it deliver an electrical charge twice. If employed, it should momentarily paralyze your opponent, giving you the opportunity to eliminate him. The dart gun comes with four darts containing blue sea snake poison. It's a paralytic. Not initially fatal, but if your target doesn't get the antitoxin, he'll eventually suffocate. Here's a hypo kit with the antidote too. Don't administer it until your target is secured. Most people have violent reactions to the antitoxin."

He looked over at Erica, frowned a moment, and then looked down into his case. "For you, miss, I recommend this .38-caliber automatic. It comes with a ten-round magazine and I'll issue you five magazines. They'll set right here in this case on your belt. I think you're better off with a stun baton. It works the same as the shock knife, but less fatal. Also, I think these gloves suit you. They have extendible claws coated in a sleeping agent. One good nick and your target is out for about four hours. Their drawback is you have to get up close and personal with your target, so be careful. Also, remember to retract them when you're done. You don't want to scratch yourself or a teammate accidentally."

Erica glanced down at the assortment of weapons and then began attaching the various holsters and ammo pouches to her flight belt. It felt odd to be storing weapons instead of packages for delivery, but nothing had been normal since that day at the *Temple*. She noted Sophie was inspecting her ammunition before snapping the revolver closed and returning it to its holster. She acted like she'd been carrying one all her life.

Sophie called back over her shoulder. "Don't forget to lock your holster before we take off. You don't want to get into a situation and find out it fell out miles ago."

Erica surreptitiously clicked the lock shut. "I won't. It's just like securing a package. 'Always double-check before flight.'"

Sophie gave her an approving nod. "Those electro-rods shouldn't affect our flight, but I'd recommend trying a few maneuvers when we first take off to get used to them. Between them and the larger wings, it may take a bit to get comfortable."

Erica fought the extra weight from the wings as she tried to keep their tips from dragging on the ground. "At least we'll have time to get acclimatized en route. It's going to be a long flight after last night's."

Sophie nodded again and then went to speak to Phil. Erica turned around to see Toby still standing there, rummaging in the case. "Are you joining us? Shouldn't you be getting ready?"

Toby looked up, surprised. "Uh, yeah, but I don't fly. Don't have the eyesight or the coordination for that. So, Stu and I will be following along on the motorcycles with spare gear. Hey, I have a question for you."

"Sure, what's on your mind, Toby?"

"Have you ever fired anything other than blanks at another person?"

"It shows that badly, huh?" she said, staring down at the table.

"Hey, don't feel bad. I've been with the Vengeance for six years and never fired a single weapon except at the range. I'm the team's armorer. I make and modify weapons, but I normally stay behind when they go on a mission. This is an unusual situation, though, so Phil agreed to let Stu and me come along as long as we stay out of the way."

"What's so special about this mission?"

Toby blushed all the way to the roots of his hair. Erica had always thought that was a legend but he proved her wrong. "Ah . . . well . . . you see . . . it's kind of hard to . . . well, Crystal and I have been dating. I can't just sit back and not do anything."

Erica recognized Toby's discomfort talking about himself, much less a relationship, with a stranger. She was honored he'd let her in on his secret. She hadn't heard Crystal mention him, but then again, she couldn't remember Crystal talking about anything not specifically about a project. Crystal's hyper-focus was legendary when pursuing a new project.

Toby's voice caught Erica's attention. "Anyway, here. This might be useful." He reached into the case and pulled out something resembling an oversized pistol. Erica examined it and realized it was a double-barreled shotgun cut down to pistol size. He handed her a case for her belt and motioned for her to open it. It contained six black cartridges and four red ones.

"If something goes horribly wrong, this should work as a backup weapon. The black cartridges are smoke grenades. It won't cover a lot of area, but if you're indoors for any reason, they'll fill a room. The red ones are buckshot. You want to hold it at hip level, put one hand on top of the barrel when you pull the trigger. If you try to fire it like a pistol, it'll come back and tattoo you right between the eyes. It's not for distance shooting, but up close, it's a devastating weapon. Just point and pull the trigger. It'll do the rest."

"Point and pull. Got it."

Erica waited while Toby fixed a holster on her right hip. He showed her how to draw the weapon safely, where the weapon's safety catch was, and how to reload it quickly. Once he finished, he packed his gear back into his case and hurried over to the motorcycle, still blushing. She spotted Sophie and Phil looking at a map pinned up on the wall. Sophie was pointing out different things to him, so Erica decided not to bother her. She took the opportunity to get used to the weapon cases attached to her flight suit. Bad enough she had to learn how to walk and balance in these oversized wings, much less with all this ballast.

Once the meeting broke up, Phil motioned for everyone to head outside. Erica joined Sophie as the small team cut between the buildings toward the parade field. Once everyone had gotten quiet, Phil stepped into the middle of the group.

"The initial plan is to travel directly to the mountain. Sophie and Erica will use the glider wings to gain as much altitude as possible and conduct overwatch for us. Three miles out, we'll drop down and fly nap-of-the-earth until we start up the slope to the camp. Depending on what we spot, we'll either enter the camp hot or we'll land on the reverse slope, drop wings, and infiltrate through the surrounding woods."

He glanced around and waited for everyone to acknowledge what he'd just said before continuing. "Stu and Toby will be taking the same trail the convoy went yesterday. Their job is to try and spot anything overlooked yesterday. They'll join us at the camp after we've secured it. Sophie and Erica will join us after we know what the situation is and we'll adjust the plan based on what we find."

The team quietly discussed who was doing what if they had to take the camp by force. Phil let them talk for a bit and then rapped on a wall to get their attention again. "I doubt they'll be there. The *Lynx* crew has never struck me as foolhardy, but then again, they've never had the balls to assault the Angels directly either. Their strategy might be to remain in place, counting on *us* assuming they'd depart as soon as they could. If they're that foolish, we'll teach them the error of their ways. If they are gone . . . we'll figure out where they went and take the fight to them. Any questions?"

To Erica's surprise, she heard her voice breaking the silence. "If the camp is occupied, then Sophie and I remain on observation duty?"

"Absolutely. If the camp is occupied, that airship will be around somewhere. I don't know what kind of weapons the *Lynx* has mounted, but I have no desire to be caught between pirates hiding in those buildings and the airship pounding us with cannons. You're our best chance of coming out of this alive."

Erica felt her back straighten at Phil's words. She caught herself becoming excited about the entire mission. Her senses felt sharper as the Vengeance team moved into position and Toby and Stu fired up their bikes. With a wave, the two techs headed off toward the mountains. Then it was their turn.

The two women stepped away from the pack and spread their wings to the fullest extent. Unlike their regular wings, it was going to be harder to lift off the ground. Thankfully, Crystal had equipped these harnesses with 75 percent more thalisium to help provide initial lift. Erica felt the wings catching the soft breeze blowing through the camp and flapped her wings in long slow strokes, building up speed as her feet lifted off the ground.

These wings were not as responsive as her usual set. It felt like the tips had to move much farther to complete an entire sweep. Still, once she was airborne, it only took a small movement to gain or lose altitude. With a couple of strokes, she was moving almost as fast as her original wings did at full speed. It was going to take some time to get used to their balance, but she saw how effective these wings would be in these open spaces. They'd be useless within Southwatch proper, unfortunately.

Erica couldn't imagine why Crystal was working on them. They were obviously for flying the coast or making deliveries to Atragon. No, that didn't make sense. Those runs were normally handled by merchant marine vessels, or in the case of Atragon, submersible vessels.

Sophie caught up with her and the two took turns maneuvering at low levels. Once they both were comfortable, they signaled the Vengeance team and began circling to gain altitude. Sophie waggled her wings and Erica fell into her usual trail position, climbing into the slightly overcast sky. Below, she saw the six flyers move to a medium altitude, spreading into two V-shaped formations.

After a while, she lost sight of them and concentrated on her own mission. *Hang in there, Crystal. We're coming.*

Chapter Sixteen

I wish I could see what's going on. Between the clouds and the distance, all I can see is some blobs moving around against green and gray. Crystal really needs to make telescopic goggles for whoever is going to use these wings. Still, with today's weather that might not help. These clouds are thicker than last night's. It feels like a storm front is moving in, but the winds are manageable, so far. I hope Sophie's having better luck than I am.

Erica checked a small gauge on her harness and saw the oxygen tank was nearly three-quarters full. Gliding in circles around the mountaintop had skewed her sense of time. It could have been hours, but the wings made her flight so effortless she couldn't measure time that way. She loved the fact she only had to flap about twice per circuit. The wings caught so much air she had to remind herself occasionally not to stall out.

I know these are impractical, but this is flying. Just a few strokes and the wings do all the work. I have to keep an eye on the wind, though—if there's a gust, I'm going to gain or lose altitude in a hurry. Still, I could get used to this.

Erica stretched her back muscles and then her leg muscles. That was the hardest part about gliding, trying to keep her body parallel to the ground to minimize drag. With their regular wings, they were flying faster, so the body normally flowed into the right position. Doing lazy circles above the mountain forced Erica to rely on the harness more to keep her legs in position. She felt the straps cutting into her thighs from the constant pull of her legs.

Two slow flashes appeared on her wrist-com and she returned the signal. There was no sign of the *Lynx* anywhere, which was good as far as she was concerned. It would have been simpler if Crystal and the others had been here. They could have just gotten in and out, but that was a forlorn hope. The best they could hope for was that the pirates were sloppy enough to leave clues to where they had gone. Otherwise, the Angels would return to Southwatch and wait for the ransom demand. Lady Orisaka was *not* going to take that very well.

Her stomach caught as she hit a small air pocket and dropped through the clouds. She spread her wings to max and leaned forward to regain control. She knew she'd only fallen a few hundred feet, but it felt like an eternity. After a few gut-wrenching seconds, the wings bit into the wind, bringing her out of her headlong dive. She let out a long sigh and climbed back onto station.

The clouds closed in and the air temperature dropped slightly. Every instinct told her to land soon. The air felt wrong—this was going to be a bad storm—but she kept climbing until she saw Sophie ahead of her. She angled her wings in that direction and forced her way through the rising wind to join her flight leader.

Sophie rolled slightly to keep Erica in sight as she moved inside Sophie's track. Erica motioned toward the clouds and then made a tentative sign toward the ground. Sophie shook her head and held up five fingers.

Five more minutes?

Erica's thoughts must have shown on her face because she could see the frustrated look Sophie gave her even through the oxygen mask and goggles. Sophie nodded emphatically and Erica allowed herself to peel off and maneuver back into position opposite Sophie's circuit. She wasn't sure what was going on but Sophie must have a reason for staying aloft.

Erica climbed higher and then allowed herself to sink through the clouds. The clouds were moving in thicker now and it was getting harder to find patches of open sky. *This is not good. The only way I'm going to spot that airship is flying right into it. I don't know what Sophie thinks we'll accomplish in five more minutes, but she's the leader. She must know what she's doing.*

She couldn't smell the air with her oxygen mask in place, but she felt the moisture forming in the air around her. She couldn't spot any thunderheads, which was a relief, but flying in a storm of any kind was always tricky, much less with unfamiliar wings. At least the rain would be nicer to fly through than a storm in the Dark Cloud.

Nothing like a little toxic waste water coating your flight suit and goggles while you're delivering a package down a narrow passageway to keep your attention on the job.

Wait.

Something was below her—something big and dark moving through the clouds. She couldn't see Sophie, so she broke off her circuit and headed toward Sophie's position. Erica flew through the thickening clouds for a few minutes, but there was no sign of her

141

flight leader. She signaled to the ground she'd seen something and then began gliding toward whatever was below her.

She went through her checklist as she descended. *Where is my emergency wing release? Where are my weapons? Where is the oxygen tank release?* Going through the checklist helped calm her as she kept her glide under control in the buffeting winds. She broke through the clouds and spotted an airship's balloon beneath her. Something looked different from the other night, but then again, she'd never seen the *Lynx* from above either. She let the craft pull ahead of her and then took a position above and behind, taking advantage of the blind spot on most airships.

Moving closer, she saw three stacks inflating the massive balloon, keeping the airship afloat. Still, something felt wrong. She fought the wind currents to remain in the airship's blind spot while signaling the team below.

To her surprise, they signaled her to land immediately. She asked for a confirmation and the signal was repeated. Puzzled, she let the ship pull ahead and then flew down in a tight spiral until she could see the camp. The team had put out landing lights and was rigging a temporary anchor and winch. She swooped in and made a somewhat graceful landing given the crosswinds. Bringing her wings in tight, she hurried as the field in front of her lit up from a huge spotlight out of the sky and an anchor rope came snaking out of the clouds.

The Vengeance team hurriedly worked the winch as the airship slowly descended from the clouds and took up a position about twenty feet above the camp. The winds made it difficult to hold the ship in position, but a rope ladder descended and three people climbed down.

She heard Phil's voice over the noise of the winch and the airship's engines. He pointed toward the main building. "Halgrim, you're needed over here."

The heavens opened up and the rain that had been threatening all afternoon drenched everyone. One of the people from the airship opened an umbrella for one of the others to duck beneath and then Erica joined the gaggle rushing toward shelter. The water coated her goggles and someone ahead of her opened the door. She stumbled in out of the rain along with the others.

Once the newcomers passed her, she yanked off her goggles and glanced around the dimly lit room. The one person she was looking for was missing, so she grabbed Phil by the shoulder. "Have you seen Sophie? I lost sight of her about the same time I saw this airship."

Phil motioned for two of his team. "Has Zwyer hasn't reported in?"

"No, Phil."

"Grab Zeke and get up there. If she had comms failure, bring her back. If you can't find her, start a search and see if she ran into trouble. Keep in contact with Toby. I'll have him set up his long-range wireless, just in case."

"That won't be necessary."

A familiar voice stopped everyone in their tracks. Erica turned to see Lady Orisaka standing there. There was no misunderstanding the ferocious look on her face. She was flanked by a middle-aged man in a business suit and, to Erica's chagrin, Jessica Black. "I hate to ask this, but would everyone except for Flight Leader Vetrano, Angel Halgrim, and Technician Blake relocate to another building? We need to speak to them privately. Flight Leader Vetrano will brief you on your new mission afterward."

The Vengeance members clambered over the furniture in their haste to fulfill Lady Orisaka's orders. Jessica secured the door behind them. The others took seats near Lady Orisaka and sat quietly until she was ready to speak. She paced around the room, not resembling the normally placid leader of the Angels, until she finally took a deep breath and sat down in the middle of the group. She spoke in a soft, but determined voice. "I don't know any way to sugarcoat this, so I'll get right to the point. What happened yesterday was no accident and neither is Zwyer's absence now. We have more than sufficient reason to suspect Sophia Zwyer was working with, if not for, the pirates of the *Bloody Lynx*. We must assume they now have both the creator of the glider wings as well as a working set."

"That's a serious charge, Chairman Orisaka," the unidentified man said, running a hand through his salt-and-pepper close-cropped hair. "I was led to believe Flight Leader Zwyer was one of your up-and-coming members."

"That was never in question, Ambassador Bogdanovich. Zwyer is a talented flyer and leader. Still, the evidence I've been presented with leaves little doubt. The fact she fled when she saw our airship merely confirms what I've been told. It appears Zwyer's past has come back to haunt her."

"I'm sorry, Lady Orisaka, but her past?" Erica looked around to see if she was the only one confused by that statement, but only Jessica seemed to know what that meant, and she was reveling in that knowledge. Erica wanted to slap that smug look off Jessica's face, but she knew that would only make matters worse.

Lady Orisaka looked at the floor and then directly at Erica. "Yes, Halgrim. What we're about to say *will* be held in the strictest confidence. Am I clear?"

"Yes, ma'am."

Jessica leaned back in her chair, reveling in being the center of attention. The agent opened up a black briefcase sitting next to her chair and pulled out a sheaf of papers. Flipping through a couple, she selected one and began reading to the assembled group. "Zwyer is not originally from Southwatch. Her mother moved here when she was ten and Zwyer grew up in the Underground, It was not an easy time for Zwyer or her mother. Southwatch can be rather cruel to people who are unfamiliar with the unique nature of the town. It took her mother quite a while to adapt to living beneath the Cloud, much less to get a job in the town. I have no information about her father."

Erica broke in. "What does that have to do with Sophie being involved with what happened yesterday?"

"We believe while she was living in the Underground, she spent time with the Brickyard Bangers, one of the numerous youth gangs that infest the city," Jessica continued as if Erica hadn't said a word. "Zwyer has no record with the Southwatch Police, which is probably how she managed to get her position of trust at the Angels. Still, there is anecdotal evidence of her involvement in gang activities. General nuisance activities one would associate with bored kids and maybe some petty larceny. However"—Jessica paused for effect, which made Erica sigh deeply—"former members of that gang have rather extensive criminal records. Several are prominent within the Southwatch underworld. In fact, her old gang leader is the subcommander of the *Bloody Lynx* pirate group. They say he runs the smuggling portion of the operation, bringing things in and out of Southwatch and distributing them through the city."

Erica broke in as Jessica shuffled through her papers. "But she also moved out of the Underground when she hit high school. She told me her mother moved to Midtown Bakerstown to get her as far away from the Underground, and specifically Bricktown, as she could afford. Sophie graduated with honors from high school and the Royal

Polytechnic College also. Does that sound like someone still involved with criminal gangs?"

Lady Orisaka made a small motion with her hand, catching Erica's attention. "I fully admire Sophie's skill and intelligence. She would not have been chosen to be a flight leader right out of training otherwise. However, let Miss Black finish her report. There will be time to discover the *entire* truth after this."

Erica fumed but sat back in her chair. She knew better than to fight openly with Lady Orisaka, especially not in front of these people. However, she took her cue from the way her employer had stressed the word "entire" and realized there was more going on than she knew. The information Jessica had presented so far shouldn't have convinced Lady Orisaka either. She wondered what else the Black Watch agent had up her sleeve.

"Apparently your friend neglected to tell you about the gentleman she's been seeing the past eight years. Has she ever mentioned Darren Freeman before?"

Erica paused, not sure where Jessica was going with this. "No, I've never heard Sophie mention that name before. She's my supervisor, so she's not in the habit of sharing personal information."

Jessica pulled out a photograph and handed it to Erica. It looked like it had been taken in a portrait studio. The picture showed Sophie and a young man sitting on a settee, both looking rather uncomfortable—as if they were unfamiliar with the fancy clothing they were wearing. Erica had to examine the picture a few times to convince herself it was Sophie. The woman in the picture wore an evening dress and had her hair down—two looks she'd never associated with the stern flight leader.

Erica handed the picture back to Jessica. "You've got a picture of Sophie and a young man. Does that surprise you? She's young and attractive. I'd be more surprised if you didn't have one."

"The young man she's sitting next to is Darren Freeman. He's a mechanic on the *Bloody Lynx*."

Erica stared at Jessica. "You, of course, have evidence Sophie knew that?"

Jessica laughed, but there was no humor in the tone. "Halgrim, your dogged defense of your flight leader is a credit to you and Lady Orisaka. However, you have to face facts. Sophie is working for the enemy—the enemy that kidnaped two of your companions and, might

I remind you, made an attempt on your life the other night. For all we know, she's also been behind the attacks on you within the city."

"No."

Jessica stopped and looked at her. "No?"

"No. I'm not convinced Sophie's involved with the pirates, but she was not involved with my abduction. The way I was kidnapped and interrogated, and the way they cleaned up after themselves, it was more likely the Black Watch did it than any band of pirates. Way too professional and slick, and if it wasn't the Black Watch, then there's another professional group in town."

"We'll discuss your impression of the Black Watch another day, Halgrim. What we need to focus on now is where have they taken their captives and when will we hear from them?"

Erica looked over at Lady Orisaka, but her boss's face was impossible to read. She half-listened while Phil went through his own interrogation, trying to sort things out in her own mind.

I wish I knew what's going on. Why would Lady Orisaka come out here just to deal with a pirate raid? Why would she bring the Black Watch along, especially since she barred them in the first place? Besides, they're the baron's private police force and this definitely isn't Southwatch.

Then a sudden thought caught her attention. *Why would they have a dossier on Sophie anyway? How many Angels do they have under observation?*

And what the heck is the ambassador doing here? I realize it was his daughter who died up there at the Temple. *Who invited him here, the Black Watch or Lady Orisaka? It's weird running into him right after Tony suggested I seek him out. Speaking of which, I know Tony said the* Bloody Lynx *was asking questions about the incident, but how could that be tied into the raid on our convoy?*

Too many things are happening for coincidence. Something's not right and I'm never going to feel comfortable until I get to the bottom of this.

Lady Orisaka's questions to Toby caught Erica's attention. "Blake, you probably understand Crystal's experiments better than anyone else in my employ. You prepared the glider wings for their mission today. Do you believe they were a finished product and if so, could someone else replicate them given a set to reverse engineer?"

"The lady flatters me. Crystal is in a class by herself when it comes to design."

"Yes, yes, but the question, please?"

Toby thought before answering. "No, I don't think so. I noted places where Crystal obviously used inferior-grade material in the wings. She never commits actual bessum implants until she's certain everything is ready to go. She prefers to use a mixture of ceramics and aluminum in her prototypes."

"Wait a minute," Erica broke in. "You sent us up to that altitude with inferior equipment?"

Toby pulled back into his chair at Erica's vehemence, but then he straightened his back and his voice got stronger. "Trust me, what is considered inferior for Crystal is superior to most developers' best work. I would have been perfectly willing to fly with those wings . . . if I wasn't afraid of heights."

"Halgrim, I don't think Blake would have let you fly if he had any doubts about their airworthiness. However, if I understand what he's saying, the wings you flew were not optimized," Lady Orisaka said quietly.

"You are quite correct, my lady. While still superior to the only other manufacturer of wings in Dalriada, the wings in use today were approximately sixty percent capability. With proper materials assigned to the wings, I could guarantee increases in altitude, speed, and ability to remain on station before the thalisium would need to be recharged."

Lady Orisaka waved a hand at him. "We have no doubts about Crystal's abilities, Blake. Thank you."

Toby looked down at the floor, his ears turning red. When he looked up again, Lady Orisaka tapped the tips of her fingernails together before continuing. "So, the question becomes, if they have the minimized wings but they have Crystal, can she modify them to reach maximum potential?"

Toby smiled before answering the Angels' leader. "No, I don't think so. The material she works with is exotic. You are probably one of only three people who would use those materials in Southwatch. The other two work at the Polytechnic University and the Imperial Coast Guard. Neither of them would sell the material to anyone, much less a pirate. Also, there's only one person who exports that material and he's, let's say, discriminating about who he orders it for. There is

147

also only one merchant in Southwatch who serves as his contact here in town."

"Very good. You will let me know who this exporter is in your written report."

Lady Orisaka began questioning Phil again and Erica let her thoughts drift. After a while, the meeting was brought to a conclusion. Lady Orisaka handed Phil a package and gave him instructions to stop by her cabin later with his team. They walked to the front door and Erica saw the last of the vehicles being winched up into the airship. Now that the ship was hovering stationary overhead, it was easy for Erica to recognize it as the *Enkeli*, Lady Orisaka's personal airship.

That caught Erica's attention. Normally, the airships of Aerie were permanently moored above either Downtown or White Cliffs. Even though the *Enkeli* was moored near one of the outer rings, it was not an airship designed for casual flying. It was Lady Orisaka's home. For her to bring it showed how important this was.

Once everything was loaded, the winch and platform descended one last time and the personnel on the ground climbed aboard. The crew ensured everyone was secured before bringing the platform aboard the airship. It was a smooth trip, even with the rain, and soon everyone was inside and being handed towels so they could dry off before going to their quarters.

The chief steward announced a light meal had been prepared in the main dining area, but Erica was ready to call it a night. She followed a servant to a room with two beds and sat down. She glanced at the bed and felt tears begin to well up. She knew Sophie would have been her roommate for the return trip.

I still don't believe it. Sophie would never betray the Angels like that. She pushed herself and all of us in her flight harder than anyone else in the group. We were going to be the elite delivery team among the Angels. She wouldn't sell us out like that.

She had just wrapped her arms around her pillow when there was a tentative knock at her door. She wiped away her tears on the corner of the sheet and moved to the door to see who would be calling on her. The door slid open with a little pressure and Ambassador Bogdanovich was standing there, looking very nervous.

"I'm sorry, miss. I know this is rather awkward, but could I possibly have a little of your time?"

Erica was too shocked to object and stepped backward into the room to let him enter. He was unlike the other ambassadors she had met in her short time in the Angels. Most were distinguished older gentlemen who generally did not travel anywhere without either their wives or their retinue of toadies. Ambassador Bogdanovich was a handsome middle-aged man who obviously took care of himself. She would have guessed he was an athlete instead of an ambassador if she had met him elsewhere.

"Thank you for your time, Miss Halgrim. This has been a very rough time for my wife and me."

Erica motioned to the chair tucked under a small writing desk and positioned herself on the edge of the bed closest to the door. "I am so sorry for your loss, Ambassador. I wish I hadn't been hurried away to provide testimony on the incident. I've wanted to speak to you before now, but there just hasn't been an opportunity."

"Yes," he replied, staring at the door as if expecting someone to interrupt them at any moment. "I requested to meet you once before, but Lady Orisaka informed me you are on restricted duty. I thought I'd take advantage of this opportunity to speak now, if you do not mind?"

"No, that's all right. What would you like to know?"

The ambassador looked nervous and bent closer toward Erica. "I know what the official reports say. However, I also know official reports may be edited to ensure the Empire is shown in the best light. Personally, I don't hold the Empire at fault. Still, I have to know the truth, not some whitewashed story. What happened to my daughter? Why was she on that gyrocopter? Who was she with? How did she fall? Was she still alive when she landed? Did she say anything?"

He started pacing around the room, his hands clenching and unclenching behind his back as he moved. From the precise steps and the way he held his body, Erica changed her opinion from athlete to soldier. She started to answer and then paused, wondering what he'd been told up until now. Taking a deep breath, she let it out slowly to calm her rapidly beating heart. She told him what had happened, starting with meeting Tony Blaylock and continuing through the attack on her as they had descended through the Cloud afterward. She didn't bring up her subsequent kidnapping, the later incidents with the Black Watch, nor the assault on Eve. Although she felt for his loss, he was still the representative of another government and she couldn't see how those events were associated with his daughter's death.

149

She finished her tale and he sat back down on the chair. It was as if someone had stuck a pin into an inflated version of him—he just seemed to collapse into himself for a bit. He sat there so motionless and unresponsive, she was about to call for the ship's doctor. As she rose from the bed, he stirred. He went over to the small dresser and unclipped the crystal water decanter and poured himself a drink. Silently he motioned to her and she nodded in agreement. He poured her one and then refilled his glass before sitting down again.

"Your story is close enough to what I was told. Some of the details you've added I did not know, but it does not substantially change my interpretation of the events. I wish you had gotten a better look at the man on the gyrocopter, if it was a man. For your edification, I have individuals attempting to track him down, but it's the proverbial needle in a haystack. Southwatch is so reliant on air travel—there are too many pilots and too many places that rent vehicles like that. Still, I will learn the truth soon enough."

"I hope you do, Your Excellency. If something were to happen to someone I loved, I would move heaven and earth."

"I believe you would, which is why I hoped to speak to you. There is another thing I would like to address, but this is not the place. I will discuss lifting your flying restrictions with Lady Orisaka for a specific event. I would like you to join my family for dinner at the embassy as my guest." He glanced around again and then leaned forward. No sound came out but it was easy enough to read his lips: *"Michael recommended you to me."*

She tried to keep her voice calm as she replied. "As you stated, I am under flight restrictions, but should Lady Orisaka change her mind, it would be an honor, Your Excellency. I am fond of your nation's cuisine and I have heard from some who've attended your parties your chef is second to none."

The ambassador clapped his hands together. "Excellent. Now, I shall gird myself for battle with your employer. Here's to a dinner party in your future."

He lifted his half-empty water glass to her in a salute. Erica lifted hers in return and then escorted the ambassador to the door. She watched him walk down the hall toward the main cabin of the airship and she carefully shut and locked her door before preparing for bed. She found a nightgown in her size in the dresser and soon she was stretched out on the silk sheets of the bed and the night passed without her knowledge.

Chapter Seventeen

The storms still raged through Southwatch two days later, sending a deluge of dark sludge down the window as Erica glanced out over the city. Far below on the streets, people dodged in and out of the milling crowd, their umbrellas glistening in lamps fitfully attempting to break through the gloom. She noted the Dark Cloud seemed even lower today, pushed toward the earth by the weight of the rain filtering through it.

A sudden flash of lightning cut through the sky, startling her out of her contemplation. She turned back to the window and started again as an apparition suddenly appeared behind her. She spun around to find Christina standing in the doorway watching her. They both looked at each other with uncomfortable expressions before Erica mustered up enough energy to speak.

"Hey."

"Hey, yourself," Christina replied. Erica watched her roommate come to a decision, set her jaw, and plunge into her speech. "Look Erica, you haven't left this room in three days. Don't you think it's time to get out and do something?"

"What's the point? Crystal is still missing so I can't train. Sophie's still missing and everyone thinks she's deserted to join a pirate crew. I can't contact Michael and I'm grounded pending investigation. Plus, it's raining sludge. I don't see the attraction in going out into that."

"Listen to yourself. My roommate doesn't just give up like that."

"Your roommate hadn't been put through hell recently either."

Christina paused and then gave Erica her I've-got-you-now smile. "What if I told you I found a restaurant you might like? One you may have visited before?"

Erica flopped face-forward on her bed but something in Chris's voice made her pause. She gingerly lifted her head to see the grin on her roommate's face. "A restaurant . . . I've been to before? One where I didn't get a chance to finish my meal?"

"Could be. I hear they have a special guest dining there tonight. It'll be quite the social event. Simply everyone who's anyone will be there. A friend said they might be dining there this evening. But, if you just want to mope about the room, I guess you wouldn't be interested. "

Christina turned to walk out the door, but Erica jumped off the bed and let out an unarticulated growl. "For Goddess's sake, don't just stand there. Help me pick out something to wear while I get cleaned up. I can't go out looking like this. I must look like death warmed over."

"I wasn't going to say anything, but the gravedigger stopped by a few times to check on you."

She heard Christina going on about something, but couldn't hear her roommate over the noise of the shower. There were only two people who knew about that particular restaurant adventure. Given the not-so-private altercation she'd had with Jessica on the *Enkeli* the morning they had docked at Southwatch, she was pretty sure Jessica wouldn't be inviting her to dinner. Especially since it had taken two of the Vengeance to keep her from ripping that smirk off that blond bimbo's face.

Furiously toweling off and finishing her toilet, she came out to see Christina had selected an understated outfit for her. Chris moved closer and whispered, "I think it would be best if *we* looked like we were going shopping. If you get too dressed up, your shadows might wonder what's going on. Besides, we're going to a clothing store first. There's no sense in getting dressed up just to try on more clothes. Think of this as urban camouflage."

Erica nodded and spoke in a normal tone. "Clothes shopping?"

"Yes. There's this darling boutique you'll love. We *definitely* want to stop there before dinner."

Erica wasn't sure where Christina was going with this conversation. Some of it was pretty clear, but other things, especially the tone she was using, made her wonder if her room was being monitored. She decided to wait until they were in a more secluded area to figure out exactly what was going on here.

"You know, it's been quite a while since I bought anything new. That might be just the thing to perk me up."

"That's the spirit," Christina said gaily. "You've been entirely too mopey lately. It's time we went out and had some fun together. I can't remember the last time we just kicked back and enjoyed ourselves."

"All right, but I'm keeping an eye on you tonight. No champagne for you."

"Awww!"

Erica gave her that look. "Just because I'm grounded doesn't mean you get to do what you want. You've got a full day tomorrow, if I remember correctly."

The two chatted like that all the way to the front door and, Erica realized, Christina's good mood was infectious. She really was starting to feel like her old self. She paused at the main door, though, and glanced through the glass before going outside.

"Is there a problem, Erica?"

"Just checking for vegetable carts."

The two women laughed before rushing out and flagging down a passing people mover. They hurried onto the large car and found their seats as the driver set it in motion and it lurched forward. The car bumped against the narrow rails in the street and the conductor issued them tickets. They took turns looking out the window and talking as the mover trundled its way through the rain-soaked streets.

Erica caught herself checking the faces of the people getting on and off. She knew it was ridiculous, but every time she left the Angels' building lately strange things happened. Christina and she made it a game, trying to guess what this or that person did for a living or where they might live. It settled her paranoia and helped pass the time as the mover crawled through the early evening traffic.

Finally, when the mover reached University Heights, they got off at a busy intersection. The rain finally was letting up but they still huddled under their umbrella until they reached a building. She made her way through a crowd of children rushing into the street and followed Christina. They stopped at the coatroom and dropped off their rain slickers and her umbrella before following the press of people to the elevators.

The glass-walled elevator was dimly lit for the first twenty floors as they made their way through the interior of the building. However, once they hit the twenty-first floor, the building opened up into a large atrium surrounded by balconies overflowing with plants. A large crystal lamp hung from the sky-blue ceiling and people moved in and out of the stores and homes on the balconies as if enjoying a world without the Dark Cloud. Christina and Erica enjoyed the view from the elevator car until they reentered a dark shaft. At the fifty-second floor, they stepped out of the car into a small maelstrom of shoppers.

Christina spotted the department store and tugged on Erica's arm. The doorman held the door open for them and they hurried inside. The variety of items amazed Erica. Unlike the typical shops on the Streets, this department store was huge and staircases led from the main floor to additional sections on the four floors above. Even from the entrance, she saw clothes, furniture, entertainment devices, and housewares carefully displayed to catch the eye of the hurried shopper. Each stairway had a number of assistants ready to guide the shopper deeper into the store to find just the perfect item. Erica heard faint music being piped throughout the store and felt an almost childlike glee at the chance to go visit the various rooms. They wandered through the first floor viewing the different items. While not as exotic as the shops in the Aerie, there were still fashions and items from around the world here.

Christina led her to one of the upper floors and through a draped doorway. A saleswoman met them before Erica's eyes had a chance to adapt to the dimly lit room. From the tone of her voice, it was obvious she thought they were in the wrong area and wanted to herd them back into the main room as soon as possible.

"Welcome to Madame Truesby's, where we stock the finest in fashions from not only Dalriada but the finest from Cassyran, Coritanian, Tacedon, and Castran designers also. We carry the rarest silken garments from Moenia. How may I help you two ladies?"

Christina continued examining a hem on a nearby dress with a dismissive look on her face, acting as if she hadn't noticed the woman's approach. She let the hem fall with a flick of her fingers before straightening up. Finally, she turned to the woman. "My friend needs a new dress—something suitable for dining in the Heights, yet stunning enough to attract the attention of a certain young man. I hope you have something satisfactory."

Erica blushed and waved her hand at her friend. "Christina!"

The saleswoman looked at the two young women with a matronly stare. Erica felt like the prize cow at a county fair, but Christina seemed oblivious. After a few moments, the woman motioned for them to follow and led them deeper into the showroom. She waved an arm and a series of small spotlights illuminated the various dresses adorning the mannequins in the room.

"We have a number of dresses that may meet your needs. The question I have to ask is, what is your budget? After all, this *is* a rather exclusive line. Before we begin making any alterations, we will insist on payment in full."

Christina moved closer and whispered in the woman's ear. Erica couldn't hear what her friend said, but there was no mistaking the effect. The older woman turned pale and then bowed at the waist. She called into the back room and suddenly the two women were swarmed by a bevy of saleswomen. Chairs miraculously appeared behind them and a tray of drinks and finger foods arrived moments later.

"Now, miss, what kind of dress do you prefer?" the head saleswoman asked.

The next several minutes were a blur to Erica as people seemed to appear out of nowhere. A young woman seemed to have no other job than to fill her glass. A manicurist pulled up a small stool and began working on her nails. Another person came by and measured her feet before disappearing into the darkness of the showroom. She watched in fascination as models came by in various dresses to show off the latest styles. Once she identified some styles she was interested in, two tailors appeared—almost as if by magic—to take her measurements. She wound up trying on seven different dresses under the watchful eyes of the head saleswoman and Christina.

They narrowed it down to two dresses and Erica turned to Christina for advice. "What do you think?"

"Both."

"Both? Christina, I'm not certain I can afford either of them. How am I going to buy both?"

"You're not. They're my gift. I thought you could use some cheering up, so I'm paying for these. Or at least my father is."

"Your father?"

Christina asked the head saleswoman how long it would take to tailor one of the dresses for this evening and to arrange for matching dress boots, hat, and handbag. With a quick nod, the saleswoman bustled away with both dresses. Erica continued to stare at Christina in amazement. Christina finally noticed, then glanced down at the floor, before shyly raising her eyes to her friend, her cheeks flaming red as she seemed to fight for the right words. "Ah, you've heard of Blackwolf Aetherworks?"

"They specialize in miniature aether machines that complement larger steam equipment. Our wings use a variant motor of theirs Crystal tweaked."

"Dad gave Crystal the plans for the original motor. In return, Lady Orisaka and he split the profits for the miniaturized motor. He is one of the owners of Blackwolf. He helped them with their original stake for forty percent of the company."

She looked down at the floor again, reminding Erica of a small child caught in the cookie jar. "I've got a charge account here, so that's partly why I brought you here. I had a different store in mind initially, but I remembered you're not supposed to go to Dayside, so that was out. Besides"—she paused and gave Erica a conspiratorial smile—"there's another reason to bring you here."

Erica was processing the fact she didn't know her roommate as well as she thought and missed Christina's last statement. That was, until her friend nudged her with an elbow. She blinked a few times to clear her head and tried to focus. "What other surprises do you have in store for me today? You're marrying the lord mayor's eldest son?"

"Ew, no. He's only ten. No. Remember our discussion earlier about dinner?"

Erica felt an eyebrow rise as she stared at her friend. "Yesssss?"

Christina moved closer. "There's a back door leading to a staircase from this particular department. I've used it before when an old boyfriend wouldn't take no for an answer. Luckily, Madam Leroux is very strict about not letting gentlemen enter the gallery. Anyway, a certain gentleman we both know informed me of a hidden door on the landing below this floor. There's an elevator there. We're to take it to the twenty-ninth floor and someone will meet us there to escort us to dinner."

Erica nodded. She wanted to rush to the stairway and head downstairs, but she knew she had to wait for the final fitting and Christina settling the bill. Soon, Christina signed a slip of paper for the head saleswoman and made arrangements to deliver Erica's other dress to Angels' Headquarters. Once Erica had changed and passed Christina's inspection, her roommate led her through the back door and into the stairway.

They stood at the top of the landing and listened to ensure someone wasn't approaching before they made their way down to the landing below. Erica had to steady herself in her new boots. She didn't normally wear heels this tall, but according to the shoe seller, they were the latest style and perfect with her new dress. When they reached the landing, her roommate reached up and twisted one of the lights on the landing to the left. A small panel slid back and Erica heard the elevator car rising to their floor.

The elevator slid into position and Christina slid the folding door to the side. They slipped into the tiny car. Erica guessed it was designed for just one occupant, so with the two of them in there, it was a tight fit. Still, they managed to get situated and depress the lever to descend to the twenty-ninth floor.

Reaching the proper floor, Christina pulled the lever and brought the car to a stop. The door slid back, revealing a storeroom. The boxes and crates were arranged to both hide the entrance to the elevator and provide a passage along the back wall. Theo waited near the corner and did the best imitation of a smile a mechanical man could as they approached.

"Ah, Miss Erica, Miss Christina, so glad you were able to make it. If you'll follow me, we'll soon join your dining party."

"Theo, can you tell me something before we go?"

"Certainly, Miss Erica, if I can."

"What's with all the secret elevators?"

Theo paused before answering as if gathering his thoughts. Erica knew that wasn't needed given his mechanical brain, but it was an affectation he had assumed to fit in better with humans. "Given the way Southwatch has grown over the years, these buildings have been gutted and remodeled to support the population. Occasionally, shafts, rooms, and even entire floors have been blocked off and lost. Master Michael and some of the other storms search for these lost areas and repurpose them. Of course, they're not the only ones."

"So, Michael and his friends aren't the only ones who use these passages?"

"Oh, certainly not, Miss Erica. Many criminal gangs in Southwatch use them to transport goods from the Underground to other sections of town without being discovered. Master Michael suggests the Black Watch and the military have established their own lairs within the city too. It is truly a no-man's-land. But we do need to go, the others are waiting."

"Others?"

"I'm not at liberty to say . . . Master Michael's orders. If you'll follow me."

The two women accompanied the bronze mechanical out of the storeroom and down several floors. Erica soon recognized the familiar smells from her earlier visit as Theo opened a door to an unmarked store with the curtains pulled down. Once inside, the manager escorted them to a dimly lit small room off the dining area.

"Well, two lovely ladies, Michael. You didn't mention Erica was bringing a companion."

"Tony?" Erica blurted out in surprise as her eyes adjusted to the dim light. Michael rose to escort the women to their seats and she noted with surprise there were three people at the table. The renegade pilot leaned back in his chair with a grin on his face. The third figure remained seated with a hooded cloak concealing its features. Michael rose to give her a hug, but Erica stopped him with a gentle push in the center of his chest. Grabbing his arm, she pulled him away from the table until she was certain they wouldn't be overheard.

"Michael, who in the hell is that hooded person?"

"An acquaintance. She's Southwatch's premier cybernetic expert, but she prefers to remain anonymous."

Erica found herself flustered at Michael's nonchalance. "After all the stuff that's been happening, you just thought you'd invite someone who won't reveal their identity *just like that?*"

"I'm sorry, Erica, we were in the middle of an experiment when I learned of your return, and I thought it would be rude to just dismiss her. Of course, if you want her to leave…"

Erica saw the concern in Michael's eyes and found herself shaking her head. "No, if you consider her a friend, then I'm not going to make a scene. Just give me a heads-up next time. I'm not really in the mood for more surprises."

Michael looked embarrassed and nodded in agreement. "You're right. Tonight is supposed to be a special evening."

When they returned to the table, Tony spoke up. "I'm so glad to see you're all right, Erica. I was sweating it when I heard the *Bloody Lynx* was involved."

"There were a few close calls, Tony, but for the most part I was never in danger. I still can't believe Sophie is involved. She helped me escape from the pirates' trap. If she was really working with them, why didn't she let me get taken like Crystal and Flight Leader Kail? Something else is going on."

Michael helped seat Christina and her before returning to his own. "That could be. But let's enjoy dinner first and we'll discuss things in a bit. If I recall correctly, you didn't get to enjoy your meal last time. That's why I had them prepare a special dinner tonight."

"Just for me? Michael, you didn't need to."

"Maybe I didn't need to, but I wanted to and that makes all the difference. Besides, there are things you need to know, Erica. Christina is not here by accident either. I specifically need her if we're going to get ourselves out of this situation."

Tony piped up. "Seems your boy here and I have drawn more attention than is healthy. So, if we want to stay upright, we need to get to the bottom of this while we can."

Erica leaned forward, looking at Tony. "But, what's at the bottom of this, Tony? You were in the *Temple* with me, but you seem to know more about this than I do. At first, I thought it was just a simple accident, but it's obviously more than that."

"I *didn't* know any more than you did at first, Erica, but I've got connections you don't, as I mentioned the other night. I don't know all the players myself, kid, but I recognize some. The *Lynx* crew and I have worked together before—that was after I... left military service... but it's always been small stuff. I have a knack for finding information and they have a knack for paying well. It's been a profitable relationship until now. However, they've never been involved with something this big before."

They paused at the knock on the door and waited for the servers to bring in plates heaped with food. The headwaiter set several bottles of wine around the table before escorting the other servers out. The diners indulged themselves on the exotic food and Erica allowed herself to be carried away by the unusual combinations of meat, vegetables, and spices. While they made small talk during the meal, Erica noted the hooded figure avoided joining the conversation.

After the last plates disappeared, the owner returned to speak with Michael. Erica couldn't hear the conversation, but the owner nodded and then walked out, locking the door behind him. Michael leaned back in his chair with a serious look on his face.

Erica prodded him with a question. "Michael, do you have any ideas about what's going on?"

"Perhaps. At least why Crystal was kidnapped. Those new wings were a joint project between the two of us."

"The two of you?" Christina blurted out. "She never mentioned anything about it."

"I'm not surprised. We went through the Royal Polytechnic College together a few years ago. She went to work for the Angels and I went freelance. Still, we both have an interest in clockwork devices, especially miniaturization. We were working on several sets of wings, some for speed, some for long-range flight. We even designed some to see how small we could make them and still generate lift. After all, some places within the Cloud can only be reached by flying—if your wings are small enough to fit in the passages."

"So, you were involved in the testing I was doing?"

"Not directly, but that's how I knew where you were at the test range. I couldn't go myself, but Tony has been a useful addition to my team."

"Your team?" Erica glared at him. "Just what is going on here, Michael?"

"I'm not running a spy organization or anything like that, Erica. However, I have contacts all around the city. Remember, I like being a freelancer. Well, as I said back at the train station, storms are a valuable commodity. Some people don't appreciate the fact I like working for myself. These people don't like taking no for an answer. That means I need my own people—people who find information or run errands while I stay as far out of sight as possible. Believe me, if you weren't involved, I'd avoid this situation entirely. Too many people are taking an interest in my activities these days."

"But, what's the purpose of these experiments and new designs, Michael? Why all the secrecy and why are so many people after them?"

"I can't tell you everything yet, Erica, but your employer is not the only person interested in winged flight. You know the Imperial Air Corps has been experimenting with it. However, they have not been able to overcome the weight distribution issue. It's a simple matter, though, if we—"

Erica recognized that tone of voice and cut him off before he could go into a multi-hour lecture on the dynamics of flight. "Yes, Michael, so you're designing these for the Imperial Air Corps."

"Not exactly."

"What does that mean? You're not designing them for another country—are you?"

"Science recognizes no arbitrary lines on the ground, Erica, you should know that. But, no, I'm not working for another government either. There's a consortium of scientists who're trying to design both new wings and new pilots for dangerous missions. After all, you've met Eve, haven't you?"

"You're building mechanical flyers?"

"Why not? What's the biggest danger the Angels have in Southwatch?"

Christina popped up with an answer. "Flying through the Cloud. Most injuries and deaths, to not only the Angels but gyrocopter pilots and glider pilots, happen while making the passage from Darkside to Dayside. Not to mention gangs use the limited visibility to set ambushes and such."

"Exactly. We're attempting to automate the ability to move items through the Cloud without risking people's lives. We don't expect the aeronauts to replace human flyers, but in specific areas or on specific missions—like mapping the terrain of the northern continent, Thule—they'd be perfect."

"But couldn't they also be adapted for war, Michael?" Erica asked, with a concerned look on her face.

"Absolutely, which is why we try to maintain as much secrecy as possible. However, there's no such thing as perfect security, not with as many pieces as we have in motion. We know the Black Watch knows about this project, as do agents from Cassyra and Celacti, so we have to move cautiously with our research. We've tried to camouflage much of it under the guise of other projects. That's where you came in, Erica. Since you were grounded, it seemed like the perfect opportunity to get as much testing done as possible, especially with your strong flying qualifications."

"Thanks, I think. But, how does that tie into the incident with the Coritanian ambassasdor's daughter?"

Tony spoke up then. "We're not sure it does. These may be two separate incidents blurred together. We still don't know why she was on that 'copter or who she was flying with. If anyone knows, they're keeping their lips sealed."

Tony took a drink of wine and then a grin spread across his face. "Of course, Michael and his team import some of their more exotic minerals from Coritani, so there may be a connection after all. Coritani also has been supplying trace metals to Atrigon for those special servos they're building for Michael. Now, the Atrigonese don't know they're building them for Michael, but that's their problem, not mine."

Erica raised a hand to cover her smile at Michael's shocked expression. "How . . . how did you know about that?" he sputtered.

"You are a brilliant scientist, Michael, but I know people. It's amazing what you learn when you know who to speak to and who to listen to, especially in Bricktown. Those sea rats hear lots of things they don't necessarily understand. It takes someone like me to put all the random pieces together. That's how I make my living, after all."

Michael harrumphed and sat back with his arms crossed on his chest.

"In fact, I have a bit of information I think you *all* might be interested in—say, a lead on where the *Bloody Lynx* might be docking in a few days?"

Erica shot out of her chair and leaned across the table toward the pilot. "What? How—never mind that. Where will it be? Are Crystal and Sophie aboard?"

"I don't know that, Bright Eyes, but I can say the *Lynx* will dock in White Cliffs four nights from now. They're bringing a special shipment for a customer and then departing for the Gray Mountains, where they lay up most of the time. They're only expected to be in Southwatch territory for six hours at most. So, if you want to raid them, that's your best chance."

The person under the hood spoke for the first time, startling Erica. She'd almost forgotten the person was there, they'd been so quiet. "That would be incredibly foolish. A group of flyers small enough to avoid being spotted would be overpowered by the airship's crew, and a large enough group would be spotted, giving the pirates the opportunity to destroy any clues to their base."

The voice sounded mechanical and Erica wondered if they were using a device to disguise their voice. She stared at the figure, but given the volume of the cloak and the angle of the hood, there wasn't any way to determine if it was a man or a woman. Of course, it could

163

be a mechanical. Erica shuddered as she remembered rumors of androids, mechanicals inhabited by the spirits of people who'd died.

Michael took the suggestion in stride and nodded in agreement. "I think our guest is right. It's more important to track that ship to its base in the Gray Mountains. I suggest one flyer could approach the ship while it's moored and attach a tracking device to it. Then a small squad would be able to track it back to its base and affect a rescue there."

The hooded figure nodded slowly and then Michael turned to his other companions. "Erica, I think you know some people who might enjoy a chance at the pirates."

She thought about the Angels of Vengeance team and nodded savagely. "I can guarantee that, provided Lady Orisaka will authorize the mission."

Michael nodded. "Let me work on that. Even though Crystal was the front person for this project, I have had some dealings with your employer. Also, while you were at the base, Tony installed a tracking device in Eve. I've tried to get a fix on her frequency, but the transmitter has a limited range and low power to avoid alerting anyone else to its presence." He reached under the table and pulled out a narrow box, which he handed to Erica with a smile. "If you're within a couple of miles, this will let you know."

There was a soft knock at the door—two sharp raps followed by three that were spaced out. Michael frowned and turned to the group. "I swear that woman is either part bloodhound or she's found a way to track one of us. Erica, Christina, have the Angels take a blood sample and ensure you weren't injected with something traceable."

Erica glanced at the door in fear. "Michael, what are you talking about?"

He sighed and continued. "Jessica Black and her boys are nosing around. At least we finished our meal this time. Erica and Christina, say nothing to anyone. We'll contact you when we have more information. If all goes well, Lady Orisaka should be assigning you a mission in a few days. If not, we'll make other plans."

"But, Michael . . ."

"No time, Erica. We need to leave now. Follow me."

He led the group to the back of the room where a panel slid back revealing what might have been an old fire escape once upon a time. Now, it was a narrow metal stair running between two walls into the darkness. He pulled out a pair of small electric torches and handed one to Tony before he led the way down the stairs. The women, Theo, and their cloaked companion followed while Tony secured the door behind them.

They descended ten flights of stairs before Michael paused. "Erica and Christina, go through this door here. We'll go to another landing. We shouldn't be seen together. No sense in making it easier for our pursuers. We'll be in touch soon."

Erica didn't want to be separated from Michael, but she recognized the truth in his statement. Theo opened a hidden panel and they slipped into a small alley between two stores. From the smell that assaulted their noses, it was obvious this was used by the neighboring stores to store their trash cans.

The two women wasted no time in exiting the alley and mixing in with the crowd. Christina looked like she had a million questions, but Erica knew they'd have to wait. She led her friend into several more stores where they purchased accessories to go with her new dress and a few new books to read. After a bit, they returned to the ground floor and recovered their coats and umbrellas for the return trip back to Angels' Headquarters.

Chapter Eighteen

"Are you sure you want to do this, Halgrim?"

Erica fixed the goggles on her face before facing the technician. "Yes. Even without Crystal, I need to get better flying with these wings. Please ensure the harness is right and then let's commence the test."

The technician tugged her harness one last time to check the fastenings, then gave her a halfhearted thumbs-up, though his expression said *It's your funeral.* As he moved to the controls, Erica tested the wings one last time to ensure the servos were drawing enough power from the small motor on her back. Satisfied, she extended her wings to catch the rustle of air in front of her. She gave the technician a nod and slats in the far wall pivoted, exposing a mesh screen. The air stirred as the large fan behind the mesh spun, becoming a headwind that slowly increased in velocity, forcing her to lean forward to keep her footing as the air picked at her wings, trying to push her back. She fought the instinct to tuck her wings in around her and concentrated on her task.

When she couldn't maintain her feet any longer, she hit the controls. The wings flexed as the servos kicked in and she leapt forward in her harness. The wings bit into the wind and she forced herself to ignore the restraints and fought forward. She attempted to move the wings faster and faster, as if through sheer willpower she could break free of the restraints holding her in place.

Once certain she'd reached the maximum speed possible given the restraints, she waggled a hand at the technician. He hit a series of switches and the floor sank into the ground as the ceiling retracted. The flashing light at the end of the test center went to solid amber, signaling Erica she could begin the next portion of the test.

A series of lights began flashing on the far wall and Erica forced herself to match the angle and slope of the lights, bringing her wings into line with the glowing lights ahead of her without losing airspeed. She felt the sweat trickling down her forehead as she dove around imaginary obstacles, shifting altitude and pitch at an instant's notice. She thought she'd reached her exhaustion point when the amber light flashed again, announcing the last section of the test.

Now it gets interesting.

She adjusted the setting on her test goggles. Dark glass flipped down on her goggles and suddenly she felt like she was zooming through the Cloud. She waggled her wings at the technician and took a deep breath.

Now, instead of bright white lights, dim red and amber lights appeared on the wall, which was faint and blurry through the darkened lenses. Erica pushed forward, diving and twisting through the imaginary obstacles, as she tried to avoid the temptation to anticipate where the next obstacle would occur. Instead of complete rows of lights, there might be a horizontal line with only a small gap in the middle, forcing Erica to pivot ninety degrees to slip through the narrow passage. Then partway down the passage, the entire wall would light up along with a section of the floor or the ceiling, compelling her to turn in midair to fly up or down a small chimney to reach open air.

Just as she felt her concentration wavering from the strain, a slow flash of amber lights signaled the end of the test. Erica flipped up the dark lenses from her goggles and tried to focus on maintaining good flight posture while the ceiling and floor returned to their normal positions. When she felt the fan shut down, she lowered her legs and fluttered to the floor. If not for the harness, she might have collapsed, but she let the harness take the strain of holding her upright as she fought to catch her breath.

The technician hurried over and released Erica from her harness, escorting her to the nearby examination table. A member of the Angels' medical staff ran diagnostic tests, checking blood pressure, oxygen levels, heart rate and so on. Once the medic gave her a clean bill of health, some water and fruit, and an appointment for a follow-up, she was allowed off the examination table and was aided over to a padded chair next to the technician's desk. She sat there, feeling her muscles slowly begin to relax from the strain, and waited for the technician to return. He wandered back with two sets of papers and a puzzled look on his face.

"I've got your results here. The first set is from your 'daylight' flight and the second is from your 'Cloud' flight. Rather remarkable, if I do say so myself."

"So I did all right?"

"You did fine—if you're a cat with multiple lives. During the daylight obstacle course, you managed to follow the pattern with a score of eighty-five percent. There were only five or six instances where you failed to react to a change in flying conditions within the recommended time and three of those, you probably would have corrected just in time to miss the obstacle."

"That's not too bad."

"That's not too bad if you ignore the fact you would have died at least three times hitting them at that speed. Still, considering it was the first time you ran that particular obstacle course, you did well."

"And the Cloud flying?"

The technician flipped through his papers, rubbed his chin, and then shook his head. All in all, he was the perfect picture of confusion. "That's the strange part. While simulating flying within the Cloud, your score was perfect. Not only did you react well within tolerances, the test noted you began shifting to meet an oncoming obstacle before the lights changed. Normally, candidates who try to anticipate changes drive themselves into obstacles. On the other hand, you seemed to know instinctively what was coming before it even happened."

"I was trying not to guess. I tried to only change my orientation once the light changed."

"Perhaps you thought that, but according to my data, you maneuvered into the proper flight position split seconds before the lights changed. It's the oddest thing I've ever seen."

Erica started to say something else but there was a sudden flurry of activity at the doorway and a secretary scurried over to speak to her. "Lady Orisaka would like to have a word with you."

"Okay, let me get cleaned up and—"

"Regardless of your current state or what you are involved in, you are to report to her immediately. Those were her exact words. You *will* follow me." And with that, the secretary turned and walked off at high speed. Erica shrugged and stumbled off in the wake of the rapidly departing secretary. The woman never looked back to see if Erica was having issues keeping up with her. However, Erica noted where she was heading and guessed Lady Orisaka was in her regular office. She forced herself to try and keep up, resting a hand on the wall as necessary to keep her balance on her shaky limbs.

After a few minutes, she caught up with the secretary waiting near the office doorway. The secretary looked down her nose as if offended Erica hadn't kept up and then walked in, announcing Erica's presence. Erica heard a muffled reply and the secretary waved her through the outer office into the meeting room.

Lady Orisaka pointed to a chair at the table and waited for Erica to get seated. She motioned to her aide, who brought over an envelope and set it down in front of Erica. Erica stared at it in confusion and then looked up at her employer.

When the older woman spoke, there was no questioning the mixture of surprise and anger in her voice. "Miss Halgrim, can you please explain this?"

"I'm sorry, Lady Orisaka. I just came from the test lab. Can I please explain what?"

"Your invitation to dine with the Coritanian ambassador this evening."

Erica looked at her employer as if she had sprouted a second head that was speaking a foreign language. "My what?"

Lady Orisaka sat back down at her desk, folding her hands in front of her face and glaring at Erica over her interlocked nails. "This arrived a little while ago addressed to me. It specifically requests I lift your flight restriction to allow you to join the ambassador at his residence in the Aerie this evening. Halgrim, you and I need to have a little discussion."

Erica was slipping her wings on when she heard the door to the launch room open. She spotted Lady Orisaka speaking to one of the technicians as she finished tightening the harness holding the wings to her body. A command rang out from the head technician and, as one, the technicians filed out of the room, leaving the area to the two women. Erica gave her harness one last tug and walked over to her employer.

"You remember my instructions?"

Erica nodded. "Yes, ma'am. Go directly to the Coritanian embassy, mingle with the guests, listen closely, speak little, leave as soon as I politely can, and come straight back here."

"Very good. At least you listen when I'm here."

"I listen to you often. I am not used to receiving quite this much attention from my employer."

169

The older woman paused and walked to a small bench nearby. She motioned for Erica to follow her. "Halgrim, this is not a normal situation. I believe in giving my flight leaders and flight commanders as much leeway with their personnel as possible, so I can focus on the big picture. However, you have become part of the biggest picture this organization has dealt with since I created the Angels."

"I'm sorry to have caused so much trouble, ma'am."

Lady Orisaka gave her a warm smile. "You are not the cause of the problem, Halgrim. If you were, I would have fired you long ago. Still, there is no question tonight's invitation has something to do with the unfortunate incident that provoked the events of the past few weeks."

Erica decided to share some of the ambassador's last conversation with her to Lady Katsumi. "You are probably correct there, ma'am. During our flight back from the camp, the ambassador expressed an interest in speaking to me about his daughter's death in a place he was sure certain people couldn't listen in. I think he's highly concerned by the Black Watch's involvement in this issue. Although, a formal dinner does seem a little overboard."

"Be careful, Halgrim. There are more things going on that you realize. I have gone to great lengths to cultivate the Coritanian ambassador's good graces. I intend to open a branch of the Angels in his capital city by this time next year. I cannot openly defy him, but I do not condone this dinner engagement. He is not content to work within the confines of the Southwatch legal system to discover the truth behind his daughter's death. I am afraid he may do something, or attempt to do something that will put both himself and you at risk. I fear this is not simply a social call."

Erica nodded and then set her face in a serious expression. "I promise not to do anything to embarrass the company while I am there. This invitation caught me off guard too."

Katsumi looked at her, a tired but honest smile still on her face. "I'm certain you will do fine, Halgrim. Attending a formal dinner will draw less attention than if he asked for your presence alone at his embassy. Remember, you are attending this as a representative of the Angels, so your manner and speech must be circumspect. You may rest assured the Black Watch will be there, uninvited of course. Nor would it surprise me to find agents from other countries there in an 'unofficial' capacity. You may be approached by a number of people for various reasons. Trust no one—no matter how friendly they seem.

Also, we still have no idea who kidnapped you. There's no guarantee they will not make another attempt. It could happen en route, on your way back home, or even inside the embassy. Be alert."

"Am I still allowed to enjoy myself?" Erica asked, trying to lighten the mood.

"Within reason, yes." Lady Orisaka nodded slightly before continuing. "Under normal circumstances, being invited to an embassy dinner is one of the social highlights of a person's life. The event will be glamorous and you may never have a chance to meet people of power and authority in a relaxed setting like this again. It will be almost fairy tale–like in some ways, but do not let your guard down. It's unfortunate there are so many cross-currents going on right now. If I could send an escort, I would, but since the embassy is considered Coritanian territory we cannot send armed personnel there. We're not even allowed to add shock sticks to your wings. If you get into trouble, you'll have to fly your way out."

Erica pulled herself to attention. "I understand. I'll do my best to avoid any situation that may arise."

"I'm sure you'll make us proud, Halgrim. We'll speak again when you return."

Erica stood and watched as Lady Orisaka left the launch room, and then saw the technicians scurrying back in to resume work. The head technician gave her wings one last examination and nodded in approval. He motioned to the launch pad on the roof and Erica followed him through the large glass doors at the end of the room. He took one last set of readings from his test equipment and then gave her the signal to go.

Erica walked to the edge of the launch platform, which resembled many of the other balconies in the surrounding buildings with one major exception—no railing. She waved to the tech, pulled her goggles tight over her eyes, and then stepped off into the dimming light. The wind rushed past her as she plunged headfirst toward the street below. She made sure her posture was good and then flipped her wings open, catching the rushing wind in the feathers. She felt the wings snap taut as they bit into the wind and then the thrill as she shot upward, climbing with strong beats, using the momentum she'd built during her fall to propel her toward the pulsating darkness overhead.

She climbed upward in a lazy circle, gaining height with every beat of her wings. It was going to be a challenge going through the

Cloud in the dim light of late afternoon, but the joy of just getting to fly again was worth the challenge. She checked her rebreather and saw she had a full reserve on the cleansing chemicals. However, she remembered Lady Orisaka's instructions and soon began climbing as quickly as she could toward her dinner engagement in Downtown Aerie.

A few minutes after beginning her ascent, she broke through the lower layers of the Dark Cloud. The swirling winds were working in her favor, pushing the Cloud around and revealing obstacles before she encountered them. She began a typical climb, zigzagging through the various walkways and overhangs that jutted out over the boulevards many floors below. She found familiar landmarks in the half twilight and decided to stick with the normal route instead of the shortcuts she had learned during her time with the Angels. If there was a chance in running into trouble, it was probably on the less-traveled routes. Even if Lady Orisaka couldn't send an escort, Erica suspected Angel Security was positioned along her flight plan . . . just in case.

She checked her rebreather one more time and saw she had more than enough time for her trip up and back if she didn't linger. She spotted a familiar sight, an old forgotten gargoyle that knelt at the ninety-third floor of the Amber Star building. She always admired the carved gargoyles lining many of the buildings' corners. Some were ornamental and some served as rain spouts directing overflow away from the buildings onto the streets below. Seeing this particular gargoyle told her the sky was clear above to the top of the Cloud. She swooped by and patted the acid-stained statue for luck and angled up until she was in a vertical climb.

Breaking through the Cloud, Erica was treated to a sight few Darksiders ever had the opportunity to enjoy—the sun setting against the darkening blue sky, the rays of the sun gleaming against the underside of the bessum-lined airships, sending golden rays ricocheting across the top of the Cloud. She glanced to the south and saw a paddle wheeler in the bay, struggling against the outgoing tide as it tried to reach the Docks before dark. A few stars twinkled in the far eastern sky and, above, the golden airships of the Downtown Aerie began to glow bloodred in the dying light of the sunset.

Now, there's *an ominous omen.*

Erica began a lazy spiral to gain height and soon rose through the mooring cables and walkways to reach open air above Downtown

Aerie. She spotted the green and gold lanterns that identified the Coritanian embassy and angled down to the landing ledge near the main walkway.

A man in Coritani livery opened the gate on the landing just before she arrived. "Good evening, Miss Halgrim. I am Esteban and I am to be your aide for the evening. I will guide you to your changing room and guard your gear while you are dining."

"Thank you, Esteban. I've never had an aide before. I'm usually the one fetching things for my superiors."

"Trust me, Miss Halgrim," Esteban said, with a conspiratorial tone in his voice, "tonight you are one of the spotlighted guests."

Chapter Nineteen

Erica hesitated at that news. "Uh… maybe I should…I mean …"

Esteban laughed. "Not to worry, Miss Halgrim. Just relax and be the charming young woman I suspect you are. After all, the ambassador seemed quite taken with you. He suspected you might be uncomfortable this evening, so he assigned me to make everything as easy for you as I can."

"Thank you, Esteban. I don't mind admitting I'm nervous about tonight. Lady Orisaka impressed upon me to be on my best behavior."

"I'm certain she did. But why are we conversing out here on this drafty balcony? Come in and let me escort you to your changing room. Do you require any assistance getting out of that contraption of yours?"

Esteban's question caught her off guard. "Oh no, I'll be fine. I've taken this on and off so often since I started training, it's second nature now."

"Very good, miss." Esteban held open the door that led into the airship as she entered. The hallway was lined with a warm, dark wood that was not native to this area and it had fine, luxurious woolen carpeting leading deeper into the airship. The servant led her down the corridor until they reached her room. He held the door for her until she entered and shut it behind her, remaining on station in the hall. It wasn't as large as her bedroom back at the Angels' facility, but it was sumptuous for an airship's stateroom. She hurried out of her flight suit and cleaned up, washing the soot and grime from the Cloud off her skin and hair.

There was a knock at the door and Erica heard a woman's voice. "Miss Halgrim? I've here to help you with your dressing."

Erica inched the door open and saw a young woman in Coritani livery standing a respectful distance from the door. "You're what?"

The young woman spoke in a soft voice. "I am Raquel and I am here to aid you. Esteban thought since this was your first dinner at the embassy, you might want some assistance with your clothes and makeup."

Erica eased the door open enough for Raquel to enter. The young woman immediately grabbed one of the large towels and began

174

wiping down Erica's shoulders and hair, while the Angel squirmed from the attention. "Really, Raquel, I can towel myself off."

"Yes, Miss, but it will be easier to get your hair ready this way. It's already so short, it's almost dry. I need to set it quickly. Please do sit down."

Erica fumed but allowed herself to be led to the vanity. Raquel began putting curlers and rods into her hair and then began setting a number of different bottles on the vanity, picking some out and discarding the others. She took one look at Erica's face, saw something she didn't like, and immediately grabbed a bottle of some clear liquid and began daubing around Erica's eyes.

"It is so unfortunate you must fly through the Cloud. Your skin is beautiful, but the Cloud leaves such a resin behind." She paused and then smiled. "There. Now the makeup will set perfectly."

The next half hour was either the most excruciating or the most luxurious time of Erica's life. She chafed at being washed, combed, patted, poked, and then squeezed into a corset before Raquel helped her into a turquoise-colored sleeveless bustle dress with large poofs at the shoulders. After adding waves into her short red hair, Raquel applied her makeup, helped her with yet another pair of high heels taller than Erica was used to, attached a diamond choker around her neck, and placed a single strand of diamonds on Erica's head like a small circlet. As a final touch, Raquel gave her long, white gloves that rose above her elbows and a fan embellished with angel wings to carry.

Raquel took a few steps back and looked Erica over from head to toe. "There. Now you are ready for your grand entrance."

"If I don't kill myself trying to walk in these shoes. My dress was long enough, did I really need heels?"

"It is the latest fashion. One cannot be seen in last season's clothes and make a good impression."

Erica decided that she appreciated her simple flight suit and flat boots more than ever. Still, she admitted, she looked like a princess in the full-length mirror. It was too bad Michael couldn't see her this evening, although, she admitted, social etiquette wasn't his strong suit.

Raquel let herself out and a few moments later, Esteban knocked at the door. She found him standing there with his hands clasped behind his back. He nodded approvingly. "Dinner will be served in about an hour. You'll want to take this opportunity to mingle with the guests before the actual event begins."

"Thank you for everything, Esteban. Is there a way to secure this room after I leave?"

The older man paused before answering. "I have the key to lock the door, but I assumed you would want me to guard your belongings while you were at dinner."

"Do you suspect something might happen to my gear?"

"Absolutely not, Miss Halgrim," Esteban answered, raising his hands in front of him. "Still, with the number of visitors on the ship this evening. I cannot vouch for everyone present. The ambassador made it clear you are to be provided every possible service to ensure your comfort . . . and your safety."

She smiled at Esteban's ferocious look when he said that last line. "Very well, I entrust you with my well-being this evening." She moved closer and dropped her voice, forcing him to lean closer. "Any last-minute suggestions? I've never attended a soiree like this except as part of a performing group. What's on the agenda and what's expected from me?"

He smiled, enjoying this role. "First off is the reception. As I said, it's a chance for people to meet and greet, but do be careful. Since you are the new person, most will be interested in you and not always for good reasons. Gossip is air in the Aerie, after all."

"Gotcha. Keep all my responses polite and to the point."

"Indeed. Dinner will be a multiple-course affair. There will be small talk throughout the meal, but restrict your conversation to those closest to you. Afterward, the guests will return to the lounge. However, many of the small groups you will see have been prearranged, so do not attempt to enter one without being invited. This is the time the ambassador may wish to speak to you privately. I know that's why he invited you, but circumstances may dictate what happens. If after an hour the ambassador has not summoned you, you're free to return to your quarters or leave. Although"—he paused again and chuckled—"I can't imagine flying through the Cloud in the dark. I've taken a few glider rides during the day and visibility was bad then. I can't imagine what it would be like trying to fly through that now."

"It's not as bad as you might think, Esteban. Mostly we fly predesignated routes after dark. We practice them enough during daylight hours, so it's almost second nature by the time we try it at night. Besides, the Cloud has a strange luminescence. Depending on the weather, the Cloud is brighter when it's dark than during the day. However, I will plan on staying overnight unless the party breaks up early. I think Lady Orisaka would be happier if I was not traversing Southwatch by myself at night."

Esteban chuckled, drawing a sharp stare from Erica. "Ah, yes, the ambassador mentioned your recent misadventures. Now, don't look at me like that. He did not go into details, but believe me, anything associated with the Angels of Steel makes the gossip rounds these days. Ever since the dreadful incident at the *Temple*, I'm afraid all of Aerie has been spending good money getting the latest gossip from Darkside."

"I . . . see."

"But, as I said, I am more than happy to remain here on guard, should you desire. You should hurry, though. The guests are arriving in the lounge as we speak. You *really* do not want to be the last to make an appearance. Just tell the servant at the entryway who you are. He'll announce you before you enter."

Erica felt a sharp knot in her stomach at the idea of everyone staring at her in this outfit. "So, you don't mind watching my gear?"

"My dear, that's my job—to make sure your stay is enjoyable and worry-free. Go and have a wonderful evening."

Erica nodded gratefully and hurried to the lounge. She managed not to break into a run in her desire to get there, or to break her ankle in these new shoes. Stopping at a strategically placed mirror, she made sure she was presentable and then found the servant waiting by the door.

"Hi, I'm Erica Halgrim."

The servant checked a list and nodded. "Ah, yes, Miss Erica Halgrim of the Angels of Steel, guest of the ambassador. I must say, I don't recall anyone other than your company's owner attending one of these dinners. I hope you'll have a good time."

Before Erica could ask him about Lady Orisaka's earlier visits, he stepped forward and spoke just loud enough to be heard over the small string orchestra playing in the far corner. "Miss Erica Halgrim of the Angels of Steel." There was a small pause as those already in the lounge turned to acknowledge her presence. A few of the ladies lifted their feathered fans, hiding their mouths as they exchanged words, while some gentlemen smiled and bowed as she walked toward the center of the room. She had reached one of the couches when a young man walked over to her.

"Excuse me, Miss Halgrim. Might I offer you some punch?"

Erica noted the young man was impeccably dressed, but she was certain she'd seen him before. Recalling Esteban's suggestions, she allowed herself to be led to the far side of the room to a table loaded with drinks and finger foods. A large ice sculpture of an eagle dominated the table. The young man deftly snagged two cups of punch from one of the servers and handed one to her.

Erica took a sip before speaking. "I'm sorry, but you look familiar. Have we had the pleasure of meeting before?"

He laughed before responding. "Not officially, but I believe we have a mutual friend in common. Christina and I met at your performance at the *Temple*, if you recall."

"Oh my goodness, you're the Air Corps officer Christina's been dating." She paused as his name came to her. "Geoffrey Kingston. I didn't recognize you out of your uniform."

He laughed again. "They do let me out on occasion. However, my commanding officer likes us to attend these functions from time to time. Says it's good preparation for future promotions. Hopefully, you won't get too bored. These things tend to drag on for hours."

"This is my first time attending a party in the Aerie. I doubt I'll be bored."

He gave her a knowing look. "These parties are seldom exciting, but sometimes conversations do get spicy. It's generally safer when they're boring." He glanced around the room as if surveying a battlefield before taking a sip of his drink.

She lowered her voice and spoke in a conspiratorial tone, trying to match her companion's mood. "That sounds ominous. Are the ambassador's parties that dangerous?"

"Only to the reputation, Miss Halgrim, only to the reputation. Keep your wits about you at all times. That's why I suggested the punch instead of wine or champagne. You never know who's trying to make points with someone you've never met at your expense. One of these events cost me a promotion simply because I held a door open for the wrong young lady. It seems someone who wanted to spend time with me assumed we were a couple. She mentioned a few words to someone who knew my former commanding officer. A few weeks later, the promotion list came out and there were five names on the promotion list. I was number six."

"That's horrible."

"That, Miss Halgrim, is life in the Aerie."

He started to say more when two middle-aged women bustled over like miniature hurricanes. "Ah, Geoffrey, my good boy. I was *so* hoping you would be here. These parties are *so* boring when you're on duty. I think you've missed the last four of these and we did so miss you."

"My duties do not always allow me to attend, Lady Miranda, which is unfortunate since it deprives me of the joy of your company. And Lady Gwen, you look lovely this evening. May I please present Miss Erica Halgrim. She represents the Angels of Steel this evening."

The second lady held up a pair of glasses mounted on a long stick and gave Erica a once-over. She seemed perturbed Geoffrey had been speaking to her, but she quickly hid that behind a smile that failed to reach her eyes. "Oh, you must work for that delightful Lady Orisaka. I do so love watching the Angels perform at our celebrations. Which division of her company do you run?"

Erica returned the woman's smile and ensured her voice remained cheerful. "I'm in Deliveries, my lady."

"I see. I say, those women are so brave the way they flit about the city on those metallic wings. It's not very ladylike, if you ask me, but I'm sure when one doesn't have real opportunities, one does what one must."

Erica gritted her teeth in her smile. "Indeed, my lady."

Lady Miranda held the back of her hand up to her mouth before chuckling. "Now, Gwen, not everyone can marry into the family of the largest ship owner in Southwatch. There are only so many eligible bachelors, you know."

Lady Gwen nodded conspiratorially. "And we're working to keep that number down too."

They both laughed and Geoffrey gave Erica a glance as if to say *See what I mean?* He visibly nodded to Erica and then addressed the two women. "Now, ladies, perhaps we should find a seat? I'm dying to hear what you've been doing since I last saw you."

Erica resolved to send Geoffrey a gift for rescuing her before she could get Lady Orisaka or herself into trouble. She had the servant refill her glass of punch and then wandered about the room, visiting with people here and there as the room filled with guests. She took Geoffrey's lead and confined herself into letting the nobles and aristocrats talk about themselves and spent the majority of the time listening to the latest gossip. Occasionally, she had to deftly escape from a few of the nobles who made subtle, and not-so-subtle, hints about rendezvousing after dinner. After a bit, she spotted the disapproving looks from the wives of these same gentlemen and attached herself to a group of ladies so busy discussing those who hadn't arrived yet they hardly noticed Erica. She decided it was a safer occupation than visiting with the men—young or otherwise.

To Erica's relief, the ambassador and his entourage appeared and dinner was announced. Erica followed the crowd to the door where a servant soon guided her to her table. She looked in horror at the table layout with six different forks, three different knives, and so on. But, as the courses arrived, she followed the lead of the closet person and survived the dinner with no blatant faux pas.

Again, most of the dinner conversation circled around those who were sitting at other tables. Still, being the newcomer, her dining companions seemed interested in what Erica did. She knew no one wanted to hear about delivering packages, so she focused on her recent experiences with the research department. That caught the attention of a couple of the men sitting near her and they began to wax at length about their experiences in the Imperial Air Corps and the Imperial Navy. The older gentlemen went on about how airships just weren't built up to standards these days and so on. Erica listened politely and nodded at the right times, glad to have the attention off her again.

The dinner wound to a close after the sixth course and one of the servants came by announcing dessert and coffee would be served in the lounge. Erica began following the group when a servant tapped her on the arm and asked her to follow him. She left via a different exit and found herself in a cozy room with a small fireplace. The room was done in dark woods and heavy furniture. It felt out of place on an airship, but comfortable all the same.

There was a soft knock at the door and then the ambassador and Geoffrey entered. "Ah, my dear, I'm so glad you were able to accept my invitation. I apologize for the short notice. I gather from the rather curt reply I received from the lovely Lady Orisaka she would have preferred prior notice, but it couldn't be helped. Things are moving and, well, some things can't be helped."

"She hates being caught off guard, Your Excellency. However, I appreciate the invitation. I've had a wonderful time so far."

The ambassador plopped down in the chair behind the desk and motioned for the other two to sit. "That's kind of you to say, my dear—kind, albeit a polite untruth. These parties are dreadfully dull, but they're expected, so I try to be a good host. Nevertheless, I hope you'll be able to visit again under less 'formal' circumstances. Oh, and bring that gentleman scientist you hang out with along with you. I suspect Geoffrey and he would have much to talk about."

Erica tried not to let her mouth hang open. "Ah . . . thank you, Your Excellency. I'm certain we'd love to visit again. Perhaps a smaller meal too." She smiled at him and then touched her stomach. "After all, I do have to maintain flying weight."

The ambassador laughed. "Yes, I remember those days on active duty when I had to watch my weight." He glanced between Geoffrey and Erica and then continued. "You seem surprised Geoffrey is here."

"Yes, Your Excellency. After all, I only met him earlier and he's a member of the Imperial Air Corps. I really didn't expect to see him here."

"Please, call me Pavel in here. 'Your Excellency' seems so overly formal for such an intimate gathering."

Geoffrey spoke up. "I'm afraid appearances can be deceiving, Miss Halgrim. I *am* in the Imperial Air Corps, but I am neither a pilot nor a crew member. I'm actually with Air Intelligence Wing. We are providing assistance to the ambassador regarding the unfortunate incident we're all familiar with. My position was already known to the ambassador, as are many of his people here in Southwatch and elsewhere."

"You're *not* working for the baron?"

Geoffrey smiled before answering. "Since he is a loyal subject to his Imperial Majesty, I'm not working against him. But I do not report to him nor do I report to the Black Watch."

Erica blushed and swallowed hard before responding. "Ah, you've heard about that."

"The intelligence world is a small one, Miss Halgrim. We don't always like each other but we know each other and word gets around. Besides"—he smiled at her—"Christina has been very worried about you."

"Please, both of you, call me Erica."

Geoffrey smiled again and she caught herself enjoying that sight. Then a thought crossed her mind. *He had better not be using Chris to get information on the Angels. If he hurts her, he better find a place to hide because he'll learn what the meaning of hurt really is.*

He must have seen her expression change because he answered her unspoken question. "And no, I met your roommate before the incident. I would have asked her out anyway. However, it did give me an opportunity to keep an eye on you as best I could, I will admit that."

"I'll trust what you say—for now."

The ambassador broke in, rubbing his hands together. "Now to the reason I brought you both here. Miss Hal—" He stopped himself and then continued. "Erica. I have spent a great deal of time and money to get to the bottom of my daughter's death. While I don't know the name of the young man who piloted it, the gyrocopter she fell from belonged to a pirate ship—one I believe you're familiar with."

"The *Bloody Lynx*?"

"The very same. However, my sources suggest my daughter was on that gyroscope voluntarily. To my surprise, she was dating a young man without my knowledge. Whether she knew of his profession is of little consequence now. But the manner of her death concerns me."

Erica nodded. "I met this young man briefly. He was scared away before we could talk, but he claimed it was, and was not, an accident. He implied he had to take evasive maneuvers and she fell during those maneuvers. I do not know if he was trying to avoid an accident or something more sinister. I believe he did not intend for her to fall."

"I can believe that. According to your statement, there were two gyrocopters following the black one into the Cloud. I believe you even described it as an aggressive pursuit?"

She thought back to that day, then slowly nodded. "They were following closely, but they did not seem to be with the lead gyro. My first instinct was it felt like a pursuit." She paused for a second and then let a self-depreciating grin form on her face. "I'm sorry if I sounded conceited there. We practice synchronized flying and flying in formation so often, I can tell whether people are working with or against each other just watching how they fly."

"I'd be more surprised if you couldn't," Geoffrey said, as he unrolled a map on the ambassador's desk.

Erica waited, wondering what was going on. She helped clear the desk and found some items to secure the corners of the map. She recognized the area shown—the Angels' training camp was on the southern border and the test site was around the middle. Geoffrey picked up a ruler from the desk and began pointing at the map.

"You know these two places. Can you point out the spot where you encountered the *Bloody Lynx* when it was airborne?"

"It was cloudy, but as best I can figure, Sophie and I encountered it about . . . here." She tapped the map to the northwest of the test site. "We were taking a random route to get away from the camp. We were surprised an airship was out in that weather."

The ambassador examined the map closer. "That also ties in with the information my sources gave me. It is believed the pirates have a base somewhere in this region in the Oghden Mountains. In fact, if I were a pirate airship, I'd consider using this formation here." He pointed at a place on the map and Erica could make out a faint label on an oddly shaped ridge called "The Whale."

"What makes that so special?" she asked, looking from one to the other.

"The land flattens out here just behind the whale's head," the ambassador replied, pointing at the other symbols on the map. "In fact, according to the map, there are a number of caves, some quite large. It's conceivable one could land an airship there, deflate the cells, hook the ship up to a steam tractor, and pull it into the caves to keep it safe from accidental observation."

The ambassador rubbed his hands together. "This reminds me of my days as a scout pilot. Coritani was at war with Traveria and I spent a lot of time flying around mountain ranges looking for enemy formations. We built a base similar to this for our scout fleet. Geoffrey could probably tell you all about it. We know Dalriada had people watching the war on both sides."

"Now, Ambassador, you know I can neither confirm nor deny any Dalriadan activities, even those from thirty years ago," Geoffrey said with a smile. Erica could tell this was part of their typical give-and-take from the ease each of the men felt with the other.

"Of *course* you can't, Geoffrey. You see, Erica, sometimes the best secrets are the ones both sides know but cannot admit." He smiled even more broadly before continuing. "It's one of the best kept secrets of diplomacy. We all know each other's secrets, but we pretend we don't so we have 'negotiating points.' Diplomacy is about admitting you know that they know that you know, so let's figure out the best way to make our rulers get along."

The intelligence officer poured himself a whisky from a cut crystal bottle on the shelf near the ambassador. "That's a very cynical view of the world to have, Pavel."

"Nonsense, Geoffrey, it's really quite refreshing. Cuts through a lot of the acrimony and the faux indignation. I need X, you need Y. I know you need Y, you know I need X. So, the negotiations become how much X can I get from you for the least amount of Y I can spend. It's just business at the ultimate macro level."

"As I said—a *very* cynical look at life."

Erica saw they were about to slip back into a running argument and spoke up. "But, what does this have to do with the *Bloody Lynx*?"

"Oh yes, quite right." The ambassador reached into his desk, pulled out two sealed bundles, and slid them onto the desk as Geoffrey rolled up the map and sat it on top of the bundle. "I think it would be wise to present this map and these bundles to Lady Orisaka as quickly as possible. I will make arrangements for Geoffrey to visit her in a day or so. Of course, what Dalriada does with this information is beyond my control. After all, I am only a visitor here."

He smiled at her before continuing. "Still, it wouldn't surprise me to hear rumors of the Imperial Air Corps and the Angels of Steel cooperating on a mission of national importance in the near future. In the meantime, the other set of documents there are in regards to Lady Orisaka's business proposal. I have received word back from the Coritani government that they are disposed to look favorably on her proposal—especially since it went forward with my highest endorsement."

Erica bowed to the ambassador. "She will be pleased to hear that."

"Quite. Anyway, I think if you hurry, you may meet this young man again and, with any luck, find the truth of what happened that day. Regardless, I *must* know what happened. You and Geoffrey are my best hopes. I would recommend you return directly to your quarters. Whether you remain until morning or leave soon is up to you, but I wouldn't return to the party. I don't mean to make disparaging remarks about my guests, but personally, I trust some of them about as far as I could throw the *Temple*. Come to think of it, I think returning to your mistress this evening might be safest."

"Safest? Flying through the Cloud at night might be safer than sleeping on this ship?"

The ambassador shook his head sadly. "My dear, how badly do you want to wake up in the morning? I trust my staff, but that's as far as it goes. I make no guarantee of your safety once word gets out about those documents—and I guarantee word *will* get out."

Chapter Twenty

Erica waited on the entryway to the airship while Esteban helped her get her wings settled into the place. "Damn, it is dark out here, miss. Are you certain the ambassador advised you to fly home in this?"

"He was quite adamant, Esteban. Don't worry. Like I said earlier, we practice these runs all the time. I don't normally fly at night by myself, but it shouldn't be that bad. As long as I enter the Cloud at the right spot, it's pretty straightforward."

The older man looked rather dubious, but he knew there was nothing he could do to change the situation. He insisted she explain her safety procedures and ensured all her straps were tightened and buckles fastened. After he couldn't come up with another reason to delay her flight, he gave her a quick, fatherly hug and retreated to the open door of the airship.

"Do be careful, Miss Erica. I've gotten rather fond of you. We would love to have you come back under more pleasant circumstances."

Erica nodded and adjusted her goggles. She plugged them into the power unit on her chest and waited for them to warm up. The night took on a familiar greenish glow as the crystal lenses reacted to the electrical stimulation and amplified the light almost a thousandfold. It was another of Crystal's inventions, one that had saved more than one Angel who'd navigated the skies of Southwatch at night.

While the goggles began to focus and sharpen the images around her, she tested her wings. While she was certain Esteban prevented anyone from coming near her gear, she still went through her preflight checklist with a fine-tooth comb. Only once she was satisfied did she step to the end of the landing and launch herself into the inky blackness below her.

She let herself fall until she was certain she'd cleared the guy wires and mooring ropes holding the airships in place before spreading her wings to catch the air. The metal-and-ceramic wings bent slightly between the uprush of the air and the downward momentum of her body. Her wings begin to push upward, regaining some of the height she'd lost in her plunge. She circled Downtown to ensure her goggles were working fine. After her third circuit, she spotted her entry point. She checked her breathing apparatus one last time before swooping into the swirling blackness.

Regardless of what she'd said to reassure Estaban, it was a completely different experience to enter the Cloud at night. She thought back to the various tests she'd taken with Crystal. That same sensation of almost knowing where the turns were before she reached them came back and she let her training carry her downward. Her goggles magnified what little light managed to break through the Cloud, but for the most part, she was flying blind.

Staring ahead, she suddenly had to wing over to the right to avoid a large stone gargoyle that appeared on the edge of her peripheral vision. A shiver ran through her at the near miss. She couldn't believe she'd forgotten about something like that.

Wait a minute. Unless I'm on the wrong course that shouldn't be there.

She cautiously flew upward to examine the gargoyle. She approached the spot she'd seen it, but there was nothing there. She checked the ledge, but there was no sign anything had ever rested there. If it had fallen, there should have been rock chips or something but the ledge was clean.

You're imagining things, Erica. Calm down and stay on course. Gargoyles don't just get up and move. It was a trick of the dark and the goggles.

She folded her wings and let herself pick up speed as she plunged into the darkness. Suddenly, the brick of the ledge she'd just been hovering above shattered. Seconds later, the echo of a shot reached her. She snapped her wings into their widest spread to halt her descent and then slowly flew into the shadow of an overhang, glancing upward.

Gargoyles are one thing. Someone shooting at me is another. Who the hell would be in the Cloud this time of night? Why are they shooting at me?

The package of documents that hung in her pouch silently accused her of being naïve. Whoever it was must have followed her into the Cloud. No one could wait there on the off-chance she'd come this way. Somehow they had a way of tracking her.

Erica was glad she insisted on taking her regular wings instead of the ceremonial pair Lady Orisaka had suggested. Even without the shock sticks, she was at least comfortable with these wings. Ceremonial versions were not designed for heavy stress.

That's only going to help a bit. That was a high-powered rifle. They've definitely got me in range.

She pushed off from the wall at a sharp angle and felt the rush of wind as another rifle round cracked off the brick wall near her. To her horror, she heard a stuttering noise and instinctively ducked as more masonry pelted her. Someone had an automatic rifle here too. Realizing she had to dodge at least two pursuers, she dove hard into the darkness, hugging one of the walls to minimize the chance of them catching her between them.

She fought to keep the picture of the city in her mind as she swerved from side to side and from building to building, trying to find the shortest and safest way out of the Cloud into the city below. However, whichever direction she went, it seemed one or the other pursuer was right there behind her. It was almost as if they knew the city as well as she did.

At first, she was afraid her unknown assailants were herding her toward another group until she realized the bullets were too close. They were trying to kill her. Her only chance was to hide and then figure out a path to safety. Simply running blind through the Cloud was only going to get her killed.

With a sudden push of her wings, she flipped onto her side and squeezed down a narrow passage between two of the nearby buildings. She dropped a few floors and then swung around the building, coming to rest next to a gargoyle. Folding her wings tightly around her, she tried to blend into the deep shadows surrounding the stone figure.

She didn't like to admit it, but after a night of dining and conversation, she wasn't at her flying best. The adrenaline rush was keeping her one step ahead of her pursuers, but that could only last so long. She could *not* afford to get into a long fight with anyone.

If it wasn't for the Cloud, they'd have caught me by now. It's limiting where I can go, but it's limiting their ability to coordinate. If I can keep ahead of them, I should be able to break out of the Cloud soon, but I'll have to get down to street level fast. I can't let them catch me in Midtown air. The walkways are farther apart and I'd be an easy target.

She heard a slow beat of wings nearby and pulled herself tight against the gargoyle. A shadowy figure slowly flapped down the street. Erica recognized the style of wings her pursuer was using—it was about three generations behind hers, which meant they probably were Imperial military. She'd heard rumors a number of military warehouses had been raided near the capital, but she hadn't expected them to turn up in Southwatch.

She watched as the flyer did lazy circles to remain in place, obviously waiting for something. A few minutes later, she heard the familiar "whop" of rotor blades and a dark one-seat gyrocopter circled around a building and headed toward the waiting flyer.

"Any sign of her?" the winged man asked, struggling against the wash of the gyrocopter.

"Nothing. She may have headed farther into the center of town. I'll head toward the Steamworks. You circle around and look for her. If you see her, fire twice and I'll head toward you."

"Don't let her get away."

A cruel chuckle came from the gyrocopter pilot. "Don't worry. I have no intention of returning to Solly empty-handed."

The gyrocopter rose into the air and pivoted toward the center of the Downtown area. The winged man waited until his companion was lost to sight in the swirling miasma and flapped down a side street before disappearing around the corner of a building. Erica waited until she was certain they weren't lurking around before easing out onto the ledge and then diving down into the waiting darkness.

She began making her way down toward street level, dodging from walkway to walkway as she descended. She pulled up short as she encountered a net strung between two of the walkways. The netting was close-knit and there were items sitting near the middle that could have fallen from Aerie.

As if I didn't have enough to worry about, I hadn't even considered scavengers. It wouldn't surprise me if those were sticky nets too. She shook her head to get the image of human-sized spiders out of her mind and then checked her surroundings. *I may have lost them, but I may have lost myself too. I need to find something familiar so I can get down from here without crashing headlong into something.*

She carefully made her way through the maze of netting until another shot ricocheted off a nearby walkway. She dove to her right and zigzagged down a gap between two buildings as she heard two shots in rapid succession and knew the gyrocopter would be returning. She flew around a corner as another shot whipped past her. She spotted a narrow passage and landed. Folding her wings behind her, she raced along the narrow ledge, hoping she could reach the far end before her pursuer spotted her because there was no place to hide in the narrow corridor.

She neared the end of the passage when something inside her screamed *Stop!*

She dropped and slid on her rear, pressing her hands against the wall to slow her down. The edge was coming closer as she slid on the cold stone, but she was slowing. She held her breath and then realized she had come to a stop with her feet hanging out over the edge.

She scrambled back into the passage, ducked down to minimize her shape, and glanced around. No one was waiting for her but just beyond the exit to the passageway hung a glistening rope net between two buildings. If she had dove over the ledge as she had planned, she would have been hopelessly ensnared in the webbing, just waiting for her pursuers or the scavengers to come get her.

She checked her rebreathing equipment and saw she had approximately an hour of clean air left. If she had gotten trapped, she probably would have suffocated in the toxic fumes before anyone found her. She felt a cold shiver run down her back and thanked the Goddess for that premonition.

She stepped out onto the ledge running around the building and pressed her back against the wall to help maintain her balance. She sidestepped toward the corner and then knelt there, looking out over the intersection. She did her best to pretend to be just another gargoyle as she scanned the area for her pursuers. A familiar weight in her sleeve pocket gave her an idea but it would be tricky to pull it off.

Tricky? More like insane. Still, I don't see any other way out of this. Even if I reach open air, I'm not sure I can get to street level before they pin me down. And I'm not counting on the local Rangers to come to my aid. They're too busy looking for pirates in the Aerie. No, I'm on my own here.

She needed to know where her pursuers were before she could implement her scheme, though. She spotted another gargoyle on the corner of the building across the way and frowned. Either she was completely lost or someone had been moving gargoyles around inside the Cloud. She shook her head in disgust. *Focus, Halgrim. Worry about statues when people aren't trying to kill you.*

She waited until she heard the unmistakable whop of the gyrocopter's rotor blades as it cruised nearby, looking for her. She found a loose stone on a nearby ledge and carefully threw it down the street at a building. The rock clattered along the stone facing of the building and the sound of the rotors immediately became more strident as the gyrocopter increased its speed heading toward the sound.

She flew toward the sound, acting like she was trying to sneak down the open street. When the gyrocopter turned the corner, she waited until she knew the pilot had seen her before she reacted. She spread her wings and climbed as the gyrocopter climbed after her. She continued to climb until the gyrocopter was in position, then went into a steep dive. The gyrocopter pilot pivoted the nose of the gyro down and sped after her.

She maneuvered from side to side, trying to make certain he couldn't get a clean shot at her. He snapped off a few shots, but she ignored them as she picked up speed in her dive. She felt the gyrocopter closing, but at the last second she rolled to her right and spread her wings, clawing for the sky to avoid the scavengers' net.

The gyrocopter shot past and she saw the pilot pulling frantically back on the stick as he realized what was stretched across the path ahead. It had taken her a while to hack through the net with her father's pocket knife and restring it vertically across the path. There wasn't time to react before the gyro ripped into the net. The sticky strands of rope enveloped the cockpit and wrapped themselves around the rotor. She smelled the burning gears and bearings as the rotors seized and the gyrocopter plummeted, disappearing into the Cloud below. She wasted no time flying down the street, looking for another spot to hide.

However, she wasn't quick enough.

"Stop right there. Hide-and-seek is over. Land on that ledge."

She turned to find her winged pursuer had landed on a nearby walkway. His rifle was trained on her and there was no way he could miss at that range. Erica flapped slowly over to the other end of the walkway and landed.

"That wasn't very nice, what you did to my friend. I was supposed to bring you in to see some people if possible, but I guess

I'll have to report you had a little accident. Couldn't be helped in the Cloud."

Erica glared at him through her goggles. A small bank of thicker pollution was wafting down the street at him, making it harder to see him in the dim light. "Isn't it going to be hard to explain a bullet hole in my body? I'm not sure what kind of accident I'm supposed to have that would account for that."

"Oh, there won't be any bullet holes. Now, strip your wings off."

"What?"

"See, your wings had a catastrophic failure. Like my friend, you're going to learn what it feels like to break out of the Cloud in free fall. Let's see how long you can scream as you see the ground heading toward you."

Erica crouched lower, her wings spreading almost without her consciously doing it. "That's never going to happen. You want my wings? Come and take them."

The man flipped his rifle over like a club and started advancing toward her. "Fair enough. It's not like they're going to notice a few more bruises on you when they find your body. If they ever do . . ."

Erica made a break for the edge of the walkway, but the man was quicker than she anticipated. She bent her knees and felt the butt of the rifle pass mere inches over her head. She tried to push past him but he recovered from the swing to get in her way and then kicked out, striking her in the stomach. She felt the air go out of her lungs and fell hard onto her back.

He loomed above her, aiming the rifle butt at her exposed face. She tried to roll to the side, flinching away from the strike, until she realized nothing had happened. Opening her eyes, she saw the man hoisted into the air, large hands surrounding his throat and his feet kicking feebly in the air. After a bit, his feet hung still and then his body fell to the walkway.

To her horror, a large gray being stood there, its muscular body indistinguishable from the stones of the buildings around her. It glared at her with large red eyes and its horns glistened in the dim light. She shrank away and pushed herself backward along the walkway until she was far enough away to safely scramble to her feet.

The being lifted an arm and pointed toward the ground. "Go," it said in a gravelly voice. Turning around as if she wasn't there, it picked up the man it had just killed and spread its own wings, lifting the burly man as if he weighed nothing, and slowly flapped into the darkness until he was swallowed up by the Cloud.

Erica tried hard not to scream all the way back to Angels' Headquarters.

Chapter Twenty-one

"You really saw a gargoyle?" Christina's eyes widened as she sat on Erica's bed the next morning. "That's incredible. I've heard rumors they were real, but no one ever claimed to meet one before. What was it like?"

"What was it *like*? Chris, it strangled a man with its bare hands right in front of me."

"A guy trying to kill you. It sounds like it was trying to protect you. It may not have been a knight in shining armor, but . . ."

Erica flopped back on her bed and shuddered. "We are not having this conversation, Chris. It killed someone with no more emotion on its face than you would have stepping on a bug. Actually, I've seen you try to step on a bug, so erase that image. Still, I'd really like to not talk about that."

Chris got a dreamy look on her face. "Right, you got to meet Geoffrey. Isn't he something else?"

Erica tried to choose her words carefully. "He's something. He's definitely not what he appears to be on the surface."

It was Christina's turn to flop on the bed and close her eyes. "I know. Not only is he a war hero, he's also intelligent, sensitive, and he's got plans beyond being in the military. I think there's nothing he couldn't do if he put his mind to it. I can't wait for you and Michael to join us one of these evenings."

Erica prayed she never looked that goofy when she was talking about Michael. But then again, Christina was a romantic. She sat up and glanced around the room for her shoes. "Hopefully, once all this is over, I'll be able to have normal evenings again. I swear, I'm living under a cursed star or something. Everything has been happening to *me* lately."

"Ooooh, maybe you should visit one of those fortune-tellers. She could see if someone has put the evil eye on you."

"Oh, Christina. You and your wild ideas."

Christina rolled over onto her stomach and looked at Erica. "Hey, you saw a gargoyle. Why not believe in a little magic?"

"Thanks, I'll stick to good ol' science, if you don't mind."

A knock on the door interrupted their discussion. Christina rolled off the bed to answer the door while Erica dug her shoes out from underneath her bed. She heard a squawk from Christina and then Felicia Miles's voice in the doorway. She scrambled backward and got to her feet, shoes in hand.

The head of Security hid an amused grin as Erica hopped from one foot to the other, trying to get her shoes on while standing up. "Halgrim, please sit down and put your shoes on right. I don't want you injuring yourself on my account."

"Yes, Miss Miles." Erica flushed a deep red and nearly leapt to the bed in her hurry to get her shoes on. That accomplished, she snapped back to her feet at the position of attention. "What can we do for you, ma'am?"

"First off, you can both find somewhere to sit down and relax. Really, it's much easier to talk if you're not standing at attention. We're not in the military and we don't have to stand on protocol all the time." She smiled. "Don't tell Lady Orisaka I said that."

The two girls shared a grin and then responded in tandem, "Said what, ma'am?"

"Thanks. Halgrim, I read your report. I'm concerned about your encounter in the Cloud last night."

Christina piped up, "Yeah, can you believe she met a gargoyle?"

Erica shot her a dirty look, but Felicia smiled. "Yes, I can believe that. We get reports about them from time to time from Angels who fly through the Cloud at night. Although"—she paused briefly—"I can't recall one aiding an Angel before last night. Generally, they just go about their business and let us go about ours. You *do* have your share of adventures, don't you, Halgrim?"

"I'd be more than happy to spread them around, Miss Miles."

The security chief smoothed out her skirt. "No, it's the human attackers who have me concerned. It's not like you had a specific time you were to return from the party, nor a specific route, yet they were waiting for you. We suspect someone at the party saw you leaving and signaled them. They probably entered the Cloud right behind you to set up their ambush. So who could have seen you leaving?"

"There were people all over the ambassador's airship. The people I dealt with specifically were the ambassador himself, Geoffrey Kingston, Raquel—the ambassador's maid who helped me get dressed—and Esteban, the ambassador's aide. He remained behind to ensure no one gained access to my flying gear. He also helped me prepare to leave the airship. However, others could have seen me leaving the ambassador's study or even leaving my quarters. The ambassador implied people would be *very* interested in the papers I was delivering to Lady Orisaka and that it wasn't safe to remain on board overnight. Based on that, I suspect everyone I met last night."

Christina gave her a dirty look. "Not *everyone* everyone."

Erica kept her face impassive. "Ev-er-y-one," she said, carefully enunciating each syllable. "Chris, I have to keep an open mind. If I start mentally eliminating people, I may miss something important. If they're not in the Angels, I have to be careful around them."

"Does that include Michael?" Christina asked, crossing her arms at her roommate.

Erica surprised herself with her answer. "Yes. I *want* to trust Michael, but he's been so secretive lately. Plus, he's the one who found me after I had been kidnapped. Did he really find me because of the necklace or because he's working with the dark men? There are too many weird things going on to trust anyone right now."

Christina's eyes widened, but Felicia spoke up. "That's probably wise, Halgrim. We don't think the Angels have been penetrated, but you might want to limit any discussions about this. I'm pretty sure you can trust Miss Bronson here."

The two girls laughed before Felicia continued. "However, we are going over the package the ambassador gave you last evening. It has some interesting data in it, but like you, we're investigating it for ourselves." She paused for a second and then grinned. "After all, he's not with the Angels."

Erica walked toward the lunchroom after spending the morning with the head technician. He remounted her wing weapons and gave the gear from last night a thorough going-over. She'd spent more time in the Cloud than anticipated and he was concerned the prolonged contact might affect her gear. When she hadn't been with him, she'd been with the medical staff to ensure she had a clean bill of health. They were concerned about possible Cloud-inhalation, since her rebreather was so low on chemicals when she arrived. Also, the Angels' psychiatric staff was concerned about her gargoyle encounter. They wanted to schedule a session with her just to be certain she wasn't suffering from some sort of Cloud-induced delusion.

If I had any idea telling the truth would stir up all this nonsense, I would have just let the whole gargoyle thing slide. Everyone around here is acting like I'm either crazy or the luckiest person in the world.

"Erica?"

She saw Christina running toward her. "What's up, Chris?'

"We've got a meeting. Come on."

"Oh, for pity's sake. I'm ten feet from the lunchroom."

Chris looked at her, the lunchroom, and then back to her. "I know. I'm starving too. Still, can't be helped. We'll get some chow after it's over."

Erica followed Christina to a conference room and saw the rest of her flight there. Rachel was writing something on the blackboard as Chris and she took seats near her. They had just gotten comfortable when Rachel called the room to attention as Lady Orisaka, Flight Leader Vetrano, and Felicia Miles entered and took the remaining seats at the table. Rachel left the blackboard and sat with the rest of her teammates.

"Thanks you for your quick response, ladies. Flight Leader Walker, had you started your briefing yet?"

"Negative, Lady Orisaka, I was about to start when you walked in. I'll begin when you're ready."

"We'll begin in a few moments. I wanted to bring you all up-to-date on the current situation. I've had the chance to go over the intelligence reports the Coritani ambassador submitted last evening. I find myself agreeing with his initial analysis. I suspect his sources have identified at least one lair associated with the *Bloody Lynx*. However, you know my methods. I am not one who puts all of my faith in one source, just like none of you do only one check of your wings before flight. That brings us to this briefing and tonight's mission."

Another mission? I haven't recovered from last night yet.

Rachel nodded. "With regard to tonight's mission, there's supposed to be a slight overcast this evening and almost no moon. I think weather-wise we'll have perfect conditions."

"Indeed. Thanks to a meeting Halgrim and Bronson attended earlier this week, we know where and when the *Bloody Lynx* will be next. This is the perfect opportunity to seize the initiative back from the pirates."

Erica thought for a second and then her hand shot up to her mouth. *Oh! I had forgotten about that with everything else happening lately. I wonder who that cloaked person was? Still, whoever it was, if Michael brought them along, it must have been important.*

Lady Orisaka continued. "This will be the perfect opportunity to corroborate the ambassador's information. If we can approach the *Lynx* unobserved, we can plant a homing device and track it back to its lair. If the lair is near the Whale, as the ambassador's information purports, then we will plan a raid to rescue our missing comrades. If it lands elsewhere, then we'll turn the ambassador's information over to the Air Rangers, so they can mount a raid on that base while we focus on the *Lynx*."

Flight Leader Vetrano spread his hands out on the table and leaned forward. "I asked Lady Orisaka to let my team handle this, but she believes one of you, specifically someone trained to use those newly developed glider wings, would have more success reaching the pirate ship and planting the device. She is afraid we would be spotted using our standard wings. So, we will coordinate our two teams to provide support and backup should something go wrong with the mission."

Lady Orisaka motioned to Rachel and the acting flight leader moved to the blackboard to begin the briefing. "This mission will sound simple at first, but I think you'll agree just how tricky it really is. One of us will be responsible for attaching the tracking device to the *Lynx*. That person will leave Angels' Headquarters, fly up through the Cloud, head north along the Khyber River until you reach Blackwater Bridge, and then remain on station."

Christina had a puzzled look on her face. "Why Blackwater Bridge? The Aerie is above us. Why not fly straight there?"

Rachel paused before answering. "Because if they anticipate this move, they'll be spending all their resources scanning the skies below their ship. Leaving the city and then approaching from the north will help disguise our approach."

She faced the rest of the team. "Our mission will be to locate the *Lynx* in White Cliffs Aerie, identify whether or not the Lynx has deployed sentries or gyrocopters, and then signal the glider to approach. The person using the glider wings will be moving slowly to avoid drawing attention, which means they'd be a sitting duck if a gyrocopter spotted them."

Phil Vetrano spoke up. "My men will be in position to provide cover, but that's as a last resort. Stealth, not strength, is the theme of this mission."

"Exactly. Now, normally Halgrim would be assigned to the glider wings since she has the most experience, but given the events of last night, Lady Orisaka and I do not believe it would be the best strategy. Instead, Bronson will be flying tonight. You were Halgrim's backup at the camp. We'll see if you were paying attention."

"Hey!"

Rachel drew a quick sketch of the *Lynx* moored to a typical building. She made some notations on the blackboard from her notes and then turned to the group again. "Halgrim, Fitz-Simmons, and I will assume position in these three spots, slightly above the *Lynx*'s airbags. This should give us the maximum ability to keep the *Lynx* in view as well as providing cover to keep the pirates from observing us. Christina will need to take not only her rebreather to get through the Cloud but a supply of oxygen too. You are going to climb as high as you can safely to remain out of observation range. Once we're sure it is safe for you to approach, we'll send three short bursts to your wrist-com. You will then fly to White Cliffs at altitude and signal once you can see our lights. We will signal once if it's clear and then you will approach the *Lynx* from above. We estimate you will have three minutes to attach the tracking device to the ship and leave. Once you leave, fly north again. There will be a transport vehicle at the bridge."

"Got it. Sounds like I have the easy job."

"If you want to look at it that way, I guess you're right. You're going to be in the air for quite a while in the dark. Keep your wits about you. More than just gyrocopters and Angels fly in the night skies."

Christina suddenly didn't look so happy about her assignment and Erica suppressed a smile. Rachel continued with the briefing. "The three of us will have colored lights with us. Once we send the signal to Bronson, we'll turn on our lights and begin flashing them every two minutes. Halgrim will have green, Fitz-Simmons will have blue, and I'll have yellow. However, if anything happens—a sentry is spotted, a gyrocopter flies by—we'll shift to red. Do not approach until you see the green, blue, and yellow lights again. If you circle White Cliffs for more than five minutes and do not see any lights, assume the mission has been aborted and return to the bridge."

Lady Orisaka stood up to ensure everyone was looking at her. "I cannot begin to impress upon you how important this mission is. These pirates hold three of our members as well as valuable equipment. We must track them to their lair and attempt a rescue. If our people are not there, we will force them to tell us where they are. One way or the other, the *Bloody Lynx* will be brought to justice, but if they have harmed our teammates, well"—she paused for effect— "there is a reason why they're called the Angels of Vengeance."

She let that sink in before continuing. "However, it does the Angels no good if any of you are hurt or killed trying to make this rescue attempt happen. Take your time, be careful, and trust your training. We shall reconvene at six o'clock this evening. Until then . . ."

Erica checked her watch one last time and wondered how long it was going to take Christina to get there. *We've been here almost forty-five minutes. She should have been here by now.* She rolled to her stomach and felt the airbag lurch beneath her as she shifted. Not for the first time since she had landed atop one of the adjoining airships did she let out a small prayer the padding on the ends of their wings remained in place so it wouldn't puncture the membrane she was resting on. *At least the bag is filled with warm air. It's pretty chilly just sitting here this high in the air.*

She shifted so she could scan the walkways visible from her perch. There hadn't been a sign of sentries or hangers-on, but that did not mean they couldn't be there. The *Lynx* remained dark, as if it had been shut down for the night. There had been some movement when they first arrived, but even using the light-amplification lenses on her goggles, she hadn't seen anything for a while. She was surprised pirates would be so unconcerned about their own security, but then she hadn't seen any guards outside the other airships either. Perhaps the *Lynx* was trying to blend in.

Reviewing the briefing in her head to kill time while they waited for Christina to show up, she was surprised how different White Cliffs Aerie was from Downtown. There, many of the airships had been moored for years, but White Cliffs Aerie had expanded from small docks and been divided into quarters.

The southern quarter was devoted to the original airships and those belonging to up-and-coming industrialists and merchant lords waiting their chance to move to Downtown. The western portion was set aside for visiting airships from foreign countries, with its own customs and security area. The eastern quarter was set up like the west, except it was reserved for airships from around the Empire of Dalriada.

However, it was the northern quarter where she was hiding at the moment. This portion was dedicated to cargo ships. Customs officers moved along the catwalks during the day to inspect cargos and ensure all appropriate taxes were paid. In the night, smugglers prowled the same catwalks trying to ensure their cargo was not inspected and appropriate bribes were paid. There was a significant business devoted to moving shipments from the Aerie to the Streets and below. The northern quarter had a more lawless feel about it, which made it perfect for the *Lynx* since it had once been a merchant vessel before its capture and re-outfit.

She hadn't seen any signs of gyrocopters or gliders beyond those of the Southwatch Air Rangers as they patrolled for possible pirate raids. She found it somewhat amusing the very same forces designed to suppress pirates were providing protection for the marauders' ship. However, as long as the *Lynx* behaved itself, the Rangers weren't likely to notice it among all the other ships.

She checked her watch and then flashed her green light into the sky again. She glanced around and saw the answering lights from the other two airships near the Lynx. While not part of the original plan, they had decided to use the adjacent airships as their hiding spots; since the dirigibles were so close to the pirate ship, it was unlikely a sentry could spot the lights unless he was standing atop the *Lynx*. Vengeance snipers were positioned for that possibility. She didn't know their exact locations, but the fact they were there was reassuring.

There!

She spotted the faintest movement and barely made out a dark silhouette against the inky black sky above. Christina seemed to inch along in a lazy circle high above. Signals were exchanged and Christina changed her approach, coming in on a long, slow glide down to the *Lynx,* her wings barely moving to keep her aloft. Erica only heard the faintest whisper of noise as Christina arrived and hovered above the target. Apparently satisfied with the situation, Christina eased onto the *Lynx*.

Erica began counting down in her head, watching with concern as Christina seemed to have trouble attaching the tracking device to the ship. She caught herself starting to launch out to aid her roommate and forced herself to remain still. They were too close to accomplishing their mission to overreact now.

Suddenly, the *Lynx* lit up as lights shone out of cabin windows in the main portion of the ship. Seconds later, a series of lights illuminated the catwalks surrounding the ship's berth. There were shouts and, even from the top of the adjoining airship, Erica could hear the sound of running feet.

Crap. Chris must have set off an alarm.

She charged her weapons and held her breath as the main hatchway opened and men poured out onto the catwalk below her. Christina froze in place atop the *Lynx*, trying to blend in with the shadows. Again, Erica started to move, but she remembered the warning from the hooded figure about the foolishness of charging the raiders and held her place. There was a quick flash of red on her wrist-com and she knew the Angels of Vengeance were prepared to go into action if necessary.

Stay calm, Erica.

To her surprise, the next thing she heard was laughter. Curious, she crept closer to the edge of the ship. The men hustled onto the catwalk below and it was obvious this was no threat. From the way they moved, it was obvious they were well into their cups.

"Come on, mates. There's no sense in drinking our own whiskey when there's a tavern down in the Heights with our name on it. It'll be perfect for what *I* have planned for tonight."

"Now, wait a minute, Solly. You think ol' Pete's gonna be all right guarding the ship?"

"Perfectly fine. We're respectable businessmen, after all, just out enjoying a successful cargo delivery. Besides, who's going to mess with the *Lynx*? *Pirates?* That's what the Air Rangers are for, right?"

The men broke out in drunken laughter and cheers and followed their captain down the railed catwalks. Erica watched until they moved beneath the other airships moored in the area and their laughter disappeared into the darkness. Erica felt her heart start beating again and she tapped her comm link twice to signal "all clear" to Christina.

They all held their positions for a few more moments to be certain none of the pirates returned and then Christina spread her wings and stepped off the back of the *Lynx*, silently rising into the sky. Once clear of the surrounding airships, her roommate's shadowy figure turned north and soon vanished from sight.

Erica started to leave when something struck her. *So, that's Solly. That means the men chasing me last night were from the* Lynx. *But why? Who at the ambassador's party would be associated with a band of pirates?*

She stared at the airship and caught herself inching closer to the edge. *I wish I knew if Crystal, Sophie, and the others were aboard or not. If only one person is aboard, we could rush the ship and rescue them before the others returned. But, if they're not there, we'd lose our only chance to find them. What should I do?*

She could almost hear the hooded person talking as she stared at the hatchway. *Patience, Halgrim. Stick to the plan. This is not a game to be won in one bold stroke.* Erica shifted positions atop her airship, trying to see anything through the lit windows. She glanced down and saw her comm link blinking furiously. She realized Rachel was waiting for a response and she slapped her hand down on her crystal to send a reply. A few seconds later, Rachel signaled for the flight to withdraw and the rest of the Angels rose silently into the night to join their teammate.

Erica gritted her teeth the whole way there.

After that evening, things started moving quickly. The *Bloody Lynx* pulled out of her berth in White Cliffs a few hours behind schedule, but the tracking device worked exactly as they had hoped. The Angels of Vengeance confirmed the pirates were using the cave complex the ambassador's sources had indicated. Once satisfied the pirates hadn't found the transmitter and there was no counter-ambush in place, they withdrew to a safe spot and contacted Lady Orisaka.

That evening, under cover of darkness, a contingent from the Imperial Air Corps appeared and was quartered inside Angels' Headquarters. With their arrival, the building went on lockdown. No one was allowed to enter or leave without Lady Orisaka's personal approval. It was obvious both the Imperial Air Corps and she were determined there would be no security leak on this mission. Geoffrey's team had taken over one of the conference rooms for their office and the sentry outside the door made it clear the room was off-limits.

The next day was filled with meetings between Angel Security and the Flight Intelligence Wing members, reviewing terrain maps and the known members of the *Lynx*, who their suppliers were, who made and lost money on the *Lynx*, and so on. Most of the regular Angels were confined to the residence floors, except for Erica's flight.

It drove Christina nuts knowing Geoffrey was staying two floors below her room, but Lady Orisaka made it clear there would be no fraternizing with the Air Corps personnel, regardless of any prior relationships. Still, the two of them did seem to wander into the same break room on more than one occasion.

Based on their earlier work, Erica's flight was assigned to support the Angels of Vengeance. They split their time between working with them, attending meetings, and additional training. Vetrano arranged a crash course in physical training, hand-to-hand combat techniques, and extra time on the marksmanship range in the subbasement of the headquarters. Toby flitted between ensuring Crystal's experimental wings would be ready in time and working with each member of Erica's flight with their new weapons, both wing-mounted and personal. It seemed to Erica he was trying to out-Crystal Crystal. She hoped he wouldn't burn himself out before the mission.

By the third day of this training, Erica was exhausted. They hadn't had more than four or five hours of sleep in a row since the White Cliffs mission. She was stumbling down the hall after yet another session with Toby in Crystal's lab when a young woman from the Administrative staff caught up with her in the hall. "Excuse me, Miss Halgrim? Lady Orisaka would like to see you in the main conference room."

So close to that shower and bed. What do they need now?

She knocked on the conference room door and went inside. To her surprise, there were only two people in the room—Lady Orisaka and...Michael? Erica paused in the doorway, her mouth agape, but Lady Orisaka simply waved her forward and returned to their conversation.

"As I was saying, Lady Orisaka, these flyers I've designed would be useful for your upcoming mission. From a distance and especially in the dark, they look like oversized bats. They have the optics to see not only in dim light, but I have adapted them to pick up heat signatures. If there are guards on patrol, you could identify and neutralize them."

"Halgrim, Michael says you're familiar with these flyers. Can you vouch for them?"

"I've never actually seen them flying. However, he says that's how he found me the night I was kidnapped. Since Michael is prone to underplay his abilities, I suspect they'll do everything he says."

"There you go, my lady. After all, I feel somewhat responsible for what happened. Crystal was working on that new design based on some work I had done. If we hadn't been collaborating, none of this might have happened."

"Nonsense, Michael. I think what's happened would have happened no matter what the catalyst was. Neither of you knew all the machinations behind the situation . . . and you're not going to learn them from me right now either. Erica, I asked you to come here because there's a very special mission I need you to handle for me."

"Of course, Lady Orisaka."

The older woman looked at Erica over her long fingernails and Erica was transported back to the first interrogation with her employer those weeks ago. "Do not be in a rush to volunteer, Halgrim. You might want to learn *what* I want you to do first."

Erica bowed quickly to hide her blushing cheeks. "Of course, Lady Orisaka. What would you like me to do?"

"Better, Halgrim. I'm only asking you to do this because Zwyer isn't here to volunteer, and I know she would. Senior Lieutenant Kingston and I have gone over these plans and there's a problem. Even with the added strength of the Imperial Air Corps, we are not confident we can take the pirate base quickly enough to guarantee the safety of the captives. We need a way to divide their forces and take them down piecemeal."

Erica looked at her employer with a dubious stare. "And therefore you need me to do . . . what?"

"We need you to lure the *Bloody Lynx* or at least some of their personnel out of hiding. I'm afraid for this operation to work, we need live bait and *you're* the one thing they can't resist."

Chapter Twenty-Two

Erica watched the crowd around her as she rode the people mover out of Emerald Park. She was still a little numb about the idea of being bait. After a long discussion with Lady Orisaka, Michael, Flight Leader Vetrano, and Felicia Miles, they decided letting her go to the park was the best opportunity to make contact with someone who might relay a message to the pirates.

She didn't know why Angels' leadership was certain she would be contacted, but from the looks Miss Miles and Lady Orisaka exchanged, it was obvious they had a suspect in mind. Today, Erica's job was to be available for contact. The only instructions they gave were to start at the western lake and make her way around the park until she was contacted. She might be contacted two or three times, but she was to stick to the same story and note who approached her.

I don't think I've ever had vaguer instructions in my life. Just walk around until something happens? What happens if I get kidnapped, or shot at again, or worse? I know they said I'd be under observation, but this is worse than flying through the Cloud with a blindfold.

The people mover stopped at the entrance of the park and Erica followed the flow of the crowds through the main gates. She stopped to buy a drink from a vendor before continuing toward the far end of the park. She meandered along, taking whatever path she encountered, trying to act like someone out for a stroll. Still, she knew she was the most conspicuous person there. She wondered if the young man would be selling fish food again, but knew that chance had already come and gone.

She reached the lake and leaned against the railing, watching kids playing with their parents and young couples walking hand in hand, completely oblivious to everything but each other. In the distance, she heard a band warming up and wondered if it was the same one from those weeks ago.

She started walking over to see, but a beep from a horn caused her to jump from the path onto the nearby grass. Two young men on penny-farthings came rushing around the bend and sped down the trail, one trying to keep up with the other. She watched them weaving their odd bicycles in and out of the other pedestrians before they disappeared around a bend into a wooded area in the distance.

"Dreadfully dangerous devices, wouldn't you say, Erica?"

Fighting down the instinct to scream, she recognized the voice and tried to put a placid look on her face when she turned around. "Good morning, Jessica. I guess I didn't hear you behind me. They look like they would be fun to ride, but awfully hard to balance if you had to stop in a hurry."

"I'm sure they'd say the same thing about your wings. So, what brings you to the park today? I noticed our fish food seller isn't here today."

"I noticed that too. Strange fellow, wasn't he? Did you ever find out who he was or why he had a gyrocopter here?"

Jessica managed to keep her smile steady. "I'm afraid not. I was hoping you might have more information."

"I'm afraid this is the first time I've been back to the park since you saw me here. I don't think I've ever seen him around town either. Still, Southwatch is a huge city and I've been busy. I think I've done more training lately than when I first joined the Angels. But you probably don't want to hear about that."

Jessica smiled at her. She tried to make it a friendly one, but Erica still envisioned a shark with a short blond bob when she did. "I *was* wondering why I hadn't seen you lately. Anything special, or just general training?"

Erica started walking along one of the paths and Jessica fell into step with her. "They've had me trying out all kinds of new wings. With Crystal gone, they seem to think I know what her plans were. Honestly, I just fly them. I'm afraid aeroengineering wasn't my strong suit in college. I don't know how to improve them beyond what Michael or Crystal have taught me. Still, I've been helping the technicians as much as I can."

"That seems strange, no offense. You'd think the technicians would have worked more with Crystal."

"She's funny that way. She never wants to bring in too many people until she's sure something will work." They were passing a petting zoo and Erica slowed down to watch the kids getting to meet some of the animals. "I remember going to a petting zoo when I was a kid. I was so used to seeing the mechanical animals around Southwatch, I didn't realize they were based on real creatures. It's good they have something like this for kids nowadays. That's why I'm so glad I'll be heading back to the testing grounds."

"You're going *back* to the testing grounds?"

"Oh, yes. Tomorrow, I'm going there for another week of testing. We won't go to the mountain camp you visited. I'll be at the main camp and using the course there. I *will* get to fly along the foothills, though. I love that because there are always animals wandering around the training area. Last time I was there, I think I saw a puma. Of course, it disappeared into the woods so fast, I'm not sure if it was one or not."

Jessica seemed annoyed by Erica's sidetracks but she soldiered on, trying to be polite. "Aren't you worried about what happened last time?"

"A little, yes. However, Lady Orisaka doesn't think anything will happen this time. We're just sending a small group, it's unlikely anyone will know I'm there. Plus, we still have to run tests on the other wings Crystal developed before she disappeared. As worried as we are about her, we still have delivery dates, and like the military, it's next person up. Besides, it's a chance to fly under blue skies. I'll never pass up an opportunity like that."

Jessica paused for a moment and Erica stopped after a few steps to let her catch up. The Black Watch operative gave her a puzzled look before speaking again. "You're awfully friendly today, Erica. The last time we spoke you were a bit more . . . upset with me."

"Yes, and I really do need to apologize for that. I was so upset about the whole thing—Crystal, Sophie, the pirates—well, let's just say Lady Orisaka pointed out I was being ungrateful. Pointed it out rather bluntly, I don't mind telling you. You have a job to do just like me. You would have been remiss if you hadn't asked questions and pointed out unpleasant truths. In your job, you can't let personal feelings get in the way and I can't fault you for making me think."

Jessica seemed taken aback by Erica's apology, but she pushed on. "It's true. I'm a bit jaded, considering the people I interact with on my job. The Watch takes its job as the eyes of the baron seriously, but it's easy to get caught up in the cynicism. Perhaps I was too zealous in my duties also and we got off on the wrong foot. You have my apologies too."

"I'm glad I ran into you, Jessica," Erica said, glancing at her watch, "but I'm afraid I have to return to pack. We're leaving for camp before dark so we can get started first thing in the morning."

She sighed dramatically, "Somehow being a test flyer isn't quite as glamorous as I was led to believe."

Jessica laughed. "No, unfortunately many careers look great until you actually start. Best of luck, Erica. Let me know how things go."

"Thanks, Jessica. Will do."

She waved to Jessica and then started toward the main gate. She stopped a few times and bought some treats, but no one else approached before she reached the main gate. She smiled to herself as the people mover arrived. Lady Orisaka had been right. She had advised Erica to be polite to Jessica if she showed up and give her just enough information to catch her interest.

So, if no one else approaches me and if the Bloody Lynx *crew comes for me tomorrow, we may know the source of the leak. If they don't show, we'll have to try something else to reach them. Still, Jessica has been a second shadow throughout this entire episode. Sure, she may be trying to get to Michael, but Lady Orisaka thought she seemed like a logical place to start.*

Erica climbed onto the people mover with the rest of the crowd and made certain to sit where someone else could join her if they chose. *She did show up, though. I don't know what's going on in those meetings between Lady Orisaka, Geoffrey, and Michael, but I know they* know *more than they're letting on.*

"Excuse me, miss, is this seat spoken for?"

Erica looked up and saw a tall blond man in a business suit, his briefcase carefully tucked under one arm. She scooted over a few inches and motioned for him to sit down. He seemed familiar but she couldn't recall his face.

"Thank you. It was a beautiful day for a visit to the park, wasn't it?" he asked as he arranged himself to be more comfortable.

"It *was* wonderful. I really enjoy spending time out from under the Cloud when I can."

She noted her companion had a slight accent but couldn't place it. Then again, a number of foreign businesses and trading companies called Southwatch home. After a while the different languages and dialects were picked up by the locals and blurred together into what the rest of the empire called the Southwatch accent.

He pulled a pad out of his briefcase. She was still conscious of her mission, so she continued acting like a chatterbox, in case he might be the link to the pirate crew. "Do you get out of the city very often?"

"Actually, I'm here on a business trip, which appears to be wrapping up sooner than I had hoped. I look forward to getting home soon. I'm afraid I don't enjoy spending time under the Cloud."

"I'm sorry to hear that, but I'm glad you'll be able to return home soon. I'm from here, but I do get to get out of town every so often."

He stuck his hand into his coat pocket as if reaching for a pen before leaning closer. He spoke just loud enough for Erica to hear his next words. "Yes, Miss Halgrim, I know you do. By the way, I have my hand on a silenced pistol and it's pointed right at your heart. Please do not make any sudden moves or attempt to scream. I would hate to have to hurt you, but I will."

Suddenly, she recognized his voice. "You're the man with the lights."

He smiled. "I'm honored you remember me. It's always a pleasure to renew old acquaintances. We will be getting off at the next stop. Do not do anything foolish and walk beside me."

She tried to keep her body relaxed as she nodded in agreement. She looked for any means of escape, but the people mover was crowded and there was no easy way to reach the exit. A few minutes later, the vehicle slowed to a crawl and he nudged her. "This is our stop."

She let him guide her out the door and onto the sidewalk. He called out in a friendly tone to someone and another, much burlier man joined them, falling in on the other side of Erica. The blond man tapped her on the arm and pointed ahead as if talking to his best friend. "We're going to go to that restaurant and have a nice chat, just the three of us."

"That's really nice, but I'm not very hungry."

"Nevertheless I insist."

Deciding that going to a restaurant was better than being tied up in a warehouse, she went along for now. They entered and Erica immediately noticed how luxurious the establishment was. After a few words to the host, they were directed to a small private room off the main dining area. Her hosts acted as if nothing was going on and they allowed themselves to be seated. The staff brought drinks and menus before retreating to a discrete distance to let the group make their selections.

Looking up from her menu, Erica said, "I must say, this is a much more enjoyable detention."

"There's no reason to be savages when sophistication can be as effective," the blond man replied. "However, if you make this more protracted than necessary, we *can* default to cruder means."

"That shouldn't be necessary. Besides, I think I'd much rather stay here. That chicken dish looks divine. I assume you're picking up the bill?"

He laughed before responding. "Don't get too carried away. I am on a budget after all."

She laughed with him and then he motioned for the waitstaff. She was amazed at how calm she was, but given everything that had happened the past few weeks, she was becoming quite inured to it. They placed their orders and then the staff withdrew, shutting the door behind them. Erica noted the thickness of the doors and saw the heavily draped windows had bars on them. There was no escape from this room.

"Now, Erica, I do hope you remember what we talked about the last time we visited?"

"It would be hard to forget, since you had me repeat my story often enough."

"Very good, so we won't go over that again. What we are more interested in is what new information you may have on that subject. *Have* you learned anything new since our last talk?"

Erica took a sip of water. "Nothing specific. Probably the same rumors and hints you've picked up by now. "

"Ah, but we weren't invited to the ambassador's for dinner."

"That's too bad. His chef is outstanding. You really should try to wrangle an invitation."

The other man slapped his hand down on the table, causing Erica to flinch away. The blond man moved his hand sideways and the larger man leaned back in his chair and pointedly looked away. Her interrogator continued, his voice unperturbed. "My friend here believes you're being needlessly obtuse. While I would hate to leave this restaurant before our meal arrives, I find myself somewhat in agreement. Perhaps you'd care to fill in a few gaps for me."

Erica wasn't sure where her sudden burst of temper came from, but she knew she'd had enough. "I don't know what you're looking for, so how can I fill in the gaps? You asked about the death of the ambassador's daughter. I know she was on a gyrocopter and fell from it. I know the gyrocopter was pursued by two others. Whether those incidents are related I can't say with any certainty, but I suspect they are. I know you two are not the only people interested in learning what I know. I also know people want to ensure I don't tell anyone what I may or may not know. Whether those two groups are somehow related, I can't say either. I *do* know since that day, I have been kidnapped, shot at, been chased by a gyrocopter, managed to avoid being run over by an airship, bounced off more walls, floors, and ceilings than I want to remember and even met a living, breathing gargoyle. Now, beyond that, is there something specific you are looking for so we don't waste more time?"

"Bravo, Erica!" He gave her a mocking round of applause and then his eyes grew harder. "We need to know the name of the man flying the first gyrocopter."

"That's great. When you find out, will you let me know? I would like to meet him too."

"So, you're claiming you haven't met him?"

She held her hand up in front of her mouth before laughing, almost hysterically. "No, I certainly *have* met him. For about a whole five minutes, before the Black Watch butted in and frightened him off. I might have known quite a bit about him, but he's probably convinced I set him up and I doubt I'll ever get a chance to talk to him again. I have no idea to reach him either, to head off your next question. Personally, if you're going to be upset at anyone, I'd be mad at a woman named Jessica Black."

"I'll take that under consideration. However, there are other issues we need to discuss."

The door opened and the waitstaff came in with the meal—followed by Geoffrey and Detective Casciato. Geoffrey had a large smile on his face as they walked over to the table and sat down, opening his napkin as a plate of food appeared for him too. "Good afternoon, Douglas. This is Southwatch Police Detective Josie Casciato. We're glad we could catch you before your trip."

The blond man grimaced before looking at Geoffrey. "My trip?"

"Why yes. Oh, do try some of this duck, Josie. It is divine. While Detective Casciato was all for hauling you in on two counts of kidnapping, assault with a deadly weapon, battery, unlawful confinement, and conveying terroristic threats, I convinced her there was a better way. We've already spoken to your ambassador and it seems you've been declared *persona non grata* in Dalriada. Allen and you will depart on a ship at five p.m. today. There is a small detachment outside to escort you to wherever you're staying to pick up your gear, if you wish to collect it. Otherwise, we have a very luxurious room to hold you in until your ship leaves."

"May we enjoy this meal, at least?" Douglas asked glumly.

"Of course. We're not savages, after all."

Erica rode back to Angels' Tower with Geoffrey in a little two-seater. He wove in and out of traffic like he was racing against a clock in his head and she was afraid to speak because she might distract him. A few minutes after the trip began, he pulled into the basement garage at the headquarters and swung into a parking space.

"Well, that went rather well, I think," he said, hopping out. He hurried around to the other side and gave her a hand getting out of the small vehicle. She smoothed her dress and followed him over to the elevator. He rang for the car and then leaned against a post with an odd look on his face. "You're certainly different from Chris. She would have been pestering me about what happened back at the restaurant."

"Oh, I have plenty of questions. However, I'm still waiting for my stomach to catch up after that last little maneuver you did with the oncoming produce wagon."

"Wait a minute, you fly through the air and you get scared of someone's driving?"

Erica frowned at him. "When I'm flying, I'm in control. I'm not relying on someone who's showing off. Plus, I never fly that low to the ground in congested areas. I'd be at least six floors up if I wasn't coming in for a landing. You take chances you don't have to. Maybe that impresses Chris, but not me."

She watched his smile turn into an embarrassed grin. "Sorry, I just wanted to get you here quickly. You are leaving in a few hours, after all."

Erica entered the elevator and moved to the far corner to give him as much space as possible. Finally, her curiosity overwhelmed her anger and she spoke up. "All right. So, what was that whole scene about back at the restaurant?"

"Oh, that. That was Douglas Baldwin and Allen Evers. They are with the Hidden Chamber, an elite intelligence unit with the Kingdom of Celacti. The Celactians have been stirring up trouble for Coritani

213

for quite some time. From what I've been told about your encounter with them, they decided to take advantage of the ambassador's misfortune to get information on him. If his daughter had died under *unsavory* terms, they'd try to blackmail Pavel into divulging information or perhaps taking a less hostile position on many of the treaties Celacti has been pushing the last couple of years."

"How long have you known?"

"About them? Almost since the day they arrived in Southwatch. We have a fairly good dossier on the Hidden Chamber, just like they do on us. However, I had no clue they were behind your kidnapping until I walked in on your lunch date."

Erica thought for a moment as the elevator continued to rise. "Wait a minute, you knew they were with the Celactian government and you let them walk around Southwatch unhindered?"

Geoffrey laughed. "Of course. First off, they're employees of the Celactian embassy and therefore had diplomatic immunity until we convinced the ambassador to remove it today. Secondly, we *know* they're enemy agents. It's easier to keep an eye on spies if you know who they are. By deporting them, we're going to have to expend a lot of manpower to determine who their replacements are. After all, the embassy turns over a percentage of its staff every month, so it could be anyone from the new mechanic to the new stenographer. Sometimes it's better the enemy you know than the enemy you don't."

"I don't think I'll ever understand all of this cloak-and-dagger stuff. Your team, their team, the Black Watch . . . is there anyone who's just themselves these days?"

He brought the elevator to a halt and opened the door for her. "I think it's safe to say you're you. And speaking of you, here's your floor. You'd better head straight to the lab and make sure those new wings fit right. We're leaving at dusk. Pack light, though. I don't think we'll be gone for more than a couple of days."

"Yes, Papa."

He rolled his eyes and closed the elevator door. She saw the floor counter rise until it hit the top floor and she knew he was headed to Lady Orisaka's office to give her the latest news. At least the mystery of the men who kidnapped her was solved. Now all she had to worry about was pirates.

Chapter Twenty-Three

Erica watched the Angels of Vengeance team finish their preparations. Toby went around ensuring everyone's gear was right before the team members split up. Two Barrymore Lances backed up to the warehouse loading docks and waited near the warehouse doors. The team laid down in the bed of the truck, their wings beside them. Once everyone was in, the technicians covered them with tarps.

The plan called for the trucks to drive along the perimeter road and, one by one, the heavily armed warriors would slip out and find hide positions in the woods nearby. Whether the pirates tried to fly into the training area or assault the area on foot, the Angels would be in position to interdict them. The Imperial Air Corps had positioned a small gyrocopter carrier airship a few miles away, hidden beneath camouflage netting. At the first sign of trouble, it would be launched and then a swarm of gyros would maneuver into position. There were two platoons of Imperial Marines hidden in the main warehouses at the training base proper should the pirates manage to get that far.

Looks like they've thought of everything. However, it's all up to the pirates. If they don't take the bait, then we've got a lot of people hanging around for nothing. Let's face it, if Jessica, or someone she reports to, isn't the link to the pirates, they won't know I'm here. I'm still not sure why they think she's the link. I can't imagine the Black Watch and a pirate band working together. That's just too weird.

There was a tap on her shoulder and Erica fought down a scream before spinning around. Toby flinched away from her, raising his hands defensively. "Sorry, Erica, I thought you heard me."

"No, don't take it that way, Toby. I was just thinking about what's coming next."

"Worried?"

She tried to put her game face on, but she knew she wasn't fooling anyone. "Absolutely. But I can't see any other way to pull this off. Are you ready to get started?"

The Vengeance armorer pointed to his bench. "Here's a new set of wings Crystal was working on. They're lighter than your regular set and the sweep is drastically angled. This means, theoretically, you should be able to reach higher speeds and dive faster under more

215

control. The problem with this design is it requires more effort to keep you aloft. Since they don't provide as much lift, downdrafts or air pockets may affect you more than you anticipate. Also, with less lift from the wings, your thalisium will be forced to generate more lift, which means it will burn up even faster."

Erica walked over to the bench and picked up one of the wings. She stumbled backward as she overestimated the force required to lift the wing one-handed. After a few moments, she lowered it to the bench with a puzzled frown. "To say these would be impractical flying through the Cloud would be an understatement. What's their purpose?"

"Originally, they were strictly proof-of-concept. Crystal has always been fascinated with raptors, especially hawks and falcons. They're ambush hunters, relying on their speed to take prey before it has time to react. She wanted to see how far you could push the aerodynamics of a set of wings before they weren't useful for lift." Toby paused, swallowed hard, and then continued. "These are about as close as you can get. We didn't have time to order some of the more exotic metals needed, so we didn't reach minimum weight. Still, if these gave you any less lift, you might as well be in a nonmotorized glider."

Erica looked at the wings again and then turned toward Toby. "You said, 'originally' they were proof-of-concept. What are they now?"

"Some of Lady Orisaka's contacts expressed an interest in using them to insert people into hostile situations where speed is of the essence. Obviously this particular set of wings wouldn't support a two-hundred-plus-pound man. He'd drop like a rock, thalisium or no thalisium."

That is not *an image I needed in my head right before putting these things on.*

Toby continued as if not noticing Erica's changing expression. "We have plans to build more robust versions if this works like we believe it will. The idea is to assign wings like this to a small team. They would approach the target at night in an airship, then bail out and make a fast, quiet drop, say on top of a house held by criminals, or whatever the mission required. The hope is the attackers could seize the initiative and force their opponents to surrender before any shots were fired."

Erica thought about that for a moment. "There are probably some nonlegal way you could take advantage of wings like this too." She walked around the table, noting their construction before continuing. "In fact, I can see a pirate band seizing an airship or a regular ship by surprise at night also."

Toby grinned at her. "You're absolutely right—which, by the way, is why we're using this particular set of wings today. In fact, we let that slip when Lady Orisaka met with Jessica this morning. It seems she stopped by the office to encourage us to take some Black Watch personnel along to safeguard this test. So, not only are *you* the bait, but you'll be *wearing* the secondary bait."

"Would you like to paint a big bull's-eye on my flight suit too while we're at it?"

"Nah, that might be a bit too obvious. We're going for subtle today."

She shook her head sadly. "Toby, if this is your idea of subtle, I'm afraid to ask what you think is blatantly obvious."

"You know, Crystal says that all the time."

Erica changed the subject before she could make the obvious rejoinder. "So, I hear there's a new flight suit? My usual leather pants, jacket, and boots aren't sufficient?"

Toby's smile grew bigger. "It's a unique suit we designed for these wings. We did everything we could do to minimize drag with the limited amount of lift. It's a one-piece outfit. Your boots and gloves slip inside the body of the suit and the goggles are as thin as we can make them and still be effective. The best part is it's made out of a special breathable rubber mesh. There's almost no threat of overheating. If they try to use an electro-net to capture you, the suit should neutralize the majority of the shock."

"That sounds fantastic."

"Well, odds are the net would entangle your wings anyway, but honestly, there's not much way around that. So, we still recommend avoiding the net."

Now there's a cheery thought.

"Here you go," he said as he handed her the box. "You shouldn't have any issues getting into it. We ensured it would fit you. By the way, it zips up the front." He saw her dubious look and continued quickly, "I did mention it was an aerodynamic one-piece suit. Buttons and stuff would create drag."

She took the package, raised an eyebrow at him until he retreated across the room, and then walked into the changing room. She removed the suit, gloves, boots from the box, stared at them, the empty box, and back to the suit. She couldn't believe this was all there was, but the empty box didn't lie.

She stepped into the suit and pulled it up over her waist and then her shoulders. She hadn't considered that when he said "aerodynamic," Toby meant skin-tight. It was scandalous and sensuous at the same time. There was a cowl attached to the suit that would cover her head, leaving only her face exposed. She slipped the calf-high boots on and tucked the suit down over the top of them and then the same with the gloves. It fit her like a second skin and she wondered who had given Toby her measurements; this was too perfect a fit for something put together in the past twenty-four hours.

After making herself as comfortable as she could in the suit, she exited the changing room and walked back to the table. Toby stood there, his mouth hanging open and his cheeks turning four different shades of red. He spun around and faced the table, reaching for the wings. "Ah . . . yes . . . right, we'll probably need to readjust your harness. I had it set for your normal flight suit. We may have to tighten it up a bit to account for this new suit. Now where did I leave that . . .?"

He reached over and knocked the wings, tools, and papers off the table, scattering them across the floor. He scrambled to gather the items while Erica picked up the wings. She slipped the harness on over her shoulders and tightened the waist cinches. She had to double-check to ensure the wings were actually attached. *These wings are incredibly light. I don't know how Crystal did it, but if she could make all our wings this light, I could fly forever.*

She turned around and Toby stood there, reaching out and withdrawing his hand as if he wasn't sure where he could touch her to help tighten her harness. She tried to smile her most disarming smile at him. "Toby, you're not going to faint on me now, are you?"

"No, I'll be fine. It's just different seeing the suit on a real person instead of the mannequin. As I said, these suits were designed to minimize wind resistance. That's why they're so . . . so . . . ."

"Tight, Toby."

He swallowed hard and then rushed to get the next few sentences out. "Yes. Since the wings are meant for speed, the suit's smooth surfaces will make you more aerodynamic."

Erica decided to take pity on him before he passed out from lack of oxygen. She began flapping the wings to distract him. "Aren't there any weapon mounts?"

"We never discovered a way to mount any without interfering with the goal of speed—not even stun sticks. It was anticipated the flyers using this system would have handheld weapons or explosives. There's a spot for a small pack here"—he tapped her in the small of the back and then cautiously reached around to tap her once on the stomach—"plus a small pouch could be mounted here for a handgun of some kind."

Fantastic. They're sending me out as live bait and there's no way for me to defend myself. I hope the rest of the team stays awake because if I can't outfly an attacker, I sure the hell can't fight back.

"Toby, if these wings are designed to be used by someone leaping from an airship, how do I get aloft? They're probably not strong enough to get me into the air from the ground."

"We've got a standard balloon being inflated in the main training field. It'll take you up four hundred feet before you bail out. We figure that should give you more than enough momentum to deploy the wings and gain altitude. After you're aloft, head toward the eastern boundaries of the camp and then follow the perimeter road. There will be people monitoring you as if we were doing an actual test." He paused before continuing. "Actually, we *will* be monitoring your speed and altitude while you're on the course. Might as well get real data while we're waiting for the pirates to arrive."

"Has anyone ever accused you of being monomaniacal before, Toby?"

"Crystal. Why?"

Erica sighed. "Never mind."

The balloon flight was uneventful and soon Erica and the pilot were at the end of the tether. She felt a soft breeze on her face and saw the tether line wasn't pulling hard against the mooring. The pilot checked the altimeter one more time and then turned to Erica. "Last chance. If you don't feel comfortable, we can go back down."

"No, this is something I need to do."

He opened the door to the gondola. "Break a leg, then. We'll see you back at camp."

Erica moved to the open door. She checked her gear one last time out of habit and slipped her goggles into place. Stepping onto the small launching pad, she took a deep breath, pulled her legs in tight, tucked her arms in against her sides, and let herself fall headfirst from the gondola.

The rush of air against her body surprised her as she plummeted straight toward the ground. While she'd done free fall before, with this new suit and the new wings folded flat, it was as close to achieving terminal velocity as she'd ever experienced. She counted to ten and then spread her wings as wide as they'd go and slowly arched her back to begin the upsweep.

Terror ran through her as her body continued plunging downward as if the wings didn't even exist. As the ground grew closer, she felt her velocity begin to change and her dive flattened out about fifty feet from the ground. Then, almost without warning, she was climbing into the open sky, the wings fluttering faster and faster as she gained height.

She reached cruising altitude and only then did she realize she was still holding her breath. It took a bit to figure how just how long she could go between wing strokes before stalling, and she spent the first five minutes of her flight alternately climbing too high or falling almost out of control before she began to feel comfortable with her new wings.

Wow, that was worse than my first attempts back at basic. I wish we could have tested these in the lab before coming out here. These wings are unforgiving. She scanned the distant sky for any sign of the pirates. *It's almost too bad they didn't make their move a bit ago. My flight was so erratic, I doubt they could have gotten a bead on me.*

She was still trying to fine-tune her flying as she approached the eastern border. With significant effort, she managed to climb several hundred feet into the air and then swooped to within a few dozen feet of the ground before ponderously climbing again. She had never dived that fast before and the first couple of times she wasn't sure she could pull up in time. The first time, she almost misjudged how long it would take the wings to bring her out of the dive and pulled up at the last second, only inches above the grass. The second time, she barely regained enough altitude to avoid a clump of trees. By the time she reached the boundary, she had a rough idea what the wings could or couldn't do.

She glanced at her thalisium levels and saw she was already down a quarter. Normally, she'd have to fly a couple of hours to burn that much. *When we rescue Crystal, we've got a lot of work to do. If we can blend the diving capability of these with the wings I was testing for speed, they'd be an incredible combination. I bet we could cut delivery time through the Cloud almost in half.*

She was so lost in thought about ways to improve the wings, she almost missed the sudden buzz of gyrocopters from the east. She turned and dove as a flight of nine gyros split into three groups, trying to hem her in.

All right, Toby, you said these wings were fast. Let's see just how fast they are.

She rolled onto her side and pivoted almost ninety degrees, heading back toward the heart of the training camp. She did her best not to go so fast the gyrocopters couldn't catch her. However, she kept changing position and altitude. She didn't want to let them get an easy bead on her with their weapons.

After a bit, she started climbing and the pursuing gyrocopters spread out even farther, trying to encircle her. She reached almost a thousand feet before she spotted a lake ahead. She began angling in that direction, climbing a little higher to ensure they were still following. She felt a disturbance in the air near her and then bullets zipped past her.

Holy Goddess, they aren't after the wings at all. They're trying to kill me.

She jinked from side to side and changed altitude, but unlike the gyrocopter she'd encountered the first time she'd been attacked at this base, these seemed to be supercharged. She'd never encountered single-pilot gyrocopters this fast or agile before. Apparently they weren't worried about saving ammunition either from the way they continued to strafe her.

She reached the edge of the lake and dove toward the surface. Her sudden move caught the gyrocopters off guard and they dove in pursuit. Another burst of bullets flew past her head as she changed the angle of her dive, entering an even deeper angle. The gyros struggled to stay with her.

At the last instant, she flattened her dive, skimming just inches above the water. She heard the gyrocopters screaming as they tried to react to the onrushing water. Glancing back, she saw them breaking formation, trying to find clear sky as they took emergency maneuvers. That gave her a momentary head start and she used the momentum she'd built up in her dive to regain altitude.

These wings are fantastic for dives, but they really stink going the other direction. I feel like I'm hauling a couple hundred pounds every inch I rise.

She didn't have time to worry about where her backup was. None of the gyrocopters had taken a bath like she had hoped so she was back to dodging nine gunners on her trail. It was only a matter of time before one of them hit her. Every spin, juke, or stall merely drained her precious thalisium. She spotted a large wooded area and headed toward it. The enemy pilots seemed to guess what she was doing. Part of the flight broke off and made a beeline toward the woods, as six continued to harass her though the sky.

Suddenly, a new flight of gyrocopters rose from behind the woods and headed in her direction. They were painted in the pirates' black-and-red color scheme and Erica realized what must have happened.

I can't believe I let them herd me right into this trap. All right, but they're going to have to work for it.

She dove for the oncoming vehicles, hoping they wouldn't fire because they would be caught in the cross fire with their partners trailing her. They seemed to recognize the situation, as their formation shifted, giving her a tiny escape route. She dove into their midst, narrowly avoiding one set of rotor blades, and then folded her wings and dropped toward the ground.

She waited until the trees came closer before opening her wings, praying she could reach the shelter of the trees before the others could reverse course and join in the chase. She heard firing behind her and then the whine of lightning cannons charging and discharging. Wondering what was going on, she almost forgot where she was going. At the last second, she spread her wings and rounded off her dive, corkscrewing toward a clearing. It was close but she managed not to wrap herself around a tree as she spiraled into the clearing and stumbled to a stop. She hit the emergency release and dumped the wings and harness before running into the woods. She kept moving until she reached the edge and was able to look up into the sky.

A dogfight raged overhead between the gyrocopters and several circled overhead trailing smoke. She saw winged figures headed her direction, skimming across the ground to avoid becoming a target for either side. A large airship approached from the west. One set of gyrocopters attempted to disengage from the fight above, but it was a losing battle. As the airship filled the air over her head, it began turning to port. A horn blasted out and the new gyrocopters climbed rapidly as the airship raked the first group with a broadside from their cannons. The enemy gyrocopters shuddered as the large-caliber shells ripped through their machines. Pirate ships fell from the sky.

She saw several parachutes blossom overhead and the winged men circled the field, waiting for the pilots to land. The second set of gyrocopters forced the remaining pirates to land as the airship floated overhead like a giant guard dog. Two of the winged men flew to the edge of the woods, but she didn't expose her position until she recognized Flight Leader Vetrano's voice.

He did a double take when he saw her flight outfit, but immediately regained his composure. "Sorry we're late. Some men engaged us and tried to take out the airship about the same time the gyrocopters attacked. It seems they were aware of our plan, which should have been impossible." He stared at the gyrocopters landing nearby. "I hope those pilots have a lot of answers, because I sure have a lot of questions. These are not standard pirate tactics. They usually prefer a target with immediate profitability."

"Unless someone paid them a lot."

"There is that. Let's go."

Erica stared at him. "Go? Go where?"

"The *Lynx* base. It's time we recovered our teammates."

Chapter Twenty-Four

Erica adjusted a jacket over her flying suit and followed Rachel as they approached the cave complex holding the *Bloody Lynx*. They were following the Angels of Vengeance on foot. The Angels were to locate and protect the prisoners while the military attacked the pirates.

The gyrocopters being flown by the Imperial Air Corps were approaching from the west and she knew the Imperial Marines were coming from the north. They had the base surrounded unless there was a way out of the cave the Angels hadn't discovered.

She hid behind a rock and glanced around it to notice the pirates were preparing the *Lynx* for takeoff. The maintenance crew appeared to be going through their preflight checklist, and there was a stir in front of the cavern opening. There was a whistle and people began preparing an area for the gyrocopters to land. A buzzer sounded and a door in the airship opened, exposing a slowly extending ramp.

The Angels' gyrocopters swooped in from north to south and then circled for a landing. Just as the first one touched down, another suddenly developed engine trouble and plummeted from the sky, trailing a huge cloud of smoke. It crashed a few feet away from the cave mouth, belching smoke and fumes into the air.

Flight Leader Vetrano waved his hand and the Vengeance moved as one toward the cave opening. Rachel let them get about fifty feet ahead and then motioned her flight to follow. They hugged the canyon, taking advantage of the confusion. They only had a few minutes before the Marines began their assault.

There were a few close calls, but Erica and the others made it to the cave mouth. The cave complex was lit by soft electrical lights on the walls. She heard the throbbing of a generator in the distance. Phil motioned at three of the Vengeance. They almost melted into the walls as they moved forward in the dim light. There was a soft yelp and then silence. They heard two clicks and then Phil motioned everyone to follow his men.

Turning the corner, Erica tried not to look at the man lying at her feet. Necks were not meant to move in that direction. Now was not the time to get squeamish, though. If they didn't reach Crystal and the others in time, that might be considered a good way to die.

They checked a few side tunnels as they traveled deeper underground. Finally, they saw a tunnel branching off to the right and a large chamber straight ahead. An alarm went off, nearly deafening them as it echoed through the cave system. The attack had started.

"Rachel, your people take this passage. We'll take the main chamber. Go." He didn't pause to see if they were following orders or not as his men tossed flash-bang grenades into the chamber and then went rushing in.

Rachel didn't waste time with orders but simply bolted down the corridor with Kim, Erica, and Christina right behind her. Rounding a bend, they found four wooden doors wedged into natural openings. Rachel turned and pointed at Kim and Christina.

"Go back to the corner and make sure only our people come this way. If you see someone, don't bother warning us. We'll hear your weapons."

Erica pounded on one of the doors. "Crystal, are you here?" She heard a faint cry from the next one down. "Rachel? Down here."

Rachel and she crowded around the door. "Is anyone in there with you?"

"No, but the others are nearby. I've heard them."

"Stand back," Rachel ordered, and fired two shots that broke the lock. Erica pulled the door open. Crystal stumbled out, hands out in front of her as she strained to see who was there.

"Crystal, where are your glasses?" Erica asked, grabbing her by the arm.

"They took them. They only let me have them when I'm in the lab. That way they were sure I wouldn't escape if they forgot to lock my door."

Soon, they had Flight Commander Kail out of her cell and were coming up to the last cell, when Erica stopped dead. A familiar voice greeted her from the other side of the door—a voice Erica hadn't expected to hear.

"Hurry up, Halgrim. Let's get out of here before they set off the self-destruct charges."

"Sophie?"

"We'll talk later, Halgrim. We don't have much time."

"You betrayed me, Sophie. Why should I trust you? For all I know you're waiting in there with a weapon."

There was a momentary pause and then Sophie's voice came through the thick, wooden door just barely loud enough for Erica to hear. "Erica, there's no time to explain, but believe me, I did not betray anyone—at least not anyone in the Angels."

Erica's emotions warred between her anger at Sophie and the faint hope there was a logical reason her friend acted like she had. Finally, she came to a decision and warned Sophie to stand back from the door. She took out the small shotgun Toby had issued her and blew the lock off.

Even with her hand atop the barrel, the recoil from the small weapon nearly knocked her over backward. She reached through the opening, pulled the door open, and motioned for Sophie to come out.

Erica held the shotgun at waist level as Sophie rushed out of the room. "You saw what it did to the door? That's what will happen to you if you're lying, Sophie. I can't afford to trust you yet, but I won't leave you here either."

"Thanks, Halgrim."

"Don't thank me. We're not out of the woods yet."

Crystal turned to the group. "We have to go to the main cavern. I have to recover Eve and the wings."

"I thought they didn't take any wings?" Christina stated with a confused look on her face.

"They didn't, besides the ones they took from Sophie. Somehow, they had designs and parts waiting for me. They were using Eve to test them. I can't understand how they got access to my designs."

Another explosion echoed down the tunnel, reverberating off the rough-hewn walls. Rachel shrugged as if to say *Why not? We've come this far*, and motioned for everyone to wait at the bend of the tunnel. Erica took up a position at the back of the group to keep an eye on Sophie. After a few seconds, Rachel signaled them to follow her.

A quick rush down the main tunnel took them to the central chamber. The sounds of fighting came from the far side of the huge room, but it was hard to make out what was going on, as many of the lights had been destroyed. A ricochet striking the ceiling caught Erica's attention and she glanced up. Among the stalactites was a small shaft of light—an opening that led topside. She could have sworn there was nothing there when they scouted this area earlier.

Crystal stopped them just inside the door. "Be careful. There are openings in the cave floor. Some aren't too deep and they use them for storage. Others, they weren't sure just *how* deep they go and they use them as garbage pits. If you fall in, we might not be able to get you back out. Stick close to the wall and follow me."

Crystal led them through the dimly lit cavern toward a large stack of crates, behind which was a makeshift laboratory equipped with gear, tools, and wing parts. "They set up a small wall of crates here to separate my lab from their normal maintenance work. They said it was for my safety, but I noticed only a couple of the pirates would watch me from the catwalks above. It was mostly Eve and me here."

Probably heard how dangerous being a test subject for Crystal could be. I wonder how many got hurt before they isolated her.

Crystal grabbed her glasses off the table and pointed to the right. "Ah, there's Eve."

Eve stood against a stone wall, her eyes glowing—so they knew she was operational—but she made no move to join them. Puzzled, Christina moved to the cybernaut and then called back, "A little help here? Eve's chained to the wall."

Another loud explosion echoed down the main tunnel and the Angels quickly divided into teams. Crystal, Sophie, and Rachel grabbed plans and parts, while Kim and Commander Kail gathered the finished wings and stacked them on a two-wheel cart. Erica went over to assist Christina.

"It's good to see you again, Erica."

"Good to see you too, Eve."

There was some give in the chains around Eve's waist so Erica grabbed a metal rod from the table behind them and began twisting the links. "I don't see any other way to get you free. Let me know if this hurts." Erica realized what she had just said and glanced at Eve. She'd never seen a cybernaut smile before, but there was no questioning Eve's expression.

"I appreciate your concern, Erica, but Crystal did not install pain receptors in my body. Otherwise, I wouldn't be able to crash as often as I do and walk away." Eve lowered her voice. "Thank you, though."

"Uh, right." Erica tried to fight the flush she knew was creeping up her cheeks.

Between the two women, they managed to torque the chain enough to finally free Eve. The cybernaut thanked the two before moving over to help pack the lab.

The sound of running feet caught their attention and the Angels ducked behind the crates to hide. In the dim light, Erica realized someone was running along one of the catwalks. She glanced up and saw it led to a door high on the cave wall. Then she realized there was another man pursuing him. As they grew closer, Erica recognized the two. The man with a large sack thrown over his shoulder was Solly, the captain of the *Bloody Lynx*.

The pursuer was Tony.

Erica watched the two men with a feeling of trepidation. Tony caught up with the fleeing captain and Solly pivoted and swung the sack, catching Tony on the shoulder. Erica caught her breath as he teetered on the catwalk, gamely hanging onto the rope railing that ran alongside.

Tony regained his balance and barely ducked the next swing. He drove his fist deep into the pirate's stomach. Solly doubled over, and the sack went flying over the edge of the catwalk to crash on the ground near Erica, scattering gold coins and gems across the cave floor. Solly recovered quicker than Erica thought he could and caught Tony with an uppercut, knocking him onto his back, then dove at the smaller man to wrap his fingers around Tony's neck. Tony got a foot into Solly's belly, flipping the pirate over him. Solly landed heavily on the catwalk but quickly rolled over onto his stomach. The two men climbed to their feet and warily approached each other.

Erica looked away from the fight and noticed Eve standing near, as if waiting for instructions. "Eve, do any of those wings work?"

The cybernaut gestured to the set being loaded onto the two-wheeler. "Those are operational. They're not optimized for you, but they should allow you to reach the catwalk with minimal issues."

She heard a cry of pain but there was no time to see who it was. She rushed to the cart and snagged the wings out of Christina's hands. "I need these, thanks." She struggled into the unfamiliar set of wings, but then felt someone helping her adjust them.

"Thanks."

To her surprise, it was Sophie. "Be careful, Halgrim. Solly is dangerous on his good days. Now he's desperate. That makes him even more dangerous."

"Understood." Erica thought for a second and then handed her .38 automatic to Sophie. Her former flight leader's eyes grew wide but she took the proffered weapon. "Cover me. I'm counting on you in case anyone tries to interfere."

Rachel stuck her head around a crate and saw what Erica was doing. "Halgrim, what the hell is going on?"

"Gotta help a friend."

Before Rachel had a chance to reply, Erica climbed atop one of the crates with a boost from Sophie. She could see only the occasional flash of light in the distance and the distant sounds of gunfire. She took two running steps and dove off the crate. As she fell toward the floor, she spread the wings and began flapping them. Slowly and ponderously, she rose into the air toward the catwalks overhead.

She searched for a path through the spiderweb of catwalks closer to the cavern's ceiling. A shot rang out, followed by a scream. A body tumbled from a nearby catwalk, and a scoped rifle narrowly missed her and clattered on the cave floor. Solly jerked his head around, trying to figure out where the shot had come from, which gave Tony an opportunity to tackle the larger man around the waist and drive him backward onto the catwalk.

Erica spotted the opening she'd been looking for and dove for the catwalk. Just as she landed, Solly tried to shove Tony off to go after her. Tony recovered quickly, interposing himself between Solly and Erica. Frustrated, Solly rushed the mercenary, grabbing him in a bear hug. Erica could almost hear Tony's ribs cracking as the huge man applied more pressure. She pulled out her shotgun, but there was no way to deal with Solly without hitting Tony. She took a couple of steps back, hoping an opportunity would present itself.

Tony screamed as his ribs were compressed even more by the large man. In a desperation move, Tony brought his hands viciously against the sides of Solly's head, compressing the air in his ears, rupturing his eardrums. Solly stumbled back, loosening his grip. As Tony twisted to escape the grasp, the huge pirate missed a step and their combined momentum took them over the rope railing.

Erica screamed as the two men went over the side. She dove over the railing after them, tucking her wings in, trying to reach Tony before he crashed to the ground. He flattened out to increase his wind resistance, trying to give her a chance to catch up, but to her horror, she saw Tony disappear into a dark spot on the floor—one of those openings Crystal had warned her about. Solly's scream suddenly halted as bone crunched against stone as he hit the floor next to the opening.

That sound jolted her and she saw the same cave floor rushing to meet her. She flared her wings and arched up as hard as she could to avoid pancaking on the floor. But the speed of her dive and the unfamiliarity with these wings conspired against her. She slammed into the ground, the impact driving the air out of her lungs and sending her skidding on her stomach out of control. She heard the screech of a servo as she struck something in the darkness and the right wing was ripped out of the harness, sending her pinwheeling across the floor. A second later, her right arm smashed into something unyielding, and she felt her arm go numb from the shoulder down. Before she could scream, the side of her head slammed into something and her vision exploded into a million stars.

From far off in the distance, she heard the sound of feet running toward her. She cautiously lifted her head and felt blood running down the side of her face. The cave went in and out of focus and she put her left hand down to steady herself. She pushed her tongue against her teeth and was happy none of them moved. She tried to get up on her hands and knees, and realized someone was kneeling beside her. She could see Sophie was speaking, but she sounded like she was talking through water.

". . . Halgrim, can you hear me? Take it easy. Let me check you out."

The sight of Tony disappearing came back to her and she jolted back to full awareness. "No, Tony's over there. He might be hurt."

"*You* are hurt, Halgrim. You've dislocated your shoulder and I'm certain you've broken your arm in multiple spots. The Goddess knows how many other injuries you have. I have to evacuate you now."

"No . . . you don't understand. Tony . . . he went down a hole . . . near Solly's body. He might still be there. We need to save him."

Somehow, Erica stumbled to her feet, her right arm hanging by her side, the mismatched wing throwing off what was left of her balance. She shuffled toward the hole before she felt Sophie's arm slip around her waist and her left arm being raised over her former flight leader's shoulders.

"If you're going to ignore me, I might as well keep you from doing more damage to yourself. Come on, show me where you think he went down."

The next thirty feet were the most excruciating steps Erica ever took. By the time they reached the lip of the hole, Sophie was nearly carrying her, but Erica refused to stop moving. They passed the broken body of the pirate captain. A glance told her he'd never be a threat again. Erica lowered herself near the edge of the hole and leaned out over the opening.

"Tony!"

A faint voice came from somewhere in the Stygian depths. "That you, Erica?"

"Are you all right? We'll be there in a moment. Sophie'll get a rope for you." Before she could say anything else, she realized Sophie had left already. She inched closer to the edge and tried to see into the darkness, but there was nothing to prove he existed except for his voice.

"That's a nice thought, but you're wasting your time. I don't think I'm going to be able to hang on that long."

"Damn you, hang on. Sophie will be back in a second. We'll come down after you."

He let out a low moan before responding. "I appreciate the sentiment, but there's no point. I'm pretty torn up and I'm not sure how much longer this ledge will hold. Listen, you need to know something."

"Tell me once we get you out of there."

A wave of nausea and darkness swept over her and then there was silence. Erica was afraid he'd fallen while she'd zoned out, but Tony's voice finally reached her, sounding even farther away this time. "Erica, find Vic Candal and protect him. He's the gyrocopter pilot we were looking for. He was in love with the ambassador's daughter. They were sneaking off for a ride when someone else tried to kidnap her. She fell off his 'copter because she wasn't buckled in. He's here in the crew."

Another wave of darkness washed over her. "Tony, that's great. We'll be cleared and the ambassador will know the truth."

The voice in the darkness sounded even more tired. "No more looking over your shoulder, kid. Did you say Sophie's with you?"

"Yes, Tony. I don't know where she is, but she'll be right back."

"Talk to her, Erica. She knows more than I do." There was a pause and then a soft voice called out. "Take care of yourself, kid."

"Tony?"

There was no answer.

"TONY!"

Blackness reached up to consume her and the next thing she knew, Sophie was hauling her back from the edge of the hole. "Erica, are you all right? You damn near went headfirst down that hole yourself. What's going on?"

She tried to speak to Sophie, but she could hear her words slurring. "Tony, have to get to Tony. He's—"

"Gone, Erica. I couldn't find a rope but I did find an electric torch. There's no one in the hole, Erica. I couldn't see him and I couldn't see the bottom. If he fell, we may never find the body."

Erica felt her eyes watering, but she refused to accept what Sophie was saying. "Tony can't be gone. He's a survivor. Must be a trick."

She looked up at her former flight leader and then blackness closed in on her vision from all sides and then she didn't know anything at all.

Chapter Twenty-Five

"Erica."

Erica fought down a wave of nausea. She couldn't feel anything and her limbs didn't want to cooperate as she tried moving them.

"Erica, wake up."

There it was again, that mechanical voice. Where had she heard it before? Why was it so hard to think? She knew she'd been in a bad accident, but she'd never felt like this before. "Who's there?"

"Ah, good. You're awake. We need to talk before Dr. Lopatka comes back. This can only be between you and me."

"Who are you? Why can't I see you?"

"Who I am is unimportant, Erica, but we've met before. We shared a lovely dinner a few weeks ago. As to why you can't see me, or anything, it's because your eyes are heavily bandaged. You suffered a severe concussion, amongst other injuries, and the good doctor doesn't want to expose your eyes to light quite yet. Your limbs have been restrained for the same reason."

Some of the events of the fight came rushing back. "Tony. Did they find Tony?"

"I'm afraid I don't know anything about that. No one has mentioned that name to me. But, as I said, time is short and we need to come to an understanding."

"Understanding? What are you talking about?"

The voice continued in an even tone, its mechanical sound infuriating Erica as it hid the person's identity. "It's simple, Erica. You're badly hurt. So badly hurt, I'm not convinced you're going to survive it without help. Michael and the doctor are doing all they can, but it may not be enough. Therefore, I am here to offer my assistance, but unlike Michael, I require payment for my services."

"Payment?"

"Oh, I'm not asking for money, Erica. That's not important. However, if I assist, if I help Michael do what needs to be done, then someday in the future, I will ask for a small favor. I would like to think that if you give me your word, you'll honor our bargain."

Erica laughed in spite of the pain. "This is obviously a delusion, a dream brought on by the painkillers. But, sure, o great subconscious of mine, we'll agree to a deal. After all, if I'm dead, it'll be awfully hard to collect."

The mechanical voice sounded almost amused. "Hard? Yes. Impossible? No."

Erica felt a momentary flash of fear, but the voice was too monotonous to take seriously. "I've heard the tales. People who live on with their souls embedded in a mechanical body. Don't they call them androids? Parents use those stories to scare little kids into not doing dangerous things. Or maybe you're telling me you'll turn me over to the fae? I hear they have a prior claim on Southwatch and lie in wait to capture an army to try and seize their ancestral homelands." The more she thought about it, the more amused she became until she was almost hysterical. "Urban legends, tales to scare children. Nothing more . . . nothing less."

The mechanical voice continued, taking no note of Erica's hysteria. "All legends have a kernel of truth in them, Erica. Do not be so quick to discount what you have not encountered. After all, were you not saved by a gargoyle? Why would he do that? Perhaps there are more things going on in Southwatch than you know. But time is growing short. Do you agree to the terms of the deal? I help save your life, you owe me a favor."

"Under one condition."

For the first time, Erica thought she heard a hint of frustration in the monotone. "You're in a poor position to bargain, Erica Halgrim, but let's hear your condition."

"Whatever this favor is, it cannot cause harm to either Michael or the Angels of Steel. If I have to choose between them and myself, I'll pick them every time. Agree to that, and I'll owe you a favor."

There was a pause and Erica listened carefully. She had almost decided she was alone when the voice spoke again. "I hold Michael in the highest esteem. While we may move at odds with each other from time to time, there is no animosity between us. I will agree to your conditions if you agree to mine."

Erica nodded almost imperceptibly. "Done."

There was a soft rustling and then she felt a sting in her arm. Before she could react, the world began receding. Just as she faded into a whirlpool of blackness, she heard the voice again, but it sounded miles away.

"That shot will remove the memory of this visit. You will not recall this until you are given the antidote at a time and place of my choosing. The only thing you have to worry about now is surviving the ordeal to come. *That* I cannot help you with."

There was a low roar in Erica's ears and then she disappeared into the blackness once again.

Chapter Twenty-six

"Erica? Are you awake?"

"No, I'm asleep and having a nightmare someone's asking if I'm awake." She tried to roll away from the annoying voice, but couldn't move. Unconvinced she was awake, she forced her eyes open and immediately closed them tight to avoid the harsh lighting right over her head.

She cracked her eyelids open and realized she was in an unfamiliar room. To the left, she saw odd machinery on a nearby table with tubes and wires leading to her body. To the right, standing just inside her peripheral vision, was Christina, who paced back and forth, wringing her hands.

Christina moved closer and whispered, "How do you feel?"

"Like I did a Crystal test without the restraining harness and protective gear."

"If she can joke, she's going to be fine," Michael said, moving into view on her left. "Welcome back from Morpheus's grasp, Erica. We wondered when you'd get tired of sleeping."

"How long was I out?" *Wow, my voice sounds horrible.* "Can I get something to drink?"

Christina moved out of her field of vision as Michael came closer to the bed and took her left hand into his. "The doctor kept you under for five days. It was pretty touch and go. You suffered critical injuries, both internal and external, when you pancaked in the cave. They took you off the medication yesterday, but you woke up on your own just a few seconds ago."

Christina returned with a small glass of water. "Here, lift your head."

Christina helped Erica take sips. Once she'd finished, Christina took the glass away. "The doctor said you shouldn't drink too much when you first wake up. You're going to be in recovery for a while yet."

"Recovery?" Erica motioned at her restraints with her head. "So that's what they call this imitation torture chamber?"

Michael leaned forward, a serious look on his face. "Darling, you nearly died in that cave. Sophie did everything she could, but she's

236

not a combat surgeon. Along with all your other injuries, your right arm was irreparably damaged. We had to remove your arm at the shoulder."

Erica's eyes flew open and she pushed up as hard as she could against her restraints. "My arm? But I can feel it." She felt her fingers flexing as she formed a fist over and over again. "I can feel the restraints holding me down. How could my arm not be there, Michael? That's a cruel joke."

The pain on Michael's face was palpable as he placed a hand on her shoulder and tried to comfort her. "Calm down. The doctor doesn't want you to get excited."

Her voice rose in pitch and her eyes widened even more. "Not get excited? *Not get excited?* Michael, you're telling me they amputated my arm. I don't believe you. I *can't* believe you. Without my arm, I'll never fly again." She slammed her eyes shut and fell back against the pillow, her energy spent. "You should have just let me die."

"But that would be a waste of one of my best flyers, Halgrim."

Erica moved her eyes to the right and saw Lady Orisaka and Dr. Lopatka coming into the room. The Angels' founder moved up next to the bed. "Didn't you say you can feel your arm?"

Erica's eyes watered. "Don't they call that 'phantom limb syndrome'? People who've lost limbs sometimes believe they still feel them years after they were amputated."

"Dr. Lopatka, please release her right arm."

"As her physician, I highly recommend against this." Dr. Lopatka began to say something else when she caught the look on Lady Orisaka's face. She swallowed hard and moved over to the bed. Erica could feel her doing something down where her wrist used to be.

That's impossible. I shouldn't feel anything there. Why would you restrain a limb that's not there?

"Lift your arm, Halgrim."

Tears welled in Erica's eyes. "That's a cruel joke, ma'am."

"*Lift* your arm, Halgrim." There was no mistaking the command in her voice.

Erica couldn't see why Lady Orisaka was being so cruel, but she flexed her shoulder muscles and tried to lift her arm. To her surprise, she saw an arm rise, but as she looked closer she saw a faint line going down it. In the quiet of the room, she heard the faint whirr of

237

servos in her shoulder and elbow. She turned it palm first and lowered it closer to her face. The "arm" moved as naturally as her original one had, but there was no question—it *was* mechanical.

"Oh my Goddess, what have you done? What *have* you done?"

Michael leaned forward. "Saved your life, Erica and made it possible for you to fly again."

"But . . . but, how?"

"Thank your boyfriend, Halgrim. He called in several friends who he did not bother introducing me to." Lady Orisaka frowned at Michael, who immediately began tinkering with the machine next to him. "They met with Dr. Lopatka and her team and two days later, they reappeared and you went into surgery. Nine hours later, I was allowed in and all of Michael's friends and their equipment had disappeared like they'd never been there. My security people are still trying to figure that out."

Erica wiggled her fingers and then reached out to touch Michael's arm. There was a sensation as her hand closed around his and she realized she was feeling his arm—actually feeling. "How. . . ?" she started to ask as Michael raised a hand to stop her.

"You always said I was a miracle worker, Erica. I'm really not, but my friends come close. Thank your employer too. She donated the bessum and other extremely rare metals to create the bones, servos, and sensors in that limb."

"Don't worry, Halgrim. We'll take it out of your salary."

Erica's eyes snapped open, but the smile on Lady Orisaka's face told Erica her boss was pulling her leg. Her head drooped and Dr. Lopatka shooed everyone out of the room. Erica gazed at her new arm in wonder until her eyes became too heavy to keep open and she drifted off into a dreamless sleep.

Erica walked out of the therapy room and leaned against the wall. It had been two weeks since she had woken up from her surgery and Dr. Lopatka finally agreed she was strong enough to begin physical therapy. She needed to learn how to use her new arm effectively and strengthen her shoulders and chest muscles to work with the mechanical arm. Dr. Lopatka was teaching her basic maintenance also. It was going to take a while to learn all of the things she had to do to keep her new arm in good working order.

She saw Crystal walking down the hall, her head down in a book. "Hi, Crystal. How're you doing?"

"Oh, hi, Erica. I was going to look for you after my meeting with Dr. Lopatka. She thinks you'll be ready to resume training in a couple of weeks."

Erica felt her face flush. "That soon? I thought I'd be doing physical therapy for a while."

"You are, but part of your therapy is learning how to fly again. That arm is close enough in weight and structure to the old one, so there shouldn't be any major aerodynamic issues. It's a matter of strengthening your shoulder muscles to handle the wing harness."

Erica repressed a shudder. Even though she didn't remember much about the accident, the idea of running into something and reinjuring herself was terrifying. However, the chief medical officer had just talked to her about that. She was convinced the longer Erica put it off, the harder psychologically it would be to get back into the air.

Crystal smiled, lost in her own world of testing. "Don't worry, I've developed a brand-new testing harness for you. It should minimize stress on your shoulder until you're strong enough for a standard system. Dr. Lopatka and I will monitor your progress together."

"Has the doc ever watched your testing sessions before?"

"Come to think of it, no. But I assured her I take safety into consideration."

Erica managed to keep silent. *I think your definition of safety and the doctor's are somewhat different, Crystal.*

Crystal walked off and Erica made her way to her room. The closer she got to her door, the more her workout settled into her aching muscles. *If today was the light day, I'm not sure I'm going to survive this.*

Entering her room, she saw Christina and Sophie deep in conversation, which ceased when she walked in. An awkward silence settled over them. Sophie glanced at Christina and then motioned for Erica to join them. Erica sat down on the end of her bed, wondering what was going on.

Sophie broke the silence after a few seconds. "Christina told me you'd be out of therapy soon, so I decided it's time we had a chat."

It took Erica a few moments to figure out which emotion was going to win out—she was mad, happy, disappointed, hopeful, and sad simultaneously. Finally, she settled on cautious optimism and kept her voice even. "All right. What would you like to talk about?"

Sophie glanced at Christina, who motioned for her to go on. "You were still unconscious when Lady Orisaka debriefed the rest of the flight. You know I deserted my post the night after Crystal was kidnapped."

"Yes, I remember. I also remember defending you against Jessica Black's accusations that same evening. I swore up and down you couldn't do something like that. And *where* did I find you? At the pirate camp. You *lied* to me and you *betrayed* me, Sophie, pure and simple. Don't be so surprised that I'm not welcoming you back with open arms quite yet."

Sophie winced, but swallowed hard and continued. "I don't blame you for being upset. In fact, I hate to say it, but I'm glad you're this upset. That means it should have worked."

"What should have worked?"

"I left because Lady Orisaka ordered me to undertake a special assignment. I was to link up with my old boyfriend, who was working on the *Lynx*. I had talked to him about deserting for a while. She made sure to make a big deal about the situation to make it look real."

Erica knew she was staring at Sophie, but she didn't care. "You're kidding."

"No, Erica, I'm not. The lady noted the increase in pirate and gang activity around Southwatch the past year. She also noted specific communities and businesses being targeted and how their losses led to big profits for others. She assumed this was a big push by an unknown criminal organization. Crystal's kidnapping merely accelerated our timetable. When the Angels of Vengeance arrived, there was a message for me from the lady to start the operation."

Erica felt herself getting caught up in Sophie's story. "And of course, since you'd grown up in the Underground, you were already a suspect. Does Lady Orisaka have an idea who's behind this new organization?"

"Angel Security tracked it to the highest levels of the Aerie."

Erica scoffed. "So one of the elites is involved? That's no surprise. Half of them were robber barons or worse earlier in their careers. There are more wealthy merchants and industrialist in the Aerie than nobles these days."

"If it was only that simple. There are rumors this could be traced to elements within the Southwatch government. However, there's no solid evidence. Lady Orisaka needed something tangible to go to the baron—or over his head, if need be. That's where I came in."

Erica smacked her fist into her other hand. "I knew something was going on. The fact Jessica already had your file when Lady Orisaka arrived says she'd been planting the seeds of you deserting. I should have realized something was up right then."

"I'm not sure where Jessica fits into this, but Lady Orisaka knew I had dated Darren Freeman when I was in college. I met him when I lived in the Bricktown Underground and we kept in touch after I moved. I know Mom wanted to make a clean break from the Underground, but Darren was one of my best friends, so we found a way. He was going to Royal Polytechnic the same time I was—" Sophie awkwardly paused and then continued, speaking faster and blushing. "Well, let's just say we were very close until he went into the Imperial Navy."

"And then?" Christina prodded.

"He wound up getting cashiered out of the Navy. He bounced around from airship to airship, usually getting into trouble after a few flights. From there, he drifted into flying with the *Bloody Lynx*. That's when Lady Orisaka's security people suggested I get in contact again. He's no innocent, but he's no bloodthirsty killer either. He works as a mechanic. At first, I was able to get basic information from him, mainly so the Angels wouldn't run afoul of the *Lynx*. After the incident at the *Temple*, Lady Orisaka thought we'd discover more if I went to work on the ship myself."

Erica sat back, staring at Sophie. "I never saw you as a spy, Sophie."

"I never did either. Apparently I wasn't very good. I rendezvoused with the *Lynx* that evening according to plan. Darren vouched for me with Captain Packham. While they were naturally suspicious, things went well at first. Then, about a week later, they jumped me on my way to breakfast. My wings were confiscated and I was locked in that cell you found me in when they weren't interrogating me."

"By the Goddess, Sophie, what happened?" Erica asked, holding her hand up to her mouth.

"Somehow, they knew about my mission; I don't know how. Hell, I didn't think anyone besides Lady Orisaka and Miss Miles knew—they had all the details. Anyway, they decided rather than killing me, after sufficient time had elapsed they'd 'free' me and let me return as a double agent. They'd hang on to Crystal and Commander Kail to ensure my good behavior."

Christina spoke up, her voice expressing the surprise and concern Erica felt. "What do you think happened?"

Sophie leaned back into the chair, staring up at the ceiling. "There has to be a mole in our organization. I'd been careful reestablishing contact with Darren. I knew we'd be under observation, so I always met him in out-of-the-way places, mostly in the Underground. Places where I *would* go to keep our meetings secret from the Angels. That was easy. He's still a sweet guy at heart, but he's in over his head. He's so frustrated at the world, it's easy to manipulate him, for good or evil."

"Sounds like you still think a lot about him," Christina said.

Sophie smiled a faraway smile. "Yes, I do." Then she sobered up. "But until he gets his head on straight, we have no future. I'm not the scared kid from the Underground anymore."

"Do you think he betrayed you?"

"No, they locked him up elsewhere. The *Lynx* crew accused him of selling out. Angels' Security is investigating the leak, but Lady Orisaka has a theory. That's why she wants us to meet this afternoon."

Erica leaned forward, staring at Sophie. "Deep down inside, I knew you couldn't betray us, Sophie. Jessica Black kept using the fact you weren't born in Southwatch and you grew up in the Underground to convince us you couldn't be trusted. Sounds like she needs to get out and see the city more."

"I'm not surprised, Erica. The Aerie looks down on the Underground, literally and figuratively. Attitudes like that push me to try even harder. Every flight I make perfectly or every test I ace is another thumbing my nose at those high-and-mighties up there."

Christina motioned to Erica. "Every time you talk about this, you mention that Jessica person. Have you noticed that?"

"Yeah…yeah, I do, don't I?"

Sophie and Erica waited in the main conference room, fidgeting. Lady Orisaka's secretary *had* admitted them, but it was strangely empty.

The two young women stood near the conference table, awkwardly staring at things as they waited.

Erica checked her watch one last time. "Are you sure this is the time the meeting was supposed to start?"

Sophie moved away from the table to examine a picture on the wall. After Erica asked the question again, she started, as if she'd been lost in thought, before replying. "It must be, otherwise the secretary wouldn't have let us in."

"Oh . . . good point."

There was a rustling at the door and Lady Orisaka came in, flanked by her security chief and a gentleman Erica had never seen before. Lady Orisaka motioned to the table and Sophie and Erica hurried over and took seats across from the trio. Felicia Miles began speaking while the girls were getting seated, continuing an earlier conversation.

"Suspicions are not going to be sufficient. We require solid proof if we're going to act," she said, snapping a folder shut on some papers for emphasis. "It's not that we don't have suspects; we have an overabundance of them. What we don't have is a smoking gun—something tying one of our suspects to the act."

Lady Orisaka nodded, folding her hands together and tapping her fingernails. Erica had been in front of her employer enough lately she'd learned it was a sign Lady Orisaka was agitated or annoyed. Either way, Erica decided to remain as unobtrusive as possible.

"I'm afraid I agree with my esteemed colleague, Lady Orisaka," the man said. His manner of speaking and accent told Erica he was from St. Louis, the Imperial capital. "This is a delicate matter. If we go forward with the evidence we currently have, there is no chance under the Cloud we'd get a conviction. We need something substantial to ensure success. Either that, or we simply table the entire matter until a better opportunity arises."

A flat, toneless voice came from Lady Orisaka. "No. There will be a resolution and it will come soon. Somehow they've imbedded themselves within the Angels and that must be exorcised."

The more unemotional the Angels' founder spoke, the more upset she was. The look in her eye made Erica almost feel sorry for whomever they were talking about. Lady Orisaka looked at both of her companions and continued. "There must be something we've overlooked. Maybe we're being too clever and overlooking something blindingly obvious. We have evidence, circumstantial I agree, but it's too overwhelming to ignore."

The man coughed politely before speaking. "Perhaps I didn't make myself clear, my lady. We agree with you. However, this is what we do for a living. We're going to have to overcome the baron's proclivity to see the best in people. That's why the evidence must be clear and unambiguous."

The security chief pivoted in her chair to face the gentleman. "I didn't think the baron was so naïve?"

"Don't get me wrong, dear lady. When properly motivated, the baron takes the defense of his lands quite seriously. However, he is a firm believer in 'innocent until proven guilty.' Personally, if I wasn't in my current position, I might agree with him—but I'm not, so I don't."

"Like I said—naïve."

Lady Orisaka made a small noise and the two refrained from continuing what was probably a long-running argument. She turned to the two young women sitting across from her. "How are you feeling, Halgrim?"

"I'm tired, ma'am, but I'm starting to get my strength back. I'm training with Dr. Lopatka to get back into action as soon as possible."

"I'm glad to hear that. For your information, we recovered a treasure trove from the pirate base and rescued the prisoners. Casualties were low and I think we can safely say several criminal gangs in Southwatch are about to suffer a surprising number of arrests and convictions. However, with the death of Captain Solomon Packham, we lost the link to the person behind this."

"I thought you had a 'strong idea' who that was, ma'am."

"I did and I do. However, as my esteemed colleague here says, 'a strong idea is not evidence.' We're going to need more than a hunch, a logical conclusion, anything that won't stand up to scientific examination."

Sophie sat up. "Lady Orisaka, you said you recovered information from the pirate base. Have you shared that information outside of our organization?"

"Yes, the Air Intelligence Wing has a copy of everything we recovered. Actually, they recovered most of it from the caverns after the fight; they were nice enough to share with us. I'm certain they shared the information with the other realm within Dalriada. After all, some of the information pointed to events happening outside Southwatch."

"The next question I have is, who currently has control of the *Lynx*?"

Miss Miles leaned forward, a sharklike smile on her face. "A small contingent of Imperial Marines holds the pirate base. The Angels of Vengeance are investigating the ship and the caverns for anything missed in the confusion of the attack."

"If the military holds the information, we can assume the other side has it. I don't mean to cast aspersions on their loyalty or capabilities, but it's obvious someone with power and influence is involved here."

"Your point, Zwyer?" Lady Orisaka had stopped clicking her fingernails and had focused her attention on Sophie.

"Ma'am, if *we* control the *Lynx*, we could leak something to your suspect—say, we'd found something on the *Lynx* we'd missed earlier. Something encoded that we'll be working on there. It's too important to take a chance transporting it elsewhere."

Erica spoke up. "And if your suspect is the person I suspect, there is something we could add, something they'd be unable to resist, even if they thought it might be a trap."

Lady Orisaka's eyes bored into her. "And what would that be, Halgrim?"

Erica knew what the reaction would be the second she made her suggestion. Still, there was no turning back now.

"Michael."

Chapter Twenty-Seven

"I *cannot* believe you volunteered me for this, Erica. I am a scientist, not an Imperial secret agent. I do not skulk around in alleys with an automatic equipped with a silencer looking for arch-villains. Nor do I hobnob with the high and mighty in my formal wear, or seduce beautiful female spies over a glass of fine scotch."

"Really, Michael, where *do* you get these ideas?"

Michael looked up from the machine he was tinkering with on the desk. "I read it in a novel. You don't think I just work on mechanicals all the time, do you?"

She eased out of the well-stuffed chair and draped herself over his back, resting her head on his shoulder. "No, but I always guessed you spent your spare time reading technical manuals for fun."

He shuddered. "Seriously? Have you ever read one of those things? They read like they're written for monkeys by slightly more educated monkeys."

"Be nice, Michael. You need to act like you're helping us decipher something that will lead us to the people behind this. We turned on all the interior lights because we want whoever's out there to know where we are."

"Look, you joined this quasi-military organization. I didn't ask you to serve as live bait to flush out pirates. Your boss was the one behind that. Why are you asking me to do this?"

She walked over to the door and glanced down the gangways, but there was no sign anyone was on the ship but them. "I don't know, Michael. Maybe because I want this to be over? I want a normal life again? I'm tired of being afraid. I don't think that's too much to ask for. If you object, why are you here?"

"Why am I here? That's a silly question. Because you asked me to come. Because I want this to be over as soon as possible. I want you to be happy and carefree like you were before this started."

She glanced at her mechanical limb. "I'm never going to be like I was before this started."

Michael rose from his chair and took her in his arms. "Darling, you're perfect just as you are. Don't dwell on this," he said, touching her arm gently. "It doesn't change how I feel for you one iota. You're the sweetest and bravest person I know. I'm sorry . . . I'm afraid. Not for myself—hell, this is less dangerous than most of my experiments. I'm afraid for you. I don't like them risking you again so soon. You've done enough. I'm tired of you being at risk and I want to do something to make it stop."

She hugged him back, trying not to squeeze too hard with the right arm. Once she had her emotions under control again, she pointed at the device on the table. "So, what does that do?"

"Well, since there's nothing to decipher, I needed something to do. So, I made a space detector. From what I've read about this ship, it was a cargo vessel. That means it started out as open bays and a small crew quarters. Obviously, the *Lynx* has been heavily modified. Therefore, not unlike Southwatch proper, some areas didn't fit their plans—a corner too small to turn into room, a curvature in the wall, and so on. Those are perfect places to hide things, which pirates and smugglers are good at doing. This machine will let me know if there's an opening behind the wall. And"—he paused for dramatic effect—"if there's an opening, there must be a way to reach it."

She wrapped her arms around his shoulders. "And you say you wouldn't make a good spy."

He smiled back. "I wouldn't. I'd be the guy designing the gear the spy would use."

"I'll keep that in mind."

"Anyway, it's about done. Give me a minute or two to calibrate it and we can test it right here. After all, if something's hidden on the *Lynx*, it stands to reason the late Captain Solly would keep it nearby." He pointed over his shoulder at a bag on the captain's bed. "Could you get me that? Since I couldn't bring my assistants, I guess you're my volunteer."

"But why do I have to be Theo?"

He mimicked her voice. "Because I asked you to?"

She threatened to throw the bag at him, but she laughed instead and brought the tool bag over to him. She spent the next few minutes learning the arcane language of tools as Michael asked for this thing or that without bothering to explain what they were. After a bit, he simplified things by simply asking for them by color.

Several minutes later, he held up the machine to the light, pressed a few buttons, shook it, and then pressed a few more buttons. "Hand me the screwdriver with the orange handle and we'll be done."

247

She handed him the oddly shaped tool and he tightened one last screw. He flipped a switch and a series of lights came on. The strange machine made small beeping sounds as he picked it up and walked to the door. "See, we know this is a door, ergo it's a shallow wall with open air behind it." Michael tapped a button and waved a wand-like device up and down the wall. Erica saw the lights flash red and Michael smiled as if to say *It worked.*

Carefully, they worked their way around the room. At first, the lights stayed green whenever Michael tapped the button. He paused a few times to recalibrate the device, just to be sure it was working. They made good progress around the room but there was no reaction from the machine. The only times it alerted them were at known sites—the wall along the gangway and the door to the captain's clothes closet.

"Nothing so far," Erica muttered.

"Nothing so far for the walls, but there're two more surfaces to inspect." He bent over and slowly waved the wand a few inches from the floor. He worked his way around the room and behind a screen that separated Solly's bedchamber from the rest of his room. When they reached the bed, he lowered himself to his stomach and waved the wand underneath. Around the center of the floor, the red lights lit up like the electric lights outside a bar in the Underground.

"But the bed is bolted to the floor, Michael. How did he get under there?"

Michael brought his hand up to his chin as he began scanning the area with his eyes. With a sudden move, he rose and approached the headboard of the captain's bunk. He waved his hands like a magician and pushed his finger against a discolored knot in the wooden frame. There was a small audible click and the bed rose into the air on hydraulic pistons.

"Voilà!" Michael crowed.

"Well, don't just stand there preening, Michael. How do we open that?"

"I can do many things, Erica, but I am not clairvoyant. I'll have to examine it first."

Erica raised the back of her hand to her forehead and leaned backward, fanning herself with her other hand. "What? You have a weakness? I'm so disappointed. I'm afraid I'll have to start looking for the perfect boyfriend all over again."

"Oh, har-dee-har. I wonder how hard it would be to find a less melodramatic girlfriend."

"Melodramatic? I'll have you know I went to drama school for years. I am an *artiste*."

"You're something, all right," he teased and climbed underneath the raised bed. Erica moved closer, but a soft noise caught her attention. *Footsteps? But no one's supposed to be on board.* Lifting a hand to get Michael's attention, she motioned toward the door and then tiptoed to it. She listened closely, but there was no further sound. She wasn't sure what she had heard, or if she'd really heard anything, so she motioned for Michael to resume what he was doing.

He pulled some tools out of his pocket and a magnifying glass and began poking at the floor. Her curiosity was eating her alive, but that faint noise made her uneasy. She leaned against the wall close to the door and tried to watch it and Michael simultaneously.

He lay on his stomach, balancing his upper torso over his elbows as he worked on the wooden floor. He made a tripod for his magnifying glass with some of his tools while he manipulated two other tools, one in each hand. It felt like the whole world had stopped but Erica knew only a few seconds had passed. Michael made a self-satisfied noise and then reached down and pulled. A section of the wooden floor rose, revealing a large opening partially occupied by a metal safe.

He eased the safe out of the hole and sat down, his legs dangling into the opening as he examined the object. "*This* may take a bit longer," he muttered to no one in particular. He shifted his magnifying glass and then looked back at Erica. "Could you bring me the blue-handled screwdriver from my bag of tools?"

"Of course, Michael," she said in her best Theo imitation. He scowled for a second before breaking into laughter.

"All right, all right. Next time I'll sneak in a few winders to fetch and tote. Now, the quicker you bring me that tool, the quicker I can get this safe open."

Erica knelt to watch, fascinated how Michael manipulated his tools on the safe's lock. Within a few minutes, his movements became more assured and then there was an audible click. He reached down and pulled the small handle upward, exposing the square opening.

"Ah-ha! And what do we have here?"

249

Erica watched Michael pull three items out of the hidden container: a small leather sack, a rather nasty-looking electro-gun, and a sheath of paper, carefully tied together. Erica grabbed the papers and stepped around the screen, walking toward the desk—

—and stopped dead as Jessica stood in the doorway, a small air gun in her hand. It looked like a toy, but Erica had no doubt it was lethal.

"We keep meeting at the oddest places." Jessica strode confidently over to the desk and pulled up a chair.

"I hear we have company, Erica."

Jessica glanced over her shoulder in Michael's direction. "Don't get up on my account, this won't take long. Erica, I believe those are mine."

"Jessica, aren't you out of your jurisdiction? I'm pretty sure we're a good twenty miles outside Southwatch."

"When it comes to Southwatch, there is no limit to my jurisdiction, Erica. You should know that by now."

Erica's eyes narrowed as she stared at the woman casually sitting at the desk. Her left fist clenched in anger and she took a step forward. "I think you can take your jurisdiction and—"

Jessica waved the gun and smiled, but there was no warmth in it. She snapped her fingers and two hulking men in airship crew fatigues stepped in, moving to either side of the door. From the scars and bent noses, Erica knew these men weren't only used to fighting, they enjoyed it.

"You see, Erica, unlike you I am not stupid enough to rely on just one person to protect me—even a scientist as brilliant as Michael. These gentlemen, and several more, are going through the ship to ensure our conversation is uninterrupted. It was child's play to slip past the Marines. Oh, your so-called Angels of Vengeance are a little preoccupied at the moment. Seems there was a cave-in while they were investigating something in one of the tunnels. Oh, don't worry, they weren't nearby, but it'll take them a few hours to dig out."

"You've planned this rather well, haven't you, Jessica?"

Jessica preened a bit as she motioned at the desktop. "I like to think so, yes. You have surprised me a time or two, but now the games are over. Will you hand me those papers or do I have to become . . . unpleasant?"

Erica continued with a bravado she certainly did not feel. "These must be important if you're willing to come into the open to secure them." She sat down on the edge of the desk and opened the string holding the letters together, forcing Jessica to either look at Michael or her. She scanned the first page and then flipped it onto the desk in front of Jessica. "Hmm, payment for services rendered. What do you know—a pirate who kept accurate records. How unusual."

Jessica's smile never wavered. "Yes, quite. Solly assumed he might need written evidence in case something happened. 'A place to begin negotiations,' he used to say. He thought I would bail him out if he ever got into trouble to keep those papers out of circulation." Her face twisted in anger. "He was stupid. If he had become a threat, I'd have broken his neck myself. Your deceased friend saved me the job. Actually, saved me two jobs."

"Oh?"

"You really are naïve, aren't you? Tony was dead as soon as he stepped on the balcony with you. See, novelists assume covert operations happen and then everyone shakes hands, takes their money, and goes away vowing never to say anything. Makes a great story." Jessica let out a mirthless laugh. "And that's just what they are: fiction. No one says anything because almost everyone involved is dead when it's over. Covert Ops are dangerous enough, but we don't mind making a mess if there's a way to blame it on someone else. Your friend was a marked man the day he started nosing around in this affair."

"I can't believe the Black Watch could be so cold. You're supposed to protect Southwatch." Erica's anger rose as she stared at Jessica's smug look.

"Grow up, Erica. This is a dirty business. Still, you're working from a mistaken point of view, my dear little Angel. See, there's the Black Watch—Southwatch's elite security force, which answers only to the baron. And then there's the Darkness. We ensure the purity of the Black Watch. We protect the barony. We're not beholden to any one baron."

Erica tried to channel the calm she's had back in the park the last time she had to deal with Jessica, trying to ensure Jessica's attention was on her and not Michael. "The Darkness?" A small snicker escaped her in spite of her attempt to smother it. "And Michael accused *me* of being melodramatic earlier. However, since you're

251

telling us this, I'm certain you have 'unfortunate accidents' arranged for us too?"

Jessica laughed an honest deep laugh this time. "Oh, you're such a literal child. How you escaped our traps before, I'll never understand."

Her voice grew colder as she stared at Erica. "No, you little idiot. If we were going to kill you, I'd have shot you the second I walked in. I told you not to believe those novels. I am not monologuing for your benefit. There is no last-minute rescue coming. Besides, I think I've been very clear about my intentions. We want Michael and having you will ensure his cooperation. There are many projects he's involved in that would be quite useful for our cause."

"Do you think I'd betray the Angels just like that?"

"No, I don't think you'd betray the Angels any more than your partner, Zwyer, which is why you aren't going back to the Angels. In fact, you aren't going back to Southwatch. You'll be relocated to a small village in the Gray Mountains. As long as Michael cooperates, you'll be well taken care of and he'll be able to visit on a regular basis. If he chooses not to . . . we're not responsible for accidents that might happen in that rugged terrain. With any luck, they might find your body in the spring thaws."

Erica kept reading the bundle of documents and tossing them in front of Jessica. "You said you're not so stupid as to rely on one scientist, so that means you have a storm of your own. However, he or she can't be as good as Michael or you wouldn't have been pursuing Michael this hard. So, who's the poor shlub and does he know he's getting the heave-ho?"

A voice from the doorway caught her off guard. "Hardly, Erica. I like to think of it as we're adding a new piece to the puzzle. Since we couldn't keep Crystal, we figured we'd recruit her mentor. Didn't you know that Michael's been working with Crystal for about five years now?"

"Toby?"

"Hiya, Erica. See, this proves we're serious. We wouldn't burn my cover if you were going back to the Angels. Besides, you're going to be busy in your new home. We're doing our own wing research and building our own flying corps. We're even recruiting our own instructors. I believe you encountered one of our trainees a few nights ago."

"We weren't formally introduced, but he made an impression."

Jessica raised her head to peer at the partition. "Michael, you're being awfully quiet. Don't you have anything to contribute? Michael?"

She bolted to her feet and from the expression of anger and frustration, Erica knew something had happened. Erica stepped around the desk to look behind the screen and saw a slightly larger hole in the floor near the safe and no sign of Michael. *Only you, Michael. Only you.*

Jessica rushed to the opening and stared down into the blackness. The hole was just large enough for someone Solly's size to squeeze through, but where it led was anyone's guess. "Thad, Leo, go after him. Don't let him get off this ship. Toby, keep an eye on this . . . thing. I'll alert the rest."

She rushed out the door as the two large men moved forward to examine the narrow passage. Finally, one stood up and pointed at Toby. "You're gonna have to go after him."

Toby waved a hand at the man as if dismissing a small child. "You heard Jessica, I'm supposed to watch her. Go find someone who's smaller. I'm not chasing a guy down a rabbit hole."

The two men muttered and Erica knew it was a good thing they were more afraid of Jessica than how much they wanted to wipe that smirk off Toby's face. They lowered the bed to ensure Michael couldn't double back, and ran out of the room.

"Welcome to the team, Erica," Toby said. "I think you're going to like it. In fact, there's a good chance you'd wind up being chief instructor before you're done. After all, when I'm not playing the poor simpering armorer for the Angels, I'm the commandant of the flight school. And given the way you looked in that flight suit the other day, I think there's a very good chance you'll move up quickly under my tutelage—if you follow my drift."

I'll give Toby credit, he's one hell of an actor. I really bought his timid, shy act back at the camp. "Aren't you interested in Crystal? I don't want to come between you and her, after all," Erica said, moving closer to Toby. *At least, now I know who the mole is.*

He leaned back against the doorway, leering at her. "I'm afraid you're confusing me with the character I play. You, your roommate, Bronson, even that Amazon, Zwyer—now that's the kind of woman I'm interested in. Crystal? She means one thing to me: access to her plans and her techniques. She's a brilliant woman when it comes to designs and aerodynamics but she's a child when it comes to relationships. Sometimes, it's all I can do to not run screaming out of her lab. I can't see why Michael tolerates her. He probably spends half his time dealing with her self-inflicted issues." Toby paused and nodded toward the escape hatch. "At least Michael has great taste in women."

Erica moved closer, causing him to step back. She smiled and he overcame his caution and moved closer, meeting her just inside the room beyond the doorway. "So, you really don't care about Crystal at all?" she asked in a slow, soft voice as she put her arms around him.

"Crystal is a colleague. A talented one for certain, but nothing more than that."

"That's wonderful. Then she won't be too brokenhearted, don't you agree, Toby?"

Toby started to say something—until her mechanical hand seized him by the neck and she squeezed as hard as she could. He grabbed her arm with both hands, but his fingers couldn't get purchase on the artificial skin. By the time he tried to reach for her human body, he was already turning purple. Just as his body went limp, she felt a tug on her shoulder.

"That's enough, Erica. Let him go."

"He's a threat, Michael. I have to be sure."

"No, Erica. Not like this. You're not like them."

She took a deep breath and willed her hand to open. Toby's limp body dropped to the floor. Michael checked his vital signs and shook his head. "He'll live, but I don't think he's going to enjoy swallowing anything in the near future. Help me stuff him in the closet."

They used a couple of shirts in the closet to bind and gag him. As they shut the door, Erica's knees nearly gave out as the adrenaline rush ended.

"How did you get out from under the bed?"

"There was a button to raise the bed in the hole. But explanations can wait. Come on, we need to get out of here before those thugs get back."

Michael grabbed his machine and the papers Jessica had left behind and rushed to the door. He motioned to Erica to grab the electro-pistol from the floor and they headed for the front of the airship. Making their way around the first corner, he paused to pull up his jacket in the back and remove an unusual-looking pistol from a hidden pocket. "The storage area just went a few feet farther under the floor, but it was enough to make it look like a tunnel. I knew those guys were too big to follow, so I just curled up in it and pretended I'd disappeared."

"You took a big chance. What if Jessica had come after you?"

"She's not the kind to get her hands dirty, especially if she's got others to do it for her. I've studied the *Lynx*'s plans. There's a good spot to hide down this passage."

They hurried along, hoping their plans for taking down Jessica and her friends weren't completely shot. There was no way to know how many people Jessica had or how many of their own allies were still out there. Until they encountered someone they recognized, they had to assume everyone they met was an enemy.

Footsteps pounded closer in the passageway ahead and Michael eased open a nearby door. They slipped inside, leaving it open just enough to watch who went past. Three large men in dockworkers' clothing and two smaller guys, who wouldn't have looked out of place working in a bank or a lawyer's office, went rushing past with their weapons at the ready.

"Looks like they're heading to the captain's quarters. It's not going to take them long to alert the ship. How many charges does that electro-gun have?" Michael asked, double-checking the weapon he had with him.

Erica glanced at the meter on the side of the weapon. "Ten. I've never seen anything like this before."

He rattled off information about the weapon, in the detached voice he affected when he was more nervous than he wanted to admit. "That's a Westminster ES-80. It's an antique, at least forty years old. Modern weapon technology made pistols that large obsolete. But it's worth probably close to ten thousand crowns at an auction."

Erica gasped. "That's more than I make in three years' work." She held the weapon away from her as if afraid to get fingerprints on it.

"Well, when you get to be that age, maybe you'll be worth that much too. Now, let's go. The forward cargo hold is ahead and to the right. We should be able to find a place to hide in there."

Before she could make a snarky rejoinder, he grabbed her hand again and hurried down the hall. They had to double back a couple of times as they ran into locked doors, but eventually they found a way to get into the cargo hold without being seen. They crept along the wall toward a stack of crates, shifted a few around to make an opening to hide in, and waited.

They hadn't been there long before two of the men they'd spotted earlier eased the door open and entered. Erica barely saw them in the dim light, but they had obviously done this type of work before. They moved through the hold using hand signals. One moved while the other held their weapon at the ready and then the first covered the other one's attempt to catch up. They covered the far end of the hold in that manner, searching all the crates and anything covered with canvas. Erica tried to see if anyone was near the door, but it appeared the two were the only searchers.

Well, Toby, let's see if your marksmanship training was worth my time.

The two men approached their hiding place and Erica took aim at the one farthest away through a gap in their crates. She felt Michael shift into place near her, but she didn't let herself get distracted. Just as she was squeezing the trigger, there was a shout from the doorway. "There's trouble at the main hatchway. Jessica needs you there now."

The two men sprinted up the passageway. Erica and Michael waited for a few minutes before Michael pulled out his plans of the *Bloody Lynx* again and motioned for Erica to follow. His detection machine powered up and he ran the wand over the metal floor toward the front of the hold. After a few seconds, the red lights began flashing.

"I knew there had to be a hatch up here to get cargo in and out while the inspectors were examining the main holds. A typical smuggler's trick."

She decided to ask how Michael would know about smuggler's tricks, typical or otherwise, another time. "What do we do once we get it open?"

"We lower ourselves to the ground and link up with the Marines. Jessica's right about one thing. Backup would be a great idea." There was a commotion in the passageway and they rushed back to their hiding spot. A host of people came pouring in led by Jessica Black. She motioned to the right and left and they began dragging crates and boxes around and hiding behind them.

A voice Erica hadn't expected to hear came through the door: Phil Vetrano's. It cut through the noise and babble in the room like a knife. "Give it up in there, there's no way out of that hold."

"What are we going to do?" one of the men asked Jessica.

Jessica's voice snapped at them like a whip. "There's got to be a way out of here. I don't believe any pirate ship would have a hold without a smuggler's port. Keep them busy while I look for it."

The man looked dubious but he turned and ordered the men to shift around the room to cover the entrances as Jessica began dodging around items, heading in Erica and Michael's general direction. Erica watched Jessica pull a sheet of paper out of her coat pocket and head directly toward the opening Michael found moments ago. She pulled out a hidden switch and a hatch silently opened. There was a faint grinding of gears as something was lowered from the opening. Jessica reached inside her long coat and came out with several glass containers. She took careful aim and threw them, starting with the group of men farthest away from her.

The glass containers burst open, sending thick green smoke around the cargo hold. There were sounds of confusion, choking, and the thud of bodies hitting the ground. Jessica's shark smile returned as she started down the opening before the gas could reach her.

As soon as she had disappeared, Erica and Michael rushed toward the opening just ahead of the sickly green fog. Spotting a ladder, they climbed down after her. It was a short climb, and Jessica rushed across the cavern floor toward the opening, Erica right behind her, leaving Michael to secure the hatch. She'd only gone a few steps when Jessica spun around and snapped off a shot. Erica ducked but kept coming. Jessica stood there, silhouetted in the doorway to the cavern, squinting into the dim light.

"Give it up, Jessica."

"I don't think so. They may have defeated this cell, but no one back on the ship will ever talk again. I'll link up with another cell back in town. There's always another."

Erica inched her weapon into a firing position, hoping the darkness behind her would mask her movement. "You're not going anywhere. You're not going to torment Michael and me anymore."

"Only one of us is walking out of this cave. What are you going to do about it, little mouse?" Jessica asked, raising her own pistol at Erica's shadowy figure.

Erica's finger tightened on the trigger of the electro-pistol. The weapon discharged, sending a brilliant blue bolt into the darkness, blinding her. She dropped to her knees in a futile attempt to avoid being hit by Jessica's return shot. She waited for the spots to clear from her eyes and realized Jessica had missed her. She looked ahead and saw the shadowy shape of Jessica lying on the cave floor, a column of smoke rising from her chest.

Erica started to move forward, but Michael stopped her. He told her to watch the pirate ship and signal for help while he checked out Jessica. Erica glanced over her shoulder to see Michael covering up Jessica's head and chest with his coat. He jogged back to where she was standing and simply shook his head.

"There was nothing I could do. At least she died instantly."

Erica fought down the bile in her throat and stared at Michael. "What do we do now?"

"You get the Marines. They can hook up with the Vengeance and deal with the poison gas in the hold. I'm going to disappear before I get dragged into this any further. No offense, but this is going to involve a whole bunch of city and Imperial officials and I'm not comfortable in those situations. Here." He handed her a small piece of paper. "Here's the frequency to contact me. When you're free, get to a crystal set and send on this frequency. Theo will be standing by to come get you."

"But, Michael—"

"Sorry, darling. Hate to save Southwatch and run, but you know me, I hate being the center of attention. See you later. The Marine camp is that way."

Evening found a small tent city set up outside the pirate camp. There was no moon out, so when Erica looked up, it was almost as dark as being beneath the Cloud. However, unlike the hum and murmur of the city, the only sound was the soft thrumming of the *Lynx*'s engines as the technicians finished venting the poison gases from the ship.

There was a rustle near her tent and an Imperial Marine stepped out of the shadows and asked her to accompany him. Erica found herself being led to the main tents where Lady Orisaka, Dr. Lopatka, Miss Miles, and the unknown gentleman from a few days before waited. Lady Orisaka motioned for her to take a seat at the large table and Sophie and Flight Leader Vetrano were escorted in a few moments later. A vehicle pulled up outside and Geoffrey Kingston and Ambassador Bogdanovich entered, making their apologies for being late.

Lady Orisaka rang a small bell and people in Angels' uniforms entered the tent to serve an elaborate meal. Everyone attacked the food with a gusto mirroring the palpable relief of knowing a crisis has passed. Once the dessert course had come and gone, Lady Orisaka stood up and waited for the various conversations to subside before she spoke.

"Thank you all. I think it's safe to say this has been a harrowing experience for not only the Angels of Steel but the city of Southwatch too. Erica, you'll be happy to know that the papers Michael and you found conclusively prove what we suspected." She gestured toward her mystery guest. "Mr. Samuel Wright informs me the Black Watch is initiating a purge of the Darkness from within its ranks. He passes on the baron's sympathy for this unfortunate incident."

"Mr. Wright is with the Black Watch?" Erica blurted out before she realized she was speaking out loud.

Lady Orisaka looked annoyed for a moment, but then she fixed her smile back on and continued as if this was the topic she'd intended to speak on. "Mr. Wright is the public face of the Black Watch. We have had some frank—and I think useful—discussions regarding the interests of the Black Watch in the Angels. Based on our common experiences, they will *refrain* from attempting to infiltrate the Angels again."

Mr. Wright lifted his wineglass toward Lady Orisaka in a toast and then looked around the table. "Know that your organization, and specific people within it, has both the baron's greatest regards and mine. Your people showed courage and devotion to Southwatch that will not soon be forgotten."

"We appreciate the baron's good wishes and are pleased to have been of service," Lady Orisaka responded, bowing her head slightly to Mr. Wright. She turned to the ambassador and nodded also. "We know the actions of the past few weeks cannot replace the loss of your daughter, but we hope the apprehension of those involved in her death will help to start the healing process."

The ambassador let a small sad smile play on his face for a moment before he stood up. "I want everyone here to know I appreciate all you have done. I have had many intense conversations with Mr. Candal. I have no doubt he was in love with my daughter, and had the best of intentions regarding their relationship. I have spoken to the baron personally and Mr. Candal will be relocating to Coritani. We believe a new position in a new land will give him a chance to start over. I suspect he will become a valued member of my staff in time."

Erica smiled at that news. If the ambassador was taking him in, that said a lot about the young man. Then to her surprise, the ambassador mentioned her name as he continued.

"Of course, this could not have come to pass without the bravery of Miss Erica Halgrim. While I'm certain this is not a path she ever could have foreseen, she showed the tenacity to see this incident through to the end and helped discover the truth. To be blunt, if she had not driven herself, and the others around her, to excellence, we might never have known who was behind the death of my daughter nor of the threat this shadow organization posed to Southwatch."

"Your Excellency is too kind," Erica said. "If not for my friends and companions, I certainly would have failed. All of you contributed to what little success I had in this matter."

The ambassador made a motion for everyone to stand up. Erica rose, not realizing what was going on, until the ambassador was handed a scroll and began reading. "Let it be known that by order of his majesty, King Dmitri IV of Coritani, and approved by his imperial majesty, Emperor Louis IV"—he added as an aside—"that Erica Halgrim has been elevated to the Order of the Golden Angels of Coritani as its founding member. If Miss Halgrim would please approach?"

Erica stood there dumbstruck until Sophie pushed her in the back to start moving. She slowly approached the ambassador, waiting for someone to tell her the punch line of the joke, but Geoffrey motioned for her to stand next to the ambassador. She blushed as Geoffrey opened a small box and a thick golden chain with a figure cast in gold with mechanical wings spread wide was slipped around her neck. Erica froze for a moment while the assembly applauded and then retreated to her seat with as much dignity as she could muster.

The ambassador quickly poured himself a little more wine and then lifted his glass. "And now that we have embarrassed Lady Halgrim enough for the moment, I would also like to raise a toast to Lady Orisaka for not only her excellent organization, but for her excellent eye for talent and for her ability to inspire such loyalty from her people."

A hearty chorus rang out from the table for Lady Orisaka. To Erica's surprise, she thought she saw the faintest red appear in her employer's cheeks too.

Through the noise and applause, Erica heard a small commotion outside. Then she realized the *Bloody Lynx*'s motors were revving up. She ran toward the door of the tent, closely followed by Sophie. The *Lynx* pulled against its mooring lines and the steel pegs ripped loose from the earth as the craft lumbered skyward. The Marines rushed about beneath, but the *Lynx* had already risen too high for someone to climb aboard.

With a snap, the *Lynx* broke free of its last restraint. The airship ponderously rose into the sky and then something flashed in the glare of the spotlights. Erica heard something hit the ground nearby. A Marine grabbed it and brought it to the assembled guests. It was a wrench with a note attached to it. Lady Orisaka examined the note, shook her head, and then pointed to Erica.

Erica took the piece of paper and Sophie moved closer and read it over her shoulder.

Dear Erica,

Sorry to scare you, but I wanted everyone to think I was dead (again). It's much easier to operate when people aren't looking for you. I told you I always wanted my own airship and since Solly's dead, I don't think he'll mind me borrowing the Lynx. *I figure, with the current cargo aboard, I should be able to properly outfit the ship and hire more crew than I have now.*

Don't know when I'll get back to Southwatch, but I'll look you up when I do. Until then, safe flying!

Tony Blaylock

Erica stood there, looking up into the dark sky as the undermanned airship lumbered into the sky and to the northeast, sailing out of the range of the spotlights. She realized Sophie was standing behind her, staring up into the same patch of sky. "Do you ever wonder what it'd be like traveling around like that?"

Sophie shook her head slowly. "There's too much of Southwatch to still fly through, *Lady* Halgrim."

Erica waved her hands in front of her. "Oh no. Don't you start that. It's 'Erica' or 'Halgrim' and nothing else. When the doc clears me for training, I expect nothing less from my flight leader. Besides, between the two of us, there's nothing Crystal can throw at us we can't handle."

Sophie gave her an evil look. "I'm glad to hear that, Halgrim. I turned down a promotion to the Angels of Vengeance to stay with you all, since I don't think Rachel or you are ready to assume command yet. By the way, I talked to Crystal yesterday—when you're finished with physical therapy, she wants to go back out to the training camp and complete the tests she didn't get to run. She thinks you could use the extra flight training, and I agree." Sophie patted Erica on the left shoulder. "Sounds like you got lazy without me to keep an eye on you. I'll whip you back into fighting trim in no time."

Erica flexed her mechanical arm and looked at Sophie. "Bring it on."

About The Author

Richard C. White is a science fiction and fantasy author whose works include the noir-urban-fantasy collection *Chasing Danger: The Case Files of Theron Chase,* the fantasy-adventure collection *For a Few Gold Pieces More,* the fantasy-adventure novel *Harbinger of Darkness,* and the nonfiction book *Terra Incognito: A Guide to Building the Worlds of Your Imagination.* His contributions to various genre anthologies include *Thrilling Adventure Yarns 2021, Liberty Girl: Fight for Freedom, All for One: Tales of the Musketeers, The New Adventures of Rocky Jordan,* and the Origins Game Fair anthologies *Monsters, Robots,* and *Space.*

As a media tie-in writer, he's written for the *Star Trek, Doctor Who, Battletech,* and *The Incredible Hulk* franchises. His novel *Gauntlet Dark Legacy: Paths of Evil* was a best-selling tie-in for his publisher. His latest tie-in works are *One Night in Freeport* and *Storm Wreck* for Nisaba Press (Green Ronin Gaming).

Richard is a member of the Science Fiction and Fantasy Writers of America and the International Association of Media Tie-in Writers. Additionally, Richard serves on the SFWA Writer Beware committee.